A Mystery Tale from the Hood

Durty South Grind

c-4
4/16

ALSO BY L. E. NEWELL
The Grind Don't Stop

STREBOR ON THE Streetz

A Mystery Tale from the Hood

Durty South Grind

A NOVEL BY

L.E. Newell

SBI

STREBOR BOOKS

NEW YORK LONDON TORONTO SYDNEY

SBI

Strebor Books
P.O. Box 6505
Largo, MD 20792
http://www.streborbooks.com

ISBN 978-1-59309-351-8
ISBN 978-1-4516-0799-4 (e-book)
LCCN 2010940493

First Strebor Books trade paperback edition March 2011

Cover design: www.mariondesigns.com
Cover photograph: © Keith Saunders/Marion Designs

10 9 8 7 6 5 4 3 2 1

Manufactured in the United States of America

For information regarding special discounts for bulk purchases, please contact Simon & Schuster Special Sales at 1-866-506-1949 or business@simonandschuster.com

The Simon & Schuster Speakers Bureau can bring authors to your live event. For more information or to book an event, contact the Simon & Schuster Speakers Bureau at 1-866-248-3049 or visit our website at www.simonspeakers.com.

Acknowledgments

First of all, I'd like to thank GOD for not allowing me to give up on myself—for inspiring and continuing to inspire me through the trials and tribulations to keep pursuing my dream. For without GOD's guidance I couldn't have developed one word, one sentence, phrase or idea toward the beginning and the ending of this project.

I'd also like to thank my mama, Mama Marion—how she likes to be called—for birthing me and my sisters, Janet and Debra, who have continued to support me despite my hardheadedness to do the right thing. I'd also like to thank my nephews and nieces who've stuck by me, too.

To Robert, we call him Bobby "Hollywood" Washington; you would, too, if you ever met him. He's a character, my main man, adviser and manager, who has certainly played a pivotal role in getting all this done; and David Hamm, my agent, who's been super major in getting this work to the reader.

To my buddies from back in the day, who traveled hand in hand through the triumphs and failures of surviving the street life. I choose to leave them unnamed for obvious reasons.

Special thanks goes out to all the writers I have used to teach me about how to write by reading their works over and over again until I got it right. Nikki Turner, Zane, Michael Baisden, Omar Tyree and countless others. Oh yeah, and Charmaine Parker, thanks, lady. Thanks, guys and gals, for without your brilliant styles I wouldn't have been able to develop my own.

And finally to Sister Michelle Renee Donaldson, my inspirational adviser, who has continuously encouraged me throughout the years that I could accomplish whatever I set out to do despite the odds as long as I put GOD first and foremost in my life. She's always saying that GOD is in my corner and heart, and with Him, all things are possible. Thanks, Chelle, you are wonderful.

The Beforemath

The sexual tension of sweaty bodies permeated the room with a musky aroma. Exhausted, Sparkle rolled lazily off Mercedes' drenched body, his most recent conquest. He felt his dick throb anew with lust as he squinted at the oval ceiling mirror. He admired the glistening skin and long slope of her narrow back as it flared to her round ghetto booty and thighs. A tingle flushed along his spine when she cooed in a husky voice, "Oooh, baby, that was some real long dicking you put on me there. I was getting so raw and it was hurting good." The petite red-haired stripper's firm breasts were still rising rapidly as she moaned through the final stages of leg-trembling climaxes.

With an exhausted, pleased sigh, he smiled. "Was it, girl? Whew! You had me putting in some real work dere," he whispered between gasps.

His attention swayed to one of the drawings on the far wall he'd sent his boy over the years. Suddenly the hairs on the back of his neck began to tingle. He wondered if it was his imagination or if he had heard a crunching sound, like someone walking softly through dry leaves outside the window.

"Yeah, honey, daddy, we…" Shortie Girl, still breathing heavily, began. She froze when he reached over and put his hand over her mouth. Her eyes bulged with surprise.

His street instincts snapped to full attention. "Shh, be quiet for a sec, girl," he whispered. "Listen, you don't hear that?"

Her eyes swirled wildly with fear and before she could mumble, he placed his finger to her mouth and eased out of the bed naked. Creeping to the window on the balls of his feet, he eased the curtain back slightly. An adrenaline rush surged through him when he saw a shadow edge around the corner of the house. When he turned around, Shortie had sat up in the bed with the sheet pulled over her breasts, her nipples outlined through the dampened sheet. Even in the dark he could see her fearful eyes. He motioned, signaling that everything was going to be okay.

Sshhing her once more, he crouched and tiptoed to the closet, his instincts on full alert.

Making as little noise as possible, he eased the door open and reached into his leather coat hanging on the back. With tension rising by the second, he pulled out his own personal equalizer, a Glock nine-millimeter pistol. Squinting with anxiety, he quietly cocked it, placed it firmly on his hip and crept to the bedroom door. He gently turned the knob. Cautiously he peeked around the doorsill and quickly jerked his head back. Seeing no one, he pressed against the wall and edged toward the kitchen, where he felt the predators were headed.

Suddenly, with an ear-shattering thud, the door flew open. Two dark figures zipped through and quickly spread to each side. He immediately raised his gun and fired at the splitting hunters. Return fire thundered back and he hit the floor, getting off several shots of his own. One of the intruders' bullets sent wall plaster splattering across his face. He started belly crawling backward toward the bedroom but froze when rapidly fired shots zoomed over his head from behind. The surprise of another shooter sent shivers down his spine, sending him to another level of panic. One of the intruders grunted in pain when the hot lead bit into his flesh. A relieved sigh escaped Sparkle's lips when the two attackers sprinted out of the door.

Sparkle's head jerked back and forth between the kitchen and living room in desperation. His breath caught when a silhouette emerged out of the darkness. With raw nerves, he squinted at the shadowy figure. The sound of a familiar voice came in a whisper. "Yo, Ace, you aight?" The tone was quite anxious.

Sighing heavily, Sparkle released the pent-up air in his chest before replying in a shaky voice. "Uh-huh, who dat? You, Rainbow?"

"Whodafuckcha think it is, nigga?" Rainbow snapped back. "Man, who in da hell you done pissed off now, dude?"

"Wheew! You got any idea who the hell dem niggas was?" Sparkle spat as he sat up and began wiping the sweat off of his brow.

"You must not have heard what I said. But anyway, naw, dog, I ain't got no idea who it could've been, but we sho nuff gotta find out, that's for sure." Rainbow breathed sporadically.

"That's fer damn sho." Sparkle twisted some of the tension out of his neck, braced his back against the wall to help boost himself up off the floor, and then stood up in the doorway.

Rainbow eased out of the shadows of the living room with his head swerving to make sure he wasn't near one of the windows. Clad in one of his monogrammed silk robes, it showed that he had been there for a while. He cleared his throat before he spoke in a hoarse voice, "I think they've split, dog." His brow wrinkled as he paused and tiptoed to the window. He eased back the curtain to take a quick peek. "Heard a couple of car doors slamming and wheels screaming down the street."

"I think ya hit one of dem bastards," Sparkle whispered.

"Yeah, me too; dats why dey split the way dey did. Uh-huh, could swear I heard one of da muthafuckas grunt," he spat.

"Oh hell yeah, one of them did. I'm gonna make a run outside to make sure everything's safe. You check out things in here." Sparkle wrinkled his nose and nodded before heading toward the door.

"Dontcha wanna cover ya naked ass first?" Rainbow smirked.

Sparkle looked down at himself and tried not to look so embarrassed as he headed back to his bedroom. He muttered over his shoulder, "Aw fuck you, man," as he stepped across the sill.

In the dim light of the room he could see that Mercedes still had the sheet pressed to her breasts. "Is everything aight?" she whispered in a childlike voice. "Those shots sounded like a cannon going off."

He walked on the balls of his feet to the chair beside the bed. He picked up his dark-green baggy shorts and a light-green polo shirt and dressed. He slipped on a pair of tan Timberlands. He eased the gun into his waistband and covered it up with his shirt. He gave her what he hoped was a reassuring smile. "Everything's under control, shortie. Lay back and chill. I've gotta go check outside but I'm pretty sure they've split."

Before he could walk out of the door, Mercedes sat up on the edge of the bed. She snatched a red floral blouse from a bedside chair and slipped into it. Smiling demurely, she picked up a pair of faded jeans and stood up to put them on. As she wiggled her creamy hips from side to side pulling up the pants, he let out a long sigh. His mind went mushy all over again. *Mmh-mmh, baby girl's got one phat juicy-juicy,* he thought.

In terms of ghetto butts, Honey's was apple bottom phat. You could set a cup on it while she did her sashaying thang without spilling a drop. It was the first thing he'd noticed at a strip club when she worked the pole on the circular center stage. To accompany that awesome asset, she had large doe-like eyes that made her look innocent and cute.

What really turned his dick into a massive boner that night was her exotic expressions in mounting stages of climax as she undulated on the pole. She had concentrated on him and had gotten so deep into the dance that he felt that they were actually fucking. He could actually see the cum soaking through her outfit. He had never felt such an experience and pulling her had proven to be a real plume in his hat. Right off the bat, Mercedes had blended so well into the hustling scams he and his down-ass old chick Violet had practiced on a nearly daily basis.

"Ya'll got any idea who dem dudes was?" she purred. Her little girl voice broke the trance of her curvaceous frame.

"Huh, what did you say?" Sparkle shook his mind clear.

"Ya'll got any idea who dem dudes was?" she repeated with a look of concern.

A frown creased his brow. "Naw, baby girl, but we're gonna find out; that's for sure."

Her eyes brightened with relief and she smiled seductively up at him, slithered off the bed and floated over to press her sweet softness against his body. His heart skipped a beat when she leaned her red curly head on his chest. Her whole body trembled as she caressed him with her sultry eyes and pushed her pelvis seductively against his swelling hardness. She sighed. "You ain't gonna be away too long, are you?" Her warm breath rolled along his neck and her long lashes tickled his skin. "Because I ain't finished with you yet."

He caressed her arms, gave her a gentle kiss on the forehead and held her away at arm's length. "Just got to make sure whoever that was is gone," he said in a reassuring tone.

As he turned away, he heard Rainbow yell from the kitchen, "Yo, Ace, come check dis here out."

He smiled down at her lust-filled eyes and reluctantly turned away to leave. As he made his way toward the kitchen, he shouted, "Yeah, partner, whatcha got?"

Rainbow was squatting at the door, staring intently at an object just inside the sill in a shiny puddle of what appeared to be blood. It was real hard to be sure in the darkness. To get a better look, he squatted down beside his boy, "Looks like a bracelet, huh?"

Rainbow nodded quickly. "Yeah, uh-huh, 'pears to be. Check dis out." He pointed outside the door. Sparkle could see a trail of blood speckling over the sill and along the dirt path beside the house, disappearing at the edge of the grass.

Rainbow took a gold pen out of his robe, lifted the bracelet out of the blood and held it up to the moonlight. Under closer inspection they could see the initials

"JJ" engraved in gold letters on the inside of the silver-plated woven jewelry. Rainbow's face was full of curiosity. He arched his eyebrows at Sparkle.

Sparkle hunched his own shoulders. "Got any idea who da fuck dis belongs to?"

"Shit, dog, your guess is as good as mine," Rainbow spat.

Sparkle shook his head. "Dog, we got to get on this here right away. There ain't no telling who is behind this."

Rainbow's expression left little doubt of his intentions, especially when he cocked his gun and started caressing the barrel. His eyes narrowed as he took a deep breath, stood up and clutched Sparkle's elbow to pull him outside. "Hey, chill a sec, dog." He nodded toward the house. "We haven't known dese hoes dat long."

"Hey, whatcha saying, man?" Sparkle looked back toward the house.

"Come on, playa, one of dem hoes in dere might just be down wid dis here shit." Rainbow paused with his ear cocked to the door, his eyes squinting with a coldness that would chill the blood of most regular niggas; especially those that didn't know him. He licked his lips before continuing, "Man, I done told ya a hundred thousand times, don't be trusting none of these bitches." He poked Sparkle in the chest to emphasize he was serious.

Sparkle nodded in understanding and reached into his pocket to pull out a crumbled pack of Kool cigarettes. He cuffed the lighter between his palms as he lit one. He needed to calm his nerves, still not absolutely sure those niggas were gone. Pondering what he'd just heard, he leaned against the door, sucking in a deep drag and exhaling slowly. "Okay, dog, I see whatcha saying. Uh, who da fuck you got in there anyways? Shiiit, how long ya'll been here?"

Rainbow cocked his head to the side the way he always did when he was puzzled about something. He was tossing around the whos and whys of what had gone down. Even after Sparkle had asked the question again, he still kept that blank look on his face for about thirty seconds. "Huh, oooh, yeah, uh, I got one of the twins in there." He continued to look into space.

"Shit, man, which twin?" Sparkle asked in a more serious tone.

"Hell, Bro, I don't know dem bitches apart. Anyways, what difference does it make which one it is?" He started frowning in irritation with the bullshit talk; it didn't have anything to do with what was going on.

"Yeah, bow, you right, man; it don't make no difference which one."

He punched Sparkle playfully in the side and spit menacingly. "Check it, dog, fuck des hoes. We gotta get on the trail of who dis 'JJ' nigga is, for real yo."

Sparkle took the bracelet off of the pen and twisted it around to examine it more closely. "Man, the only 'JJ' I know is that nigga that used to mess with my sister, Debra. Do you think he got the nerve to try something like this? Because I don't."

"Dude, I think everybody got the nerve except you and me," he stated matter-of-factly.

"Then we gotta get on this. Where ya wanna start?"

Rainbow wrapped his arm around his boy's shoulder as they headed back into the house. "Tell ya what, let's get dressed and take a ride to Decatur. Somebody damn sho gotta know something."

CHAPTER ONE
Breaking the Chains

It was another humid day in the summer of 2006 in the rural woods of southern Georgia. The sun was finally starting to break through the daily density of fog at the Valdosta State Prison. The sounds of the stirring of the inmate population inside the life-choking, razor-wired fences found Sparkle awakening to the final day of his bit and hopefully the beginning of a new life in the outside world.

The irritating clanging of chimes over the PA system was really starting to irritate him. He rolled over and squeezed the hard plastic-covered pillow as tightly as he could over his head to block out the persistent noise. He tried squeezing his eyes tight but that didn't work, either. Finally, he realized that more sleep was out of the question and sat up in the bed. It had been well over a year since he'd given up eating early in the morning. He had begun feeling nauseated and occasionally had thrown up after devouring that godforbidden slop. Getting to the chow hall certainly wasn't a priority for him.

A sharp rapping on the door was followed by the voice of his chain gang running mate, Skeet, yelling at the top of his lungs. "Yo, Sparkle, get yo ass up, man!" This did away with whatever rest was left.

Sparkle fell back on the bed, turned over on his stomach and pulled the wool cover over his head, shouting in a grumbling tone, "What?"

Skeet rapped harder. "Hey, man, come on; get yo ass up, nigga. We got some thangs to kick around afore you raise up outta here."

Sparkle, still in a sleepy haze, thought, *Aw man, I'm getting outta this dungeon today. Man, let me get up outta this here rack.* He had a big smile spread across his face. He peeked over his forearm and focused on the door's frosty sheet of Plexiglas where Skeet was still yelling, "Come on, man, get up and splash some water on that ugly-ass mug and get the funk outta your mouth." He was cheesing hard through the pane. Sparkle could only see his teeth and big bulbous nose. Even though he was looking directly at him, he continued rapping and yelling, "Come on, bitch, get yo ass up. It's time for you to roll outta this dungeon."

"Ugh," Sparkle grunted and frowned from the nasty film of morning mouth coating his tongue. Smacking his lips, he sighed and yanked the cover off his head and glanced menacingly at the door.

He sat up and rubbed the crusty sleep out of the corner of his eyes with the palms of his hands. Breaking out into a big smile, he began rubbing his knees and reached under the plastic mattress for his crumpled pack of Kools.

After taking his time lighting up, he took an extra long toke and started waving Skeet away from the door. "Yeah, yeah, I'm up, man. Why dontcha go get that fat butt boy of yours up." He stretched and yawned. "I'll be with ya'll in a few."

Skeet rapped his gnarled knuckles on the pane one last time. "About time, nigga; I'll be out at the basketball court. And don't have me out there all morning waiting on your jive ass, either." He gave him a staunch salute before disappearing.

"Yeah, yeah." Sparkle pressed his fist to his mouth and stifled a yawn. He stood to stretch his five-foot-ten, coffee-brown frame, twisted the kinks out of his neck and staggered to the wash basin to handle his hygiene.

With Skeet's footsteps fading, his thoughts flowed to the image of a sweet, young filly hunching up under him, giving up husky sighs and pussy aroma from his hard grinding fuck. He smiled at his dull image in the metal mirror and splashed cold water on his face. He brushed his teeth, picked out his mini fro and started putting on his prison whites for the last time.

Several minutes later, he checked the creases in his pants as he exited his room. He strolled down the catwalk toward the winding stairs. As he reached the steps he heard an all-too-familiar voice grumbling in a country drawl.

He immediately felt that old tingling of hatred run up and down his spine. He knew it wouldn't do any good to ignore it, so he slowly angled his head sideways to acknowledge the voice.

Old "Chew Tobacco" Jones was grinning at him, displaying a row of brown, crooked teeth. The big burly country hick, his distinctively foul body odor disturbing the air, placed a swollen hand on the railing. He tapped his ever-present nightstick along the wall as he approached in a rolling gait.

In a skunky wisp of air, he said, "Damn, boy, you trying to ignore me or sumthang?" He stepped a few feet closer before continuing with a nasty sneer. "You best to keep yaself oudda trouble now."

Sparkle pinched his nose and spoke, holding his breath between clenched teeth. "What's up, Stank Breath Chew Tobacco?"

The CO's face turned beet red as he frowned and growled, "Whaddafuck you say, nigga boy?"

Sparkle pinned him with cold-killer eyes and blasted his funky ass. "Cracker-ass, redneck bitch, who gave your dumb hillbilly ass permission to speak to me?" He paused and rubbed his nose again, letting it sink in. "Get the fuck outta my face." He turned away to stifle the laugh that was boiling up from his gut. A look of total shock spread across Jones's face.

A red-faced, neck-throbbing Jones grabbed his throat as if he were about to choke on his wad. His neck got puffy red as he opened his mouth to say something but nothing came out. He shifted his head back and forth, checking to see if anybody was watching this boy belittling him. Then he gritted, showing all of his tobacco-stained brownish teeth. He pulled back his nightstick to strike before Sparkle leaned in closer to him and hissed, "Yeah, stanky muthafucka, do it and let's go see the magistrate."

The hillbilly opened his mouth again to speak but Sparkle cut him off. "Yeah, bastard, I said it. I'm a free man today and if you hit me with that damn thing, your ass is gonna do some time. Yep, some muthafuckin' time in here with these killa niggas that you been fucking over all these years."

With the stick frozen in midair, he squinted his hate-filled eyes, heaved and lowered the stick. "You black bastard, you better hope that your sorry ass don't ever come back this here way again. Your ass will be mine."

"Bitch-ass cracker, your funky ass better pray that I never see your ugly mug on the other side of these fences." Sparkle's deadly look sent a shiver down the CO's spine. He backed away with trembling lips.

Sparkle cocked his head to the side and scratched his chin, and then took a deep breath to keep from laughing. Turning abruptly away he started walking down the stairs. He could feel the fire snorting out of Jones's nose, along with the hate darting from his eyes, burning a hole in his back.

He didn't give a fuck how Jones felt with all the fucked-up shit he used to do. Brushing the confrontation out of his mind, Sparkle continued out the door. Immediately, he spotted his boy Skeet and his kid Lil'

Jack in an animated conversation. They were seated on a bench beside the basketball court. As he strolled toward them, they broke out in wide smiles.

Skeet nodded toward the sidewalk and the pair walked up ahead of him. Sparkle got dap and backslaps from dudes congratulating him for surviving his bit and wishing him well on his return to the bricks. He eventually passed all of the well-wishers and walked between Skeet and Lil' Jack, placing an arm around each of their shoulders.

Lil' Jack smiled up at him and said in a squeaky voice, "Damn, big bro, you finally gonna get the chance to be a hood star again, huh?"

Sparkle blinked several times as he returned the smile. He'd always been amazed at how much Jack smiled like a girl. Hell, he was shaped like one, too. He used to joke with him all the time about him being a mistake of nature. For a moment Sparkle thought of what a helluva pimp Jack would make on the ho stroll on Auburn Avenue. He'd personally pumped enough game into his head to pull it off, too. A lot of dudes around the joint didn't realize how coldhearted the little fella was.

Because of his friendship with Skeet, they had become really close. Even though Jack was a near replica of the sexy diva Toni Braxton, he'd always treated him human without any of the homosexual bullshit involved. Sparkle figured he really appreciated it; he never acted feminine when they were alone. Often Skeet had him boy-sitting whenever he was at work in the gym or out hustling drugs and parlaying tickets.

He rubbed Jack's curly head. "Little bro, I'm going out there to do the straight-and-narrow thing." He winked.

"That's good man; that's good." Jack nodded.

When they got halfway down the long curved sidewalk, Jack spotted one of his sissy friends. He patted Sparkle daintily on the shoulder. "Hey, I know that ya'll two probably got some things ya'll wanna kick around before you leave. I'm going to holla at Miss Queenie over yonder, so take care of yourself, handsome." He twisted his little hips in the direction of his partner.

When they got out of earshot of the throng of niggas hanging out in front of the mess hall, Skeet nudged him in the side. "Ya know dat thangs are gonna be rough out der, my nigga; ya sure you gonna be able to handle that for me?"

Sparkle could tell that Skeet had doubts about him coming through with the drugs they had discussed over the past few months. "Homefolks, all you got to do is let me know that you done sent that package request to your sister and I'll be on that thang right away." He put his arm around his shoulder. "Make sure that you keep these niggas outcha business, so we both can get paid."

Skeet cocked his head to the side with his sneaky smile. "Yeah, man, we got this plan down tight and I sho nuff gotta keep these nosey-ass snitches outta my shit." He paused to scratch behind his ear. "Man, I hate to make you feel like I'm doubting you and shit. But you know how damn near everybody who gets out be claiming dey gonna do des and gonna do dat. And folk never hear nothing from them; go straight ghost on a nigga."

Sparkle stopped about ten yards from the entrance to the main control office and pulled him by the wrist. He stared straight into his eyes. "Yo, peeps, you remember that day when you cracked that fool upside the head? He was set to steal on me about that slum-ass reefer he was trying to gorilla down my throat?"

Skeet lowered his head and started massaging the bridge of his nose, listening intently.

"Well, baby boy, that alone is enough to keep my mind on the struggles you gotta go through in this crazy house. So you can count on me, dog. Word is bond, like it's always been with us."

"Yeah, I feel you, man." He continued to look down in shame for doubting his main man.

The captain who ran the control room came out the door. "Say, man, they been hollering for you on the walkie-talkies for about a half-hour now. What's up, you ain't ready to go home or something?"

"Hell yeah, I'm on my way now, Captain." He turned away from him and embraced his buddy one more time. "My nig, I gotcha. Have your sister holla at a nigga when she get the paperwork," Sparkle whispered.

Skeet grinned like a black Cheshire cat. "It's on the way as we speak. Hell, that there's a wrap; make sure you take care of yourself out there."

"Shit, dog, that's automatic. You stay strong up in this hellhole."

"No choice, partner; no choice."

Sparkle rubbed his chin as he squinted at his boy and then looked around the compound for the last time. "Man, I sho' ain't gonna miss this place here."

"Yeah, man, I feel you on that there." Skeet nodded, following his gaze.

Sparkle lifted his chin and gave Skeet one more brotherly hug. He headed into the control center, toward freedom.

⊡ ⊡ ⊡

A couple of hundred miles to the north, an individual was tossing and turning in their sleep, struggling with the constant nightmare that punished and punished, year after year.

The hot balmy breeze did little to stop the sweat from stinging the child's eyes. The heat was unbearable. The countless number of mosquitoes nibbling on little arms, legs and neck couldn't be swatted away, no matter how often and hard they swung. They kept biting and biting, growing bigger and bigger as the child's blood flooded its stinger mouth, like a hypodermic needle pumping a junkie's vein. The child got woozier as its life flow oozed down its arms.

The foggy faces of lust-crazed men poofed into view and leaned closer to the terror-filled eyes, which quickly began fading in and out of focus. Ever so close, yet out of reach. A white one with stubby hairs rubbing harshly against the child's burning skin, followed by a black one that ogled as slobber ran out of the corners of his mouth. His head angled from side to side like a lunatic; a brown one, then a yellow blurring in and out of vision.

The faces continued to swirl madly around as the mosquitoes got bigger, jaws snapping and gnawing on the child's ever swelling arms. Suddenly all the different colored backs appeared altogether in a hideous mass, sweating and stinking as they came into focus, going up and down, followed by a blood-curdling scream.

The individual's eyes shot open, a body consuming fear was causing the air to come in rapid gasps, hands rubbing vigorously all over the body that was drenched in flowing sweat, desperately trying to wipe away the icky feeling of total despair. He sat up in the unfamiliar surroundings, wondering how he had gotten there, brushing away oily hair that was plastered to the sticky forehead, before burying his head into his hands, scared to death as to why this kept happening. Tears from decades of suffering rolled down swollen cheeks, puffed with pain, wondering if the nightmares would ever stop; nightmares that were constantly increasing in frequency and intensity. Damn, something had to be done to make them stop. There was only one way to make them go away. And it would definitely come to pass. Please come to pass before insanity took over.

CHAPTER TWO
A New Beginning

The noonday sun cast eerie shadows on the freshly painted wall when Beverly Johnson picked up the persistently ringing telephone. Atlanta's newly appointed police chief listened intently to the familiar voice on the other end of the phone.

Only moments earlier her mood had been really upbeat as she had given the city designers the final instructions on remodeling her office. At least now it had a little bit of a woman's touch, with flowers and beautiful paintings to remove all of the masculine overkill.

Subconsciously, she looked at the reflection on the blank screen of her laptop. The image of a proud black woman brought a bright smile to her eyes; the first ever appointed as the head of the department of public safety in a major American city. And why not, this was the same city where Martin Luther King Jr. had begun knocking down all those racial barriers so many years ago.

She sighed and blew air upward that ruffled the ever-present bangs that rested on her brows. She pinched the bridge of her rather pointy nose and hung up the phone, pondering over the message that had brought a mixture of both joy and disturbance.

"Damn," she muttered and started punching keys to verify what she had heard. As usual the particular source proved to be reliable. With contrasting emotions buzzing loudly in her mind, she pushed away from her desk and walked to the window overlooking Peachtree Street and the downtown Atlanta skyline. It was the only city that she had ever really known. A city that she loved and had been entrusted to keep safe.

She closed her eyes, wondering whether this was the start of a dream come true or the continuation of a never-ending nightmare. What was she to do? How long could she continue to live a lie? Folding her arms across her ample bosom, she looked to the clouds, thinking of all the people that believed in her. What would they do, especially her political enemies, if the truth about her past ever really came to light?

She sucked on her teeth with the confidence that had gotten her to the status she now enjoyed. After a moment of meditation, she ran her manicured hands across her forehead and knuckled the corners of her eyes, pressing imaginary wrinkles. She spoke much louder than she thought. "We'll just have to make sure that nobody finds out."

"Never find out what, bossa lady?" a voice stuttering with an oriental accent called from the doorway.

A shiver of fear of being discovered ran down Beverly's spine as she jerked around. Quickly regaining her composure, she spat venom. "Lieutenant Woo, how many times have I told you to knock?" She paused to place her hands on her hips. "Knock and wait for me to tell you that it's okay to come in."

The petite Vietnamese officer, the feared leader of the dreaded Black Cat drug enforcement team, squinted her cheeks and smiled. "Bossa lady, you aight? You ain't never told me that." She hunched her shoulders meekly and eased through the door.

She had only taken a few steps and opened her mouth to speak further, but Beverly cut her off. She advanced aggressively toward her and growled, "Lieutenant Woo, I still did not tell you that it was okay to enter."

Woo's eyes widened and she raised her hands in a defensive posture as she backed up. "Do you want me to go back out and knock first?"

Beverly rubbed her forehead as she stared down at the floor for a brief moment before she spoke over her shoulder and turned around to walk back to her desk. "Naw, come on in and this had better be good."

Lieutenant Woo stepped forward timidly toward the chief's large desk and placed papers on it. "Is it okay for me to sit down?" After receiving a curt nod from the chief, she eased into the chair and patted the papers. "I need authorization to hook up with the Red Dogs over in Decatur to straighten up those hotels along the county borders."

Beverly's eyes squinted in concentration as she placed a hand over her mouth and leaned back in the seat. After watching Woo swallow a lump down her throat, she nodded for her to continue. Woo hunched her narrow shoulders and leaned forward. "That's it, bossa lady; I want to clean up the whole strip on I-20. From Little Vietnam to Lithonia. What else is there to say?"

Beverly pyramided her hands across the bridge of her nose, cocked her head to the side and stood. "Okay, go do your thing." When she didn't get an immediate reply from the diminutive lieutenant, she sat back down and started shuffling some of the paperwork that was piled on her desk.

Woo sat puzzled for a few seconds and then pushed the papers further across the desk. "Thanks, but aren't you forgetting to sign the papers?"

Beverly didn't take the time to look up and waved her dismissal.

Woo blinked a couple of times and mumbled, "But…"

"But what?" Beverly said sternly.

"Are you going to authorize these or not?"

"I just did and I'm sure that you're going to do an excellent job." She paused to lean back in her chair and stared back at her. "Oh yeah, and the next time that you come in my office, I'd really appreciate it if you would knock and then wait until you are welcomed in. Understood?"

Woo gathered up her papers. "Understood." She slowly got up to leave. When she arrived at the door and started to turn around to speak, the chief's hand was pointing toward the door. The expression told her that it would be useless to say any more, so she sighed heavily and left.

When she closed the door, Beverly stared at it for a minute, wondering why she had come to her office. Espccially when she knew that her staff handled that sort of thing. Was she trying to get closer to her since she was now the chief instead of one of her colleagues? Hell, she couldn't really blame her for that. Or maybe she was being a little too paranoid because of the call. *Check yourself, old girl, ain't no need to start getting all unraveled now*, she thought and then dug into her black purse to retrieve her cell phone. She punched in some numbers.

"Might as well make sure that the playing field is all clear," she hummed to herself as the phone rang. "Hello, you know who this is. There are some things I want you to look into."

✠ ✠ ✠

A half-hour after entering the control room, Sparkle rolled down the window to catch the breeze in the old prison van. He watched the rural Georgia countryside en route to the bus station. Old gray-haired Sergeant Jones gave him a bucktoothed smile. "Yo family's going to be waiting on you at the bus station in Atlanta? That's where you're going, ain't it?"

Sparkle was way too deep in his own thoughts to be paying him much attention. Sarge cleared his throat and repeated himself. Sparkle blinked. "Sorry about that, Sarge; my mind was way out there. Ah yeah, they'll be there when the bus shows up. I think my sister said the bus would hit town around noontime."

"That's good, man, that ya family be sticking wid ya and all." The van shrieked to an abrupt stop and Sarge took the time to light a cigarette. The sudden stop caught Sparkle by surprise and forced him to brace against the dashboard. He was about to shout a number of obscenities before he looked up and saw an old country convenience store.

Sarge let out a stream of blue smoke in his direction. "Dat dere's da bus depot; you near about there now, home, I mean." Sparkle shot a frown at him, wondering why he had stopped so far away. Sarge didn't acknowledge the frown as he reached across Sparkle's body to open the glove compartment. Having no idea what this hillbilly was up to, Sparkle leaned back in the seat. Sarge smiled at his reaction. "What's wrong with you, partner?" he snorted in response. He pulled out a flask and took a big gulp of some rot-gut home brew. He aahed and belched loudly, and then to Sparkle's surprise, offered him a taste.

Sparkle gathered himself together. "Thanks, Sarge, but no thanks. I'd rather keep my head on straight now."

Sarge harrumphed, took another big swig, aaahed again

and wiped his mouth with the back of his knuckled hand. "Just thought I'd offer. You were one of the few guys back yonder that acted like he had some sense."

Sparkle forced a smile at the so-called compliment. At the same time he was thinking, *This droopy-jawed mutha-fucka's gotta be out of his godayum mind if he thinks I'm gonna drink sumthang after his... uh, uh, damn what's that mutt's name...dam...Uh-huh, the one that used to slobber all over everything. Oh yeah, that fucking Hooch, Turner and Hooch, that big nasty drooling mutt with Tom Hanks... Oh hell to the naw.*

"Whatcha thinking about, son? I say sumthang funny?" Sarge grimaced, puzzled why Sparkle couldn't appreciate his good-natured gesture. *Hell, how many boys do he think could even get an offer to share a drink wid me*, he thought as he harrumphed and took another big swig.

Sparkle shuddered slightly; struck between insult and common sense, he chose the latter. "Naw, Sarge, I was sorta getting away from any mind-blowing stuff, if you feel me." He paused to nod at the flask. "And from the smell of dat there and the way you aahing and shit, I really don't think I could handle it."

As he expected, that drew a smile out of Sarge, so he continued, "Now if you wanna score me one of them root beer sodas out of that machine over yonder, I will gladly touch glasses with ya."

The wrinkles eased out of Sarge's brow as he chuckled. "Aw, fella, you right, what's wrong with me?" He tapped the side of his head with the flask. "And here I'ma C.O. and offerin' you some rot-gut home brew."

Sparkle smiled innocently, hunched his shoulders and spread his hands out.

Sarge smiled back. "T'ain't much correcting in that, huh?"

"No offense, but it sho ain't."

Sarge nodded. "None taken. Come on, let's get you on home."

Sarge escorted him to the counter where a gray-haired, leather-skinned, chew-tobacco gal cashed his twenty-five-dollar state check. Sarge handed him his bus ticket to Atlanta. "Take care of yourself, son. Don't let me see ya this way again."

Sparkle saluted him as he drove off in a cloud of dust. He turned to the lady, who was whittling on a piece of wood. He bought a cherry Slurpie and went to sit at a rickety wood table with a red-and-white checkered cloth. After a five-minute wait, he looked over at her. She was still whittling away, eyeing him nonchalantly. He nodded toward her and then pinched his nose. "You don't mind if I wait on the bus out on the porch, do you?"

She grumbled what he took for a yes and headed toward the door. Opening it, he turned back to her. "How long is the bus gonna be?" She held up all ten fingers without muttering a word. Taking that to mean around ten minutes or ten o'clock, he went outside and sat in a wooden rocking chair on the other side of the soda machine. He started rolling a joint out of the ounce of reefer he'd hidden in his socks earlier.

He had a pretty good buzz by the time the bus pulled up in front of the store a half-hour later. Since the bus was nearly empty, he eased his way to the backseat and stretched out. He began daydreaming about the things he had to do in the forthcoming days.

Before he'd even realized, he had dozed off. The next thing he knew he was being shaken awake by the driver after they had pulled into the station in Macon. He placed a collect call to his sister Janet's house. Her boyfriend, Kenny, told him that she had already left for the depot on International Boulevard.

He casually walked to the counter and asked the cute little red-head cashier, "How long before the bus pulls out for Atlanta?"

She blinked her bright green eyes and smiled. "You got about a forty-five-minute wait."

He wondered if hers was a set smile. He looked down at his prison garb, feeling that she had to be accustomed to seeing dudes in the cheap light-blue shirt, khakis and brown fake leather shoes. *What does it really matter?* he thought as he turned away from her and headed for the seats.

After squirming around to get comfortable, he started scanning the room. Immediately, he noticed a familiar figure wheeling the knob of a video game. Cocking his head slightly, he squinted to make sure. Shonuff, it was

Soft, his little gambling buddy from back in the joint in Columbus. He'd been named such because of the magic he could do with a deck of cards. Nodding with a high-cheeked smile, he crept up and gently tapped him on the shoulder. "What's up, little muthafucka?"

With a jolt Soft turned around with a stunned look on his face and leaned away. Recognition set in and he broke out in an ear-to-ear smile. "Whodafuck, aw, man, tell me it ain't so. Sparkle?"

"It's so, little guy." He was all smiles.

"Well, I'll be damned. What it be, dog? Yours was certainly the last face I expected to see today. Man, when you get up? Where you go after we split? Aw, man, what the fuck; fucking Sparkle, wow!" Soft shot off in rapid succession in a squeaky feminine voice. Yeah, his boy was gay. Well, at least he was back in the joint. Sure didn't appear to be anything like that now.

"Yeah, Soft, it's me, nigga; what the fuck's up?" Evidently Soft hadn't taken the time to notice his get-out-of–the-joint gear, so he spread his hands down his body. "Man, don't tell me you've been out that long that you don't remember this shit here."

Soft leaned back and blinked his eyes. "Damn, man, I didn't even pay attention; all I saw was your face."

Sparkle smiled. "Yeah, tain't nutten but a come-up this morning, partner, from down there in Valdosta." He leaned back and eyeballed his boy up and down before adding, "Shonuff look like you doing good for yourself."

Soft dusted some imaginary dust from his collar and the front of his outfit down to the knees. "You like?"

The *dun-de-dun* of the video game caught his attention and he jerked back around to resume playing. Sparkle noticed that he had a slightly different look from what he remembered when he'd seen him last in Columbus. Replacing do-rag, pressed-down hair was a curly do, cropped bald at the temples. He was wearing a light-brown coverall about three or four sizes too big, with tan Timberland boots. The oversized outfit looked rather jazzy and disguised the lankiness of his frame. The huge gold rope dangling down his neck and Rolex watch hanging on his wrist showed that he was definitely successful in whatever he had gotten into.

He waited for him to complete his game, which was obviously frustrating him. "Yeah, hell yeah, I like your outfit, dude," Sparkle whispered. "Shit be fly for a mug." He reached over and ruffled his hair. "Looking good, baby, looking good. So whatcha up to, partner?" He made a real show of checking him out.

Soft smirked at the admiration in his eyes, ran a finger under his nose and sniffed. "A nigga's gotta do what a nigga's gotta do." Then he took a quick peek around the depot. "Well, you know, I be kicking a little weed here, a little coke there and a little boy to a select few. You know, to keep the ching-ching fat in my pockets." He rattled the few coins in his pocket to emphasize his point.

"Tain't a thing wrong with that." Sparkle twisted his mouth downward and nodded. *Fly as this nigga done got, I knew he had to be slinging sumthang. But godayum, dis nigga's a walking pharmacy. I wonder if he's gonna throw a nigga a little sumthang.*

"Last time I saw you, dog, you were Georgia skinning with JJ, Pull and that Buckhead crew on the yard."

Suddenly, as if he was reading his mind, Soft sniffled. He looked over his shoulder and whispered, "Come on, dog, let's hit the bathroom right quick; getcha head tight before you hit the ATL."

Sparkle stretched his neck in a circle and smiled. "Shit, sho ya right, curly top, you da man. Where you lead, I'll follow. I'm right behind ya."

They exited the bathroom a few minutes later, wide-eyed and shiny from sweat. Sparkle eyed the big clock on the far wall. "JJ's probably at the bus station with my sisters, Debra and Janet, now. Dat nigga sounded really eager for me to sho when I talked to him on the phone the other day. Sho hope he got something nice lined up for a nigga, ya feel me." He bent his head toward the big window to see if his ride had showed up, and turned back to Soft. "Check this out, man, how about giving me your digits and I'll holla atcha after I get settled down a bit."

The corners of Soft's eyes wrinkled for a second before he took out a matchbox to jot his number down and handed it to him. Then he took a quick inspection of his Rolex and licked his lips. "Hate to hit and run, but my girls should be pulling up right now. And I got to take a package to some white dudes out in the burbs." As if on cue, a horn started blaring from outside on the dock. His head jerked toward the sound. "Come on, man, that's them right there."

Aw hell naw, he didn't just dis me like that there, Sparkle thought before he shook his head, wondering if the coke they had snorted had him tripping. He shook the thought out of his head and followed him out the door.

When Sparkle had reached him, Soft held up his hand, indicating for him to wait as he continued on to a shiny red Escalade parked at the far end of the building.

Sparkle froze in his tracks. *Damn, shortie done really flipped the script on a nigga, for real yo*, he thought when he saw three sexily clad honeys get out the car. They greeted his boy with kisses on the cheek before one of them handed him the keys to the ride. All he could do was smile in admiration; it was evident that Soft was handling his biz.

Before the thought had cleared, Soft was headed back toward him. He slapped a piece of paper in his mitt, gave him a hug and whispered, "Yo, dog, give me a holla when you get yoself situated. I'll explain the quickness later on, but right now I got to jet, yo."

The sound of the bus revving up let him know that it was time to get on board. They embraced and slapped each other on the back. "I'll be calling ya in a day or so," Sparkle said over his shoulder. "Might have some good news for ya. And of course you ain't gotta explain yourself. I feel ya, dog."

"That'll work, you be chill, partner. I hate to roll on you like this but impatient money's waiting." He hunched his shoulders as he spun around, then got into the ride and sped off the dock.

"Last call for boarding to Atlanta," the bus driver yelled. Sparkle stepped up his pace and followed the last few people to board. He again made his way to rear of the bus.

After settling into his seat, the scene quickly changed as the bus sped through the city to the outskirts. Three-story buildings and housing projects turned into peach groves and farmland. He let the window down to catch the breeze and then unfolded the piece of paper Soft had slipped him. It contained an 8 ball of the powder they had snorted in the bathroom. *Good looking out, little buddy, good looking out. Damn, this be some good shit, too.* He took a few blasts and then eased back in the seat to continue enjoying the scenery.

The sun was at high noon as the Atlanta skyline came into view on the horizon when the bus hit Spaghetti Junction, a virtual maze of intersecting interstate highways, outside of downtown.

The sight of the Peachtree Towers' revolving restaurant warmed his heart with memories. He and his partner Rainbow had run their episodes of the "fly in the soup scam" for free expensive meals. He laughed to himself at how easy it had been to fool the waitresses and waiters simply by toting a briefcase and wearing a three-piece suit. Usually they hadn't had to use the scam; only act like they were important. The workers automatically had presumed they'd pay; however, they rarely had.

Sparkle was still caught up daydreaming when the bus pulled into the Greyhound station on International Boulevard. Debra's man, JJ, whom he had done a bit with in Columbus, was standing at the entranceway as he passed to the unloading dock. He pushed the window down to holler at him, but the bus turned the corner before he had a chance.

No sooner had he touched ground than he was bumrushed by a horde of squealing little sweethearts. "Uncle Larry, Uncle Larry," was all he could decipher. A sea of dainty hands pulling on his pants legs had his heart in an uproar. All were vying for his attention, with their wide-eyed excitement. It took all the effort he could muster to keep his balance. As he bent down to scoop up one in his arms, he caught JJ's eyes and nodded to the wiggling one in his grasp.

JJ smiled. "My nig, that's Brittany, Krystal's little girl, in your arms." He proceeded to point to each of them. "And that's Candace and Man, Kym's kids; and Ebony and Mike, Debra's little runts."

After a few moments of confused bliss, he noticed a dark-brown Mark IV parked a few feet away. He presumed it was Janet's ride. Through the fingers of a little hand clawing at his face, he saw Debra in the passenger seat beaming an angelic smile.

He looked over to his niece, Krystal, who was leaning on the hood of the car smiling at his predicament with the kids. "Niecy, could you please help me out here, girl?"

The volume of her laughter shot up a couple of scales. "Aw, man, they all happy to see you. Enjoy the moment; you can handle it."

He smiled at the dark-skinned cutie pie dressed in a jean suit bedazzled with rhinestones. She was looking as sweet and innocent as ever. He spread his arms wide apart. "Come here, girl; let your old unc get a hug." Without a moment's hesitation she embraced him and her daughter in a loving squeeze. Holding Brittany in his arms, he allowed the crew to steer him to the car. Janet, his oldest sister, was at the steering wheel.

Debra leaned out of the window and yelled, "Aight, skinny-ass nigga, come give me a hug, too."

He gently put the squirming Brittany down and leaned on the car window. "Damn, girl, you could at least get out of the car."

He put his hand on the handle, but Janet pushed open the driver's door and smiled. "Get out, my ass; you better get your narrow butt in the car. I ain't got time to be out here all day."

He harrumphed and reached in the window and gave Debra a big hug. *Always rushing to wait, that's Janet.* He loved her death, even if she was bossy as all out. He stared at Debra as they separated. She was smiling and as always he was stunned by her beauty. If you would split the years between Ciara and Chante Moore, you'd come up with Debra. She blew him a kiss and he could see in her eyes that she was blitzed to the gill. Without a word she handed him an El Producto filled with reefer and already lit.

Before he could get two good tokes, Janet hollered over her shoulder, "Godayum, Debra. Couldn't ya'll at least wait 'til we ain't around the children."

Debra pushed Sparkle's face and smiled. "Uh-huh, yeah, Mr. Sparkle man, you can't wait."

He looked at her and put his hand over his youth to stifle the laugh erupting from his stomach and stuttered, "What, I can't. Aw, hell okay." He frowned at the back of Janet's head.

"Thank you, godlee," Janet harrumphed and added, "And I ain't got to turn around to know you sneering at me, bony-ass man, so you better come around here and give me a hug or something."

He pulled back from Debra's tongue-poking-out-face, crossed the front and bowed his head toward her. When she turned her face sideways to offer him her cheek with her arms raised, he jerked the door open. A look of shock crossed her face as she lost her balance. He scooped her out the car and embraced her in a bear hug.

She immediately started cursing, "You crazy mutha-fucka."

Before she could get it all out he swung her out of the car and started swirling her in a circle. He could keep it up for only a few spins because she had gotten big as hell. He staggered to a stop before they both hit the pavement. He released her and barely got out of the way of a wild left hook before he sat her against the car. She made a feint and started chasing him, but realized it was useless after only a couple of seconds. She slid back into the car huffing and puffing. All the kids were rolling with laughter.

He slid into the backseat and Debra blew him a shotgun up his nose. He pressed one nostril with his index finger and inhaled deeply until he started to gag.

She reached across his shoulder and started pounding on his back, until his face was mashing into the back of the seat. Janet popped him upside the head. "Ah-ha, that's whatcha get. I done told ya'll not to do that stuff around the kids anyway."

He coughed. "See there, BooBoo, I told ya to wait." He back-handed the spittle from his mouth and chin. Debra sucked another good toke and rolled her eyes at Janet and said, "Aw godayum, let's get outta here." Reluctantly she put the blunt out.

"About time." Janet pouted.

"I said okay, Grandma," Debra spat, as she suddenly pressed her back into the seat.

"Grandma, my ass. All these kids around; damn girl," Janet growled as she spun angrily around.

"Hey, I said okay. I put it out, so you can stop yo bitching," Debra said as she crossed her legs and arms.

Janet reached back and slapped Sparkle upside the head. "And as for you, fly-ass nigga, you ain't been out but a hot second. Can't you chill on that? Man, we in downtown Atlanta. My God!"

He held up his hands in surrender, reached over Debra and yanked a giggling Brittany onto his lap. "Let's roll then, ya'll."

Brittany wiggled and giggled all the way to the Chandler East apartments where the rest of the family waited to welcome him home.

He admired the skyline as they rolled down I-20 and passed some of his old haunts in Atlanta and Decatur.

Thirty minutes later they piled out of the car. His nephew, Stacy, and niece, Kym, tackled him to the ground. He looked up the sidewalk; these were the same apartments where he used to stay with the twin sisters from Washington, Georgia.

He smiled, recalling the sweet honeys; especially how down they had been with their hustles. He silently wondered how they were doing, since he hadn't heard anything about them for several years. He made a mental note to track down their whereabouts. Those surely had been some good times, getting high and getting plenty of digits with his boy, Rainbow. One of the twins had ended up being one of his fastest steppers in his ever-revolving stable.

Sparkle got up off the ground and then he and Stacy had a hugging and shoving match up the walk to Debra's apartment. Stacy was draped in a number 38 Georgia Tech football jersey and wore denims bunched around his gold-trimmed Nikes. He was the spitting image of his daddy, Sam, a top player who drove the honeys wild with his squinty-eyed smile and Mack man mentality.

There was a five-player Tonk game in progress when they entered the apartment. Sparkle's initial instincts were to join in the game. He fought off those urges to complete the greeting and to chow down on some fried chicken, fish, spareribs and cornbread; all finger-licking good. He washed down the food with ice-cold Heinekens. Sparkle, Debra and Stacy disappeared into the kids' room. They smoked a couple of blunts before everybody started leaving. It was indeed a blessing to be home.

CHAPTER THREE
It's Rolling Rocks Time

"**I** hear that that nigga Sparkle is about to hit the bricks," a silhouetted figure said out of a haze of blue smoke from the shadows.

"Uh-huh, he should be hitting the city in a little while, if he ain't already here," the other figure in the fedora-cocked acey-deucy responded.

Silhouette cleared his throat. "How long you think it'll take afore he hooks up with his boys?"

"Ya can't really tell. He may chill for a day or two. Then again maybe even a week or so; hell, your guess is as good as mine."

Silhouette got up from behind the desk and started pacing the floor; the hard face was deep in concentration.

Fedora frowned suspiciously before reaching across the table to pluck the smoking blunt out of the ashtray. He took a few tokes, then hacked and coughed from the acrid scratching caused by the harsh smoke. "Well, how ya wanna play it?" He coughed and sniffled. "Whatcha wanna do; wait 'til they all get together?" He coughed and sniffled again. "It don't make me no difference, know what I'm sayin'?"

Silhouette squinted nervously and sat back down, wondering how far dude could really be trusted. He plucked the blunt from his dangling fingers and took some tokes. "Let's sit back and see what happens. He may get away from the game altogether and go straight."

Fedora leaned back in the chair and folded his arms across his chest. "You really think that he's gonna do that, huh?"

Silhouette gave up a snorted laugh and spat, "Hell naw, to tell you the truth, I'm sorta hoping he does. It'll be a lot easier taking care of the other two instead of all three of them at the same time. From what I've heard, these niggas ain't nothing to be playing with."

"Uh-huh, yeah, you probably right about that there. Hell, they ain't nothing to be playing with. Ain't no need for us to even pretend they are." Fedora shifted in his seat, obviously getting slightly uncomfortable.

Silhouette shifted in the shadows as well. "Yeah, you right, be-cause if something happens to the other two, he's definitely going to get involved."

"Okay, so what we do is wait 'til they get together." Fedora took a deep breath and raised the Glock from the table and aimed it out the window. "Pow, pow, pow, yeah, we wait. And be ready for whatever *whenever*."

"Yeah, and be ready," Silhouette grumbled. He took another deep toke before he got up to leave the room.

Fedora watched him leave and then pulled the empty chamber out of the gun, and replaced it with a loaded one. *Damn, you can't really trusty anybody in this damn city, on the real.*

✠ ✠ ✠

After the last of the family had left, Debra and JJ went into the bedroom and left Sparkle to chill on the couch in the living room. The excitement of being released and the following activities had him spent and snoring in no time.

It seemed like he had just closed his eyes when he felt somebody shaking his shoulder. He stirred groggily, yawning and knuckling his eyes before was able to focus on whoever had awakened him. "Yeah, what's up, nigga…" JJ placed a firm hand over his mouth and *sshed* him. Sparkle glared at him angrily and mumbled, "Whadda fuck, man?"

"Come on, dude, keep your voice down," JJ whispered with his face twisted. He looked down the hall to the bedroom.

Sparkle pushed JJ's hand from his mouth. He waved his head back and forth, indicating that he understood and was cooperating.

JJ grimaced at his aggressive motion and backed away slowly to the closet.

A slightly woozy Sparkle sat up on the couch and eyed him curiously. *Man what's wrong with this here fool, waking a nigga up like that?*

JJ, who didn't notice the aggravated look on Sparkle's face, kept peeking back and forth between the hallway and the closet. When Sparkle started to get up and ask him what all the tripping was about, JJ waved him back down. He opened the closet door and then reached down to the floor and up to the shelf.

When he turned around, he had a shoebox pressed to his stomach. He started tiptoeing toward the dining room table, then paused to look down the hall again.

Whaddafuck's up with this nigga? Shiiit, the way he acting is starting to make me all nervous and shit. He looked at the grandfather clock in the corner and saw that it was one o'clock. He yawned, realizing that he was bone tired.

JJ got to his full six feet and retied the sash of his robe. His bald head was shining, even in the dimness. He was one quick-witted dude, but had the annoying habit of overflowing his sentences with street slang; probably to portray the image of always being hyper hip. But the jittery way he was acting now wasn't hip at all.

Sparkle frowned as he watched him take out some baggies. One contained a lot of blocked cubes that reminded him of macadamia nuts. In the others were some smaller bags and some glass tubes. JJ didn't mutter a word as he took one of the cubes and placed it in the glass tube and lit up. He proceeded to suck the smoke greedily through the tube until all of the fumes stopped. Then he held his breath for what seemed like at least thirty seconds. When he exhaled, extremely slowly, Sparkle could see the euphoria spread across his face.

He wiped away some beads of sweat that had instantly appeared on his forehead. "Ooo-wee, that be some bomb shit there, dog, some real bomb shit." He wheezed as he sat back in the chair. "Go ahead, dog; do one of them muthas. Take your time though because that's some potent shit, for real."

Sparkle was curious and got off the couch to join him at the table. JJ *sshhed* him, as if he'd never caught the message. Sparkle sat up, getting a grip on his pissed-offness, feeling like JJ was overdoing it with that *sshhing* bullshit, but his curiosity kept him quiet.

Eyeing him suspiciously, Sparkle pulled out a chair and sat down. With a still sleepy voice, he asked, "Yeah, man, what the fuck is up?" As he eyed him intently, it dawned on him that the nuts reminded him of free-basing coke.

The unmistakable aroma of cocaine whiffed through the air. He pinched his nose and rubbed his neck and chin.

"Wave the lighter back and forth over the rock and when it starts to melt, start sucking up the smoke." JJ motioned for Sparkle to try as he continued to look toward the bedroom.

The rock started sizzling immediately and Sparkle sucked in the smoke. Exhaling slowly he soon felt that old familiar rush of cocaine bliss erupt into his brain. From seemingly far away, he heard JJ's voice, but the coke had him already zooming to Scottieville. The buzz was simply a buzz.

After a few moments he was able to decipher what he was saying. "Be sure you hold the smoke for a while before you exhale." Hell, he'd already done that; dude was tripping or was it him? JJ paused and leaned back in the chair with his forearms folded across his knee. "Now pinch ya nose. Uh-huh, that's the way. Now slowly let the smoke out."

Sparkle nodded and squeezed one eye open to see him still looking down the hall. *This nigga's tripping, yo; ain't even watching me. Oh, well…* The exhilarating effect of the coke had hit immediately with a rush; it felt like he was getting a nut.

His mouth flew open and his eyes bucked wide. "Oooh-weeee, man, whaddafuck?" He wiped a river of sweat off his brow. "Feels like freebasing coke; godayum, this shit be good."

JJ squinted at him. *Damn, partner was down for a helluva long time. No wonder he acting so strange.* "Yeah, dog, that's exactly what it is."

"No shit, where you come up with this, yo?"

JJ looked at him like he had lost his mind. "Come on, dude, you did a pretty long bit but it won't that fucking long. I know you had to hear how lethal this shit done got."

"Damn, man, this here's some really good stuff. And yeah, I heard something about it for years, but you know how it is in that dungeon. You never really know."

JJ turned his nose up a tab. "Yeah, man, this be the shit. Yep, rock cocaine, and the bitches be whatever to get a hit of this shit." He got up and looked down the hall again before he continued, "That's what it is, dog; the same from back in day when yo ass was freebasing, except folk be using stuff that's a lot more potent these days. And like I said, the honeys be giving it up big time, for real, yo."

"For real," Sparkle repeated with a smile spreading from ear to ear. "A nigga could really use a shot of pussy, for sho."

"Hey, man, that's exactly what we getting ready to do. But first we gotta bag up some of this stuff. Might as well clock some dollars while you get your nuts out the sand."

"True dat; true to muthafucking dat." Sparkle grinned hard as hell and started rubbing his crotch vigorously.

JJ got up from the table, put a finger to his mouth and tiptoed back to the closet.

Starting to feel a little jittery himself, he also looked down the hall to Debra's bedroom. *Damn, he sho don't want Boo Bear to know.*

As if he were reading his thoughts, JJ said, "Man, no way we can let Debra know we doing this shit. Man, she really be tripping; especially with little Ebony and Mike around."

Sparkle got up from the table and went to sit back on the couch. He felt real good. "Yeah, I can't blame her. So what's up now?"

JJ reached into the shoebox and took out some miniature Ziplocs in various colors. He placed them in separate piles on the table. Immediately Sparkle started fingering them. JJ watched him for a moment and got up to peek around the corner again before he crept into the kitchen.

Damn, dude's starting to give me the creeps. I've gotta watch his ass, Sparkle thought.

JJ tiptoed back to the table, placed a saucer on it and poured a load of the cubes in it. He took the time to light up one more hit before he got down to biz. "Check this out, dog, pick out the bigger ones, like these; they are twenties. Put them in these brown bags. And the smaller ones; they are dimes, so put them in the red ones."

Sparkle, his mind focused on getting some pussy, immediately responded by picking up the bags, opening them and sliding rocks inside. JJ nodded in approval.

They worked in silence as they bagged up at least a couple dozen before JJ gathered up the stuff and put the remainder back in the shoebox. He quickly placed the box back in the closet and grabbed two jackets. He tossed Sparkle a jean jacket and put on a khaki one.

After easing down the hall to check on Debra and the kids one last time, JJ waved for Sparkle to follow him, *ssshing* him once again. He quietly unlocked the door and slipped out the apartment.

Enough of that ssshing, *fool, like I don't know that we sneaking out of here*, Sparkle thought as he tiptoed behind him.

The paranoid effects of the coke were starting to make him trip, too, as they walked across the field to the other side of the complex. Both of them kept taking turns looking back toward the apartment.

Damn, this jitteriness must be contagious, fucking with this here rock, Sparkle thought. He followed JJ up the steps to a second-story apartment where he rapped on the door. They started to feel the chill in the air. An impatient JJ rang and kicked the door at the same time when there was no response. He shouted in the crack of the door, "Come on, girl, I know yo ass in there."

Sparkle wrapped his arms around himself as he glared up and down the door. He zeroed in on a shadow that passed across the peephole. He smiled, nudged JJ and pointed to the peephole. "Man, what kind of folk you dealing with here, dog; playing peek-a-boo games and shit?"

JJ rolled his eyes and snorted angrily. Huffing he kicked the door harder and shouted again, "Damn red-ass bitch, I can see your stupid ass at the peephole. Whatcha playing these games for?" He started to give it a more vicious kick before Sparkle pulled on his coat sleeve. JJ's head whirled and he growled over his shoulder, "What?"

Sparkle nodded toward the door. "Listen, dude, somebody's pulling the chain; check it out."

JJ leaned toward the crack and snorted. "About time. Damn, a nigga gotta freeze out this bitch, fucking with your tired ass."

The door opened up a few more inches only to be closed back just as fast.

"Damn," they said in unison and looked at each other bewilderedly.

A soft feminine voice eased through the crack. "Whodat widcha, playa?"

"He's wid me, my brother-in-law; Debra's brother."

That didn't faze her. "And?"

"And what?" JJ retorted, starting to get pissed.

"And whaddafuck he want?" she asked suspiciously.

JJ took a deep breath and pinched the bridge of his nose. "Clown-ass geeking bitch, he with me. You gonna open the door or what?"

JJ and Sparkle heard another voice whispering.

A naturally suspicious Sparkle nudged JJ's shoulder. "What's the deal, yo? Why they doing all that whispering and shit?"

JJ hunched his shoulder and raised his brow questionably. He started feeling a little antsy and then said angrily, "Looka here, Dee, you either open this damn door or I'm taking this new bomb I got down to Shorty Mack's crib."

Sparkle nudged him again. "Who the fuck is Shorty Mack? Don't tell me it's the same nigga who used to run that fake hash scam around Buttermilk Bottom back in the day."

JJ nodded with a smile. "Yo, man, this bitch here be up most of the night. And all kinds of geekers be flowing through her spot on the regular. So this be a good spot to nest in. Money, then pussy; money, then pussy; in that order. You feel me?"

"Oh yeah."

JJ snorted a short laugh and punched him on the shoulder. "Yeah, dude, she ain't the finest bitch around but she be a freaky-ass ho. And I know you ain't about to be choosy about getting those nuts of yours out the sand. I got to turn a dollar in this bitch, too."

Sparkle rubbed his hands in excited anticipation and smiled. "You sho nuff right about that there, partner. Let's do this." He elbowed him in the side and nodded at the door.

JJ chuckled and reached into his pocket. He rummaged through the bag and took out six rocks and handed them to him. "Split these with her after I leave." He reached back into his pocket. "Here's a key to get back in the crib, but make sure that you be real quiet; know what I'm saying?"

Another shadow rolled past the peephole, followed by mumbling. The door cracked open again and a shock of curly red hair eased out, followed by a set of green eyes and pouty red lips on a light-skinned face. The eyes zoomed in on Sparkle and the long eyelashes batted daintily as those luscious orbs traced up and down his body.

Damn, dis ho got some sexy eyes, whew, he thought and then posed to let her check him out. An appreciative smile started to crease the corners of those lips. JJ cleared his throat with a harsh grunt to break up the mini lust fest and then pushed the door open.

Dee stepped back and put her hands on her ample hips and frowned. "Nigga…"

She didn't even get to finish as JJ barged past her into the apartment. "Nigga, my ass, bitch; you gotta nigga out here damn near freezing with this stupid shit you be pulling." He spun on her and added, "In here geeking hard for a bitch, ain'tcha?"

"Nigga, how was I supposed to know it was you; X-ray vision or sumthing? Hell, a bitch ain't supposed to check, what?"

JJ gritted on her before he continued to spit, "Hell naw, not after I done told you that it's me."

She stuck her head under the porch light to make sure that nobody else was out.

"Ho, it's cold as hell out here. Get yo ass out the way and let my nigga in. Damn, a nigga be looking out for your stupid ass and you be acting all silly and shit. What the fuck's wrong with you anyhow?"

She put her hands on her hips again, eyeing them both up and down before she rolled her eyes. "Ain't a damn thang wrong with me. Who be this bigga wid ya, yo?" Her voice sounded a little harsh but there was a slight smile on those sexy lips as she looked into Sparkle's eyes.

He stepped by her, shaking the chill off his bones. He eyeballed her curves. *JJ be bullshitting. This bitch here be shake-a-booty fine.* He felt an ache in his groin, eyeing her hips pressed into a pair of crushed velvet shorts; the kind that cling snugly. Even though every nerve in his body was about to burst, he hid this initial reaction well. All his bitch training from way back in the day kicked in. He could see right off the bat that she wasn't the type of bitch a man should show any weakness to; unless he wanted to be eaten alive by her charms.

Sparkle followed JJ further into the apartment, eyeing her voluptuous figure. He nudged JJ in the side as he passed by him. Without turning JJ nodded to let him know that she was the ho he was talking about.

She was sorta tall for a honey. He found himself staring her nearly eye to eye. He quickly judged her to be at least five-seven or eight with an oriental slant to her eyes. She reminded him of the Vietnamese mountain gals back in the war. The kind of girl they used to call "cat eyes" when he was a snotty-nosed brat. Her red hair was cut close to the side with puffy curls on top; the kind of style he dug on a woman. She had a slight hint of a mustache and sideburns, enough to be ultra sexy on a ho. And a small pert nose sat above red pouty lips. The killer was that she stood on her legs in a way that made a bitch's ass fold crease overlap into her thighs. Thighs that were spread wide apart, displaying a sexy vee between her legs.

Feeling and then seeing the direction of his gaze, she smiled into his eyes and stuck her 38DDs right up to his face. Her cleavage was to the max in a red halter top that also revealed her bellybutton set in a chunky but not fat stomach. He saw her swollen nipples and flared nostrils.

As he stood there mesmerized by the electricity shooting between them, somebody called her from the rear of the apartment. When she twisted her body slightly in that direction, his gaze automatically shot straight to that ass. The kind of ass that you could rest a cup on easily without having to worry about spilling one drop. A donkey ghetto butt, for sho. The coke must have really had him tripping because this ho's ass was glittering from the light. Her waist dipped in real deep, right at the top of her phat swell of ass cheeks. His dick refused to stay cool inside of his jeans.

She headed toward the rear, but not before she shot a heavy lidded gaze at his crotch. It was a *"yeah, nigga, this ass looks good"* look on her face; a "come and get it smile" on her lips. They parted seductively. "Damn, you welcome to come in, nigga." She sucked her teeth and gave them one of those jazzy snake rolls with a neck snap.

JJ started rubbing his arm to kill some of the chill as he peeked over Dee's shoulder. "Who dat dere, girl?" He nodded toward a little dark-skinned runt standing behind her.

The runt stepped from behind Dee, turned her mouth

down and eyed them suspiciously. "Is ya'll niggas holding? I hope it ain't none of that garbage that other nigga brought over here a little while ago."

JJ looked around Dee for a better look and snorted. "And who you be, short and sassy?"

She snaked her body around Dee with her nose all tooted up. Then she put her hands on her hips, licked her lips and with a sassy flair, slid a designer-nailed finger under her nose before she smiled. "I be Ruby. Why you got those greedy eyes on me like that? Geez, a bitch gotta get interrogated just to score some shit?"

JJ looked at her and pinched his nose. "Naw, shortie, it ain't gotta be like that. Ruby, huh…okay, little Miss Ruby, let's get away from this door and see what we can do for you."

"Well, come on then." She swirled her narrow hips and pranced toward the bedroom. She was a nice little package, with the kind of perky attitude that made dudes want to control her. But it was easy to tell that little Miss Sassy wasn't havin' it, with her ink black skin, small curly fro and pixieish demeanor. She had that *make a nigga squint* kind of sex appeal that was enhanced by a balloon butt that jiggled like Jell-O in some daisy duke jeans. She sashayed down the hall the way honeys did when they knew that male eyes were scoping that ass.

She took a few steps and spun around like one of those rip-the-runway-models. "Well, whatcha waiting for, playa? Let's do this."

JJ had gotten caught up sweating her hourglass figure, but shook it off. "I gotcha, shortie girl, I gotcha. Go ahead; I'm on my way."

As they were heading down the hall a harsh voice hollered from the room. Dee ignored it, which didn't set well because the first shout was followed immediately by one with more intensity. Dee gritted, put a little more harumph in her strut and screamed, "Muthafucka, you ain't gotta be hollering out like you in some kinda jungle!"

An even harsher reply followed. "Well, damn, girl, folks trying to get on back here!"

She stopped short of the door and when Sparkle tried to walk past, she tugged him by the sleeve. He looked down to the long designer nails wrapped around his arm and smiled. She bumped him slightly with her hip and cooed, "So, you be Debra's long-lost brother, huh? Looks like sexy runs in your family, don't it, cutie pie?"

He felt a tingle run along his groin as he looked into her eyes and got a whiff of her scent. "Shit, Red, you leaning back with a helluva lot of sexy oozing out of your ass, too."

"Ooooh, I can tell I'm gonna like you a lot already."

"Uh-huh, I sure do hope so. I could really enjoy a sexy mutha like you in my life, that's for sure."

Her eyes lowered to the budging lump in his pants and she smiled. "I can see you ain't gonna be hard to get along with. Mmmph and from here I can tell you are definitely a real man."

Sparkle's dick started to throb in his pants. She didn't waste any time leaning into him, pressing her softness right on his hardness and moaned. She reached up and ran her fingers along his neck. The tingling increased as he reached down to rub that phat red ass.

Just when he felt himself starting to drool from the head of his dick, the voice from the back bellowed again.

He heard JJ grunt from down the hallway, "Ahem, ya'll horny muthas wanna handle a little biz first?"

Ruby moaned, "Yeah, bitch, I know you hear them folk back there wanting to get it on with your nasty ass."

Dee sucked on her teeth and flicked her a dainty wave before she elbowed her way between the two of them. JJ patted her ass as she passed and ogled at the way each of her ass cheeks jiggled in her Spandex. "Good God, girl, how in the hell you manage to hold all that up all day? *Damn*."

She tooted her nose up at him. "Very well, nigga; very muthafucking well. Now come on and handle your business because I got things to do, yo." She fluttered her long lashes at him, faked a lustful shiver and licked her lips.

"You one nasty ho, Red." Ruby rolled her eyes as she went into the room.

"Fuck you, bitch; fuck you." She gritted at Ruby before she whirled on JJ. "Okay, playa, you acting all anxious and everything, so let's ease on up in here and see what this bomb is that you screaming about."

JJ halted her swill by pressing his palm on her nose.

"Freeze wid yo shit, go-getter. You know that shit ain't gonna work with me, shawtie." He stepped away and looked at her like she was a maggot or worse.

She was well versed in the game and knew that she had to maintain at least a spark of respect for the new fly in the soup. She parried that blow by snaking her head around his palm and smiled. "Nigga, if you wanna play superfly, you can take your fucking bomb to Shortie's. A ho ain't nowhere near desperate like that." She tooted her nose up and whirled into the bedroom with bitchy attitude; she was still the queen of her castle.

"About muthafucking time, ho," was the greeting by a chorus of folk ready to get their buzz on.

JJ, having known her since their kindergarten days, could only smile at her comeback and let her get her shine on. Besides, he didn't really want to deal with Shortie and she was aware. He had to let her sample the goodies before he could sell even one sack in her spot. Still he had to maintain his swagger in front of the geekers in the room. "Come on, you pretty red muthafucka, but don't think you gonna hold me hostage up in here." He frowned and walked to the other bedroom down the hall and stepped in.

"That's right, home front, do the queen bee right, do her right." She flung her head back and wiggled her Jell-O butt on by him and pushed the door all the way open. Before she stepped all the way in she whirled on Ruby and sneered, "Be back in a sec, bitch."

Ruby wrinkled her nose. "You stank, girl; you stank."

"Whatever." She smiled, popped her finger in a large circle and closed the door.

Five minutes later JJ whipped out of the room smiling from ear to ear and headed to Dee's bedroom. He chirped at the geekers. "Okay, boys and girls, what ya'll hitting for? The bomb is here; the bomb is here."

Dee came out moments later, rolling her eyes at Ruby and wiping the corners of her mouth with her baby finger. She smiled at Sparkle and went into the bathroom. After all she couldn't get up on the new fly with dick breath, knowing she'd be working her magical skills on him shortly.

Ruby turned her nose up when Dee passed and hissed, "Ho, you ain't nothing but a stank ho."

Dee popped her fingers three times skyward and frowned. "Tell me something I don't know, bitch, with your sluttish tar-baby ass." She wrinkled her nose, batted her lashes and closed the bathroom door with a girly flair.

Sparkle, knowing he had a little wait coming, smiled at the catfight banter and went to sit at the dining room table and crossed his legs. His jaws clenched as he lusted at Dee's tremendous ass. *Godayum, dat red-ass ho must have the bomb diggety in those pouty lips, the way she shook bro off so quickly. Shiiiit, a nigga got to have a sample of that there for sho.*

He casually looked around the room. *Hmmm, baby girl has got to have some pretty good taste, too.* He checked out the décor of the room. A red leather couch, anchored by matching loveseats, were in a circle, with pink flamingos on each end. A huge kidney-shaped glass coffee table sat in the center. A seventy-two-inch flat-screen TV was on the far wall over a wall-length aquarium. He squinted at the marine life swimming in the clear blue water. *Damn, were those miniature sharks?* You bet and also a couple of jellyfish. Set all around the room were dozens of feminine whatnots and a few family portraits. There were long glass lamps shaped like flower vases with red lights that gave the room a really cozy feeling. It was the last thing you'd expect in a junkie's crib.

JJ stuck his head out of the room and motioned for Sparkle to join him, breaking his little revelry. As he stood up Dee came out of the bathroom and smiled at him and headed to the back. He bypassed Ruby, who was obviously locked in some deep thoughts. He wondered what she was thinking about, all stuck in her own little world. When he entered the room he saw several groups huddled together passing glass tubes among themselves.

Dee was really laying some dude out as he crossed the sill. "Well, I'm here now, nigga, so what's up?"

Leaning against the door was a tall, dark-skinned dude in a used brown silk suit with an angry frown on his face. Another tall lanky fella, who was leaning against the dresser drawer in a tan jean outfit, waved money in the air toward JJ. "Let's see what you working with, soldier. I could use a good fifty if you running them." He flashed a mouthful of dull gold teeth.

JJ merely nodded at dude and spoke to a light-skinned brother who was sitting on the edge of the bed. "Yo, Tee, my man, what's up, man?"

Tee, who had a set of big pink lips, green eyes and a snooty disposition, shifted his weight on the bed. He squinted at JJ and said in a nasal twang, "Trying to get on, dude. You holding some good shit, I hope?"

JJ took the time to light up a Newport cigarette, and then took a few long tokes before he surveyed the room. "Yeah, I got a little bomb here; whatcha hitting for?"

Tee leaned over to whisper to short dude beside him who looked like he had been geeking for days on end. The fella nodded and went into his pocket to pull out a roll of money.

Dee, who had stationed herself at the door to the bathroom, braced her hands on her ample hips. "Nigga, I thought you said ya'll was broke," she said in an angry tone.

Tee spoke up for the both of them. "Bitch, I didn't want your dirty ass playing games with my ends. Hell, everybody knows how you do when you get broke yourself."

She strutted to the bed and placed her crotch directly in his face. "Naw, nigga, how I be doing?"

He leaned back on the bed, wrinkled his nose and

wiped his hand across his mouth. "Come on, bitch, back your damn pussy outta my face."

She leaned forward, practically right in his face and spat, "Whaddafuck you say?"

"I said," he paused and took a deep breath, "aw, don't worry about it. All I want is some good shit; that's all." He leaned around her and looked at JJ.

Dee straightened up and snorted. "Which one of ya'll gonna serve this bitch?"

JJ stepped menacingly toward Tee. "Nigga, didn't I just ask you what you hitting for?" He cut his eyes at the short guy and then back at Tee before he pulled out a leather pouch from inside his jacket. He rummaged through the baggies of twenties. "Flip money, Reggie, here it is. My shit on display but like I told this nigga here, I got dimes, twenties and boulder fifties."

Reggie eyeballed the pouch like he was struggling to get out of a straitjacket before he licked his dry lips. "Well, what kind of deal can you swing, nigga?"

"Hey, ain't no deals. I told and showed you what I'm carrying, so what the fuck is up; you scoring or what? I ain't got all night to be bullshitting around; you either do or you don't, simple plain, dog."

Tee and Reggie shifted their eyes toward Dee. "Man, I heard ya, but this be her crib and she like to act like she running thangs and shit."

Dee started to say something but JJ put his hand on the small of her back to stop her. "One more time, man. I got dimes, twenties and fifties. What's up?"

He gritted on Reggie like he was something out of the gutter, not about to allow no game right off the top. He was a pure snake from dealing with him in the past. "Nigga, I know you of all people ain't coming at me with that work-a-deal bullshit. You don't cut nobody no slack whatsoever when you on, so it ain't about to happen."

Reggie massaged his salt-and-pepper beard, and being the old grizzled veteran of the streets, he couldn't give up on the first try. He came back at him with a quickness. "Playa, playa, now you know that we been doing this here way too long for you to be going square on me now."

JJ cocked a brow and spat, "Nigga, please, you always come at folk with that pissant con. Then again, fuck that bull you talking. You can get two of these boulders, ten dimes or five of twenties. Nuff said, whatcha gonna do?" He held out the dope in his palm.

Reggie knew that he wasn't going for any of his bull; especially in front of all these folk who also wanted to score. "Aw, aight, dog, if you gonna handle an old friend like that." He reached into his palm and started fingering the rocks.

JJ frowned, his patience wearing thin. "Aw, man, fuck dat. They all the same size." He snatched the bills out of his hand and picked out five dimes and gave them to him, ignoring his grunted reaction. Then he straightened up and looked around the room. "Next."

With a quickness, three people made their way over to him, practically pushing Reggie out of the way and flashing money.

Sparkle leaned against the dresser while checking the action. No sooner had JJ served one customer than another was flashing dollars in his face. The fast-paced activities brought back memories of when he was slinging coke and heroin on Auburn Avenue with his boy, Rainbow, in Buttermilk Bottom. *Boy, homey's really clocking the bills*, he thought as he counted dollars right along with him.

CHAPTER FOUR
Sexy Dee Works Her Magic

Sparkle tried to concentrate on his boy getting down. But his attention kept getting drawn to Dee's ass shaking like Jell-O every time she shifted her weight in her animated confrontation with Tee. When she started pacing back and forth, each ass cheek seemed to rumble on its own axle. His dick kept jerking at his zipper like it was trying to take a sniff at the wide gap between them. Sensing him checking her out, she eyed him out of the corner of her eyes. She started posing at an angle so that her titties and ass curved up and out for his full inspection.

Catching the lust glittering in his eyes, she threw him a sexy smile and purred, "Hey, fellas, how about one of ya'll check to see if I bolted the chain back on the door."

JJ looked at her like she had lost her mind, but turned and reluctantly went to check it out anyway. She sneered at his departing back and locked in on Sparkle's eyes, seductively lowering hers to the ever-growing bulge in his pants. Her nostrils flared as she ran a wanton tongue across her lips and walked up to him. Faking like she was watching JJ check on the door, she whispered so that the others in the room couldn't hear her. "Mmm-mmm, where did JJ come up with you, sexy-ass nigga?"

She rolled her golden cat eyes up and down his body and put some extra dick-throbbing sway into that sexy ass as she walked to the hallway bathroom. He was caught up in the motion of her hips. He didn't notice JJ had walked up to him until he'd nudged him in the side. "Hey, man, don't let all that honey-coated sex appeal fool ya. Dat bitch is a real dog. Believe that shit there, partner."

Sparkle gritted at him, irritated that he had picked him to be some kind of weak-ass nigga. "Yeah, bro, I done figured dat much, but damn she be fine for a mug. Don't worry about me, dog, 'cause I got my mental on at all times."

"Yeah." JJ smiled.

"Hell yeah." He smiled back.

"Uh-huh, but take it from me, the bitch has got some of that super-duper pussy and head and ass. She know that shit, too, so keep yourself on point, dog. That's all I'm saying, for real, yo."

"I bet she do." Sparkle smiled in anticipation.

"Yeah, you bet right, but it's for all comers who keep the biggest package of this shit here." He flashed the bag of rocks he'd taken out of his pocket. It was time to get paid so he waved away the nonsense conversation and nodded toward the people in the room. "Come on, dog; let's go get the rest of this here scratch."

There were groups in clusters but Sparkle zoomed in

on a trio of honeys sharing a glass shooter in the far corner. One of the girls had a remarkable resemblance to Dawn Robinson, that sexy redbone that used to sing with EnVogue. She happened to be one of his favorite fantasies while he was doing his bit. Another was dark with a tight afro, aight as far as aight goes. Then there was a coffee-and-cream-colored older broad with short hair. She had her back to him so he couldn't get a full look at her face.

There was another dark-skinned honey in a plaid skirt and white blouse sitting at the upper end on the other side of the bed. She was busy stuffing a big piece of rock in a shooter. He stared with interest as she took long tokes, and beads of sweat jumped off her forehead. As she pulled off the shooter, he smiled knowingly when her eyes bucked open when that shit hit her. *Ain't that a bitch. Must be some kinda epidemic going on with all these girls with green eyes.*

His eyes flickered with a smile when the Dawn Robinson look-a-like hollered at the older broad. "Damn, Violet, you gonna suck the char boy out of the bitch, ain'tcha?"

Miss Coffee-cream ignored her and continued to suck on her glass dick a few more times before she said between gasps of breath, "Ho, I done told you that I gotcha, so cool yo ass down."

A big black dude in some bib overalls with dreadlocks grumbled from the other corner, "Aw, greedy-ass ho, give up the dick like folks do you."

Coffee-cream stretched her neck around and frowned.

"Fuck you, Daveyboy, ain't nobody asked your broke ass for a damn thang."

Dee got fed up with not being the center of attention and strode to the front of the room with her hands on her hips. "Look here, ya'll, why the rest of ya'll sitting around holding on to that raggedy-ass money, you can see the man's got the bomb. What ya'll gonna do? Folks ain't got all night waiting for ya'll."

Daveyboy and Coffee-cream stared at each other before she arched her brow and stood. Sparkle thought he'd heard somebody call her Viola, Violet or something similar. Yeah, that was it: Violet. She passed her shooter to her partner and started walking toward them with what he took for as a sexy smile. "Hey, honey, what ya'll players hitting for here anyway?"

JJ, aware of the game she was playing, sniffled and jacked up his jeans. "What's up, V? We got dimes, twenties and boulder fifties. What ya'll be wanting?" He reached in his pocket and displayed the rocks. "And it be the bomb, old gal, you know I don't be playing with you about this shit here. It's some new shit from Miami called Peruvian golden flake. Let me warn you though, this shit is some instant hurling shit, playette."

Violet rolled her eyes at him and walked over to Sparkle, giving him a personal version of her sexy smile. "And who you be, playa?"

He looked her up and down. "Who the hell *you* be, player?"

"I be Violet. Folks holla for Lady V when they be wanting all kinds of fly shit. Maybe someday you'll need some fly shit, so let's see up close what you working with." She fluttered her eyes seductively, followed by a sly wink.

Sparkle took an instant liking to her upfront style but kept his approval in check. Something was telling him that he had to work some real player magic to deal with her. He put the chill in his eyes to show that she had to be at her best to impress him. "Let me see what we working with for the nice lady here, dog." He nodded to the bag in JJ's hand.

She rolled her eyes and pulled out a roll of bills, peeled off five twenties and flashed them at him. He turned his back to her and reached in the bag to get two fifties. He turned back around and held them out for her inspection. She reached for the dope but he closed that hand and opened the other one.

The smile left her eyes, replaced by a cold stare. He had pissed her off but he had to show her which of their personalities would rule between them. He stared blankly until she placed the money in his hand. He slapped the rocks into her hand. She turned them over and over in her hand. "So this be the bomb, huh?"

Feeling that he had proven his point, he allowed himself to smile. "Yeah."

She nodded. "Okay, player, we'll see." She put half a fifty on her shooter and put it to blaze. Halfway through the hit, the euphoria hit her like a ton of bricks and beads of sweat erupted on her forehead. "Oh yeah, this be some good shit, aight." She reached behind her to hand the shooter to her buddy.

Dee, who had retreated to her bathroom to observe the scene, waited until the flow had slowed before she sashayed across the room to lean against him. He was still enjoying the sight of Violet's reaction when he felt her sweet heat pressing against his side. Her nearness caused an immediate stirring in his groin. She was expecting a response but he waited for her to make her next move. He didn't have to wait long; he felt her soft hand start to caress his back under his jacket. It was followed by a warm wisp of air whispering in his ear, "You mean to tell me that you ain't holding nothing for your own pleasure, stud?"

He cocked his head sideways as he peeked over his lowered shoulder and flinched, stunned by the nearness of her green eyes. The warmth in them seemed to pierce through his brain and he shuddered from the tingling sensation that ran down his spine. It was only the beginning.

Dee rose up on her tiptoes, placed her small hand on his shoulder and whispered in his ear, "I want to suck that big dick of yours. JJ can handle these geek monsters. Come on, let's get away from these muthafuckas and go to the other room."

He narrowed his eyes and smiled, giving her a guttural

response. "Damn, girl, you sho ain't got no problem going at yours, do you?"

She licked her lips and leaned away. "And why should I? I see what I like, I go at it. You got a problem with that?" she purred as she squeezed his ass.

He spun to face her but was interrupted by JJ, who had taken care of his immediate biz and grabbed Dee by the elbow. "Come on, girl, I need to use the telephone."

Now this nigga knows damn well I'm trying to get it on with this nigga here, she thought. She frowned but allowed herself to be pulled down the hallway. She eyeballed Sparkle over her shoulder as JJ led her away.

JJ sighed. "Damn, bitch, can your fat ass chill for a sec? Bro's gonna be here for a while. I need to call my boy."

"Nigga, you act like you don't know where the phone is." She gritted and eased her arm out of his grip.

"Come on, girl. On the real; I need you to look out for my boy for an hour or so because I got to make a run." He took the phone off the kitchen wall and started punching numbers. "Seriously, Dee, buddy just got out of the joint today, and I can see he's got the hots for you. But I need him to clock some dollars while I'm gone. You already know that I'm gonna look out for you."

He could see her conniving little mind clocking all the rocks she was gonna get to smoke. For a split second he started having second thoughts about leaving the package. He quickly pushed those fore warnings to the side and smiled. "Dee, you one slick-ass ho, but don't let that innocent look he has fool you. My boy's been in the streets for quite a while."

"I didn't—"

He cut her off with a quickness, "Girl, shut up; cut it out. Ain't no need playing goody girl with me. Handle your biz and don't go getting all greedy and shit."

She waited until he finished with his bullshitting line and placed a reassuring hand on his shoulder. "Man, gon' take care of what you gotta do. I'm sure that pretty boy in there can handle his own. Hell, you know me; I just wanna keep my geek going." She licked her lips and waved her hand through her hair before she sucked on her teeth. "And your boy wants to get his nuts out of the sand. Ain't that what ya'll niggas call it? Hell, any way you look at it, we, me and him are using each other for what we want. The way I see it, an even swap ain't no way a swindle, huh?"

JJ sniffled and scratched his head. "Yeah, bitch, that's what we say. You a mess, you know that?"

"So go do you. I got this." Dee gave him a snappy nod, spun around and headed back to the bedroom with a sly smile on her face.

Sparkle, who had been spying on them the whole time, turned back toward the room before she could bust him sweating her. He realized that she was working him for the coke with her come-on, but he didn't give a fuck as long as he got his freak on. It was hard to do, the way her ass was yanking from side to side as she went into the bathroom. He wondered what she was doing in there but quickly shook his head to rid himself of that sucker thought. Hell, she was only a piece of ass.

"You still holding that monster, sweetie?" Violet said in a sweet timid voice. He felt her warm breath on his neck and a whiff of her sexy perfume. His lips brushed her forehead when he turned to face her, forcing him to lean away so he could focus on her face. Her penetrating green eyes caused a shiver to run down his spine. Or was it the horniness that was ready to burst?

He choked back his rush of hormone bliss and licked his lips. "Let me go holla at JJ. Whatcha hitting for, sweet thang?"

She batted her eyes twice. "Me and my girls over yonder got close to a hundred and we was hoping that you could swing us some kind of deal." She nodded toward her friends sitting on the far end of the bed.

"I'll see what I can come up with; give me a second." Sparkle headed for the kitchen to holla at JJ.

JJ placed his hand over the receiver and smiled. "Damn, they ready for some more already?"

"Yeah, man, Shawtie wants to know what you can do for her and her friends for close to a hundred," Sparkle said after clearing his throat.

"How close to a hundred they talking about?" JJ started digging in his pocket to take out the package.

Sparkle wiped his hand across his mouth, frowned and hunched his shoulders.

JJ wrinkled his brow and told the caller that he'd get back with him later, gave Sparkle a half-hearted smile and slapped him on the back before heading toward the back. When he crossed the doorsill, he turned back to him. Sparkle nodded toward the honeys huddled together, chattering amongst themselves. JJ mouthed which one and Sparkle indicated the one in the white jeans.

JJ nodded and called out to her, "Yo, Joyce, you or Violet want to holla at me?"

Violet took a last toke off her shooter, swiveled on the bed and eyed the two of them. Sparkle hadn't noticed how old she was until then, but it was all good because he preferred older broads anyway.

She was dressed to the tens in a brown calf-length silk cowgirl skirt with a matching blouse and expensive suede boots. He wondered why a jazzy broad like her was hanging with a crew of geeked-out high chasers. His eyes brightened when she stood up like a gracious queen and strode over to them.

She cleared her throat, smiled demurely at him and spoke to JJ. "How you been, playa? We've been zooming all day. Wish you would've brought this good shit over a lot earlier before we'd spent all our ends." She cleared her throat again and licked her lips. "Anyhow we down to around eighty-five dollars, so what can you do for a sister?"

JJ covered his mouth and ran his hand up and down his shirt. He studied her for a while before he nodded toward the hallway. She brushed a scented shoulder against Sparkle's chest as she passed. He tilted his head at her passing figure. For the benefit of those watching for his reaction, he held back a smile as he admired the sway of her hips. He felt as if she was putting a little extra harumph into the way she was swinging that thing just for him.

"Hey, stud, what's up?"

He stopped tracing Violet's ass and slowly veered his attention to the sound of the voice. He wasn't really surprised when he looked down at the creamy titties pressing into his chest. Damn sexy-ass Dee; she wasn't about to get any objections from him, no way. Nor was he about to turn away when she started wiggling her finger for him to follow her into the bathroom.

The sight of those sexy hips caused a surge through his groin before she reached back for his hand. He'd barely crossed the doorsill when she said in a husky voice, "Close the door, playa. Gotta keep these muthas outta my biz, you know." She turned away to let him get a real good look at that fat ass of hers while she fidgeted with a few rocks she had in the cabinet.

He forced his eyes away and closed the door, turned around and ran smack dab into her pouty lips. She gave him a shotgun so close that he could feel the heat coming from her lips without her even touching his. He opened his mouth enough to let the smoke in as her hypnotizing eyes got closer and closer.

He nearly gasped when her snake-like tongue slid into his mouth. He did gasp when she cupped his neck and started swirling her tongue around his. There was an unmistakable, lust-filled passion in her eyes when he got a firm grip on her waist and pulled her to him. She moaned with delight and floated into his body.

He felt the drool oozing from his dick as it gushed down his thigh, slippery and godayum erotic. She spread her thighs, closed her crotch around his throbbing dick and moaned even louder.

Her warm breath caressed his cheek and ear, sending tingling shocks down his spine. The heat from her crotch was unbearably hot, as she hunched slowly up and down his dick. His nose flared fire as he felt her pussy lips clutching around his swollen head.

His head started spinning. *Aw godayum, I can feel this bitch's pussy getting wetter through my pants, whaddafuck-godayum.* They reached down and cuffed each other's ass at the same time and she started moaning sweetly as her tongue picked up speed in his mouth. She started dry-fucking him.

When she gasped and froze her tongue at the roof of his mouth, he nearly went into shock. *Oh hell naw, this ho is getting a muthafucking nut, good God almighty.* Beads of sweat started rolling from his forehead to mix with hers. The intensity of her passion pushed him to the edge of getting a nut himself.

Suddenly, the door started to vibrate on his back and

he heard JJ mumbling through the door. "Oh no, he didn't." He heard and felt her mouth the words into his in a muffled reply. He fought like hell to control the trembling in his body as his knees started to buckle.

She froze in the middle of a powerful grind and backed off of him. He was either tripping or swearing that he'd felt her pussy squish as it loosened its massaging magic off his dick. *Man this bitch here has either got me punked on her pussy already or this coke is really working my ass,* he thought as he eased back off the door. She reached around him to turn the knob.

"Yo, Spark, I need to holla at you, partner. Me and my boy Percy's got to go handle some biz." JJ squeezed his voice through the crack in the door.

Damn, who the hell is Percy? he thought when JJ's face came into view after he opened the door.

As if he were reading his mind, JJ spat, "He's the nigga that I've been down with for a minute now. You'll get to meet him after we make this run." Then he looked over his shoulder at Dee. "Check this here out, redbone, I need to holla at my man before I jet." As an afterthought, he added, "Why don'tcha school him on some of these niggas for me; I'm gonna leave him some of these rocks to handle while I go reup. Okay?"

Sparkle looked over his shoulder, hunched his shoulders and stepped out. As they headed down the hall, he said, "Hey, man, I can handle this while you gone."

JJ ran a hand over his head and stared at him for a few

seconds. "Yo, man, don't let all that warm shit that red-ass bitch be throwing at ya throw you off track. She's a master at using that 'got-a-nut-off-of-feeling-you-nigga' game to smoke up as much of your shit as she can. She good at what she do, dog; I mean real good at what she do, dog." He rubbed his crotch, thinking about her skills.

Sparkle replied quickly, "Yo, JJ, gon' do what you got to do. I ain't been away from the bricks that long, soldier."

JJ smirked. "Yeah, sure you right; just feed her greedy ass a little at a time..." Before he could finish, they heard a car horn blaring. JJ pinched his nose and handed Sparkle the pouch of what was left of the rocks. "Hey, dog, that there be my nigga. I'll holla atcha in a few." He headed out the door.

The door had barely shut when he felt Dee wrapping her arms around his waist and pushing her hot pelvis against his ass.

He looked back at her. "Damn, girl, you don't be wasting no time, do you?"

She smiled into his ear. "Shit, nigga, you felt how horny you got my freaky ass. Let's go finish getting those nuts of yours out of the sand." She clutched his hand and started down the hall.

His dick surged as he admired her ass swaying seductively in front of him toward the side bedroom. As soon as the door closed, she wrapped her arms around his head and pushed her tongue down his throat. She started where she had left off and cocked her leg up to rest her hot pussy directly on his dick. The drooling started from the first hump and he felt it oozing down his thigh. She must've felt the slipperiness as she moaned, "God-ayum, baby boy, that phat dick is about to go off, ain't it?"

She didn't wait for a reply and dropped to her knees and unzipped his fly, pulling his throbbing meat out.

His full nine inches jerked around like crazy, as she moved her syrupy tongue around trying to capture it. When she did, she gripped it hard around her lips and started swirling her tongue like a twister, hungry for all of it.

His knees buckled from the sensation, feeling like he was nearly pissing with all the drool she was slurping out of it. He spread his hands and went up on his tip-toes, lifting one leg as the feeling started to boil deep in his gut. It wouldn't take but a second or two before he flooded her mouth with years of built-up cum.

Right at the point where he felt himself ready to flow, he heard a rapping on the door. It was followed by a muffled "shit" as Dee grimaced in frustration. "Damn," she said and engulfed his whole dick down her throat before pulling off. His meat plopped wetly on his stomach.

"Damn, DeeDee, can't that freaky shit wait? A ho trying to stay right out here," an angry female voice spoke through the door.

Dee snatched open the door with *goddamit* smeared across her lips.

Violet didn't let the look faze her. "Ho, ain't no need to be looking all stank and shit. Let buddy boy serve a bitch before we split." She turned to him, totally ignoring the frown on Dee's face. "Yo, playa, this ill-mannered bitch ain't even introduced us. I heard your boy call you Sparkle or something like that. Is that right? Anyway, are you still holding?"

He took a deep breath. "Yeah, sweetie, I got a little something left. Oh, and you right, my name's Sparkle; so whatcha hitting for, baby?"

She shifted her eyes toward the living room, indicating that she wanted to conduct her business in private.

Dee made no effort to hide her frustration for being interrupted in her conquest. She grunted her disapproval of the lack of respect.

Violet caught the sign but she didn't give a damn how she felt; the bitch should know better than to hide the man for herself, selfish inconsiderate muthafucka. She traced her up and down and sneered. "Ho, why you looking at me all snooty and shit?"

Dee rolled her eyes dramatically. "'Cause we was handling some biz up in here."

"Hmm-hmm, we know what kind of biz you was handling," she said, checking out the swell in Sparkle's crotch. All of a sudden a look of recognition crossed her face and she looked up into his eyes. "You done just got out of the joint, ain'tcha, homeboy?"

His eyes lowered to his clothes and then back at her.

"Yeah, baby girl, this morning; come on." He touched her elbow and escorted her to the hall bathroom, totally ignoring the protesting gaze Dee was burning in his back.

Nuts gotta get out the sand, sweetie, but digits always come first, he thought as he eyed her over his shoulder and led Violet through the door. "Okay, baby girl, whatcha got? I thought ya'll was broke."

"I ain't never broke, playa; just down a little before the next score."

He nodded in admiration of her jazziness. "Okay, I feel ya on that. So what's up then?"

She looked down and started counting some wrinkled bills, trying to stretch the creases out as she handed them to him. "Seventy-five, eighty-five, eighty..." She spoke in a little girl's voice while she blinked shyly up at him.

He'd already decided to let her go short with whatever she had. But he waited until she finished her spiel to see what kind of game she would come up with. He squinted his eyes as if he were concentrating on what to do, making her think that he was seriously considering her dilemma. "And?"

She looked away briefly, fighting back the playa-to-playa smile that was threatening to erupt; she was hip to how he was playing his role. She scratched her brows a moment before she frowned at him. "Let me get five of them boulders"—she paused to run her thumb across her lips while she studied his eyes for a reaction—"uh-huh, or about ten of them dimes, if you done run out of the twenties. That is if you can trust a bitch you just met about an hour or so ago."

He faked cleaning the crust out of the corner of his eyes, then cut them back at Dee, who had eased to the door. She was definitely checking out how he was gonna handle his biz. Sighing heavily for show, he rattled in the pouch and removed what she wanted and handed them to her. "Sweetie, I ain't been out here but a hot second and I can't really be going short on another nigga's shit. Just kick me the other twelve when you get back from wherever it is you going."

Cutting a sharp eye at Dee before she cuffed the rocks in her hand, Violet palmed the bills into his upturned hand.

He felt an odd wad of paper in the money, but didn't show any sign that he was aware and put the loot in his pocket.

"You ain't gonna count it?" she said with her head cocked curiously to the side, wanting to make sure that he noticed the note she'd slipped to him.

"Damn, sweetie, you just counted it for me, didn't you?" He winked to let her know that he had.

She nodded and looked around him at Dee. "Yo, Dee, me and the girls gonna roll out. We'll be back in about an hour." She turned her attention back to him. "You gonna hang for awhile, ain'tcha, playa?"

He looked back at Dee as he nodded at her.

Dee frowned impatiently, but he didn't let her grit

bother him; even if his dick had started jumping in his jeans from the thought of her wanting to return to what they had begun. Besides, he was sorta digging old cream-and-coffee, feeling some positive future dealings with her. Plus, the old player in him wasn't about to let one bitch dominate his options.

Violet ignored the frown as well. Despite the circumstances, she was digging dude and wasn't about to let a selfish-ass ho dictate how she did her. She cleared her throat. "Hold up, homeboy, I ain't finished yet."

He didn't see them getting into a catfight; even if it was one helluva ego boost to have two hoes vying for his attention. He enjoyed the thought for a second and then he decided to play both sides of the fence like a real player would. He slid a couple of rocks into Violet's hand from behind his back.

Feeling triumphant for getting a sneak off on the slimy ho, she smiled at the back of his head. "Okay, sister girl, I'll catch ya'll in a few." She touched him gently in the back, pressed her head around his shoulder and raised her voice to the back of the room. "Yo, Joyce, Candy, let's roll, ya'll." She couldn't help herself when she looked at Dee and wrinkled her nose.

Dee wrinkled her nose back, then threw a snakehead roll and a finger pop to boot.

He smiled at their antics, hunched his shoulders and then turned to the others in the room and spread his arms.

Daveyboy popped up before anybody else could make a move and scored a c-note worth. The snake in him kicked in as he turned away with a scheming look while he checked out the dope. He spun back around, frowning. "Yo, bro, you can't make a better deal than this"—he raised his eyebrows curiously—"I done spent three bills with ya'll so *far*."

Sparkle, a veteran of the junkie's mentality, wasn't about to start this scoring game with him right off the bat. He pinned him with an ice cold stare. "Yeah, partner, and you got your three bills' worth, too."

Daveyboy retorted, "Damn, baby boy, no slack, huh?"

Sparkle smiled. "Not tonight, partner; maybe the next time." Before dude could respond, he was forced to duck out of the way. One of the girls zoomed past, holding her mouth en route to the hall bathroom. From the sound that followed, she didn't make it in time; vomit was probably all over the walls and everything. *Oh well.*

Violet rushed after her. "Joyce, you aight, girl?" There was a muffled response followed by the sound of tissue rolling. Violet walked back down the hall, wiping her hands with a paper towel. She walked straight up to him. "She'll be aight."

"Holla at me when you finish dealing with them stank-ass bitches. Ho can't even hold her shit." Dee huffed with attitude as she walked past them on her way to the kitchen.

"Whatever, snooty-acting ass ho with your own stank self." Violet gritted at Dee's departing back.

Sparkle waited until Dee turned the corner before he said, "Damn, babe, you sound like honey is your enemy or something. What's up with that?"

Violet hunched her shoulders and, with a smile, headed for the bedroom. "Oh no, she one of my number one partners. She just get into her bitchy bullshit every now and then. I don't really be paying her shit no attention, for real though." She made sure to put a little extra sway to her hips with her arms swinging wildly. *Bitches, whew.* She got to the doorsill and spun around. "Go figure, huh." She pinned him with a dazzling smile.

Sparkle smiled as he locked in her mental attitude for future reference. He leaned his back against the wall, thinking about the best way to handle these crazy hoes. With his options circling wildly in his mind, he heard Dee clear her throat. She was standing against the kitchen wall batting her eyes seductively. Then she harumphed and started walking toward him. She slid her hand into his and led him back to the bathroom. She squeezed his ass as soon as the door closed. He shivered when he felt her breath caress his neck and stiff titty nipples press into his back.

He turned around, pulling her into his arms and started rubbing her back as he pressed her closer. But her elbow got in the way when his hand headed toward her ass as she leaned back to look up at him. The lust in her eyes burned into his face. She began kissing his neck and snaked her tongue upward in slurpy circles under his chin. He moaned. She moaned louder. She was all over him with her tongue plunging down his throat and humping wildly at him before the lock even clicked.

Before Sparkle could get over the shock of Dee's tongue paralyzing him with passion, she was unbuckling his pants and sliding them over his knees. The feel of her wet tongue feather licking his behind and around his knee caused him to start trembling. She moaned softly at his reaction and started working her way up his thighs. She ran her tongue around his balls, up his shaft and greedily swallowed his whole dick in one gulp. His knees buckled.

The only thing that kept him from falling was the pressure she was applying that pressed him against the door. He gritted his teeth to keep from hollering out in joy when she started bobbing her head slowly up and down. She paused at the head to slurp her hot tongue around his sensitive glans several times before deep-sixing all of him again and again.

By the time that she went down for the eighth time, he was squirting years of built-up cum all over her greedy tongue and down her throat. Boy, oh boy, when she had first felt his dick begin to swell and jerk toward that nut, Dee had pulled her panties to the side and started gunning her gushy pussy hole. When the first spurts erupted, she gulped hard and moaned loudly. She cuffed his ass to press his dick so far in her mouth that the head was splashing his seed on her tonsils. She gagged for a second but that certainly didn't stop her from massaging the back of her throat with his throbbing, madly spurting dick.

Getting his nuts out of the sand, as she called it, was exciting enough, but when he had looked down after that first spurt, his eyes had bucked wide in disbelief. She was waggling her legs back and forth, fucking her hand. *Oh shit, this ho's nutting while she's sucking my dick. My God, what a fucking freak, whew!!* He sighed as he backhanded the sweat off his forehead.

Sparkle's knees were weak. The intense pleasure had him so hyped. He was surprised that he was still standing; he thought he was about to faint.

Luxuriating on the immense passion, he barely felt the knock on the door. But he snapped out of the nerve-tingling explosion when he heard a faraway voice. "Yo, bro, JJ's out in the parking lot blasting the horn for ya."

"Oh shit." They huffed between gasps and both pulled his pants up. His eyes blinked uncontrollably as he looked down at her. "Whew!! Where the fuck you learn how to do that shit there, my woman, whew!"

She smiled up at him seductively, still down on her knees. "Shit, playa, we just got started." She stood up and backed up to the bed, sat down and spread her legs. Narrowing her eyes in lust, she started waggling them back and forth, and rubbing her pussy through her soaked panties. "Man, hurry up and handle your biz with that nigga, and get back in here and stick all that big-ass black dick in this wet-ass pussy of mine."

Cocking her legs even further back and apart, she pushed her panties to the side so that he could see all her juices.

He stood there stunned with lust until another knock on the door rattled him alert. Sighing again he gathered himself and reluctantly opened the door to leave the room. He headed straight for the door, ignoring Ruby, who was standing in the hall with her hands on her hips.

He slowed down when he saw Violet standing in the hall counting some more money. Her two buddies were sitting on the sofa looking at them anxiously. "Baby, I'm getting ready to jet and I got forty-five bucks left. What can you give me to ride with 'til I get back?"

His first instinct was to straighten her but he smiled. "Baby girl, I'll, uh, the best I can do is three twenties. You can add the rest to our little debt. Then again, the short can be a down payment for our kicking-it session later on." She squinted but didn't say anything.

After a moment, she smiled. "Yeah, that'll work, but you and JJ need to get some more over here right quick. I called one of my peeps over in East Point and told them about how good ya'll stuff is."

"And?"

"And they should be over here with a big roll in about an hour; maybe less."

"Damn, why so long? Where they coming from?"

She frowned. "Damn, you geeking yourself, ain'tcha? I just told ya, East Point. Hell, it really don't matter. Can ya'll be ready when they show?"

Sparkle checked his watch and stared off into space like he was really calculating. "Yeah, we'll be ready," he said when she put her hands on her hips like she was getting impatient. "Then again, they might be out there with it now. Let me go see what's up; hold on for a minute and I'll let you know." He started to rub her shoulder but thought better of it. He stepped around her and left the apartment.

The horn was still blaring when he saw the dark Chrysler New Yorker with its lights on. As he approached, the window whirled down and JJ stuck his head out of the passenger side. "Yo, Sparkle, come here, dog. I got somebody I want you to meet."

He slowed down and cocked his head to the side to see the driver but couldn't see through the tinted glass. He finally leaned on the passenger side and peered across JJ to see a nigga glittering like new money in a red, shark-skinned silk short set peeking from under the bib of a bright red fedora. A brilliant gold-toothed smile greeted him as dude reached across the seat and shook his hand firmly.

A smiling JJ pulled their hands apart. "Sparkle, this here's Percy. Percy, this is..."

Percy interrupted him with a flip of the hand. "Yeah, yeah, partner, man, he done told me about how you just got out from down there in Valdosta. Man, I helped build that joint when I was on the construction crew some years back. Anyway, fuck that, and since he has convinced me that you're going to be working with us, I thought I'd give you a quick holla before we go get this stuff."

Sparkle pulled his hand out of the car and rested his elbows on the door before nodding his head. "Uh-huh, uh-huh, that'll be a pretty good thing to do. I'm definitely all for that there, soldier; no doubt about that."

Percy pinched his nose and pointed at him. "All good, yeah, that's all good, but look a here; I hate to sort of hit and run and shit but we gotta split." He paused to look at his watch, a gleaming Rolex. "Like a couple of minutes ago, I'll, uh, we'll kick it when we get back."

JJ, who up until that time had remained silent, said, "Yeah, dog, we'll be gone for about an hour. Oh, and by the way, you clocked any dollars yet? We gonna try to get a little more this time since you joining the crew."

Sparkle reached into his pocket and handed him the digits he'd made so far and repeated what Violet had said.

JJ nodded. "Oh yeah, I know who she's talking about. They be from way over there in East Point and College Park. It'll take them a minute or two to get over this way. Tell ya what, I'm gonna slip to the crib right quick and get you the last of this package here to hold them until we get back. Wait a sec, and you can get back to that red-ass bitch; I know she working her magic by now. Hell, you done probably already busted a couple of nuts already." JJ did a quick count of the money he'd given him, pocketed it and nodded to Percy, who immediately pulled out of the parking lot.

Sparkle waited until the lights disappeared around the corner before he headed back to Dee's. Violet and her friends were coming down the steps. She smiled at him. "Yo, baby boy, my people just called again. They said they were on the way to pick me up, so we'll be back in a few minutes."

"Okay, you know where I'll be," he said over his shoulder as he passed them. He didn't wait for a response and walked right past little Ruby standing at the door and headed for the back. He served up a couple of hundred dollars' worth before he went back to join Dee in the other room.

When he opened the door, a big smile crossed his face when he saw Dee lying on the bed buck naked playing in her pussy.

She opened her eyes and slowly took her fingers, which were glistening with pussy juice, and started licking them one by one.

He practically snatched his clothes off and crossed the floor, admiring her sweaty body. Before he could lie beside her, she got on her knees and started sucking on his thighs like a vampire.

She nibbled her way to his dick, whirling her tongue along his skin to his collarbone. She scraped her teeth across his chest until he grabbed her head and started guiding her movements. When she got around his navel, she started pulling his hairs with her teeth. *Damn*. The pleasure pain had his stomach muscles contracting and his knees buckling.

Before he realized it, she was pulling him by the waist onto the bed between her wide opened thighs. Her small hands grabbed his jerking dick and started stroking him roughly, then massaging the head with the drool that oozed out of the tip. Then she gripped it at the base, making it stretch out as long as possible.

With him damn near in convulsions, Dee worked her way back up to his ears and whispered, "Come on, nigga, ride this hot pussy with that long muthafucka. I want to watch it go in." Her voice was husky with desire.

As he lowered himself in her, he damn near skeeted as her pussy lips started engulfing his pulsating dick. He let out a strained snort as he watched her pussy slowly begin to eat his dick up. Her muscles made it seem like her hot hole was gnawing its way up his rock-hard shaft.

The pressure of pleasure was way too much for him to stand, and he started spurting cum like a fountain. "Godayum, woman, whaddafuck you doing to me…" he stuttered as his balls were drained of all their juices.

Dee cried out with a passionate purr when she felt his dick spitting, "Oh nigga, your cum is making me cum. Oh, God, that dick is so muthafucking hard, I'm cumming, baby, I'm cumming. Hit that pussy, man, don't stop. Please don't stop. Push that big muthafucka. That big Mu-tha-fuc-ka." She screamed and lifted her ass off the bed, grinding hard into his balls. She wrapped her arms around his neck and her legs around his waist and wailed over and over, "Oh shit, oh shiiit, I'm cumming again, nigga. Godayum, that fat-ass dick is all the way up in that pussy. Oh shit, oh shit, I'm nutting all over that dick again. Hit it, baby, hit it, baby, aaaaaaaaahhh-hhhhhh."

He reached under her to cuff that soft ass, spreading the cheeks and ass hole wide open and started pile driving that pussy. Her muscles were contracting around his dick so hard and fast that his dick was soon throbbing to another nut with each power stroke. She was moaning out of control now and holding on to him for dear life.

She sighed in his ear, "Kiss me, nigga. Godayum, put that tongue all the way down my throat." He maneuvered his mouth to catch her tongue, which was darting in all directions. She moaned louder and her tongue went wild twirling around his He felt his third nut streaming through his shaft at the same time that he felt her start to get yet another one. She cried out, "That's it, baby, hold that dick right there. Let me fuck on that dick now, man. Let me fuck on it. Oh shit, oh shit, that's it, nigga. Right there, oh shit, right there. That dick is so goooood, nigga, that dick is sooooo goooooood."

He looked down in time to see her pussy juices squishing along the sides of his erupting dick. All of a sudden she unwrapped her legs and arms from around him and pushed him off of her. He grunted from shock because his dick was still squirting cum. He watched in total amazement as she caught his dick in her mouth and deep throated the last spurts while she jacked her fingers wildly in and out of her gushing pussy.

His chest was heaving as he lay back on the bed, resting his eyes. The bed was soaked with their combined sweat and cum. He rose to his elbows, looked down at her, blinked several times and flinched, not believing what he was seeing. *What the fuck?* he cursed at the image of Beverly smiling back at him. Her face was turned up to him, eyes glistening with satisfaction, with a beautiful smile on her lips. She sighed. "Now that's what I needed; some real loving." He knuckled the corners of his eyes, blinked a couple of times and stared at the far wall.

A voice with a vibrating echo crashed through his lust-a-mare. *Now that's what I needed—some helluva dick slung up in this muthafucka.* She breathed heatedly with her fingers finally relaxing calmly on her pussy.

He gazed at her with half-closed lids as her features cleared through his own hazy climax. "Hell yeah, you definitely got the bomb pussy there, girl."

She shook her head along with him, "And you got the bomb dick, my man, the bomb-dick-a-dick. Now that's for muthafucking sho."

He stared through her momentarily and slipped to the edge of the bed, contemplating his next move. She sat up, caressing his back as he moaned over his shoulder. "Check this out, redbone. On the real, how long it'll take you to help get this stuff off?" He poured the remainder of the package out on the bed in front of her.

As he watched her eye the contents, he wondered how long it was gonna take JJ to get back with the rest of the dope. *Damn, those niggas have been gone for well over an hour by now. What's up with that?* He wasn't fond of having to go back to Debra's crib and leaving all that hot-ass pussy of Dee's, not to mention that suffocating head of hers. Hell, as freaky as she was, there was little doubt she'd offer that ass sooner or later. He shivered with the thought.

He shifted to her counting the dope dumped on the bed. "Looks like you got about six hundred dollars worth left, playa."

He did some quick calculating himself. "Okayeee, dig this, baby, you go ahead and do your thang at twenty percent and we'll go from there, cool."

"You mean to tell me that you are about to trust me with a package. Nigga, I be smoking this here shit twenty-four-seven; you sure you want to take a chance like that?"

Sparkle arched a brow and smiled at her. "Well, baby girl, for some reason I can't explain, I feel like I can. You and I are going to go a long way together. Call it a hunch, intuition, hell, call it whatever the fuck you wanna call it. I just feel like we need to do this together. That is, if you can find it in you somewhere to keep the money at least partially straight. And to tell you the truth, down in my heart, I feel that you will."

He got up and started to get dressed. She watched him considering things. Hell, ain't nary a soul had ever trusted her like that. And here was a nigga who she was meeting for the first time in her life doing exactly that. She twisted her bottom lip and started to laugh.

He turned to her as he was pushing the last button into place. "So what's so funny, girlie?"

"Shit, baby boy, ain't nobody trusted me with this here shit for so long that it's fucking with my head. I ain't lying." Dee shook her head in disbelief.

He spread his hands. "Well, can I trust you or what? Make up your mind now, and I do mean *right now* 'cause I'm tired of waiting on JJ to get back. I've got to go back to the crib and wash my tired ass. It's been one helluva long day."

She nodded in agreement, realizing that he was going through some shit; his first day out. Radiating a brilliant smile, she purred, "I gotcha, baby, I gotcha."

He sighed, nodding, and reached for the doorknob. Before he closed the door, she called out to him and pointed to the rocks on the bed. "Hey, I know you tired and all that, but ain't you forgetting something?"

He squinted and cocked his head to the side, left his gaze on the rocks. "Naw, girlie, I ain't forgetting a thing. I'll see ya when I come out of this coma I'm about to go in." He left the apartment and fished out Violet's note. Smiling to himself, he pocketed it and thought, *What a first day back on the bricks; what a first day home.*

Halfway across the parking lot he heard the car horn. JJ and Percy were in the car on the other side of the apartments. With eyelids heavy from fatigue, he headed toward them.

As he approached the car, JJ reached his arm out and gave him a baggie of rocks. Sparkle blinked himself alert, fingering the bag of about thirty or forty, fifty slabs. *So that's what took these niggas so long. They were probably just getting ready to come back over here.*

JJ smiled. "Yo, dog, I can see that you damn near out. Go ahead and hit them niggas who ready to score right now. Whatever you make we gonna take with us. Give them other fools about five minutes to score because our folk'll be calling us any minute now. And we gotta be on the sprint to hook up."

He stuffed the package in his coat and headed back up the stairs. JJ called out, "Man, I know that you your own man but take a good look at old lady Violet. I can see that she got eyes for you and she can cut you into a lot of good people and a lot of good thangs."

Sparkle started scratching his eyebrow with his thumb. "Oh yeah, she got it like that, huh?"

"Muuu-hmm and it ain't too many niggas that draw her attention like you did, player. I say take advantage of it."

"I can see it myself, dog. How old is honey, anyway?"

JJ cocked one eyebrow and thought for a few seconds. "Let me see, shit, V's got to be closing in on fifty but she don't know it. Know what I'm saying."

Sparkle wondered if she was the same legendary Violet hired by pimps on Auburn and MLK back in the day to school their hoes on the boosting game. He hoped so because a nigga could certainly use a fly wardrobe. She was coming on to him, no doubt, and was definitely worth pulling, but it would take patience and some well-hidden anxiety.

JJ noticed him staring off into space and grabbed him by the elbow. "Yo, man, you still with me here?"

"Yeah, yeah, I heard you, dog. Don't worry, I can handle this here."

A red sedan pulled into the parking lot. JJ looked over to Percy, saluted and drove out, followed immediately by the car.

Sparkle walked back to Dee's apartment, considering the real reason they were allowing him in their clique so easily—a situation that certainly bared scrutiny.

Violet walked down the steps with an impatient look on her face, then slowed down when she saw him. When he stepped on the curb, she said, "Honey, do you know where the apartments are?"

He took the paper out of his pocket, scanned it quickly and nodded. She was standing on the back of her legs with her hands on her hips, breasts jutting out. He couldn't help getting distracted. *My God, this old lady has got to be working with some 40 triple E's or something.*

The smile on her face told him that she knew he was hooked on them, too. "Hey, player, my eyes are up here."

He rubbed his hand over his mouth and raised his eyes. "Baby boy, I like your style, but please don't take me for one of those geeked-out bimbos."

He began a retort but she *ssshhed* him with a finger to his lips. "We could be good for each other, player. I can see you're about turning bucks and getting high; the same with me. So play with me straight, dog, okay?"

"Okay, shawtie, I feel ya, we'll stay on the real." She nodded. "I'll call you sometime tomorrow. That'll be cool?"

She looked over her shoulder when she heard the door open. Dee strode to the edge of the steps with her hands on her hips, giving them the twice over.

If Sparkle wasn't so sure that the bitch was playing hard at her game, he could've sworn that he saw some signs of jealousy. It was absolutely ridiculous since he'd just met her only a couple of hours ago.

Violet read the bitch the same way and rolled her eyes at the corny display. She turned back to him. "Yeah, let's see what it be." Without turning fully around, she smiled, this time with a glitter in her eyes. "Yo, Dee, I'll be getting with you, girl. Tell BaBa and them that we'll be at the crib if they get here before we get back, will ya?" She started up the stairs but changed her mind and headed for her ride, speaking over her shoulder, "I really don't feel like going back around those niggas in there. Could you tell my girls to come on?"

Dee lowered her head and looked under eyed at her

departing back before she shouted, "Okay, girl, I'll let them know." She wasn't about to fulfill her wishes right away though and sashayed up to Sparkle beaming. "So, my girl done lost her patience waiting on those folks, huh? Hell, she know how they be doing. It'll probably be another hour before they get over here but they coming. They always do when they've heard about a new bomb in town."

"Yeah, home girl be out," he said as she got in the driver's seat of a bright red Thunderbird.

Dee spun around and headed back up the steps, mumbling over her shoulder. "Well, come on back in. That ho done scraped up some hidden digits from somewhere."

"What she got?" He wondered why she hadn't served the bitch with the stuff he'd left with her.

"She counted out about sixty bucks but you need to go on and handle her now because she's about to roll. You know how folks get when they down to their last coins and don't want to share that last hit with nobody."

He didn't really care who she was talking about but nodded anyway and followed her.

She continued, "Oh yeah, a couple of folks called and they'll be over within the hour, so how much you holding?"

"Enough," he stated flatly, knowing this slick bitch was figuring how much she could angle.

She squinted. "Hell, that'll do, I guess." The telephone in the living room rang and she twisted away to go answer it. "Yeah, uh-huh, it's still here. How long you gonna be, girlfriend? Damn, you at the BP; shit, you didn't have to call if you that close. Girl, the shit is the bomb. You know it's good or I wouldn't have called you. ...Uh-huh, uh-huh, well, I ain't playing none this time. Naw, I don't think so, then again you might know him; yo ass be everywhere. Hey, fuck dat, you can do whatever with him when you get here. Come on, girl, I done told you the shit be good. Looka here, I ain't gonna argue with ya all night; you'll see when you get here. I'll unlock the door, just come on to the back. ... Yeah, Violet was here. Matter of fact the bitch just left a couple of minutes ago. ...Yeah, uh-huh, bye."

A couple of minutes later the door burst open with the sound of three yakking females. Sparkle and Dee got up off the couch together and met them at the door. One pale redbone and two jet-black sweeties came fast-stepping in, waving dollars. They stopped and eyed Sparkle from head to toe. The shortest one sporting a curly top cut close around the ears, wrinkled her nose, smiled and said, "Hmm-hmm, bitch, I know what your stank ass been doing."

Dee bobbled her head and spat, "Fuck you, ho, whatcha want?"

"Name's Missy, mister, this impolite-ass ho ain't got no manners," she purred with ghetto swag and held out three fifty-dollar bills like she was used to slinging large sums around. He gave her three big boulders. She examined the rocks, looked him up and down and tilted her head back. She then harumphed and stepped past them toward the first bedroom.

Palebone looked over her shoulder before she stepped into the room. "Ugh, it sho smell nasty in here. Damn, slim, you must've tore that bitch's pussy up."

Dee gritted and pulled the door shut before going into the hall bathroom.

He had served the girls a few more times by the time Dee came out looking and smelling fresh. He had already made up his mind to tap that ass as often as he could. The way she was looking now put a mortal lock on that thought.

She tiptoed to plant a kiss on his cheek. "JJ just called; said he'd be by in a few minutes and for you to be ready to roll when he honks."

It dawned on him that he didn't have the cell phone in his jacket pocket that JJ had given him. He looked down to see it in her hand. He started to say something when she beat him to it. "Here, you left it on the bed before you left to meet him the first time, and I put it in my pocket."

He stared at her as she leaned back, batting her eyes. "Damn, soldier, I'm sorry." She lowered her gaze. "It slipped my mind when those hoes wrinkled their noses at me. I'm sorry, man; forgive me, okay." She came closer and sniffed at his chin.

He smiled. *This is a real slick bitch, for real.*

"Where he at?" He spoke over the top of her head.

"He didn't say." She breathed on his neck and arched her pelvis against him.

Before she could get back in the lust groove, he heard the horn outside. It was time to blow, so he made his play to lock her in. Folding his hand around hers, he placed six of the boulders in her mitt. "Sweetie, now these are some pretty big boulders so you can probably make five twenties or ten dimes out of each one. That leaves you a lot of room for your twenty percent come back to me. This here's six hundred worth. I'll be expecting my four-hundred-fifty bucks when we see each other again." He reached down and cuffed her chin, raising her gaze to meet his. "I've been warned to play you real close to the chest, but my gut instincts keep telling me that we are going to go a long way together."

"Uh, I get the same feeling about you, too."

Damn, is that a fucking tear in her eyes? Watch yourself, player; she got plenty of game. "That's all good, so let's see if you really want to get paid and get me my four-fifty, okay." He could tell by the teary puzzling look that she wasn't used to people trusting her. He figured she was either going to make him a bundle or he'd get her to put out a lot of that super pussy to make up the difference, even if she fucked up. Regardless, he'd still have a helluva spot to sit and make a killing when thangs got slow.

"Four-fifty, yeah, I can handle that."

"I know you can, and by the way, why don't you see

if you can hunt down some of that skunk weed for our next booty call." He started to walk away but stopped when she didn't reply right away. He turned around and leaned on the doorsill, staring at her, waiting for her to say something, anything.

She put her hands on her hips and looked under eyed at him. "Yeah, I can get that."

He smiled. "With your profit."

She frowned but he ignored it and gave her the cell phone number split.

CHAPTER FIVE

It's Lettuce Clocking Time

Sparkle scanned the parking lot. JJ was nowhere in sight. Damn, he'd heard the horn himself. Hunching his shoulders, he started across the field, thinking they'd probably be at Debra's. Halfway across he saw the headlights of the car on the other side of the apartments. By the time he hit the street, he saw Percy's lanky frame leaning against the car. JJ was waving from the other side, signaling for him to follow them as they headed to the apartment.

The after-effects from the coke had him feeling jittery and looking up and down the street, thinking he was being stalked. He imagined shadowy figures moving in the car, but they were already heading up the stairs. He snapped his attention from the car and followed them. Damn, he was really tripping. He quickened his pace because the geeking was really starting to mess with him.

He shouted to JJ, "Yo, dog, wait up for me." They gave him an urgent wave as they were entering the apartment.

He thought he saw somebody duck behind the corner of the building. *Shit*, he thought. He ran up the steps before they could close the door. When he stepped inside,

JJ was opening the closet. He turned around and started laughing because of the bug-eyed look on Sparkle's face. "Aw, man, this nigga's geeking his ass off."

JJ shook his head and reached down to get the shoe-box off the floor and then walked to the dining room table. Removing a digital scale, razor blades and plastic bags, he placed the items on the table. He looked up at Sparkle like he was just noticing him. "Aw, man, my bad; sorry we sped off before you could come out. Come on, Percy, whatcha standing around for, looking like you don't know what to do?"

"What's up, soldier? Sorry about the short intro earlier but as you can see, we had to catch our boy for a bigger reup," Percy said as he put his leather cap on the table and nodded for him to join them.

"To tell you the truth, man, we was gonna come getcha after we had cut this stuff up," JJ said, "but hell, you here now so let's get busy. You ain't finished with that, I know."

Sparkle blinked his eyes and took a deep breath. "Man, I thought you told Dee to tell me to come on and I heard the car horn."

JJ had started popping open the small Ziploc bags and didn't reply right away. Sparkle stood with a blank look on his face. JJ slid the bag of razors over to Percy, who had placed six bricks of coke on the table and had begun unwrapping one of them.

JJ sat back in the chair and folded his arms. "Percy

and I go way back, partner. I'm sorry we didn't wait for you after we hit the horn, but we really need to get this here stuff cut up like right away."

Sparkle nodded. "Yeah, I heard ya earlier, dude. I just ain't used to this geeking shit; know what I'm saying?"

Percy finally spoke up. "Hmmph, that shit can be a bitch, my nigga, but you'll get back on track soon enough."

JJ said impatiently, "Yeah, uh-huh, enough of that play by play, fellows. Okay, Sparkle, here's the system, yo. Percy here hits off some fifties first and you put them on the scale. If they over point five, you trim them down to fit. And if they under, add the pieces you done already put to the side. Then you put them on this saucer here; feel me?" They nodded as one and got busy.

They had cut up one of the bricks when JJ suddenly stood up and went to the back. Moments later he was tiptoeing back, so Debra must have still been asleep. Otherwise she would've been out there cussing up a storm; especially if she knew JJ was sneaking around playing with coke with the kids in the house.

JJ spoke up to match his thoughts. "Yo, man, we got to keep it down in here. It sho won't do no good for Debra or the kids to wake up right now; know what I'm saying?"

Percy rolled his eyes like he really wasn't worried and pulled three glass tubes out of his jacket pocket. "Yo, JJ, you got any more of that charboy? I left mine in the glove compartment."

When JJ got up and returned with some fresh char-boy, Percy took three of the rocks out of the baggie and placed the dope and shooter in front of them. After a couple of good blasts, they started on the other five bricks, cutting up thirty-two eight balls weighing 3.4 to 3.6 grams.

"You know, JJ, this is a lot better than the other stuff," Percy said between gasps. "How you wanna work it?" JJ hunched his shoulders. "Okay then, since it's better and all, let's give them a .8 instead of a .10 on the dimes."

For the first time Sparkle began getting some bad vibes about him. Either the coke had him paranoid or he wasn't feeling dude. He had to stay on the alert, dealing with this snake.

JJ tossed a bag of smaller baggies at him. "Naw, my nig, we gonna keep it the same weight. Hold up and hear me out, man."

Percy had started fidgeting like he wanted to complain but JJ stayed firm. "Man, we gotta keep it the bomb and weighted better than these other folk. That way people gonna be hunting us instead of us waiting on the street corner like them other fools."

"Yeah, man, and it sounds a lot safer, too," Sparkle added.

They worked in silence for what seemed like forty-five minutes or so until two plates were full. JJ finally broke it. "Sparkle, put these dimes in the pink bags and the twenties in the brown ones." He reached back into the shoebox and tossed him some medium-size clear ones and placed them on the table. "Then put thirty dimes and twenty twenties into each of these."

They kept blazing rocks as they worked. When they got down to the last brick, JJ cut it in half, cut one of the halves into thirds and said, "This here is so we won't have to dig into the sellers."

After all the cutting was finished, Percy pinched his nose, leaned on his elbows and arched one brow awkwardly. "Yo, Spark, check this here out. Jay let me know a while back that you was about to come up. Now I don't know you personally, but I done heard some thorough thangs about you, which is all good. It's the main reason I agreed to team up with ya to get this cheddar to be had. So this is how we do this thang." He smiled at JJ. "Since you fresh outta the beast, it's understood you got to take yo time getting yo feet wet. In other words, we know that it's gonna take you a lot longer than us to get rid of this stuff. We gonna give you this here bag of fifties, eighteen of them. That'll add up to nine-hundred dollars, and if you got plans to work that slimy bitch Dee, the standard is twenty percent. So taking in her bullshit, let's just say you looking for seven hundred, which allows for shorts and that ho's lying about what she got. You feel me here?"

"Mind now that we be looking at you working these for thirty percent. So it's really up to you if you want to work that bitch or not, but we be looking for you to toss us six hundred-thirty dollars per sack. You feel me now? So by us tossing you four of these joints we be expecting a kickback of, let's round it off to a straight twenty-five hundred." He paused to let that sink in. "Dog, I know that all this is like foreign language to you right now, being you done just raised and shit, but you set your goals at that figure and we be rolling partner, okay?"

Sparkle nodded to let him know that he understood. He continued, "Now me and JJ been scoring four-and-a-half ounces or an eighth of a kilo at the reup. But now that you on the team we are gonna be shooting for the quarter kilo. That'll be fifty-five hundred to the source we dealing with right now. Which means that each of us have to come up with eighteen hundred apiece per joint."

Right off the grip that shit didn't quite add up, but hell, Sparkle definitely wasn't in the position to say a damn thing. These niggas were getting him on his feet. And on his first day out of the joint, the half slick-ass nigga was in the driver's seat; he could have his say; at least for now.

JJ saw the inquisitive look on his face, even if Percy was ego-tripping too much to do so. "Hey, don't bug, dog. We know you don't have any hoes right now, so we'll get you settled in on two, three hot spots until you can work in your own route. Oh yeah, in a couple of days we gonna get you a rental car after you get your driver's license and a cell phone."

Sparkle was leaning across the table, taking in all of what

he was kicking. He didn't necessarily like all of it but what choice did he have? He was on his dick. So he pinched his nose and sat back in the chair. "So when is the catch day? You know how long I got to get up the ends?"

"We usually try to reup every three or four days," Percy said.

"Okay. I can probably get with that, but ya'll know that I got to go handle my legal for the next couple of days while I'm blending in with ya'll on this here. Shit, JJ knows how Debra and Janet be all up in my shit firsthand."

"Whew, do I ever," JJ chimed in, "but don't choke on that, dude. We've taken into account that it's gonna take you a bit to get your routine down."

Percy cocked his head to the side and studied him for a few seconds. "I'll bring you a piece later on tonight. What kind do you prefer?"

"I can work with something that I can easily hide in my back pocket. I don't like people to know that I'm holding; you know the threat they are dealing with," Sparkle added quickly.

"I can dig that. Let's see, whatcha say about a thirty eight mini; you know something you can practically palm in your hand, around say eight or nine o'clock tonight?"

Suddenly all eyes flew to Debra strolling down the hallway rubbing her eyes.

"What ya'll niggas doing? Aw hell, why I even got to bother asking." She gritted when she noticed Percy sitting at the table trying to look innocent.

She tightened the sash on her robe, put her hands on her hips and looked directly at Sparkle. "Damn, boy, you ain't even been out a full day and you in this shit already," she said, eyeing the dope on the table.

He bowed his head and raised his hands to the ceiling. "Got to get off my dick, sis. What else can I say?"

"Muthafucka, you can say I'm gonna get a job and dodge penitentiary bricks; that's what the hell you can say and do, nigga."

She huffed and turned her attention to JJ. "Al just voice mailed you; that's what woke me up. Says they got a good game rolling over there."

"Who be over there? Damn, he could have let us know that when we met him a little while ago."

Debra was in the kitchen fixing up the coffee pot and whirled on him. "And what was you gonna do; leave me here?"

"Naw, baby, I would've called you myself so you'd know I was on the way to pick you up."

She laid the cup down and hissed, "You a lying-ass nigga."

JJ got up and went in the kitchen and hugged her from behind. "Yeah, baby, you right, I wouldn't have woke you up; especially knowing you got to be at the shop in the morning. Figured my baby needed her beauty sleep."

"Nigga, there you go lying again, knowing damn well that I ain't gotta be there 'til eleven."

He gazed back at Percy with a damned look on his

face and hunched his shoulders. "Okay, Mike and Ebony know how to get ready and go to school. Go ahead and get ready."

Uh-huh, you didn't really think I was gonna let you run that weak one on me. Did ya, nigga? She smirked on the way back down the hall. "Ten, fifteen minutes, so don't ya'll niggas go to smoking that shit with these kids in the house. And I ain't playing either."

"You know we wouldn't do that," JJ whispered.

She sniffed the air and wrinkled her nose. "Yeah, right, sure you wouldn't. So what's that I'm smelling? Some fake coke or something? Nigga, please."

Percy waited until he heard the door shut before he started stuffing a boulder in the shooter. He flicked the lighter before he looked to see the expressions on JJ's and Sparkle's faces.

"Patio dog, whaddafuck you think, she playing or something? She dead serious, man," JJ said.

He got up and slid the glass sliding door open and stepped outside. After a deep toke, he stuck his head back inside and whispered, "Hmm, this stuff be that skunk, for real, yo. Oh yeah, it's that skunk, aight. Ya'll niggas ready to roll?"

Sparkle started to nod his consent when JJ held up his hand to cut him off. "There are five hotels we got people slinging out of. All you gotta do is pick up the ends; probably sit awhile if you want to and leave them something to work with."

"I ain't got no problem with that, dog, but what's up with that poker game? Shiiiit, I wouldn't mind some of that action there." He looked at JJ and then Debra, who had gotten dressed in record time. "Ya'll know that be my drop there, dog."

JJ giggled. "Do I ever; all that money you beat me out of before we got tight."

Sparkle smiled sheepishly and hunched his shoulders. "Don't worry; Peggy will jet you over there after ya'll done finished making those runs."

Whodahell is Peggy and where she at? Sparkle thought as his brow wrinkled in confusion at the unfamiliar name.

Percy saw his confused look and smiled. "Hey, man, stop looking so fucked up. Peggy's my main squeeze. She should be here any minute now. She's gonna take you around the hotels and introduce you to the crew and then bring you over to the poker spot."

Sparkle's nose wrinkled in disgust as he stared the nigga up and down his body. Percy assumed that he'd accept whoever and whatever because he was out of the joint. The look only lasted for a moment though; he quickly realized that he definitely needed help in getting his game together. It was tough but he held his ego in check. It was probably because he didn't like or trust the nigga from the get-go.

Luckily, before he could dwell on the negative thoughts any further, his attention zoomed in on Debra striding down the hall counting a wad of bills. His baby sis had a knot of paper she was prepared to invest in the poker game. That didn't bother him one bit; he had given her the cheat game years ago. Honey could hold her own with any hustler.

Debra, who had that gambler's glitter in her eyes, slapped JJ on the shoulder. "Uh-huh, well, we got to get on over there before that tight-ass Jew nigga cuts off. Ya'll know how he gets when he senses the money getting low." She turned her attention directly to Sparkle. "Oh yeah, before I forget, I heard your slimy-ass partner Johnny Ivey's raggedy grumbling in the background when I called back."

Sparkle started beaming. "My ace coon boon is over there? Hell, let's get a move-on then. I definitely got to holla at my boy."

He stood up, pulled JJ to the side and whispered, "Let me holla atcha for a sec."

They walked into the kitchen, where JJ opened the fridge and pulled out a Pepsi. He handed it to Sparkle. "Yeah, what's up, bro? I hope you make this quick because we finished here anyways."

Between sips of the ice-cold drink, Sparkle said, "I wanted to let you know that I left six-hundred dollars' worth of stuff with Dee; you know, just to see what she do."

"You did what?" he replied in mock surprise. "Man, I told ya that bitch had the super pussy and that she has a constant flow of geekers rolling through her crib and all, but godayum, dog, I hope you ain't got weak for her already."

"Man, I got a hunch, just a hunch about her."

"Well, I sure do hope your hunch is right. Hey, man, this here is going to be a lesson on you as far as I'm concerned. And I really expect that six hundred. So that's on you, for real, dog, if she's fucked up like I think she is."

Sparkle frowned. "Okay, it's your stuff anyway, but I told her to get back at me with four-fifty."

JJ gritted. "Okay, four-fifty then, but on the real, don't expect but half of that. I told ya she's a slick bitch but then again, she smart enough not to fuck it all up. Come to think of it, she probably ain't gonna play a good lick all the way out, not right off the bat anyway. Matter of fact, she's gonna try to keep the string on ya to stay high and fuck you to death. You'll see."

He punched JJ's shoulder and laughed. "Shit, I can go for that kinda death, for real, yo. But on the other hand, I got a feeling I can handle her fine ass to be one of my bases. Hell, at least until I get my own routes."

JJ spat back in a tone full of skepticism, "I guess you know whatcha doing. You been in the game long enough; that's for sure. But on the real, partner, keep a sharp eye on her; she has a vicious bite."

"Man, all the time, believe that there," Sparkle replied with all the confidence he could muster.

"Man, I hope that you haven't gotten too rusty with all that time you did; that's all." He walked away and tapped Percy on the shoulder. "Let's roll, dog."

CHAPTER SIX

Rolling The Hotel Strip

A few minutes later, as they were leaving the apartment, Sparkle was introduced to Peggy, a honey with creamy brown skin who was parked in a Mustang behind Percy's ride. Without any fanfare, they split up. The next thing he knew, they were pulling into the parking lot of their first stop at the Red Roof Inn on Candler Road across I-20.

With a street veteran's flair, Peggy conducted the business and introduced him to a light-skinned girl named Brenda. The room was full of smokers lounging around so they went into the bathroom to handle their transaction. After a brief session of kicking it, he told Brenda to get in contact with Peggy for the time being, but things would be changing in the upcoming days. Brenda hunched her shoulders like whatever, not really giving a fuck who served her as long as she got served.

They continued down I-20 where they made stops at the Motel 6, the Holiday Inn, the Sheraton and finally the LaQuinta Inn in Lithonia. He didn't take any hits, even though the girls did. He wanted to portray a straight-up business image with them. All the sellers were girls in Percy's stable—at least that was what he was led to believe.

The ride down I-20 brought back memories of when he and a fat dude named Perry used to hijack furniture trucks. Those used to be some good licks. He'd never forgotten the time he was in Fulton County Jail looking at TV. The same dude that used to buy the whole tractor-trailer from them was on the tube slamming a jail cell, bidding to become an Atlanta City Commissioner. All he could do was nod with respect, recognizing dude as a member of the biggest gangsters of them all—the government.

Sparkle juggled the mental notes he'd collected on the honeys he'd met at the drug spots. He could be lenient with some of them and others he would need to handle with a longer-handled spoon. There was one jet-black queen named Lisa, who was six-feet-four and scored a whole sack from him for $600; some $120 he pocketed because he didn't have to give it to one of the girls. He'd never dealt with an Amazon and had no problem whatsoever when she wanted him to go to her room. She even smoked some of the stuff with him; the only one he let know that he got high. She gave him a quick five-minute head job. Not bad; not bad at all. He made sure that they traded numbers before he left. He'd definitely be checking her out in the future.

While Sparkle and Peggy were at the LaQuinta, he got a call from Dee. Since he wasn't too fond of anyone knowing his business, he slid to the lobby with the pretense of going to get donuts on display. When he was sure that no one was paying attention, he went to the phone and called girlie. "What's up, sweetie?" he said nonchalantly when she picked up.

There was an anxious tone to her voice. "I need to see you like fifteen minutes ago."

"All of that is gone already?"

"I ain't got but three dimes left. How far away are you? One of my regular customers called to let me know that he was on the way," she spat rapidly.

'Whatcha call a mint, girl?"

"At least five-hundred, for sho."

"You sound real serious there, girl," he said, not sure if he believed her.

"Hell yeah, for real," she responded impatiently.

"Damn," he said more to himself than to her.

"Whatcha mean damn?" she retorted in a doubtful tone.

"Girl, I'm way out here in Lithonia."

"So." Dee's sassiness returned.

"So." He held the phone away and stared at it.

"Yeah, so."

"Aah, godayum, I'm on my way to a poker game."

"Naw you ain't," she responded with urgency.

"Naw I ain't; why I ain't?"

"Baby, you just got to turn around and get back here," she said nervously.

He let her stir for about thirty seconds.

"You still there. What's up?" she squeaked, sounding unsure of herself.

"Okay, okay, godayum. I'll be there in about twenty, thirty minutes. Hold your ass 'til I get there."

"I'll be calling you back in twenty minutes," she assured him.

He smiled at her sassiness. Hell, he definitely wanted to keep that pussy on the ready. "Okay, girlie, see you in a few." He hung up before she could reply.

Close to twenty minutes later, they were pulling into the parking lot when the phone started ringing again.

As they headed to the apartment, Peggy said, "Ain't that Buster's BMW over there?" She nudged him in the back.

Sparkle gave her a *damn, how-am-I-supposed-to-know* look.

"Looks like it. Whatever bitches that are up in there is about to get blasted for sure. Oh yeah, big time with big boy," she added with a smile. She didn't bother to get out of the car. "Hey, fuck that. I ain't gonna be hanging out here all night while that fool be shining on everybody in eye and earshot just because he be throwing dope around like it's water. Besides, that nigga Percy be getting stupid rough with a bitch; know what I'm saying?"

The way she was acting made Sparkle think back to the days when he used to play cushion for Johnny Bee and Johnny Dobbs when pimping was real art. A nigga got a chance to fuck some shonuff sexy honeys then. *Hmm, that nigga Percy's got this bitch trained. Either that or she thought that he would tell him how she acted.*

As soon as the door opened, he could hear Dee's voice squawking obscenities. She bent her head around the doorsill and saw him. "Hey, baby, come on in. It's been a real bitch holding this fat nigga here; you ready?"

Realizing that he was at the point of setting a pattern of respect, he brushed past her without saying a word. She followed him silently to the first bedroom. He closed the door as soon as she stepped in and cuffed her ass, kissing her real hard. She gasped as he slammed her against the door. When he felt her press her pelvis forward, he pulled away and held out his hand. The suddenness of his action had her in a slight daze as she reached into her bra. He stopped her hand and roughly reached in and clutched the money. He gave her a cold stare as he placed the money in his pocket. Before she could respond, he grabbed her crotch and leaned forward to whisper in her ear, "I'll count it later. Don't say a thing."

Dee was more than a little stunned and it showed on her face. However, Sparkle didn't show any reaction to her look and leaned away. "Now what do buddy want?"

She batted her eyes. "He usually starts at a bill."

He placed a bundle in her hand. "Here you go, baby, and I've got things to do. Holla if he wants some more."

"How much is…"

"Bitch, I said I got to roll. It's enough." He planted a kiss on her forehead.

Swallowing nervously, she opened her mouth to speak but the look he gave her froze it shut. When he grabbed the doorknob to leave, she leaned against him to prevent him from going. He looked down at her lust-filled eyes. "You really got to go right now?"

"Yeah, baby, got to get to that poker game... You wanna check out a movie or club tomorrow?"

She batted her long lashes and bowed her head dejectedly. "Yeah, I guess so."

"You guess so; do you or don't you?"

"Mmm-hmm."

"Okay, I'll holla atcha then. I got to go."

Peggy was looking uneasy when he got back in the car, so he didn't say anything to her as she put the car in gear. His phone went off as they were pulling out of the lot. He looked down at the blinking light and for a brief moment, he thought of going to use Dee's phone. He had already set her on course so he looked over to Peggy. "Let's roll."

An unfamiliar female answered on the third ring. He told her who he was and she let him know that it was JJ who was trying to reach him. He wondered why he hadn't used his own phone. He hunched his shoulders and told the woman to put him on.

"Hey, baby, you on your way over here or what?" JJ asked gruffly.

"Uh-huh, we about to head that way now."

"Where you at?"

"Leaving Dee's. The bitch called while we was about to head that way from the LaQuinta."

"Is Peggy still with ya?"

"Yeah, homes, the girl's a real trooper. Some nigga was letting the coke flow like water while we was at Dee's, but she brushed that shit right off like it wasn't about nothing. I think the nigga was named Buster or something like that."

JJ laughed out loud. "Oh yeah, that nigga be buying up some shit, trying to play the super bigshot and shit. How did Dee do? She come straight with the digits?"

"Hold on a minute." He counted the money. "All here. I left her another packet."

There was a long moment of silence, followed by muffled voices before JJ got back on. "Hey, dude, go give Dee another one of those thangs because Big Buster be over there ego tripping on that impression shit. Must be a lot of honeys at Dee's.

"Okay, I'll go do that but who is he anyways?"

"Man, he be down with Junior and 'em at the club."

"Damn, that spot still kicking? Shit, me and Lah, I mean Rainbow... Damn, that nigga be changing names more than he changes hoes. Anyways we sold 'em niggas a rack of colored TVs back in the day when they was first opening up that joint; seems like a hundred years ago now."

"Uh-huh, right, well, you wouldn't recognize it now. A big black nigga named Black Don be down with them too. But it ain't like it was back in the day no more. Them young fools be shooting up the joint like it's a recreation or something. Niggas crazy, yo."

"Okay, let me go give Dee that. Tell JJ and Debra that I'm on my way. Aw man, I meant Percy; damn, I'm talking to you. Oh yeah, don't let Johnny Bee know that I'm on the way. I want to surprise his black ass."

Sparkle hung up and called Dee to let her know to meet him in the parking lot. When they rolled around the corner, she was leaning on some nigga's car with an irritated look on her face. Her arms were folded across her chest to ward off some of the chilly air.

Rolling down the window, he handed her the packet, which she slipped into her pants. Then she reached in her bra and gave him a handful of money.

"Damn, that was quick," he said, raising his eyebrows.

"That's almost half. I told ya Big Boy be buying up some shit. Why'd you bring me some right back?"

"Just had a feeling; that's all. I'll see ya later on," he said, nodding for Peggy to pull off.

Dawn was on the horizon when they hit I-20. They stopped at the Waffle House on Wesley Chapel and picked up five breakfast takeouts of waffles, eggs, corned beef and hash browns. They figured that everybody should be a little hungry by now. Sparkle devoured his on the way.

A half hour later they pulled into a circular driveway lined with luxury cars. He was impressed. They took a few minutes to take a couple of hits. As they were getting out of the car Peggy said, "You know your boy Johnny Bee is over here?"

He acted surprised. "Black ass-pimping Johnny Bee?"

"Uh-huh." She nodded.

"I didn't know you was down with Bee; what's my boy been up to?"

"You know Bee dis and dat," she said with a dainty wave of manicured fingers.

"Oh yeah, dis and dat; so he still pushing boosting hoes?"

"That amongst other thangs," she said as she concentrated on pushing the rock into the shooter.

"Other thangs, huh. Oh yeah, you know my nigga Bee aight."

"Yeah, yeah, I do." She hiccupped between gasps of sucking coke.

He watched her go silent in contemplation with a dazed look. *She must've been one of Bee's hoes at one time or the other. He always had that lasting effect on a bitch no matter who she ended up with*, he thought. "He still rolling with that slick-ass bitch, Yolanda?"

"For sho, you know dat dem two are gonna take it like that all the way to the dirt together."

"Uh-huh, from the kindergarten to the grave; that's them aight." Sparkle laughed as his mind swayed to

Beverly Johnson, Atlanta's police chief. She was Yolanda's running buddy way back in the days of their youth, and his girlfriend for life, *hmmphhed*. He wondered what Beverly was doing right then.

"How two people can stay together all these years, arguing and killing each other twenty-four-seven, amazes me."

"They still killing each other." He smiled.

"Every day." She giggled.

He leaned back, admiring her for a moment and thinking about how good home girl looked. She was a real cutie pie when you studied her for a while and had one of the prettiest smiles he had seen in a long time. But he wasn't the type of nigga to shank up on a nigga's ho unless she gave up some sign that's what she wanted. She was off limits, even if he didn't like or trust the nigga; the way he felt about Percy. Honoring principles in the game, he fell back into script. "They do go way back. Shiiiit, way back to when we used to play doctors under the blanket doing the stinky finger thang."

"Uh-huh, wid little baldheaded dicks and pussies, talking about su-la, su-la." Peggy laughed, grabbing her side.

They sat in the car lost in time, kicking it until the porch lights started blinking rapidly. A blonde-haired darky in a red dress stepped out on the porch, causing them to snap back to reality and reach for the door handles. Before they could get out, the girl said, "Ya'll coming in or what. Ya'll can't be sitting out here like ya'll on a stakeout or something. Come on, Peggy, you know good and well that this fool don't be liking that there."

"Hey, home girl, sorry about that. This here's Debra's brother, Sparkle."

"Shit, girlfriend, anybody can see Debra all over his face." She smiled with glittering eyes. Cutting the porch light off, she waved for them to follow her. They walked through the garage of the huge split-level house to a door that took them into a game room. Sparkle's eyes lit up as he took in the beautiful pool table that was the centerpiece of the room, surrounded by a couple of pinball machines, two large TVs in front of a sofa and a coffee table displaying Nintendo and Xbox game systems. On the side of each TV was a foosball machine.

He almost started toward a Ms. Pac-Man machine in the corner, having flashbacks to the days when he used to be chilling at Joe's pool hall on Auburn Avenue, helping his boy Rainbow clock dope and ho money. His mind raced with thoughts of Saturday nights on the strip overflowing with hoes, boosters and drug dealers hawking their wares. Nights that ran into Sunday mornings when down the street, lines of luxury cars and limos expelled dignitaries at the Ebenezer Baptist Church where Martin Luther King Jr. had gotten his life lessons from his pops. Of all the places he'd ever been, this was the most bizarre change of sceneries he'd ever experienced.

They passed through a red oak door into a room lined with shelves of books. There was a large-screen TV and mirrored paneling all along the wall. Several ceiling fans hung with long drawstrings and strobe lights on the blades.

When the girl saw him admiring the setting, she hit the wall switch. Red and black lights clicked on as the fans began rotating and a Janet Jackson melody began serenading the air. She clicked again and the lights got dimmer and started blinking in rhythm with the beat of the music. He was certainly impressed.

"This is the library-study-groove room," she cooed in the husky voice he recognized as the one that had answered the phone earlier.

They passed through another door that led to a room with two card tables with gamblers in thick cushioned chairs. At the larger table sat a big brother in a fedora crunching on a fat cigar. He was sitting in a circular straw wicker chair with huge potted plants on each side. Had to be Al. Beyond the gambling tables along the wall there was a craps table, a miniature roulette wheel and another Ms. Pac-Man machine.

The room was filled with gamblers trash-talking, as they tossed money around like water. JJ, Debra and Percy and two other players he hadn't seen before were at the table with Al.

"Godayum, a nigga's luck be running like donkey shit around this bitch, damn." Sparkle smiled at the familiar voice of his nephew, Stacy, who screamed in disgust and flung his cards on the table.

Sitting across from him, beaming as he raked in the pot, was his lifetime buddy Johnny Bee. "Damn, Junior, you go for that one every time." He shook the money at the other players around the table. "Ya'll people been good to an old playa tonight as usual; appreciate it. I really do."

He was immediately bombarded with curses around the table. "Fuck you. Go to hell. Kiss my ass. Move ya money, nigga; we going to the next hand."

A sweetie in an orange halter top and tinted glasses picked up the deck and started shuffling. "Ya'll crybabies need to ante a five spot on this here low-ball hand. I got to get my nephew some of them baby Jordans; let's go."

Another honey in tight braids with jet-black skin joined in the banter. "Damn, bitch, that's the only game yo ass know, ain't it?"

Halter top shot right back, "Aw, ho, you deal yours; I deal mine. Chuck your five in the pot if you in. If you ain't, shut the fuck up and let us play."

Sparkle stood, admiring the bantering for a couple of hands, before he slid up behind Johnny Bee and tapped him on the shoulder. "I really don't like the way you taking advantage of my nephew here, player."

"B" tensed up from the touch and then tilted his hat back. "Fuck you and your good-paying nephew." His eyes blinked and he shivered. He looked over his shoulder and squinted at the intruder before he leaned back in his chair and slapped himself upside the head with both hands. "Aw hell to the naw!" he yelled. "Oh my holy be damn, say it ain't so?"

"It's so, nigga." Sparkle beamed down at him.

As one, "B" and Stacy got up to crush him in a double bear hug. "Unc."

"Partner, my nigga." The two greeted Sparkle with exuberance.

"Aight, I appreciate the love, but godayum, I gotta breathe, ya'll, shiiit."

"B" beamed, stepping back. "Man, why didn't you let me know you was out?"

Stacy added quickly, "Man, I started to call you and let you know that I was coming over here, but I figured you was worn out. But shit, I'm sho' glad you showed up because this black-ass nigga done sliced my ends like they was his from the get-go."

The commotion caught the attention of the folk at the other table, where Al had just pulled in a fairly decent pot. "So that's your brother, Deb?"

She cut her eyes at him as she was counting her money. "Uh huh, yeah, dat be my big bro, Sparkle." Her eyes lit up when she saw the take-outs. "Is one of them for me, bro, 'cause I'm hungry for a mug. Good looking, uh, bro, could you throw me a few ends? This nigga's got to hit a brick sooner or later."

Sparkle jerked his head back and gritted on her but

reached in his pocket and tossed her a couple of bills anyway. She didn't even look back and held her hand over her shoulder. "Hold up there, nigga. Let me cut those if you don't mind, please."

Percy pushed the deck in her direction and mumbled, "Girl, you need to be keeping yo head in the game instead of doing all that hollering, disturbing a nigga's concentration and shit."

Al drubbed his fingers on the table and intervened. "Man, you know you got to let folk cut the cards before you deal; come on now."

Sparkle stood, playing ghost, while he was checking out their hand moves and poker face expressions as they continued the trash talk. From years of experience, he honed in on lip twitches, eye arching and posture movements; any telltale signs that most players didn't pay any attention to.

After a few rounds, JJ nudged Sparkle on the hip and pointed to Stacy, lying on one of the beanbag chairs lined against the wall. Sparkle strutted over and took a seat in the one beside him. "Bad night, huh, baby boy?"

There was a sneer on his face until he looked and saw who it was. He straightened up as best he could and said, "Yeah, Unc, shit be rough right now."

"Gets like that every once in awhile, youngun," Sparkle said with an understanding tone.

"Man, I been losing my ass off for weeks now," Stacy said as he shook his head in disappointment.

"Brighten up, baby boy, old Unc's gonna come to the rescue. How ya been doing other than having this dry run at the table? Heard ya been making babies by the car load."

Stacy smiled in his squinty-eyed way and hunched his shoulders. "Shiiiit, honeys be blowing up before I even get the dick in, Unc." He harumphed.

Sparkle laughed right along with him, glad that he was able to lift his spirits. "Son, you still a wild dog, just like your pops. Speaking of...what's my nigga Sam up to these days?"

Stacy twisted his mouth to the side and sucked on his teeth. "Man, I holla at Pops whenever I hit the News. He still be running that skag wid dat bitch Rita; no-good-ass ho. Know what I'm saying, Unc?"

"So he's still oiling that shit, huh?"

"Hey, Unc, every time that I see him he's nodding." He shook his head in disgust. His expression faded into a distant sort of look, the way he usually did when he was talking about his old man's drug habit.

"Oh yeah, I definitely know how that be."

"I sure wish he'd quit, but I know he ain't, though." Stacy sighed.

Sparkle decided to change the subject. "How many babies you got now, yo?"

"Hell, I don't know; that shit hard to keep up with. Uh, okay, let's see. Uh, three crumb snatchers that I know about for sho, a coupla I got a few doubts about, and a couple dat bitches be claiming." He squinted his eyes and ran a finger under his nose before he gave a short snort. "I know it had to be that Kym or Krys one who told you that."

"Krystal," he admitted.

"Figures, well, you know they be riding a nigga about doing dumb shit like getting married and shit," he said with a sneaky smile.

"Hey, man, you know how women are about that."

"Yep, you right; dey sumthing else wid dat mess."

Sparkle placed a hand on his shoulder. "Uh, you lose a lot?"

"About thirty-five hundred dollars in the last few days. Shit, to tell you the truth, I lost count," he replied disgustedly.

"Yep, well, let's split. I got something. Aw hell, it's time to show you a few things." He cleared his throat harshly to get JJ's and Debra's attention. "Me and Stacy about to make a run. Ya'll want anything from the store?"

Before either of them could respond, Big Al spoke up. "Hey, soldier, if it ain't too much of a bother, could you pick up a case of Heineken and Old E for me? I'll hit ya off when ya'll get back or do I need to give it to you now?"

"Yeah and naw, I can handle it. It'll be a minute, though," Sparkle said. A chorus of sounds followed them out the door. Stacy led the way to a black Cadillac with a gold rag top.

"Let's go to one of them all-nighters where I can pick

up some decks of cards." Sparkled pulled out a deck he had slipped off the table. "Mmm-hmm, Hoyles, they should be easy enough to find. Ain't there a Cub Foods or Kroger around this way somewhere?"

"Sure, about a five-minute drive down I-20."

"Okay, let's go. We can pick up the beer there, too."

They bought five red and five blue decks, Elmer's glue sticks, single-edge razor blades, emery boards, sandpaper, red and blue magic markers and the cases of beer.

As they were exiting Kroger, Sparkle said, "I saw a Thrift Inn right down the street. Can you go get us a room? Yo ass ain't all the way broke, are you?"

Stacy nodded and went to get the room after they had parked.

When he walked into the room on the balcony level, he tossed the items on the bed and sat down. "Now, youngun, you can never let anybody, and I do mean absolutely nobody, know about the things I'm about to show you."

While Sparkle began opening the stuff up, Stacy sat on the edge of the bed, toying with the TV remote. He waited until he found a station he wanted to see.

"By the way, I gave Debra these cheat lessons a year before I got out last time, and she been killing niggas ever since."

Stacy jumped off the bed with a look of shock written on his face. "You mean to tell me that my own auntie's been cheating me outta my money for all these years?"

The fire was certainly lit up under his young ass and he started pacing the floor with his jaws puffed out.

Sparkle lay back on the bed and lit a cigarette and eyed him for a moment before he resumed unwrapping the stuff. After lining the decks up, he took the razor and cut all the cellophane off carefully. Then he used the markers to place strategic marks on the cards for suit and numeration before placing them on the bed to dry.

The way that Sparkle ignored his anger, steadily continuing what he was doing, curbed Stacy's pacing and he sat on the bed to observe. To say that he looked astounded was an understatement, for youngun was straight-up dumbstruck.

Knowing that his nephew's mind was racing in all kinds of directions, Sparkle smiled. "That's the same attitude these suckers are going to have if you give them any kind of sign that you down with the cheat. Uh-huh, that goes for somebody else, *anybody* else that even sniffs at you being hip to this stuff. Hell, I've been skinning JJ for years and 'B,' too, and you know he my dog. That is, until I finally hipped him a couple of years ago while we was in that camp in Columbus. Nephew JJ don't even know that your auntie be cheating to this day."

Old slick-ass auntie. He smiled as he sat on the bed, stunned by the things he'd learned.

Sparkle cleared his throat to draw his attention back to what he was doing. "Now watch me carefully; I'm going to let you do the last deck to see if you got it."

"Okay." He nodded, turning his full attention to the lessons at hand.

He proceeded to take out the aces, kings and queens and used the emery boards to file down the edges at each corner. Then he used the sandpaper to sand down the middle of the rest of the deck. He carefully explained the process as he was going. "These, baby boy, are called slides because you take 'em like this here and slide out the cards you done fixed up. You use these mostly for Georgia skin to shoot what niggas call the curb, but they also work pretty well for three of a kind playing poker."

Next, he took out the deuces, treys and fours and marked them with very small dits on the edges. "This, way you'll know where twelve cards are in poker, and they also come in handy in skin, as you can see. And let's not forget the advantage you'll have knowing what cards a nigga's dealt and holding in tonk."

Finally, he placed the deck back in the cellophane, using the glue stick to gently paste the cellophane and stamp back together. "Usually, you will let somebody else open the deck up. But for right now, I want you to stand close enough to me where you can hand me one of these decks for the switch. You can handle that, can't you?" As an afterthought, he added, "Of course you got to do it quickly and out of sight."

Stacy nodded in understanding.

Then Sparkle took one of the decks and showed him how to run up hands, followed by doing false shuffles and cuts. "We'll do some more of this later. I wanted to give you some hand maneuvers to practice on."

He gave him enough time to get a grip. "Now, for the encore, here's how you suck most of the money out of a game when you set to roll." He gave him a sly smile and picked out five low-ball hands, arranging the cards where everybody would be forced to go in the drywood to trade cards for a better hand.

After watching him maneuver through the concept a couple of times, Stacy leaned back on the bed, smiling. "Unc, I had no idea…damn, you something else, yo. Guess I got a lotta practicing to do, huh?"

Sparkle nodded. "Yeah, nephew, I've been at this for a long time and I still got to get that practice in on the regular. And you had no idea; ain't that something else? Now Stacy, you have got to remember this at all times. Look at the hits and side dits really quickly and natural-like and never get caught staring at the deck."

"Yeah yeah, unc…damn, where you learn all this stuff from?"

Sparkle snorted a short laugh. "Man, this is how Debra and your grandma been skinning folk for years, yo."

His eyes widened in shock. "Ah, man, Grandma be cheating a nigga all this time, too?"

Sparkled laughed out loud. "Man, she's the one that turned me out and I came up with the rest over the years."

"Well, I'll be damned." He shook his head in amazement.

Sparkle held up his hand to get his attention. "Now concentrate on this here, for real, yo. When I rub my hair and scratch behind my ear three times, I want you to say something funny as hell to get everybody to look at your face. And slide me this deck here so they don't see your hands making the switcheroo, got that?"

"Yep, oh man, this is going to be sweet." Stacy gleamed, his eyes shining.

"Okay, now what I do is play down the river, sometimes with a wild card; that way I can see what I dealt everybody. And then spread the deck out like this so I can see the next four cards coming off," he added, studying his reaction.

"Oh, man, that's slick as shit."

"One last thing; when I adjust my chair like I'm getting ready to get up, I want you to be ready to switch the low ball set-up, okay? Just say something to Al or JJ, ah hell, anybody but Debra, so that their attention will be drawn off of me. It'll only take a second." He finished by popping his fingers to emphasize how really simple it could be.

Stacy smiled. "Yeah, yeah, I getcha, man; let's go get paid, unc."

"Okay, give me a second," Sparkle said before he fixed himself up a hit of coke. "Okay, I'll work the slides and shakeouts for now, to let you see this shit at work. I'll help you perfect everything later; we ain't got time right now." He took a deep breath, gathered up all the decks and headed for the door.

✠ ✠ ✠

Several hours later, Al was looking at him with a smile that curled to one side of his mouth. "Damn, Sparkle, this must be your lucky night, dude; you done hit up for at least ten g's, maybe more."

Sparkle swigged down the rest of the can of beer he had been sipping on for a while and folded his stacks of money. "Uh, can I get that beer money now?"

Al laughed out loud. "Man, I almost forgot about that." He slapped the bill on the table. "Keep the change."

Sparkle tossed the c-note back and smiled. "It's on the house, partner. No problem, soldier; I only wanted to see if you was a man of your word."

With his eyes squinted, Al studied him real hard for a few seconds. "Hey, you aight, dude, and I really enjoyed playing with and meeting ya." He stuck his hand out for a shake. "But don't think for one second that I ain't gonna get my money back."

"Just a friendly game amongst players, right?" Sparkle winked at him.

Al leaned further back, then took a long drag off of his cigar. "Yeah, yeah, sho ya right. Well, boys and girls, ya'll welcome to enjoy yourselves with my baby here if you want to, but I've got to hit the rack." He turned to Debra. "Be by yo spot between two and four o'clock, if that's cool with you, baby girl?"

"Sure, Al, you know I'll be there for ya," she replied. When he left the room, she pulled up on Sparkle as they were heading for the door. "Nigga, I know you gonna kick some of my ends back."

"I am?" he squeaked as he reared his head back with a look of surprise on his face.

"Yeah, you are." She looked under eyed at him and held her hand out.

"Shit, I got out of the way when you got your thang in and if I recall, you did the same thang with yo half-slick ass. And I ain't asked for nothing back from you."

She leaned back a little further, laughing. "You still ain't shit, is ya, nigga?"

He pinched his nose and shook his head. "Hell, two rags from the same cloth, you and I. Come on, Boogie Bear, and damn you playing big bro for a real sucker now."

"Okay, okay, but I need a few anyhow. Got to get Ebony and Mike some school stuff," she tossed back, giving him a sweet little smile, knowing she had hit his weak spot. "Don't worry about it right now. But you know that I'm about to shine on your stingy ass, right? Uh-huh, get right in front those two smiling faces and tell them that good old unc don't give a fuck if they got new clothes or not. Hmm-mmm, that's exactly what I'm gonna do, for sho."

"You good, girl. You know that? You good." He gritted at her.

"Yeah, we are, aren't we?" She winked.

As they entered the game room, Johnny Bee motioned him over to one of their foosball machines. "Got a few games in, ya nigga; it's been awhile since I done laid the Bee-law down on ya."

They played four games, which Sparkle won three to one, the same ratio when it was an everyday thang for them at the gym in the Columbus prison.

Afterward, they settled on the couch, sipping Olde English. "What plans you got, partner? You need some hoes? Some dope? Hell, you don't need no money; all them greens you pocketed in that game."

Sparkle took a long swig. "Got money; got dope. What I need is a rundown on a couple of hoes I just met."

"B" rubbed his chin with hands that looked like they belonged to a seventy-year-old man, all gnarled up and shit. "'Pends on who ya talking about."

Sparkle flicked the TV remote to a music video on BET. "One's named Dee, redbone, thick in the ass and shit."

"From Candler Road?" "B" responded immediately.

Sparkle smiled and cocked his head sideways. "Yeah, foxy ass a muthafucka."

"B" leaned back, laughing. "Ah, man, you mean to tell me that you don't remember little nappy-headed Dee from back in the day?"

Sparkle was confused and it showed as he cocked his head to the side and rubbed his hand across his mouth. "Man, I'm lost, and you got me there."

"B" coughed into his fist. "The little red bitch from Carver Homes that used to wear pink and red everything... Uh-huh, we all thought she was a fucking tomboy and shit."

He got up and started pacing the floor. After a few ups and downs, his eyes lit up in recognition. He sat down beside "B." "Aw dude, now I remember them green eyes. But shit, man, ain't a damn thing tomboy about her now, for sho."

"B" stared at him for a second and then put his hand back up to his mouth, laughing. "So you done already got some of that super pussy and head of hers, huh? Shit, that bitch has always been a super freak. Hell, I even had her working for me for awhile, until her ass kept putting that geeking shit ahead of my money and the game I was pouring into her ass."

Sparkle started shaking with laughter. "Oh yeah, she done put that thang on me and I must admit, she's definitely got the bomb on both ends." He gazed off to the other side of the room. "Man, I put a package in her hand. Hold up now, before you say anything. The bitch be smoking that stuff like twenty-four-seven, but I've got to start somewhere. Hell, might as well get some good pussy and head in the process, ya feel me?"

At that moment, Debra and Stacy came through the door. "Hey, man, what you gonna do?" Debra asked in a gravelly voice. "If you wanna hang with that black-ass nigga there, you can. Or you can roll with us and we are about to roll now, so do what you feel."

"I'm rolling with ya'll." He turned back to "B." "Hey,

dog, give me your digits so I can hook up with you in a day or so after I take care of my legal."

"No problem there, partner; you seen our nig, Rainbow, yet?"

"Naw, I ain't seen him yet." He squeezed "B"'s shoulder and then embraced his lifelong buddy before he got up and left with his folk.

CHAPTER SEVEN

Trapping A Fast-Stepping Ho

Beverly couldn't shake off her paranoia as she made the right turn off Peachtree onto Auburn. Subconsciously, she kept checking both rearview mirrors every few seconds, making sure that no one was following her. Most of her police training consisted of being alert at all times, never really knowing when something might pop off. It had become a second nature to her.

She couldn't detect anyone trailing her but that certainly didn't mean that there wasn't. Sensing she was on point, she dared not turn her head; it would be a dead giveaway that she was nervous about something. Yep, a definite no-no.

Perhaps she was putting more into the awkward feeling she had with Lt. Woo earlier. Or maybe it was the run-in she had with Deputy Commissioner Aaron Taylor and the way he always made her feel uncomfortable. Despite his position of rank a step above hers, she couldn't force herself to trust him; neither he nor the assistant police chief, Roger Jackson, better known as RJ. She hated to admit it, but they were two people she would never trust with her life.

A car horn blared loudly behind her, snapping her out of her revelry. She wondered how long she had been idle at the green light. She needed to get those icky feelings off of her mind and put more concentration into the dilemma at hand. Ever since she had started her climb in the Atlanta Police ranks, she'd made friends, enemies and forced allies. Hell, it came with the territory.

Right now, she had to fight off the nervous energy that came every time she had to go on one of these secret rendezvous. No way could she ignore a request from anyone who was responsible for her being in the position that she was in today.

Even though her loyalty to her friends often had her taking chances that could easily destroy her career, she couldn't find it in her heart to turn her back on them when they needed knowledge or her influence.

So despite the warm and cold feelings she got whenever she had the chance to see or help them, she still had to be careful, extremely careful. Thinking of Lah, Rainbow or Johnny, whichever name he had chosen to go by now, she decided to take the extra time before their scheduled meeting to pay a visit to the MLK Center. It would also give her the opportunity to double and triple check for anyone suspicious that may be following her.

She parked in the center's parking lot and took a little stroll of the historical site. Afterward, she decided to leave her car where it was and walked back down Auburn Avenue. When she got to the Ebenezer Baptist Church, she started feeling good that none of the people getting out of the many limos recognized her behind her disguise. As she watched her image in one of the cars she passed, she adjusted her sunshades and baseball cap. The faded-out jean outfit helped her to blend right in with the regular denizens of Atlanta's red light district—one she had prowled for years when she was on the beat as a rookie, sergeant and on upward through the ranks.

As she crossed the street across from the corner cab stand-poolroom, she noticed a young girl strutting her wares. Right off the top, she wondered if she was one of Rainbow's girls. *Damn, why couldn't this nigger get out of this life? He's so very, very smart. Hell, he could've been a helluva…a helluva…well, anything he wanted to be,* she thought as she watched a young couple enter the poolroom.

She pushed open the door and tingled at the sound of the bell over top of the door. Damn, she hated how that fucking bell jumped all over her nerves every time.

She spotted Rainbow immediately, sitting in a corner booth with his legs crossed, displaying a shiny pair of Gucci loafers. He was gulping down a huge slug of Heineken beer when he saw her and uncrossed his legs.

He gave her his best Max Julien smile. "What's up, Bevy girl? You looking super fine, as usual." He faked a shiver of ecstasy. "Gives a playa dreams of sweating your glory." He stood up from the table and pulled back one of the chairs, offering her a seat with a gentlemanly flair of a wave, like he was accepting royalty into his midst.

"Just answering the call of the wild again," she said, scoping out the other patrons in the room.

"Hey, you didn't really have to go through your espionage bit again, you know. That call was only that; a call to let you know that our boy done got out." He looked away, smiling brightly as he motioned for one of the girls to bring him a couple of more brews.

She sat down gracefully. "Well, I haven't seen you for awhile either, and a girl can't ever get tired of looking at a Max Julien look-alike. Have you seen Johnny Bee lately? He still holding down my girl, Yolanda, since she got out last summer?"

He ran a manicured finger under his nose and sniffled. "Come on, Bevy, you know just as well as I do that dat thang there is forever, for life, just like we are."

Smiling from ear to ear, she said, "Yep, you remember that day that she bloodied his nose when he stomped on her mud pies." She started laughing into the suds at the top of her glass.

"Look atcha, girl, suds all over your nose and shit." He flicked a napkin across the table.

She shook her head and started wiping away the tears easing down her cheeks. She took a deep breath and sat back in the chair and coughed. "Aw man, every time I think about that look on Bee's face, I flip out."

"That was some funny shit, for real tho."

"Yeah, it was." She puckered up and leaned forward

with her elbows on the table, "On the serious side, how's my baby boy looking?"

"How should I know; I haven't seen him yet, either." He picked up a saltshaker, sprinkled some on the back of his hand and started licking it off.

She frowned, disappointed, figuring that he would be able to give her a rundown.

"Whatcha frowning all up for, girl? I was just letting you know that he'd gotten out," he said as he took another long swig of his drink.

"I thought, I assumed, aw fuck it…anyway, when do you think you're going to see him?"

"Hmmm, I expect he'll hang around the family for a few days or so; hell, maybe even for a few weeks. There's really no telling… Aah anyway, I'll let him know you still got the hots for him when I do." He laughed into the glass.

She giggled for a few seconds before putting on a more serious look. "Hey, man, on the real, let your folk know that Lieutenant Woo's on the war path over there on the hotel strip. Little bitch tried to get me to sign an okay to harass my boys. Oh hell no, I couldn't do that to 'ya'll; my heart wouldn't let me."

"Oh yeah!" he said, tingling with anticipation now that she had put him on full alert with that information. That bitch Woo was truly a terror. He'd have to tell his girls to slow down for a few days. *Or at least be on the lookout for that bitch and her crew. Them niggas there ain't have no sympathy for nary a nigga when that ho gave the command.*

He cut an admiring eye at her. *Damn, all that money for tuition and love for this girl was well worth it. Mmm-hmm, to put this girl here through college was a fucking stroke of genius.* He lit up a Kool cigarette. "Thanks for the info. By the way, how's our nana? I haven't had a chance to cut her grass lately."

She smiled. "Grandma's Granny, you know; she's as sweet and stubborn as always. Matter of fact, I'm on my way over there now to check on her."

Rainbow nodded his head, full of love for the old lady who had helped raise him with nothing but affection. He sniffled. "That's a good woman there, yeah she is."

Beverly took a deep breath and sighed. "Let my boy know that I asked about him whenever ya'll hook up."

"Why don'tcha welcome him home yourself? He'd rather hear it from you instead of me."

"I can't do that."

"Why not? Why in the hell not?"

"I just can't, okayyyeeee." She moaned and stared off into space.

His loving stroke across her hand broke the semi-trance she had slipped into. His arm swept up to her shoulder and he gave her a nice little squeeze. "Hey, Bevy, I understand."

"Do you?" she wondered as she got up and walked out the door.

Rainbow waited until she was out of sight before he snatched his cell phone out of his lizard-skinned jacket and called Lady, his main broad. "Hey, baby, have you heard anything from my boy, Duke, yet?" He nodded to a few of the things she was reporting while he eyed one of his girls strolling by the window. For a second, he was tempted to call her to get whatever money she had hustled up, but thought better of it. There was always the possibility that one of those crooked-ass cops might have been spying on her. He quickly turned his full attention back to the Lady on the phone. "Check this out, baby girl, how about making a run down I-20 for me? Yeah, I want you to pick up whatever they got and reup them, if they need it. Oh yeah, and let them know that rats are in the closet."

He listened to her chattering for a while and then told her, "Naw, I'm going to let him get his feet wet first. Yeah, yeah, yeah, I know he's your favorite nigga, but baby, he ain't even been out but for a second. We'll holla at him soon enough. Uh-huh, yeah, okay, holla atcha in a bit. Bye."

Rainbow hung up and thought about his buddy, Sparkle, for a while. Then he got up and thought, *Might as well get a few things lined up for my boy for whenever he decide to holla at a nigga. Shit, it's been awhile since I pulled off a caper anyhow. Should be fun and a helluva way to get him back into the street rhythm.* He wore a full smile as he headed for his car.

✠ ✠ ✠

Several days later found Sparkle beginning to wonder when JJ would get back with Percy. He was slowly running low on the rock supply they had left him the night before. He and Dee had already smoked up a couple of fifties since he'd come over to her crib a couple of hours ago. He certainly didn't want them to think that he couldn't handle his biz or a slick-ass bitch like Dee. But this shit had him geeking hard for a mutha. He contemplated going back to Debra's. He had to squash that thought; he hadn't taken the time to get himself a key and didn't want to wake her or the kids. As high as he was right then, he realized that she'd get knee deep in his shit for fucking with this dope; especially since he hadn't even bothered to go get his legal down.

Most of the geekers had left, either because they were broke or going back on the track for some more money to score again. So Dee let him turn on the TV so he could watch some HBO or BET. He peeked at her every now and then, knowing that she was most likely scheming on ways to get him to smoke some more dope. She didn't believe him, for one second, when he told her that he didn't have any more by the way she kept throwing hints at getting a blast. After hanging around her for the past couple of days, he'd gotten used to hearing her spit game at him. It was all good, letting her spiel to her heart's content in exchange for the use of her drug hut with the almost constant flow of folk looking to score. Thankfully this wasn't one of those nights; he really wasn't in the mood for dealing with all the games that went with nearly every score.

He flicked his nose, uncrossed his legs and leaned toward her to brace his elbows on top of her soft thighs and spat, "Girlie, I know that a nigga done just set his feet back on the bricks and all"—he reached up and grasped her chin to turn her face to look directly in her eyes—"And if a playa is gonna get this cheddar the way he wants to, he needs a ho that he can really count on, even when the roller coaster goes downhill every now and then."

Her gaming switch automatically kicked on. He could see it in her eyes as she leaned toward him, smiling brightly. It raised his antenna as well. JJ's words of warning immediately invaded his brain. *That ho's a she-devil; keep your antenna up at all times.*

She had a real serious look on her face when she batted her eyelashes. "Baby, all I've ever needed was for a nigga to trust me a little. Hell, you've witnessed it yourself, there's some major ching-ching that be coming through this bitch." She sat up daintily and twisted her shoulder around sassily. "Baby, all that's ever been missing is a constant source to rely on. And being that we are playing square with each other, I've got to warn you right up top, playa: Don't be giving me stuff when you know that things have slowed down. Like on Sunday, or the end of the month, or days or nights like this one here."

He recrossed his legs, took a deep breath, uncrossed his legs again, placed his hands on his knees and twisted his mouth down. Why he want to go and do that? Home girl gave him a quick snake roll of her head, looked him up and down and said, "What, you want a ho to be real with ya, don'tcha?"

He didn't even try to hold back the smile that crept to the corners of his mouth; home girl was pulling no punches whatsoever. She was coming straight up with her shit.

He cleared his throat. "Yeah, shawtie, I want you to be real."

"So why you looking like that then?"

He wiped his eyes with the back of his hand. "Hell, I don't know. Well, to tell you the truth, I ah, oh whaddafuck, I see a lot of game in you, girl, but that's a good thang if we're gonna make it rain money in this here bitch."

"Exactly." She smiled and pursed her lips.

Suddenly the doorbell started to ring, followed by the sound of JJ's muffled voice.

Before she got up, she reached over to rub his crotch and sashayed her fat jellyroll ass to get the door. Her head angled back to make sure that he was checking her out; of course he was, recalling the way that she had put that hot pussy on him.

She had barely twisted the knob when JJ came storming through, looking all geeked up. Totally ignoring her, he walked straight over to Sparkle and squeezed his shoulder. "Come on, dog; we got a lot of things to do."

Sparkle flinched from the fingernails JJ dug in his collarbone. Grimacing just enough to let him know that shit was uncomfortable, JJ took a deep breath and removed his hand. Sparkle leaned away and started scratching his eyebrows before he ran his hand across his mouth. He straightened up and rotated his shoulders. "Shit, dog, let's do this then."

He got up immediately and followed him out the door. Before closing the door, he looked back at Dee, who had sat down on the arm of the couch. She had the nerve to try to be looking all innocent and shit. All he could do was shake his head at her good-playing ass. He walked back over to lean down, whispered in her ear and gave her ass a nice squeeze. "Don't go overboard with that innocent bullshit. I'll be getting you a nice package over here sometime tonight or early morning, aight."

She smiled over his shoulder and wrinkled her nose at JJ, who was leaning on the doorsill. She sniffed at his neck. "Whatcha want me to do if Violet and her girls come back through?"

He shot her a quick glance from the corner of his eyes, remembering the other day when he felt that twinge of jealousy coming from her. And again he smiled at the prospect with the thought of two fly, money-getting hoes competing for his attention—not to mention the money flow and comfort the competition brought. Even though he hadn't seen Violet since that first night, he couldn't quite get over the electricity that flowed between them.

"You can come over Debra's to get one of us." He looked over to JJ and got a nod; he knew he had said the right thing.

She immediately shined. "Why can't I just call?"

"Because her and the kids will most likely be asleep."

JJ frowned from the door and nodded for him to get a move-on. He got up before she could see the smile creeping to the side of his mouth. And also to avoid seeing the snake-and-eye roll that he knew was about to come.

She gave him neither and merely nodded. "Okay, I'll see ya'll then."

The two of them quickly stepped across the field toward Percy's ride that was parked down the street from the apartment. He got out of the car as they were coming and lit up a cigarette. "Yo, Sparkle, I see you are getting in the groove of things. Though a little slower than I had hoped, but you getting there."

All of his instincts kept telling him that this nigga was a pure snake. He'd use those instincts to deal with him with a long-handled spoon. He didn't want either of them thinking he was anxious to be under their rules with this dope thing. He massaged his chin as if he was in deep thought. "Yeah, playa, I feel you and I appreciate the get-up ya'll provided for me, but I'm gonna take my own time on this; I don't really know any of these folk I've been dealing with."

JJ finally spoke up. "That's on point, so what we are to do now is, instead of you just going to the hotels to pick up and deliver when we think you should, you gonna be on your own thing now. You can hang around and meet a lot of the people who be rolling through and from there you can expand. You down with that?" JJ turned around in the seat and stared at him before adding, "Ah, hell yeah, you down. Man, let's chop this here shit up and get this lettuce."

Percy turned around as well and spat. "You right, bro, be down for sure, so what we're going to do is give you a couple of ounces and you can chop it up anyway you want. Just pay us what the ounce cost and use your turnover money to score your own weight. That way you can move as comfortable as you see fit."

Percy took the time to light himself a good hit. He also was squinting at Sparkle to make sure he was getting it—he was. "Now you've got to decide what kinda paper you gonna cut your folk for slinging for you. The general idea is the same way you been dealing with Dee. Oh yeah, and bro, I can feel ya calculating, but I can tell ya right off the bat that from the beginning, you probably ain't gonna clock but maybe two hundred clean dollars to put in your pocket. I mean, like after handling what shorts you're going to have to accept; and collecting your re-up digits. But it'll get better as your clientele grows."

Sparkle, who had been clinging on to his every word, spoke up, "Hey man, 'nough said; let's get this started." He reached for the door handle but they both stayed put. "Yo, what's the hold up now, dog?"

JJ said, "Okay, before we even get out the car, the same rules apply, as less noise as possible. Chip and zip, chip and zip with no lip. We aight with this? Good; let's roll."

JJ pulled a grocery bag from under the seat and they crept up to the crib. Just as they had previously, JJ slipped to the closet to get all the working gear, while Percy went to the kitchen to get the saucers and sandwich bags. After taking a good hit, they got busy. By the time they had bagged up all nine ounces, the early morning light was easing through the drapes of the patio windows. The suddenness of Percy's phone ringing in the otherwise silent room caused all three of them to jump in their seats.

Damn that thing is loud as hell, Sparkle thought before he realized that it was probably the coke that had their senses extra sensitive.

A frowning Percy lifted the tail of his shirt to check out the number. He cut his eyes at JJ and whispered, "Man, fuck, damn, it's those worrisome-ass sisters of mine. I told them girls that I'd call them when everything was ready, damn."

JJ stifled a laugh. "Man, go ahead and answer them because you know they are gonna keep calling 'til you do. And dog, we got lucky that loud-ass phone of yours didn't wake Debra or the kids."

He didn't get the chance to finish when his attention was drawn to a yawning voice coming down the hallway. "Debra what?" she said as she appeared knuckling the corners of her eyes as she cinched the sash of her robe.

She emerged out of the shadows of the hall gritting. "What the fuck ya'll sneaky-ass niggas doing in my house this time of the night; oh shit, morning, I meant." She stopped to look at the grandfather clock in the corner of the room. "Oh hell no, not this shit here again. I done told ya'll." She grimaced angrily as she stifled the next yawn.

JJ was on his feet immediately and rushed over to her. She wasn't having it and whacked his groping arms away from her.

He put on his best jeffing face. "Come on, baby, you gonna wake the kids."

She pushed him back and stepped away, growling, "I'm gonna what? Wake the what? Nigga, please, I done told you not to be having that shit up in my house." Then she whirled on Sparkle, who was acting like he was asleep on the couch. "Nigga, ain't no need for that shit there; that fake-ass sleep ain't gonna work with me. You the first one I saw, fool, and your stupid ass ain't been out a whole week and already knee-deep fucking with this shit. What happened to looking for a job, bro; what's up with that?"

He gave up the act and sat up. "Aw, baby sis."

"Aw, baby sis, my ass. Whatcha gonna do; kick bricks right back at the penitentiary before you even get your feet wet? That's fucked up, man. You ain't even going to give yourself a chance to do the right legal thang," she nearly screamed as a tear rolled down her cheek.

Suddenly everybody's heads jerked to the hallway behind her, where Ebony and Mike were stretching and yawning.

Debra gathered herself and placed an arm around each of their shoulders. "Ya'll gon' clean yourselves up and get ready for some breakfast. I'll have something to eat in a minute; gon' now."

The mumbling pair made their way back down the hallway. Percy's phone started ringing on his side again. He already knew who it was but looked down at it anyway and grimaced.

Debra, who by now was breathing fire, whirled around with her hands on her hips and growled, "Might as well go ahead and answer it and don't be making no deals that I can hear, either." She huffed and twisted back around and headed for the kitchen to fix the kids something to eat.

Percy spent several moments whispering into the phone and nodding before he clicked it off and went to peek out of the patio curtains. He walked back to the table and grimaced. "Man, do you believe them damn girls are out there in my car, waving and smiling up at me? Damn, I thought I'd locked the damn door. What's it going to take to get rid of them monsters?"

He huffed and turned to take another look out of the curtains. His head jerked back when he looked beyond the twins, who were still waving at him. He turned back to them with an aggravating look on his face.

JJ raised a curious brow at his expression and then frowned at Sparkle, who could only hunch his shoulders in response. JJ threw his hands in the air. "Damn, dog, what's the deal? You act like you done seen a ghost."

Percy shook his head. "Man, here comes that bitch, Dee, walking across the field like she on a mission."

JJ jumped up and rushed to the patio to see for himself, before he turned back to Sparkle. "Aw fuck, she sho is. Yo, bro, go handle things with that ho before she get over here." He reached under the couch where he'd thrown the coke when the kids had appeared in the hallway, picked out one of the baggies and tossed it to Sparkle.

Sparkle snatched the bag in flight, eased it into his jacket pocket and turned to see if Debra was paying any attention. Luckily, she was reaching into one of the cabinets. He sprinted quietly to the door before she could turn around.

He smiled at the silhouette of a girl sitting in the backseat of Percy's ride. He just as quickly ignored her and put his hand up to halt Dee's progress across the field, motioning for her to turn around as he stepped up his pace toward her. When he stepped off the curb he heard the car door open and turned around to see a girl get out. Damn, honey was fine in some cut-off jeans. He watched her run up the stairs of Debra's apartment.

He blinked once or twice in curiosity and turned back to Dee, who had stopped at the corner of one of the buildings and braced her hands firmly on her hips. When he got close enough to see her face in the shadows, he saw that she was looking beyond him, so he turned his head to follow her gaze. *Whaddafuck*, he thought as he watched the same girl in a pair of white jeans follow the path of the other girl. What really fucked him up was that she was also standing at Debra's door before he blinked and shook his head, and like magic she was gone. He wondered if he was tripping, because there was only one girl again. "Aw man, this stuff done got me tripping for a bitch," he mumbled to himself.

"Whatcha say, nigga?" Dee responded when he turned back to her.

"Nothing, I just thought…aw fuck it, I thought. Never mind. I was tripping off of some real dumb shit; that's all. What's up?"

She stood with her mouth twisting to the side, gnawing at nothing, the way he had noticed folk doing while they were high on coke. She ran her eyes up and down his body like he was bugging for sure.

Her reaction only riled him up as he leaned away from her and gritted. "Girl, I asked you what was up?"

"I heardcha."

"Well, what's up then?"

She sighed and rolled her eyes. "Man, you told me to holla atcha when folk started to show up; well, I'm hollering."

He spread his arms apart. "Okay, I can see that and...?"

"And whatcha gonna do?"

He grabbed her by the elbow and steered her back toward her apartment. Damn, she smelled good. He felt that familiar stirring in his groin, but he didn't have the time. He noticed her eyes slanted toward his ever-expanding crotch and he didn't want her to get the wrong idea. He stopped on the steps leading to her door and pulled out one of the bags with fifty dimes in it before she could open the door. "This here is five hundred worth of dimes." He looked in both directions before handing it to her. "Now ten of these joints is yours, aight. Hey, girl, I ain't really got to tell you this, but you got to keep this here straight 'cause we got to make it rain green up in here if these dudes are gonna keep fronting me."

She massaged the bag for a few before she looked back up at him batting her eyes. "So how I'm supposed to get atcha when this here's gone?"

There was an instant dilemma, but he played it off. "Before the day's out, I'll stop by." He hesitated for a second, reconsidering his thoughts. "I'll call and leave you another number where you can reach me."

Her eyes narrowed while she thought of other ways to cement her game. On the other hand, she wanted him to leave so she could get a good blast with the stuff he'd given her in peace. She decided to save some of her sexy for the next time. "Yeah, baby, I can feel you being busy and shit, so I'll see you later." She didn't even wait for a reply before she opened her door and disappeared.

All he could do was shake his head. True enough, he felt her conniving mind scheming and didn't expect her to leave that quickly. He rather enjoyed her shooting him all that bullshit; helped to keep him sharp. Oh well, whatever, as long as she kept those digits straight and answered the booty call when he needed it, she could act any way she wanted to. He turned around, braced himself against the early morning chill and headed back to Debra's.

As he crossed the street, he noticed that the girl was back in Percy's car. He figured that it was the coke that had him tripping; she had on different clothes and hairstyle, damn. "Whew." He shook his head as he stepped inside. "Damn," he moaned and froze, his eyes bucked wide open. He rubbed them with his palms and then stared at the girl in braids sitting at the table. Blinking a couple of times, he headed back out the door, only to be slowed by the laughter at his back.

"Hey, bro, I know whatcha tripping on; come on back in here," JJ said.

Sparkle took a deep breath, went into a crouch and

squinted at Percy's car. Seeing the girl still sitting there, he sighed heavily, walked back into the apartment and took a seat on the couch. The girl in the braids smiled at him, then got up and went outside of the balcony doors. He turned to Percy and JJ with a confused look on his face and frowned at the sneaky smile on theirs.

His body jumped involuntarily when the sound of a shrill whistle erupted in the air. He looked over to see the silhouette of the girl waving through the curtains. She had a wicked know-it-all smile on her face when she stepped back in and returned to her seat at the table.

When the same face pushed through the door, it finally cemented what was going on. He gazed back and forth between the identical twins and shook his head at his own stupidity.

Percy got up and put his hand on his shoulder. "Man, forgive me, I should've told you about these two."

He gritted on both of them. "These are my nagging twin sisters. That one over there looking like she stole something is Cherry; and the one sitting yonder with the braids, trying to look all innocent and shit, is Sherry. Together they are my worst nightmare."

Sherry, the braided one, smiled devilishly and walked over to Percy. "Aw, big bro. Don't be talking about us spoiled brats like that; you the one that spoiled us."

Cherry, the one with the curly do, joined her sister and said in an identical voice, "Yeah, we only want to hang out with our hero brother for a while; that's all."

Percy tooted his nose up and looked away from them. "Uh-huh, I'm sure you do, don'tcha?"

"Yep," they said in unison as they crossed the room in sassy struts and planted sloppy kisses on each of his cheeks.

Percy ducked and pushed both of their faces away from him. "Yeah right."

Debra stuck her head around the corner and brushed her shoulder- length hair. She held her palms up at the guys and spoke to the girls. "Hey, Sherry, Cherry, how you doing? I'm glad to see ya. Tell your mama that I got her set for eleven o'clock tomorrow at the shop."

Cherry pushed Percy upside the head as she answered, "Yes, ma'am, I'll tell her."

Debra stopped combing her hair and under eyed her. "Girl, you ain't gotta be calling me no ma'am; makes me feel like an old lady."

"Yes, ma—" She stopped in midsentence when Debra put her hands on her hips, bucking her eyes. "Uh, yes, Miss Debra," she corrected herself with the quickness.

"Okay, that's better; uh, a little better anyway." Debra smiled, giving the dudes a nasty snake roll of her head as she whirled around and headed back into the bedroom.

JJ looked at Percy and spread his arms apart. Percy stretched his neck and started rubbing his chin and looked back and forth between the twins and Sparkle. "Yo, check this out, ya'll two demons; why don't ya'll do your big brother a favor and roll with my boy, Sparkle, here to check out those hotels for me."

They looked at each other and hunched their shoulders before Sherry said, "Yeah, we can do that, but how are we supposed to get there; catch a cab?"

"Naw smartass, ya'll can use my car. I'll ride with JJ and Debra. But don't be driving all crazy and shit. Yeah, Miss Cherry, I'm talking to you, Miss Hotrod, and when ya'll finish, come straight over to Al's."

Cherry, the obvious boss between the two, sassied up to him and bumped his hip. She flopped her arm around his neck and began toying with his heavy gold Mercedes-Benz chain. "Now, big bro, you know that we're going to handle this for you." She nodded and winked at her sister and JJ. "But ain't you gonna break a little sumthin'-sumthin' off for me and sis?" She ended with a pout.

Percy leaned away, faking a frown he knew she wasn't buying. "Why I got to give ya'll something every time I ask ya'll to do a little task for me?" He tried to maintain a serious look but that didn't last but a hot second before she mugged him in the face.

"I see you getting the royal treatment, nigga." Debra laughed sarcastically as she came out of the kitchen, wiping her hands with a towel and hollered down the hall. "Ya'll kids need to get ready to eat and get outta here." She grimaced at their muffled replies and went about fixing their plates.

JJ walked up to Debra, only to meet a frown and stiff palm to his chin; a move that didn't faze him in the least. He knew his woman, so he forced an innocent smile. "Baby, if you want to get in contact, we'll be back at Al's trying to get some of our money back that fat nigga wiggled out of us the other day."

Debra looked at him like he must have lost his mind. She put a hand on her hip and then put a manicured finger up to his face, freezing whatever he had to say as she spat, "Nigga, please, you actually believe I'm gonna hang around here like some kind of housewife. Well, you can think again; I need to get some of that ching-ching back, too." She held a finger up and waved it around the room. "Ain't nary one of ya'll niggas going anywhere until I get ready to ride with ya, what?"

Each one of them, including the twins, threw their hands in the air and leaned away from her. She mugged the whole crew and twisted her narrow behind down the hall.

The twins smiled at each other and then at Percy, knowing they had only a little time to get a hit off of him while Debra got dressed. Percy squeezed his eyes together and shook his head; he knew what they were thinking. He motioned for all of them to join him on the balcony so they could get a blast out of sight of the kids, who had gone into the kitchen to eat.

Afterward, JJ said to the girls, "Looka here, ya'll, we want ya'll to let the girls ya'll deal with at the Red Roof,

Holiday Inn and Motel 6 know that he's the one who's going to be dealing with them for awhile. All of them chickenheads should be ready for a fresh package by now." He held his head up, listening for something in the wind for a second, and then leaned against the patio door. "Wait a minute." He sighed and pushed through the curtains.

Percy took over after he left. "Yeah, my nigga, just hang with these fools so you can get a feel for those girls at the hotels, pick up the ends and give them some of this fresh stuff. They already know what the deal is, so all you got to do is get in rhythm with them."

I wonder why they haven't mentioned to the twins that I've already been to those spots. Mmm, must be another set of honeys they talking about. Yep, probably is, Sparkle thought. Nodding his head in agreement, he was definitely ready to sprout out further anyway. "Okay, I feel you on that there."

Before he could continue, JJ burst back through the curtains and slapped a new cell phone in his hands. Sparkle gave him a curious look and flipped it around in his hand before he put it in his pocket. JJ cocked his head to the side with his hand held out. Sparkle looked at the hand and raised his brow before it dawned on him what he wanted. He gave it to him. "Them hoes already know the number, just give them a code that they can use to let you know they need some more stuff. Niggas got to be careful what they say on these things, dog, you feel me?"

They were about to do another hit when they heard Debra hollering at the kids to get their things together and get to school. They knew that she was coming by the tone in her voice. They started stuffing the dope in their pockets as one by one they eased back into the living room before she came out.

Shortly afterward, she pranced into the room, dressed in a skin-tight brown jeans outfit laced with flowers and rhinestones, with a Gucci handbag slung over her shoulder. "Aight, troopers, let's go roll up some of that cheddar that fat boy's trying to hold all for himself."

Not a moment was wasted joining her as she strolled out of the apartment. JJ and Percy followed her to the parking lot while Sparkle and the twins headed to Percy's ride on the other side of the building.

With Cherry at the wheel, it took them only a minute until they were pulling into the parking lot of the Red Roof Inn. Sherry led the way as they entered the room on the third tier facing the expressway. A different girl answered the door than the times he had come over with Peggy. A bright-eyed Sherry introduced him to a perky petite red-haired honey named Carla, who was still draped in her robe with rollers in her head.

In a small Loretta Devine-type of voice, she stifled a yawn. "Pinky had to make a run last night, I, ah, figured that she'd be back by now." She spread her arms around the room in a herky-jerky motioned. "Ah, so you must be Sparkle, right, yeah, right. Anyway, she'll probably be here the next time that you ride through. I'll be sure to let her know what the deal is."

Sparkle's eyes squinted in concentration to keep up with her rapid-fire dialogue. In a way he reminded her a little bit of Left Eye, who used to roll with TLC; she had that kind of spunk about herself.

He sat down and crossed his legs and watched the girls kick the bullshit girl talk for a few minutes. "Yeah, shawtie girl, we'll see what it be like with Pinky when we see her, but right in now, how about you shooting me those ends."

The suddenness of his intrusion brought a brief frown from her pixieish face, causing her to wrinkle up her pouty lips for a second before she broke out into one of the cutest smiles he had ever seen. She spun daintily and went to the sink and reached up on the clothes rack to get a box. In quick little steps, she walked back over to the bed and plopped beside him, opened the box and handed him eight hundred dollars. While he counted the money, she sat waggling her legs with her chin anchored on the back of her hand.

Sparkle forced back a smile as he thought, *Damn, this one here sho do be acting a little too girlie for this hardcore dope game.* Those thoughts were erased immediately when he considered that under her extra-feminine exterior, there had to be a cold-hearted bitch—one with her own way of dealing with the scoundrels chasing Scottie on a daily basis or whatever else came her way.

With that in mind he froze her with a serious poker face before he smiled and said in a husky voice, "Hmmm, does this mean that you wanna work with a grand piece?"

She licked her lips and looked across the room at the twins. The girls hunched their shoulders instead of giving her a verbal comment. She turned back to him, batted her long eyelashes a couple of times and said, "Uh-huh, stud, that's exactly what it means." She stared under eyed while she waited for his response.

There wasn't much to say, so he turned his mouth down, reached into his jacket and took out the bag. He pulled out two of the $500 packages and handed them to her.

She immediately ripped them open and removed a handful of the Ziplocs, tossed the twins a good-sized rock apiece and held one out to him, which he politely refused with a smile. He had long ago decided that he wasn't going to let any of the folk working for him know that he got high or dipped into any of his packages. Their relationship had to be strictly business; no more, no less.

She stared at him for a moment, cocked her head to the side and then hunched her shoulders before she got up and joined the twins. After getting their smoke on, all three girls jumped on the bed and started playing dominoes. Shortly, folk started knocking on the door.

Like magic, Carla transformed from the dainty pixie into a hardcore, no-nonsense businesswoman right before his eyes. Like some Michael Jackson-type shit. He smiled at the instant change in her and the way she handled her biz like a little gangster ho. He would make it his business to get to know shawty a lot better on future visits.

Within a half hour, she was pulling Sparkle into the bathroom and handing him $400 with her left hand and holding out her right one for another package, which he didn't hesitate a second in giving to her.

He reared his head back and started scratching his neck as he looked down at her. "Okay, little mama, I've seen enough. Just holla at a nigga whenever you ready. Any time of the day or night and I'll get here as quickly as I can." He ended by giving her the cell number and code she needed to use.

Still set in her gangster mode, she said, "Yeah, playa, you do that. I'll be hollering in a few. You handle your end and as you can see, I got this one here."

He stepped back into the room and jerked his head at the twins. They said brief goodbyes to the people that had gathered in the room and prepared to leave. As they were exiting the room, Carla pulled his sleeve. She had turned back into Miss Sweetie Petite as she smiled up at him. "I'll see ya soon, playa. You kinda cute when you ain't frowning at a bitch, you know that?"

He flicked his thumb across his nose and smiled. "Oh yeah, we'll be seeing a lot of each other, baby girl; that's for sure." He could tell from the glitter in her eyes that she was ready for whatever with him. He planned on taking advantage of that glitter in the future. But now wasn't the time so he rubbed her gently on the shoulder and left.

Minutes later, speeding down I-20, Sherry leaned across the seat with her chin resting on her hands. "So whatcha think about our little Miss Carla, Mr. Sparkle?"

He noticed in the side-view mirror that she had a mischievous smile on her face. He took a long drag off of his cigarette before he turned his mouth down. "Shortie's got a lot of spunk and definitely be handling her biz; that's what I think." He turned in the seat to face her. "We'll see what she be about down the road."

Cherry, who had been quietly taking in the conversation, checked the traffic in both rearview mirrors before she jerked the car into the exit lane, ignoring the blaring of several cars protesting her bold move. With a sly smile, she looked across the seat at him. "Looks like little mama wanna be jumping your bones if you ask me, playa."

He pulled on his left earlobe as he eyed one twin and then the other before he burst out laughing. "It's a good thing I didn't ask you then, huh?" He grimaced.

Taken somewhat aback for a moment, she wrinkled her nose as him and snorted, "You ain't got to be so nasty with it, humph," she snarled as she snapped her head back to the road.

Not fazed whatsoever, he looked at her from head to toe. "Let's put it down to ya'll like this here: I don't be mixing business with pleasure; that is, on a regular basis." He took the time to cram a rock into his shooter and put it to blaze before he continued, "And even if I did, you probably wouldn't be able to recognize the difference anyway. Of course unless that someone happened to be you." He smiled to himself as he watched her try to hide the blush that rose to her cheeks behind her hand. *Oh yeah*, he mentally patted himself on the back as he chalked her up as future prey.

Sherry decided to kill the silly noise as she piped in from the backseat, "This next girl"—she took the time to clear her throat— "at the Holiday Inn has got a lot of dude in her." She squinted her eyes, checking out his reaction.

He took a long toke of the coke and hunched his shoulders as if to say "so."

Disregarding his so-called tough attitude, she snorted. "Just thought I'd let you know ahead of time; that's all. Anyway, they call her Sissy and believe me when I tell you that she is a handful." She shivered to emphasis her point.

Was that supposed to bother me? I think not, he thought. "Sweetie, I don't give a fuck if she thinks she's Mrs. King Kong, as long as she keeps the ends straight, we gonna be cool." He looked back and forth between the wannabe divas. "Do ya'll feel me on this? Well, do you?" He put in a little extra growl to let them know that there wasn't nothing soft about him if need be.

From the way their eyes started shifting around, he knew they had caught the message loud and clear.

They rode in silence, cruising down the Wesley Chapel exit ramp. It gave him the chance to get mentally ready to deal with the so-called dreaded man-woman Sissy, with whom the twins seemed to be in such awe. But to his surprise, when the light turned green, they streaked straight across the street. He arched his brow across the seat at Cherry. "What's the deal, yo? The Holiday Inn is over that way," he said, nodding to the other side of the highway.

She purposely ignored him until she had veered around the Stop'n'Go gas station and started down the narrow thoroughfare leading to the Motel 6 before she gave him a sideways glance and smiled. "Figured we'd introduce you to a real sweetie before you tackle the monster lady."

Sparkle brushed away the smile they shared in the mirror, as he was about to get out of the car. He stepped out to check out the surroundings and heard them whispering. *Damn girls always got some sneaky shit going on*, he thought as he stretched his arms and found himself stifling a yawn.

He'd gotten only a few hours' sleep in the past couple of days. It definitely had to be the cocaine that had kept him going. He'd run through these two spots and get them to drop him off at Debra's to get some much needed rest. If not, he'd fall out on his feet before long and that wouldn't do at all.

The gleaming twins jumped out of the car and nearly skipped-to-the-loo across the parking lot and practically ran up the stairs. He couldn't help wondering why they'd gotten so hyped up all of a sudden. By the time he made it to the balcony walkway, they were ducking into a room four doors down. Harrumphing, he wiped a hand down his face before he proceeded to the room. He entered and took a step back because the room was full of geekers sitting and standing around with anxious looks on their faces.

Godayum, all these folk this early in the morning, he thought. Carla, a jet-black sister with almond-shaped eyes, whose skin was so smooth and clear that it appeared to glow, nodded for him to come inside. She batted her long lashes up and down his frame. "Whatcha gonna do, playa; stand there all day? Get your fine ass on in here," she said in a honey-coated voice.

His cheeks rose in a smile as he looked down at her stunning, barely five-foot frame before he crossed the sill. He immediately felt uncomfortable with all the unfamiliar eyes on him and barely felt the soft hand she pressed into his shoulder. His eyes traveled slowly to her tiny multi-jeweled hand adorned with rings on every finger and bracelets of multiple designs and colors jangling along her narrow wrist. She daintily grasped his elbow and led him through the throng of staring geekers into the bathroom.

She slowly closed the door, dashing the room into total darkness before she flicked the lights. He blinked a couple of times, adjusting to the sudden glare. He flinched slightly when she reached into her flowery silk blouse into a creamy pair of forty-something, deep chocolate whammies and extracted a wad of dollar bills. She batted those long lashes at him again and gave him a pearly white smile as she handed him the money and purred, "JJ and P hollered at me a little while ago and told me that you'd be on your way over here."

She caught the trail of his eyes and jerked her head back slightly. With a short snort she looked down at her chest and back up at him before she cocked her head to the side and smiled. "Damn, you gonna take the money or what?" She braced her hands on her hips. When his eyes didn't divert from her breasts, she gave him one of those snake rolls.

He zoomed in on the money and then into her face, doing his best not to look into those hypnotizing jet-black eyes. "Excuse me, shortie, but I really wasn't expecting," he paused and stuck his head around the corner of the door before going on, "Uh, all those folk I ain't ever seen before sorta makes me feel a little uneasy; know what I'm saying?"

She ran her eyes up and down his body, with her mouth twisted up in a slight smirk. "Hmmm, don't get your drawers all up in a knot there, playa." She flipped her wrist daintily and added, "It ain't always like this early in the morning. It's just that we got a red dog alert an hour ago, and I called most of my regular folk over so that it won't be all that foot traffic roaming outside."

With obvious concern, he mouthed, "A red what?" He was confused.

She cocked her head to the side and narrowed her eyes. "Aw damn, you must've just got around this way or something, but don't worry you'll definitely hear about them soon enough. Here, man, take this money, for god's sake, and give me some stuff to keep these geeking muthafuckas from looking all crazy and shit. They been here for a minute, waiting for something to come through. Oh yeah, and make that four lots because with that alert, they gonna be hanging around for a while."

"Four lots, oh, aaah okay," he said quietly as he took the bills while reaching into his jacket and placed the dope in her outstretched hand.

To his surprise, she immediately took out one of the Ziplocs, magically produced a glass smoker's bowl and lit up. She inhaled deeply on the rock before handing the bowl to him, which he politely refused with a wave of the hand. In a nonchalant manner, she hunched her shoulders, took a longer drag and said between gulps of breath, "You gonna count that, ain'tcha?"

Snapping out of his mini daze, he said, "Oh yeah," and started rifling through the bills.

"It's all there," she said, smiling shyly up at him.

He leaned away from her. "Girlie, I'm just—"

She didn't even let him finish and gently touched his elbow. "I was just testing you, playa; it's always all there."

He pinched his nose and stared at her feeling sorta stupid, not knowing quite how to respond.

Sliding her hand slowly down his arm to rub his hand, she smiled demurely and said, "Playa, don't worry about it, you'll get to know me in a little bit, and I know ya got to be stepping fast right now, so we'll get a chance to kick it later on, aight?"

He'd barely nodded okay before she was guiding him out of the bathroom and toward the twins, who were standing at the door ready to go.

With her hand in the middle of his back, she nodded and winked at the twins. She let out a short laugh and reached around him to open the door. "I'll be seeing you soon, playa. Hey, how ya'll girls doing?"

Ignoring whatever response the twins might have made, she turned back to the people in the room and said in a hard, all-business-like tone, "Okay, ya'll muthafuckas line ya'll asses up and let's do this."

Turning to them, she said, "I'll see ya'll folks later. As you can see the herd be waiting on a bitch and I got to get to serving them before they start to getting rowdy up in here." She winked and smiled before she turned back into the room and closed the door.

As he followed the twins down the stairs, it dawned on him that he hadn't seen either of them use the phone while they were on the highway.

As if she were reading his mind, Cherry smiled, raised the hem on her blouse and patted the cell phone hooked to the side of her skirt. "It ain't magic, playa. She texted while we were on the exit ramp. Come on; it's time to meet Miss Sissy." The smirk she'd had earlier had returned. Feeling a little dumb, he jacked up his jeans and quietly followed them to the car.

✠ ✠ ✠

At that same moment, on the other side of town, the clicking from the soles of the shiny, wing-tipped tan gators dominated the sound in the room on the tiled floor in the dimly lit room as the lanky veteran street player paced back and forth. A mist of aromatic smoke swirled in a steady stream from the thick Cuban cigar clenched in the corner of his mouth, emanating from the shadowy figure sitting behind the large oval desk. Long manicured fingers, bejeweled with several expensive rings, tapped a slow beat on the highly glossed mahogany top. The soulful flow of Young Jeezy's "I Luv It," was booming, adding sparks to the tension-filled room. The seriousness of the situation was proving to be a necessary evil but his thoughts were on the lovely sexpot, who was at that very moment cuddled up in his bed in the next room. It only added to his desire to get this talk over.

"My man, why are you acting so nervous and shit?" his baritone voice boomed at the stalking figure pacing, as swirls of smoke turned into halos that rose from the shadows to evaporate into a cloudy mist that rose to the ceiling.

The intensity in his voice caused the man to slow down his pace. "Yo, you haven't known these dudes as long as I have, so you wouldn't understand."

"What's that got to do with us allowing these mutha-fuckas to disrupt our coin counting, unless of course you'll turn heartless on me or something?" The mere thought of that got the man more pissed. Suddenly, he slapped down on the table so hard that sparks shot from the cigar cornered tightly in his mouth.

He stretched his six-foot-five frame. "You ain't telling me I've got to start worrying if you can handle your end of things?"

The stalker blinked several times before he spoke. "Man, these dudes ain't nothing to play with. Either one of them would blow your brains out at the drop of a hat with the same expression as if they had spit in your face or shook your hand."

His grit was solid stone. "You telling me that I can't handle them niggas? Muthafucka, get a grip. This is my turf and ain't no nigga gonna do what the fuck he wants to on it. Fuck them, shit, fuck them straight up. You with me or what? Let me know right muthafucking now." Unknown to the stalker, an itchy finger tightened around the trigger of the nine-milli that was aimed straight at his stomach.

The stalker nodded two, three times and pushed the

black fedora back on his head. One thing was for certain, taking over the hustling lanes from this particular crew wasn't going to be easy.

As the insane eyes in the devilish face leaned out of the shadows, he began to wonder which side of the fence was safer. Even though he was nodding in agreement, in his heart he knew that neither side was.

✠ ✠ ✠

Beverly pondered over the information one of her prize detectives had just revealed to her. She was faced with an unusual dilemma, with being the top cop to protect and serve the people of her beloved hometown. As a friend and a woman reared in the ghetto, she owed an enduring loyalty to her closest childhood buddies. To help send either one or all three back to prison would be a stressful task she couldn't possibly enjoy; she didn't really think she could do it. As she absorbed the information in one ear and the humming of the police ticker in the other, she started daydreaming.

She smiled at the heartwarming memories of three snotty-nosed, nappy-headed ruffians mercilessly picking at her in the sandbox at the kindergarten on Candler Road in Decatur. They were the exact same trio that used to yank her plaits and snatch her dessert off her tray in elementary school, laughing the whole time at her protest. The same trio that used to raid her nana's grapevine and peach trees. Oooh, how hair-pulling mad she'd get at them for all of those childhood antics.

She became overflowed with warmth, when she recalled that same terrible trio that used to beat up any-body that even thought about bothering her. Any one of them would rush to mow the grass, rake the leaves or carry the grocery bags from the store. At least one was always there for her during the dramas of her teenage adolescence. She could still feel the ache in her jaws from smiling so hard when she was the only girl at her senior prom with three handsomely-clad tuxedoed escorts. And of course the overwhelming joy from when they paid for her college tuition every year at Georgia State University.

Her private reverie was abruptly snapped when the deputy chief entered her shade-drawn door unannounced. She made a mental note to discipline him the next time they were alone, but at the moment her mind was too occupied and she certainly wasn't going to discuss those affairs with him. There were too many others within earshot and she had a self-control policy not to try to embarrass her subordinates out in the open; especially those that had a lot of clout on Capitol Hill. And this certain deputy had plenty of that.

She started feeling like she was stuck between rocks when she saw that stern look on his face. Even though she was well familiar with their street names that were tossed around the precinct, she was just as aware that she was probably the only one there who knew about her connection to them. Talking about skeletons in the closet, whew.

She loved all three of them dearly, especially Sparkle, who happened to be the playground, elementary and high school sweetheart, as well as the high school sports star turned hoodlum, or vice versa. He was the curly-haired mutt who had gotten her cherry. She blushed whenever she thought of that wonderful night so long ago. The fast lane reps of her three amigos had grown right along with her rise in the law enforcement ranks.

She'd lost count of how many times she'd put her career on the line alerting the two Johnnies about raids on their drug and pimping turfs. How she had managed to keep their closeness a secret for all of these years was still a mystery to her.

That loyalty was in contrast to her belief in keeping the streets of Atlanta crime free; still it had remained strong her entire career. For years she'd maintained a private scrabble telephone that only those knuckleheads had access to with the main criteria being that there be no conversations about their criminal activities.

As she listened to the deputy chief and other detectives discussing strategies for dealing with the recent Jamaican drug invasion, she really felt the weight of maintaining that loyalty. As the horror stories of the drug wars continued to trickle in, she really didn't know if she could do it any longer.

CHAPTER EIGHT
Getting to Know the Crew

When Sparkle and the girls pulled around to the backside of the Holiday Inn, the side facing the expressway, there was a short stocky girl leaning on the ice machine with her arms folded, staring off into space.

Her expression hardened when they stepped out of the car. Sparkle stepped behind the girls studying shawtie as they approached. She was dressed in a faded blue jean outfit with a Braves baseball cap turned backward on a head of close-cropped hair. Even though she had a real baby face, her mannerism was straight-up dude.

She pushed off the machine and started walking with a bowlegged strut in the opposite direction, ending at the last room on the row. She didn't wait for them but she did leave the door open when she went into the room. They walked directly in behind her.

"Yo, J and P called over an hour ago about ya'll being on the way, so what the fuck took ya so long?" She spit in a husky voice that didn't come close to matching her barely five-foot frame. Matter of fact the way she was packed in that little body, it would be very easy to envision her as a midget.

She was leaning against the sink like she consumed the whole room. Feeling the twins' scary vibes hitting him from both sides, he gave them a short-gritted snort and stepped in first.

He lifted his head in greeting as he walked directly toward her. She certainly didn't appreciate anyone approaching her like they were disrespecting her gangster, so she hung her arms along her side like she was ready to go to war. Her defensive posture made him pause for a brief moment, but he shrugged it off and reached into his jacket to take out the package.

As she reached for it, he saw out of the corner of his eye a tall shape emerge out of the bathroom. His eyes got a lot bigger when he saw that the figure was that of a true Amazon. A six-three Diana Ross was the only way he could describe her with those big eyes smiling at him.

When she spoke, it came out just the opposite of Sissy's, squeaky and sweet, as she looked him up and down. "Mmm, how ya doing there, handsome?"

He was so stunned by the contrast of the two women that he barely noticed when Sissy slapped a wad of bills in his hand at the same time that she extracted the dope out of his grip.

While he examined the wad of wrinkled bills, Sissy turned to the basin and took two bundles out of the package.

Long'n'Lovely massaged his shoulder ever so gently. "So you're Sparkle, huh? I done heard some good things about you, sweetie."

Sparkle admired her long frame for a moment before breaking out in a smile as he replied, "Oh yeah, that's nice to hear. So what's your name, princess?" His eyes started to glitter at her vision.

She held a blush and glided her long curly nails under her chin and slowly rolled her eyes away from his lustful stare to look over Sissy's shoulder. She squinted at the rocks Sissy had spread on the basin and turned back to him purring, "Oh, I'm sorry; my name's Lisa, at your beck and call," with a beautiful smile and graceful curtsy.

He smiled warmly and leaned toward Sissy. "Damn, you sure don't talk too much, do you, little lady?" He leaned away when the vein in her neck expanded as she grunted something he couldn't quite understand. He read her grunted response as plain bad attitude, stepped back and pressed the money into his pocket with the rest.

With his business handled he felt no need to hang around, so he nodded at Slim and turned away to leave. The twins immediately rose from the bed and chair beside the radiator and nodded at Lisa as he opened the door to leave. Neither of them had uttered so much as one word the whole time, which he found really strange since that's all they'd been doing before they got there. Oh well, whatever relationship they had with the masculine shawtie was none of his business.

They'd barely stepped out of the room when three successive booms rattled the still night air. He felt both girls scrabble back into the room. Being used to violence, he calmly radared the walkway and saw two crouched figures sprinting to the corner of the building. The trailer got off two shots as an arm reached around the edge of the room pumping lead at the fleeing pair.

He wasn't surprised that the twins had darted at the first sound of gunfire for neither of them seemed to be the gangster type. He felt a small hand circle his leg, while a head brushed his knee. He smiled when he looked down to see one of the twins' heads peeking around the edge of the door with her eyes bucked wide open in fear.

It happened too fast for him to react like he normally would've. It wasn't that he was frozen in fear or anything like that. It was more like he couldn't believe what he was witnessing; especially in what appeared to be a quiet part of town, but you never know.

The echoing sound of the gunfire was still ringing in his ear as he took a deep breath and rubbed the side of his neck checking the scene. A woman's head briefly appeared at the door where the action had occurred and just as quickly disappeared. Then the door slammed. He scanned the rest of the area until he felt the stillness return. Only then did he look down at the twins and broke out in a smile at one of them still holding on to his leg. He reached down to lift her up by the armpits.

"Ya'll aight? Come on, let's get out of here before somebody calls five-o," he spat and headed for the car without waiting for a reply.

"Hey, sweetie, can I holla atcha for a sec?" He looked around to see the Amazon smiling at him from the doorway. He frowned and gently urged the twins past him and headed back to the room.

Lisa placed a piece of paper in his hand, gave him what he took to be her sexy smile. "Damn, hero, that didn't bother you in the least, did it?"

She was really impressed with his show of bravery. He heard the engine crank and looked around to see the car back out and head his way before he turned his attention back to her.

"Naw, slim, not really, but it was supposed to. I've been around a lot worse than that." The glitter in her eyes said it all: Long Tall was impressed by his don't-give-a-damn attitude.

She smiled sweetly and purred, "I guess not. Hey, call me when you get yourself a little air, aight?" Then she winked at him and quietly slipped back into the room, eyeing him seductively as she closed the door slowly.

He cocked his head to the side, smiled and casually turned to get into the car. He almost burst out laughing at the expression on both of the twins' faces. But he held it in. "Damn, ya'll, aight, a little scared, huh? Hmmm, that's interesting; now don't go to speeding out of here. There's no need to draw any attention to us under the circumstances."

Cherry nodded and slowly steered the car off the hotel's parking lot, drove slowly to Wesley Chapel and then to the interstate.

He waited until they were well on their way before he

said in a quiet tone, "Looka here, girls, I ain't had any sleep in well over a day. How about dropping me off at the crib? I'm about to drop out on my feet here. Ya'll can snooze out too if you want to."

"Sounds like a plan to me," Cherry added, rubbing a hand across her mouth to stifle a yawn.

When they got close enough to Candler Road to see the club sign jutting above the tree line, they noticed several red, blue and white lights flashing from the direction of the Red Roof Inn.

The closer they got to the exit ramp, the more he was drawn to the scene. He shivered with the thought of being so close to being caught up in whatever was happening there. There were SWAT team trucks and vans positioned on each end of the building. He stared in semi shock at the ominous, black-clad policemen pushing people into the hotel's pool. His mind immediately traced back to the confrontation with Chew Tobacco on the tier in Valdosta only a couple of days ago and the warning the hillbilly cracker had threatened him with. He shook away those visions and refocused on the activities that were happening down the slope.

Was it the combination of coke-laced paranoia and physical exhaustion that caused the eerie sensation of the dreamlike tunnel vision he was experiencing? His attention was drawn to a small figure striding amongst the army of police. As he watched mesmerized by the scene, it became clearly evident who was in charge down there. Why was he able to see and feel that way from so far away? As they drove further down the ramp, he twisted in the seat, lifting himself up off the seat and stretching his neck so he wouldn't miss a thing.

"Hey, playa, you act like you want to be down there or something?" Sherry asked from the backseat. When he didn't respond, she started waving her hand in front of his face. "Earth to Sparkle, Earth to Sparkle; come back, Sparkle, come back."

The distraction of her waving hand pushed him out of the daze he had sunk into. He stared at the hand for a few seconds before he shook his mind back to the here and now. "Damn, I'm sorry; that shit had me tripping." He sighed and sat back as Cherry pulled up at the red light.

When they passed the Pizza Hut on Candler Road, the phone started vibrating on his side. He reached down to lift the edge of his shirt and saw Dee's number flashing at him. His head swayed from side to side as he searched for somewhere that he could use a telephone when it dawned on him that he was looking at a phone. *Damn, this coke's got me all fucked up.*

Cherry started feeling jittery with the way that he was acting. "Why you looking around all crazy for?"

The smoke from his cigarette started irritating his eyes as he squinted across the seat at her. "Uh, I'm just looking for a phone so I can call this girl, Dee. She must need some more stuff or something."

She tilted her head away, wrinkled her nose and said, "So why you acting so panicky, man? We about to turn into Candler East right now. And then again, what's wrong with the phone you looking down at? Yeah, man, you need some rest for sure; you tripping for a bitch, for real. Hell, call her or we can just go straight over to her spot."

Sherry placed her hand on his shoulder. "Yeah, dude, it ain't like we on the other side of town or something."

He looked down at the hand and hunched his shoulders. "I must really be tired, whew!" He slumped down in the seat, realizing that he was indeed physically spent.

Sherry shook her head. "That's aight, playa; we know you tired. Whatcha wanna do; call her or just drop by there?"

He knuckled the corners of his eyes, took a deep breath and twisted the cringles out of his neck. "Fuck it; money calls. Let's drop on over there and see what she wants." He sat back and wiggled his shoulders into the seat to shake off the weariness.

"That'll work," Cherry spat and turned into the circular drive toward Dee's.

Sparkle sprung out of the car before it rolled to a complete stop and was on his way into the apartment. She opened the door on the second knock and chattered wildly. "Hmmm, that was quick; you must've been close by." Beaming, she stepped to the side to let him in.

Being as tired as he was, he got straight to business. "All that's gone already?"

She placed her hands on her wide hips and grunted, "Well, excuse me for your attitude, Mr. Man." She stepped back and ran her eyes up and down his obviously tired body.

His exhausted expression let her know immediately that now wasn't the time, so she eased up on the sarcasm. "I ain't got but three dimes left and one of my big spenders called to let me know that he was on his way with a mint." He sensed her eagerness to get on for whoever this guy was from that unmistakable junkie spark in her eyes.

Sparkle rubbed his index finger across his nose and mumbled, "What ya call a mint, redbone?"

She lowered her roaming eyes from side to side, uncertain of how he accepted this part of her game. Refusing to stand there feeling stupid, she said with just enough enthusiasm, "At least five big ones for a start."

"For real," he said meekly.

She probed around his lazy excitement before replying in a squeaky voice, "For real."

"Damn," he sighed, lowering his eyes.

"Whatcha mean by damn?" she said, as doubt crept into her thoughts. *Now that really would be fucked up, shit, and I've wasted all this time trying to play it real with this muthafucka...mmmph, I should have called dude down the street anyway just in case some shit like this happened,* she thought and started tapping her foot impatiently.

Reacting to her vibes, he immediately reached for the dope. His tired mind perked up as well. *Damn, this*

*conniving-ass bitch was calculating moves that damn quick.
Shit, JJ, hit this dirty-ass whore dead on the head. I got to
stretch the handle on her ass from here on out.* He gathered
himself. "Hold ya horses for a second there, shortie. I
gotcha; I'm just tired for a bitch, girl. My mind was
stuck on something else; that's all."

"Oh, my bad then." She smiled down at the dope in
his hand. She sighed heavily with the relief of his coming
through for her. She really wanted to be able to depend
on him; especially with her plans for their future.

A shiny black BMW pulled into the parking lot with
the speakers booming about T-Pain and Lil Wayne
tossing money around the club.

Cherry's arms were wrapped around the steering
wheel, with her chin resting on her hands. She was
earballing their conversation when she heard the car
pull up. Squinting, she did a double-take and twisted
sideways. "Sherry, ain't that that fat nigga Buster's ride
over there?"

Her tone excited Sherry, who had been busy filing
her nails with an emery board. With wide-eyed exuberance, she did a double-take. "I think, oh hell yeah; that's
his fat ass. Come on, girl; it's about to be a party up in
this bitch."

Cherry touched the door handle eagerly but paused
to say, "Nggg, damn. Girl, what about that nigga there?"
She nodded toward Sparkle heading for the car.

Sherry turned her mouth down frowning. "Shiiiit, what

about him? Didn't he just say his ass was tired? Well, let him gon' get some sleep. He ain't about to give a bitch a damn thing no way," she said as she was getting out of the car.

Cherry stepped out and headed toward Sparkle while Sherry went to start their game with big boy. She had to stall him long enough to at least try to talk him out of whatever dope he had left. It didn't take long as he was ready to give it up anyway.

A few minutes later, Sparkle was dead to the world, snoring on one of the kids' beds. One of his last thoughts before going to snooze land was wondering how word of the raid had gotten to Dark and Lovely at the Motel 6 so fast. As he fluttered his eyes in those last seconds of awareness, trying to stifle a final yawn, it dawned on him that he didn't even know her name. Oh, what the hell, he was sure to find it out later. Fuck it for now.

CHAPTER NINE
The City Terrorists Make A Strike

Lt. Woo strode up and down the walkway like a miniature storm trooper, gritting harshly at what she considered real vermin, ogling her menace from the chilly water of the pool. She lived for these moments of watching the frightened faces of the men and women, who by now were shivering because of the freezing water and thoughts of going to jail. It gave her an adrenaline rush like nothing else she had experienced.

As she continued to pace before the crowd of scared dope pushers and users, a small smile creased the corners of her mouth. She felt like masturbating off the power rush she was feeling. She wondered if the fools in the pool; hell, even the fools who were standing around waiting for her instructions with their guns drawn and batons swinging had no idea of her future plans of getting that nut. That nut; was there anything better? If there was, she surely couldn't think of what it could be.

Looking up at the doors on the other tiers of the hotel, she wondered if there were any more fools who would make the mistake of venturing outside. Suddenly, feeling like she was in the crosshairs of a riflescope, she instinctively spun around and zoomed in on the traffic up the wooded slope toward I-20.

"Lieutenant, whatcha wanna do with these mutha-fuckas?" Her trancelike glare at the cars lined along the thoroughfare was broken by the muffled voice of her second-in-command speaking to her through his helmet visor, as he nodded toward the people in the pool.

Her slanted eyes blinked a couple of times as she frowned at him before running her gaze back over the fools amassed in the pool. It was time to scare them even more than they already were. So she nodded for the two nearest officers to follow her, as she started stalking closer along the edge of the pool.

She waited in the middle of the throng of people, so everybody could get a good look at her. She wanted this display of power to have the full visual effect of pure fear. Menacingly eyeing her trembling prey, she bent down and waved her hands through the chilly water. While still in her crouched position, she gave a nod to the two troopers. Without a moment's hesitation, they reached down and yanked a pair of hard-looking teen-agers by the plastic cuff ties behind their backs and pulled them out of the pool.

The pain on their youthful faces clearly showed how much force the officers were using. Their bodies ended up in awkward angles as they were slammed on the hard pavement. With their feet splashing desperately in the water, their mouths shot open wide in silent screams of displeasure as they arched their necks and shoulders from the impact. No sound emitted from their mouths for utter fear had taken over. All they could do was stare up into the angry faces of the cops.

The shock was certainly not over when Woo grasped both of their chins in an iron claw grip, with her teeth gnashed and growled, "You muthafuckas think this is a joke, huh?" Her eyes flared like burning coals, searing right through their brains, as she stared down at them like she wished they were dead. Her arousal soared much more when she felt the dampness moistening her panties.

The pair was so frozen in fear that it took a moment for it to register that she was talking to them. The vise-like grip that she had on their chins was so tight that they couldn't even nod their heads. The look in their eyes showed pure fear and desperation.

That pure fear turned into something else they'd never felt before, as the anger in her eyes glazed over into lust. She had dug her nails so deep into their skin that blood started to ooze around her razor-like fingernails. Her face spewed total hatred as she leaned in closer. "Let me tell ya'll niggas this here: If I ever see either one of ya'll hanging around any dope area anywhere, I'm gonna kick ya'll faces and lock ya'll asses up for so muthafucking long, that your own families won't even recognize you no more."

Then, with panther-like speed, she jumped up and

pulled the bigger of the two to his feet by his braids. A truly amazing feat by a woman so small in stature. She raised her voice for everybody within shouting distance to hear. "Ya'll muthafuckas get one chance and one chance only to get whatever illegal bullshit off your asses." She paused to scan the whole pool area, staring at each one of them with intense fire shooting from her eyes. "Me and my men are going to turn around and I'm going to count to ten, naw fuck dat, five. I'm gonna count to five and then whoever has the nerve to try to hold on to anything they ain't got no business having, are getting dumped headfirst into that paddy wagon over yonder."

Without any further warning, she raised her foot and kicked the teenager back into the pool, leaving him to right himself as he splashed aimlessly in the water. Not a soul bothered to help him. Even if they wanted to, their hands were locked behind them just as his were.

And then she looked down at his partner. "Get your ass in the water. Now." She had a sadistic smile on her face, as she watched the struggling youth. He slipped under several times before he was able to do so. The other one flinched at her psychotic mask as she stared down at his boy and, with perspirating fear all over his face, he scrambled back into the water.

She frowned murderously at the others, raised her hand and rotated one finger. All the drug squad members immediately did an about face, the soles of their combat boots thundering loudly on the pavement in the crisp morning air.

Lt. Woo started counting. "One, two, three, four." She took a deep breath before continuing louder, "Five." The squad turned around, barking orders, and started prodding people like cattle toward the waiting paddy wagon. One by one they pulled drenched people out of the pool and patted them down. After the smart ones were released out of their cuff ties, Lt. Woo shouted into their horrified faces at point-blank range, "Run, muthafucka, run!"

A total of six out of a possible thirty something were foolish enough to try to sneak some through the shake-down. Those unfortunate few were indeed slammed headfirst into the paddy wagon and secured with ankle ties as well.

Shortly afterward, a group of officers used long-handled fishing nets to scoop the assorted drugs and other what-nots out of the pool and shoved them into large bags to be burned later on.

She smiled down at the wetness in her panties as she started walking back to her squad car and pressed a call to Chief Johnson's office. Before ducking in she took a quick glance around to see if anyone was paying her any attention. Satisfied that everyone was too busy wrapping up the commando scene, a prettier smile creased the corners of her mouth as she settled down into the seat.

She double-checked the rearview mirrors to make sure,

slowly closed her eyes and gingerly slid her hand into her pants. She eased her legs apart just enough to get her sticky panty crotch away from her heated pussy and pulled the dainty lace to the side so that she could slide her trembling finger into her wetness. A whiff of fresh woman nut invaded her nostrils, sending a shiver down her spine. Letting out a soft moan, she clamped her small caramel thighs tightly around her hand. Right off the bat, another nut started to stir deep in her stomach. She opened her mouth. "Aaaaaaaaaaaaaah." Then she started waggling her legs back and forth. This one was so intense that she couldn't even close her mouth as she thrust one, two, three fingers violently into her now overflowing pussy.

"Oh shit, oh shiiiitt nnnggg, nnnggg," she moaned just before she heard the phone being picked up on the other end. Damn, she had forgotten all about calling the chief that quick. She clamped her mouth on her shoulder, biting hard into the coarse fiber of her fatigue uniform until the feeling subsided. She heard the chief's voice answer into the receiver and blew hard into the night sky.

Gathering herself quickly, she forced herself to hide the after-tone of her climax as she replied, "First mission accomplished, Chief." She listened intently to the response. "Yes, ma'am, that makes good sense to me. Word has probably spread like wildfire by now, so we'll just let the other dealers sweat it out for a while before we strike again. Uh-huh, I agree totally; it'll be best to hit two or maybe even three at the same time as well. Yes, ma'am. Thank you, ma'am."

She clicked the phone off, lay back on the headrest and expelled the tension out of her body with a heavy sigh. Wiping the beads of sweat off her brow, she rolled down the window and stuck her head out of the car in search of her second-in-command. The only person she saw of any importance was the head guy of the Black Cats, which she really didn't like or trust as far as she could spit. Hunching her shoulders, she mumbled, "Fuck it," to herself and pulled out. She failed to notice the cracked curtain in the room on the second floor.

Clara eased the curtain closed. "Well, I'll be damned. That little psycho bitch got a fucking nut off of fucking with folk. Now that is some weird shit there." She stayed at the window a little while longer, checking out the rest of those fucking pigs as they wrapped up their invasion—paying special attention to a couple of them hidden in the bushes on the perimeter. She counted the money she'd be missing for at least the rest of that night. Fuck it; business would be back to normal this time tomorrow. Now she had to think of something to do to keep her mind off of fucking up the rest of the package.

She silently cursed those crooked bastards, spun from the window and headed to the adjacent room. Gently closing the door, she went directly to the chair beside the radiator. Flipping it over, she carefully unscrewed the foot knobs on each leg and stuck the hook of a clothes hanger in to retrieve her packages. She screwed the knobs back on, sat the chair upright and stuffed all but one of the bags into her panties before returning to the other room.

She smiled at the few big-money spenders she had called when she had first heard about the raid an hour ago. "Aight, ya'll niggas get that green out. Dem mutha-fuckas gone. But ya'll can't be leaving this room for at least another hour or so; a couple of them bastards done posted up out there in the bushes. But that shouldn't last but a little while, maybe an hour or so." The expression on her face was strictly business.

Even though the heat was on, she still had several reasons to smile but none compared to the feeling she got from knowing that some real boss niggas had her back when it came to staying a step ahead of those dope-busting bastards. Her thoughts eventually went back to that crazed-ass, horny bitch. All she could think was "whew" as she felt the hairs on her neck stiffen at the thought of being caught short by that psycho ho. Cop or not, that bitch was crazy for sure.

CHAPTER TEN
Getting Legit, Yeah Right

The sounds and smells of breakfast aroused Sparkle out of an exhausted sleep. He stretched his arms and legs, yawning and aahing at the snap, crackle and pop of his aching joints. *Damn, baby sis is sho nuff doing the do to that there. Come on, soldier, getcha lazy ass outta this rack.* He groaned to a sitting position and stretched beyond one final yawn.

He blinked a couple of times and smacked his mouth. "Damn, ugh, shit be rough," he yucked to the foul coating on his tongue. It dawned on him that he was in one of the kids' beds and he sprung up, stammering to the bathroom to get the morning crust off. On the way, he noticed a set of pants and a shirt draped across a mini-recliner. "Mmm, Boo Bear must have jacked JJ up for some of his rags," he mouthed as he sneered down at the wrinkled clothes he still had on.

Minutes later, after handling his hygiene, he put on the clothes and prowled after the delicious aromas teasing his nose and causing his stomach to growl. He had bent the corner into the dining room and said in a grumpy early morning tone, "Thanks, Boo," before pausing when he saw JJ's smiling face finishing up the remnants of a scrumptious breakfast.

"Taint nuthin, dog. Debra's gone to the beauty shop and the kids are off to school. I figured you'd think that it was her in here, but you can straighten up your face, looking like you done forgot how I used to hook your ass up back when I used to do the master chef thang down there in that Columbus joint."

"Huh!" Sparkle retorted lazily.

"Freeze frame, nigga, and just enjoy my Chef-Bo-Ardee," he added as he nodded toward the plates on the counter filled with steaming cheesy eggs, beef links, buttered toast and grits. "Go ahead. Take those there to the dining table. I'll bring the OJ and coffee."

They ate in silence for a while until JJ nodded toward the stereo system. "There's a MARTA card and a 23 Candler Road bus schedule over there. Figured you'd be heading downtown to finally get your legal on, with the way Debra got in your shit. You know, just in case you're smart enough not to go jumping in no fly ride with all that cheddar you done clocked," he said between bites of the steamy hot meal.

"Thanks, dog, a nigga's got to go ahead and handle that there as soon as possible; that's for sure," Sparkle downed the last of the orange juice, realizing that he certainly had a point.

JJ sipped on the coffee and tapped a short rhythm on his forehead with his fingers. "Oh yeah, before I forget, they done moved the social security building to that building right behind the Subway at the bus stop; you know, the one that used to be the VA." He didn't wait for him to reply as he cleared his throat. "You already know where the human resources office is at, uh-huh, and knowing your half-slick ass, you gonna play for some get-out-of-jail emergency money and food stamps just to make yo sisters think you're going on the straight and narrow."

Sparkle smiled at him. "Yeah, dog, you hit it on the head with that one there, and thanks for thinking ahead for me. That's a real good look. I'm still in a daze from all the things that have gone down in the past couple of days."

JJ nodded in agreement. "Yeah, dog, I know, taint nothing, though; you'd do the same for me, and I've definitely got your back. Oh yeah, and check this here out. When you are finished handling that biz there, that is if you ain't bent out of shape by then, holla at a nigga from wherever you at because that poker game is gonna be jumping big time over at that nigga Al's crib again tonight. I'll most likely be over there trying to get back some of the ends that weasel bit out of me the other day."

Sparkle's eyes lit up. "For real, dog? Shitt, I could use some more of that fat nigga's digits again myself."

"Hell yeah, man, it had to be at least three heavy-hitting games from the sounds in the background when I talked to his ass earlier," JJ got in as he drained the last of his coffee.

"Shit, ya'll going back tonight, huh?" Sparkle said to keep the conversation going as he started gathering the dishes. It was close to the time for him to split.

"You bet your ass, I am. Like I said, holler at me when you finish up downtown and I'll get you over there."

"Okay, my nig, that'll work. Man, let me go get myself ready for all this legal I got to handle. Oh, yeah, thanks for the clothes, man," he said over his shoulder as he headed for the bedroom.

It took him only a few minutes to get himself together before he was out the door. A couple of steps down he heard JJ calling out to him that someone wanted to talk to him on the telephone. It was his sister, Janet Bea and she had hooked him up on a three-way call with his mama in Virginia.

He couldn't even measure the joy he felt when he heard her voice. "Hey there, boy, how ya doing?"

He certainly didn't mind the "boy" coming from his special lady. He was smiling so hard that his cheeks started to ache as he beamed. "I'm getting settled in; how ya been doing? Oh yeah, and Big Mama and Aunt Aurelia?"

As he waited for her to respond, he heard some voices in the background that were unmistakably his two brothers, Jimmy and Mike, wanting to holler at him. His mother said in a voice full of concern, "You gonna do the right thing this time, ain'tcha? I can't stand too many more of these gray hairs worrying about you, baby. You know that, don't you?"

He answered, hoping it would make her feel better, although he knew that she would be bugging about him anyway. "Yes, ma'am. Matter of fact, I was on the way downtown to the DMV, social security place and of course, the employment office."

He could have sworn that he heard an *mmm-hmm* coming from one of the lines. But he didn't let who he guessed it to be, Janet Bea, being sassy, get to him.

He knew that his mama had heard it too, but she chose to ignore it as well. "That's good, baby, that's good. Just keep your head on the right path this time and stay away from those guys that like to get you in trouble. You know that we all love you, you hear me."

"I know, Mama, I know. I'm gonna do it right this time. I promise."

"I sure do hope so, baby. I sure do hope."

He took a peek at the kitchen clock on the far wall. "Hey, Ma, I hate to run like this and stuff but I've got to run up the hill to catch the bus that should be about to pull up to the stop any minute now. Tell Jimmy and Mike I'll holler at 'em soon. Gotta go; gotta go." He had heard them squabbling about which one was gonna get on the phone next.

"Okay, baby, I'll tell them. Now you call your mother every now and then to let me know how you're doing; you hear me?"

"Yes, Mama, I'll do that. Love ya."

"Love you, too, baby."

"Yo, Bea, I'm gonna call ya from the Decatur station after I hit these offices so you can tell me how to get to your house. It'll probably be around four or five o'clock, I guess."

Janet grunted, "Okay, I'll be home from work around four or so. Call me then. I might be in the mood to pick you up. I said that I *may* be in the mood; I'm not sure but I might." Her tone was sassy as usual.

"You hear how your daughter talks to her beloved brother, Mama? A lot of sisterly love there, huh?" he said with a slight smile on his face.

"Uh-huh, I heard her. Stop being like that, girl. Go ahead, sweetie, and take care of your business. I'll be looking to hear from you soon, okay?"

"Okay, I'm out. I love ya." He hung up the phone and looked at the clock before he sprinted out the door.

It took a lot longer than he expected—the whole day—to get around to all the places. He had regretted not bringing a book or something to read through the long strung-out progress. He did manage to get a temporary social security card and sweet-talked a lady at the DOC office to help him trade his prison ID card for a Georgia ID. He even talked a stern-faced old biddy at the Office of Human Resources out of some emergency food stamps and a $175 check to get on his feet. He finished off his active day getting an appointment at a downtown office on Peachtree Street to talk to some organizations that helped ex-cons to get on-the-job training. All in all, it was a pretty good day.

By the time he had wrapped up everything, he was mentally and physically spent as dusk was settling in at the Decatur MARTA station.

Sparkle was sitting on a bench in front of the bus stop massaging his tired eyes, waiting for the 23 Candler Road, when he saw none other than Ms. Violet strolling across the street. He had to blink a couple of times to make sure it was her before he lowered his head and tried his best to stifle a laugh. Just as simple as you please, home girl was waddling across the street toward him in a maternity dress. If he hadn't known any better, the size of her belly and the strained look on her face would have anyone thinking that she was about ready to drop her load right then and there.

She was halfway across the street when she looked up and saw him. From the expression on her face, it was evident that she was just as surprised to see him. She immediately swerved her eyes all around, checking out the scene before a sly smile edged to the corner of her mouth. She waddled wide-legged straight to his bench, holding a huge shopping bag in one hand, while the other one held her bloated belly in place. She plopped down beside him as a loud exaggerated sigh escaped from her lips.

She squeezed her eyes together as she shifted around on the bench, trying to get comfortable. After finally getting settled, she wheezed in a whisper out of the side of her mouth, "Whatcha doing down here, looking all spent out?"

The veteran street player in him had him radaring the area to see if anyone was paying them any attention or was within earshot before he gently reached over to touch her belly. "How's the little guy or gal doing in there?" He had a "well, I'll-be-damned" look on his face.

She gave him a smile as she looked down and started rubbing her stomach while she let out a motherly sigh. "Ah man, the little bastard has been kicking the shit out of me all day long."

He arched his brow in amazement. "Where ya coming from, a doctor's appointment?"

She played right along and rolled her eyes slightly. "Naw, I've been doing a little shopping for this new addition to my life."

He couldn't help but to laugh. "Girlfriend, you're something brand-new. You know that, don'tcha?" He was really starting to get attached to her vitality.

She was feeling something special happening between them as well as she lowered her gaze. "Not really, I've been doing it for a while now." She began looking around to see if anyone was paying them any attention before she lowered her eyes again and gently pulled back a large pleat in the dress.

He looked into the crack she had revealed and saw a large ball of plastic strapped to her body that was fully loaded with clothes bunched tightly together. He recognized it immediately as a masterful piece of boosting equipment. Looking back up into her now smiling eyes, he said, "Yeah well, I see that you've been quite busy there." He took another peek at the bundle and added, "Oh hell yeah, you've been on your job, for sho."

She let out a short snicker, cocked her head to the side and practically whispered, "Uh-huh, a bitch has got to keep the green flowing; know what I'm saying?"

He looked away down the street and stifled a yawn. "Damn, it's been one long-ass day."

She nodded in agreement, showing signs of being bone-tired herself. She bent over and rested her elbows on her knees she had spread far apart because of the contraption strapped to her stomach. "Sho nough has, hasn't it?"

"Shiiiit, long for you also from the look of things."

That brought a cute smile to her face and she flicked a wrist at him daintily. "Aw hell, honey, it's exciting and fun but sometimes it gets to be a real job, stealing folk stuff. Everything gets boring after awhile." She smiled, scanning the area as she lifted some pleats on the side of her dress to reveal the large plastic bubble contraption full of stolen wares.

Sparkle leaned forward and rested his elbow on his knees along with her. "Yeah, I guess it does after awhile." Out of his side view, he could see the Candler Road bus approaching and despite being overly impressed, he braced his hands on the bench and started to push himself up.

Before he could get up, she reached over to caress his

hand lightly and whispered, "You wouldn't happen to have a little something-something on ya, wouldcha?" Her eyebrows were hopefully arched.

He gazed down at her hand and slowly raised his eyes to meet hers. He felt them staring straight into his soul, as a tingling warmth spread throughout his whole body. Damn, he hadn't felt anything like that in many years.

After a moment, he broke her hypnotizing stare by reaching into his pocket to fumble the few rocks left over from him dipping into bathroom stalls throughout the day. He removed a couple of twenty pieces and pressed them into her small hand, grasping them firmly as he did so. He sighed heavily. "You know something, shawtie. I can't quite put my hand on it, but I got this odd feeling that we're sorta like one and the same. Like I've known you for a lot longer than I actually have; shit feels strange."

She narrowed her own eyes before she looked away shyly. "I got that very same feeling about you. Felt it the other night, too." She paused for a second as her smile rose from her cheeks to her eyes, meaning those feelings she had expressed were genuine. He also felt it as he heard her add, "You reckon there's something to this here?"

"Uh-huh, there's definitely something to it for sure," he replied as he stood up. The bus was loading its last passengers. He winked at her. "I'll make it my business to catch up with you in a few, shawtie."

"Hey, what about..." she started to say as she nodded toward the rocks palmed into her little fist.

He waved her off, got on the bus and headed for the back. After settling in the seat, he looked out the window but she had magically disappeared. His face flushed with confusion as he looked up and down the street, trying to spot her. As the bus was about to pass the corner of the social security building, he saw her easing her plastic bubble belly into the driver's seat of a green Thunderbird.

After Ms. Violet had settled into the seat, she looked up as the bus was passing by. Spotting him in the rear window, she rolled the window down, stuck her head out and waved. She even surprised herself when she broke out into a wide smile when he waved back. The smiles stayed on their faces as the bus rolled out of sight down the sloped street. She started rubbing her fake stomach, wondering if she was rushing things. She quickly decided that she didn't really care if she was; she wanted that nigga and she was going to get him.

After surviving a bumpy ride over the railroad tracks, Sparkle sat back contemplating how he was going to lock old gal in. He leaned forward in the seat, resting his elbows on his knees, having drawn his conclusion. From that look in her eyes, he already had her. It was now only a matter of when and where. And the closer to the future, the better, as far as he was concerned.

A few minutes later, when he disembarked in front of

the apartments, his attention was drawn to some loud honking from across the street. He immediately recognized Debra's bracelet-laced arm waving out of the window as she pulled into the BP service station.

"You ready for some poker, bro?" JJ leaned across the seat, shouting over some Busta Rhymes flow booming from the speakers. He waved him to the car. "Man, you got here just in time. Get your ass in the car; it's already popping over there." His head was bopping steadily to the funky beat.

Sparkle jumped in the backseat and they headed toward I-20. As soon as they made the turn onto the expressway, his thoughts immediately turned to the Red Roof Inn sign. He tapped JJ on the shoulder. "Yo dog, last night when I was heading back to the crib, there was a whole rack of police down there making folk jump into the pool and shit. Man, who in the fuck are the Black Cat and Red Dogs?"

JJ arched his brow, eyeing him in the rearview mirror, before replying seriously, "My nigga, since we got locked up, they done come up with some nasty drug squads. Aw man, those bastards are straight-up terrorizing shit; bad news, dog, real bad news."

Sparkle stared at the bust scene until it faded out of view before he responded, "You know what, dude? I couldn't help noticing a little bitty muthafucka stomping around like she was running some marshal law-type shit. Who the hell was that? I got some really fucked-up vibes watching that shit, man." He sat back and lit a Kool cigarette.

Debra shook her head, answering, "Bro, if I was you I'd stay as far away from that drug thang as I could." She paused and rolled her eyes at JJ, who made sure that he was concentrating on the road ahead. She pushed on, "Hell, even I know about that little monster bitch."

"Monster what? Monster who?" Sparkle asked, swerving back and forth between them.

She spun around in the seat. "That crazy-ass ho, Lieutenant-kicka-nigga-in-the-face Woo. Bro, that ho's got the baddest of the bad shutting shop at the thought of her fucking name. Whew, she rough, yo."

"Damn, she really some kinda bitch, huh? Fuck, she hard like that?"

"Hell yeah, she hard like that, and more," they said in unison.

Sparkle sat back; he had heard enough. It was time to concentrate on what moves he was going to use this time in the poker game.

As they pulled into Al's circular driveway, Debra said, "Hey, I forgot to tell you that your girl, Yolanda, was out here the other night. She's probably in there tonight."

"Johnny B's Yolanda?" Sparkle asked.

JJ jumped in. "Damn, those two been doing it since the kindergarten, aight they? At least that's what I done heard."

Debra spoke over her shoulder as she pressed the doorbell to the garage. "Shit, how a bitch put up with a nigga like that all these years amazes me."

Sparkle and JJ looked at each other and hunched their shoulders mouthing, *women*, before Sparkle said, "Damn, I betcha they are still killing each other."

"Every day, every motherfucking day." Debra giggled as she pressed the bell again.

Out of his peripheral vision, Sparkle noticed the curtain flutter at one of the windows. He didn't say anything, figuring it was one of Al's forms of house security. Instead he smiled. "Uh-huh, they've been doing that from way back. Shit, way back to those days when we used to play doctor under the tent blanket trying to get the stinky finger."

Debra laughed. "Ooh, ya'll was nasty back in dem days, for sho. Doing the su-la su-la, humping like ya'll was really fucking something. Uh-huh, with baby finger dicks and baldheaded pussies. I used to wonder if that old stuff was for real."

"Hell yeah, it's true. Moses and 'em was probably getting the stinky fingers and those folk up in the manger. Then again, don't be sitting up there like you didn't do it."

"Oooh ya'll, so damn nasty." Debra frowned.

"We nasty? Ya'll the nasty ones," JJ added, snickering. Debra wrinkled her nose and continued to press the button. Suddenly the porch light started blinking, causing all of them to jump before the door cracked open. A blonde, red-boned honey stuck her head out the door and looked over their heads at the surrounding neighborhood like she was expecting one of the neighbors to be playing I Spy. Seeing no one she opened the door only enough for one person at a time to pass through as she said in a husky voice, "Ya'll coming in or what? I can't stand here all night; damn."

"Aw, geeked-up-ass bitch, shut the fuck up and step yo ass back," Debra hissed as she brushed by her, followed by Sparkle and then JJ.

In the dimly lit garage, Sparkle could see that she was wearing a red silk dress, split up to the thigh, revealing a nice creamy thigh. His eyes were roaming slowly up her voluptuous figure when he felt Debra's elbow dig into his ribs. "Hey, girlfriend, this here's my brother, Sparkle; Sparkle, this is…" She paused and slapped him lightly upside the head, knowing what his freaky ass was thinking. "Nigga, can you please keep your eyes anywhere near your head? Whew. Sparkle, this here's Honey. She works at the shop with me." Debra didn't wait for either of them to respond and headed for the door to the game room.

He dove right into his mack attack. "Hi there, Honey, mmmh that name there sho do—" He didn't get to finish his initial move when JJ shoved him along.

"Hey, partner, later for that shit there. Let's get our asses to this cheddar."

There was a seductive smile on Honey's sweet face as she waved a dainty hand to let him know that there was indeed an opening if he played his cards right. With the way she was handling herself, it was obvious that she was thoroughly in the game. He chalked her up for further investigation, right along with all the others, whenever the time allowed.

He let the moment pass when he was mashed between Debra and JJ before they headed up the short set of stairs that led to the main house. Sparkle met her smile as he followed them until Debra shoved him across the sill and closed the door.

CHAPTER ELEVEN
Rainbow Works The Younguns

Rainbow and a group of rock-slanging thugs were sitting around the glass table in the dining room of his crib across from Turner Field. They were in the middle of a Georgia Skin gambling game. He started rubbing his chin with his elbow resting on the table as he studied each youngun individually. He was full of confidence, knowing they didn't have a snowball's chance in hell of winning.

Behind his ever-present aviator sunshades, his eyes glittered as he thought, *Now that's a damn shame. These so-called slick-to-the-bone-ass niggas don't have the slightest hint that I'm cheating their stupid asses to death. The fools are probably thinking that I'm laughing at all that fake-ass gangster lingo they keep tossing around.*

He forced a fake frown as he waited for the next hand to be dealt. It was a mask he constantly displayed while dealing with these young fools. He couldn't afford to let either of them ever think there was anything soft about him. For dealing with these clowns was sort of a must with keeping his ear to the pulse of the hood.

Little Bird, decked out real fly in a candy-apple red

short set, was the smallest of the crew. He tried to maintain a hard-as-nails manner to enforce the image that nobody had better take his mini size as a sign of weakness. He had already lost a considerable sum of his hard-earned pusher money, so he wasn't in the mood for any bullshit. "Nigga, will ya please stop finger-fucking the cards and let a nigga scoop a winner out of that raggedy-ass deal you just shuffled up. I need to get my baby boy some new Air Force Ones with ya'll niggas' hard-hustled money," he hollered at Billy, who kept right on rifling the deck.

Billy, a real runt of a dude himself, was slightly bigger than Little Bird at five-feet-seven inches. He was dressed in a black denim short set, with a Yankees baseball cap cocked acey-deucey on his head. He was as crazy as the rest of the young fools who thought that slinging rocks gave them the swagger to be gangster. He set the deck down, snorted as he sat back in his chair and rubbed his baby fu-Manchu mustache. His complexion was as dark as midnight, leading his crew to jokingly call him "Inky." Outside of the guys there, very few were allowed to tither along his extremely short fuse.

But the other players around the table were just as mean, or so they thought. They couldn't care less if his little short ass getting riled up. Nor were they the least concerned about him being short of his re-up money. The less he had to work with, the more their pockets had the chance of staying fat.

Rainbow leaned back in his large African bamboo chair, observing the slick back-and-forth banter of the young drug dealers. They had no idea that every deck on the table—hell, in the house—was rigged in several ways to skim them for their digits. Seldom did he have any sympathy for whatever situation they were in; especially with the way the old-timers had made him pay his dues way back in the day. Now it was his turn to take advantage of those that didn't know the game. *It's called paying your dues, nigga; plain and simple,* he thought as he prepared to study the deck for the best pick.

Sitting to Rainbow's left was Chopper, a young, light-skinned stud with a bad case of acne, whose shiny bald head, mouth full of gold teeth and thick gold rope chain draping his neck were all competing for the most glitter. His idea of style went way back to the days when gangsters sported suspenders the same color of their pants and whatever style hat they were wearing at the time. Today it was a beige derby that coordinated well with his navy blue silk shirt and gator wing tips. Rainbow had to admit that the nigga stayed fly, he had to give him that much. He was a little over six feet tall, with a well-toned muscular body that was built for the boxing ring. His feet were so big that you could surf with them. He was also one of the main shit talkers, but tonight his facial expression was one of total concentration. It meant that he was either short on his re-up money or one of his baby mamas was tripping on his ass. For whatever the reason, he was strung really tight.

Rainbow had a credo to take it light on whichever of his regular suckers appeared to have their back against the wall. He smiled to himself as he thought about his old card cheat teacher, Googie, who had always preached, *Keep 'em happy, keep 'em on the edge of being broke, but by all means keep 'em smiling.* Realizing from experience that Slim was in a strainful way, he shied away from betting him or at least tried to keep his losses to a minimum. Still he wasn't about to run away if he threw money his way.

He shifted his eyes over to the right to check out Stack-a-dime, the one he considered the most dangerous of the crew, who was shuffling his money and a sack of dime rocks from one hand to the other. The tallest of the group, he was dark complexioned as well, around six-feet four-inches with an arm span like a condor and dark penetrating eyes. He stayed clean-shaven with thick cornrows lacing his head. He wore a large plaid shirt buttoned all the way to the neck and gold-tinted aviator glasses resting on the top of his head. He was chewing gum and had the nasty irritating habit of making it pop very loudly several times a minute; especially when he was losing and right now he was losing big time, so his attitude was snotty as hell.

But not a soul around the table gave a flying fuck about how he felt as long as he kept tossing his dollars and rocks in the pot. Win or lose, he considered himself a hardcore stud and wasn't about to let the shit talking get by him, so he jumped right in there with Billy and Little Bird. "Yeah, little muthafucka, set the godayum deck down. Folk in here are serious about dey bucks, nigga. And about winning that little-ass sack of yours."

Billy, who many people mistakenly took for being gay because of his girlish looks and long curly hair, was really the deadliest of them all. He nibbled on his lips and wasted little time to reply, "Hey, fuck you, dick head. You be damn near scraping the cover off the cards as many times as you be walking the muthafuckas, so chill your big ass down, nigga." In mock anger, he slammed the deck onto the table so hard that his Omega watch snapped open and rode up on his hand, which aggravated him that much further.

Little Bird laughed so hard that spittle flew out of his white gold-filled mouth. "See there, little nigga. I knew all yo shit was cheap as hell. Uh-huh, damn, look at dat raggedy-ass watch about to jump off your arm like it don't wanna be there. Where ya get that shit from; one of them flea markets out there in College Park?"

There was a loud crackling sound as Billy rotated his neck a couple of times before he raised his arm and shook the watch back down his wrist, then snapped it shut with enthusiasm. "Okay, ya'll greedy-ass bad boys go ahead and get a card that'll help to keep my stack fat," he growled as he slid the deck to the center of the table.

"Aw hell naw, nigga. It's about time for ya'll scrubs to make a playa a real mint. Ya'll know how TLC be saying how dey don't want no scrubs. Well, I sho do," Little Bird shot back as he picked a card out of the deck first since he was the end man.

"Aw, little nigga, why didn't you cut the damn cards? You know damn well that you can't be trusting this little slimy-ass pretty boy with his half-slick ass," Stack-a-dime cried out as he scooped a card from the middle of the deck.

"Come on, crybaby-ass nigga, take a peek at that loser you just pulled out of the deck and chunk some of that money over this way. Your black ass always been a sweet lick for a player anyhow," Chopper spat angrily while he also scooped his card from the middle of the deck before sliding it over to Rainbow.

While they had been doing all that jaw-jacking, Rainbow had been studying the side of the deck for the tics he'd made days ago with the magic ink only he could see with the special glasses he had propped on his nose. He smiled inwardly as the red, green, blue and yellow dots gleaned clearly through the lenses. Immediately spotting the red ones at the bottom, he expertly scooped one of them and slid the deck over to Little Bird to make sure that it didn't bump with the ones the others had picked. At the same time he saw that Billy's and Stack-a-dime's cards were the furthest down the deck, so he started trash-talking to pump them up to toss bets his way. And with their young pumped egos, he knew that they would be chunking big dollars trying to make a quick hit.

Before the first card was turned over, he felt his Trac phone buzzing on his hip. Lifting his sweatshirt, he saw a familiar number blinking up at him. He got the attention of one of his girls, who was watching a video in the living room, to bring him a telephone. He had a thing about discussing his biz over the airwaves of cell phones. The other end picked up before the first ring was complete. He nodded as he listened for a while and then answered in a gravelly tone, "To tell you the truth, 'B,' I was really waiting for him to get in contact with me whenever he felt the need. Figured he wanted to get his feet wet in his own time; you feel me." He listened for a half minute or so. "Tell ya what; drop a little hint on him to see if you think he's ready and I'll get back with ya'll later and we can see where it goes from there, aight. Yeah, cool, partner. I'll holla."

He locked off and put his concentration back on the game and immediately went straight back to the trash-talking. It was time to bring the game to an end. He had gotten enough enjoyment out of toying with these kids. And talking with "B" reminded him that his main girl, Lady, was on her way back from scoring his package from his boy, Duke. He had to go and resupply his crew of girls scattered around the city. He wasn't about to lump these young niggas' dope with the bomb he usually sold, leaving it for his girls to do, instead of digging into the stuff to be sold.

Less than a half-hour later, the game was dwindling down to the end when he heard the voices of Lady and Princess coming through the door from the hallway.

Billy and Stack-a-dime were the only ones left at the table when the girls entered the room. Little Bird and Chopper, with their broke asses, were sitting on the edge of the couch watching some porn videos with a couple of his other girls. They had their hands in their pants, rubbing themselves. Like that shit was going to turn them hoes on. *Dream on, fellas. Them girls there are cold as freezer ice.*

Lady and Princess eyeballed them disgustedly before they broke out in smiles when they saw all the rocks overflowing out of the crystal ball mirror beside Rainbow on the table.

Lady, at forty-something, was still sporting a youthful girlish figure. Only the crow's feet in the corners of her eyes gave away her real age. And Princess, who had just gotten picked up by Lady at the Motel 6, strutted pure sex appeal as she stepped into the room dressed in a skintight cream-colored denim outfit with a red flowery blouse and red cowgirl boots. Her sexy attire was in stark contrast to her jet-black skin tone. With her brick-house shape she was definitely bootylicious.

The similarly dressed pair glided along like they were on a model runway. They batted their long eyelashes at all the younguns.

"I see ya'll young and dumb ballers done donated ya'll hard-earned goodies to my baby again," Lady said. "Ya'll just so good to us. Thanks." She swirled in a circle and curtsied with her arms spread out wide. "I really do appreciate ya'll generous contributions. I really do," she added in a Southern belle twang.

They all shouted at her in unison, "Fuck you, you old biddy!"

"Ugh, such nasty manners from ones so young. Begone," she said with a flip of the wrist as she pranced over to the table to give Rainbow a big hug. "Honey, toss me a couple of them there bags so I can see what these good boys are working with anyways." She pushed her ass out in an enticing angle to fuck with them.

Rainbow pushed the crystal ball to the edge of the table and she scooped out a hand full. "Ya'll boys stay good now." She smiled at them as she and Princess disappeared down the hallway, with their asses jiggling and their mouths giggling.

Rainbow pushed away from the table and stood up to stretch the cramps out of his neck, arms and legs before he addressed the boys. "Yo, fellas, it was really nice having ya'll over for some entertainment, but I'm gonna have to call it a night because me and the girls have got to get ready to make some runs."

Reluctantly, they all rose, mumbling amongst themselves and headed for the door. Stack-a-dime was the last to leave. He turned to face Rainbow as he was about to close the door and said angrily, "My man, I don't know exactly what you're doing but you're doing *something*."

Rainbow pinched his nose and rubbed his chin as he stared the youngun down. Seeing that tactic wasn't doing any good, he forced a smile. "Youngun, I'm betting my scheme; that's all."

The anger in Stack's voice was undeniable, as his eyes narrowed and his nose flared. "Scheme, my ass. Sooner or later, I'm gonna bust your ass and when I do…" He edged a little closer to him.

Rainbow stepped toward him and gritted. "And then what, muthafucka, and then what?" He inched his hand to the small of his back for the ever-present Glock braced in his waistband. Instant death stared at the youngun.

Stack instantly knew that he had overstepped his boundaries and recoiled as his eyes lowered to Rainbow's hand movement. Despite his tingling fear, his gangster wouldn't allow him to be outright punked, so he maintained his menacing stare. "Just keep your shit tight, partner; just keep it tight." He gently backed out of the door.

Rainbow knew that he was scared and was maintaining his killer swagger for the sake of his crew and his own self-esteem. "Whatever dog, whatever," he spat with fire in his eyes as his hand eased off the trigger.

"Uh-huh, yeah, whatever," Stack spat back and spun around to follow his buddies with his coattail swinging angrily in his wake.

Rainbow slammed the door behind the angry stud and thought, *Man, these muthafuckas must think that I've gotten soft or something.* He headed for the bedroom. With the same steam boiling in his brain, he rapped sharply on the door. There was a quick muffled reply. This fired him up just that much more and he kicked the door, shouting, "Girl, what the fuck you got this damn door locked for? Them younguns are gone. Bitch, open this muthafucking door." For a brief second he considered kicking the door in.

There was a shuffling of feet and more mumbling before the door was snatched open by Princess, her face creased in a frown.

"Splack," the sound of the slap upside her head echoed in the hallway, as Rainbow viciously slammed her against the door. She boomeranged from the force of the blow into him like a rag doll. Still very much pissed off, he grabbed her around the neck and hair and slung her into the bedroom dresser.

His longtime pimping instincts had his foot raised in the air to deliver more punishment as Lady screamed out at him, "No, Rainbow, no!" She rushed over to grab him by the waist. The pleading look on her face curbed his anger. He took a deep breath and gently lowered his leg. Still, he felt compelled to let Princess know that he wouldn't put up with any defiance whatsoever.

"I'm chill, baby. I'm chill," he said evenly. Lady looked up with tears running down her cheeks to see the calmness on his face and unwrapped herself from around his waist and placed a trembling hand on his shoulder.

He gave her a weak smile, gently brushed her hand off of his shoulder and bent down to carefully lift Princess's face. His smile was warm but his eyes were blazing fire. "Baby girl, don't ever approach me in that manner again." Her ogling fear let him know he was in full control. "You feel me, baby girl? I said, do you feel me?" She nodded shyly. Grimacing, he lifted her up by the armpits and walked her over to the bed. *Damn, why these hoes got to keep testing a nigga? Why?* He gently sat her down on the bed and left the room.

He walked calmly into the living room and took a seat on the couch, picked up the remote and clicked on the porn video. He unzipped his fly and motioned toward his newest addition to his constantly revolving stable of hoes. As she gently wrapped her juicy red lips around his massive dick, he casually succumbed to the sensation, thinking, *Damn, playa, you must be getting too old for this game; you can't even remember this bitch's name.* He wiggled his ass enough to unstick his nuts from his thighs, smiling at her bobbing head. *What the fuck difference does it make? A nigga can't be expected to know all these muthafuckas' names, as long as they prove to be money-making machines. Aaaaaah, do your thang, girlie; do your thang.*

✠ ✠ ✠

Beverly was consumed with pleasant thoughts of preparing a scrumptious meal for her beloved nana, as she watched the elevator lights blinking down to the garage floor. It had been a pretty okay workday, except for the disturbing report of the overzealous Lt. Woo on her drug excursion into DeKalb County. She felt sorta icky because it was one of the areas her boys operated; she really didn't want anything to do with it. True enough, Woo had curbed the drug traffic in a positive sense in Fulton County. Even though she was a bit uncomfortable with some of her tactics, she had to smile at the results. From the police's point of view, the little monster's tactics definitely worked.

Her thoughts shifted to Sparkle when the doors opened and she headed toward her car. As she cruised along the pavement in her pigeon-toed stride, she wondered when she would get the chance to see him. And as usual she felt her heart flutter with the excitement of possibly feeling herself melt in his embrace. *Why can't that fool see that I love his hard-headed ass? Whew! I pray to God that I can convince him to give up the street life this time,* she thought as she inserted the key into the ignition.

Plack, plack, plack. She jumped nervously from the sudden rapping on her windshield. Before she could adjust her senses, there was another. *Plack, plack, plack.* A second tingling ran down her spine as she swerved her head to locate what was causing the noise. Her anger surfaced immediately when she recognized the face of the deputy chief, looking like Norman Bates, smiling dumbly at her.

The nerve of this mutherfucker. She reached for the door handle and intentionally shoved the door hard into his midsection. "Man, what the fuck is wrong…" She caught herself before she could finish the statement and got out of the car. She stood there for a moment, pinching her eyebrows to regain some of her composure. She responded in a chilly tone and with clenched teeth, "What is it, Deputy Chief?"

R.J. Madison III set his briefcase on the pavement, then rotated his neck and shoulders backward. "Chief, please excuse me for scaring you like that. I didn't mean to upset you, but you did tell me to keep you abreast on the townhouse you were interested in." He leaned his elbow on the roof of the car. "I tried to catch you in your office but your secretary told me that you had already left. And when I saw the elevator door closing, I guess I got a little overanxious and ran down the stairs. I certainly didn't want you to leave before I let you know that one will be available in about three weeks. Most of them are going to be furnished, but I figured that you'd want one that you could do yourself. Am I right to assume that?" He blinked several times, looking very sincere.

Only then did she notice that his chest was still heaving from the exertion of running down the stairs to catch her. That made her start to feel sort of guilty for slamming the door on him so abruptly. She ran her hand from her forehead down to squeeze her neck before she shut her eyes tightly and took a deep breath. "Excuse me, R.J., for being so jumpy. I've been through a very stressful day. I'm sorry for blowing my fuse on you like that." She was too damn tired to smile.

He hunched his shoulder as if to say that's okay, that he understood, before he adjusted his tie. "Yes, ma'am; apology accepted. I surely can understand the stress... hell, I go through it myself, but anyway I wanted to inform you that you can at least start the paperwork whenever you want to. I realized how badly you want to move your grandmother out of the hood."

This pompous bastard. How dare his pampered white ass talk like my old neighborhood ain't fit for living? she thought. "Uh, thank you, Mr. Madison. I'll get my banker on it first thing in the morning. Uh, please don't let me forget, okay?" she said sweetly with a glittering smile that she was finally able to force, even though she didn't feel it. She closed her door, put the car into gear and pulled out of the parking facility.

As he watched her drive away, he reached into his suit pocket to get his cell phone and punched some numbers. When the phone wasn't picked up right away, he immediately repunched the numbers. He waited five more rings and was ready to snap, when he heard a soft female voice answer demurely, "Excuse me, but Al is rather busy right now. May I take a message?"

R.J. held his face away from the slightly familiar voice and contemplated delivering a threatening message before he thought better of it and clipped the connection. He mumbled to himself as he headed for his car on the far side of the garage, "That motherfucker knows godayum well he was supposed to let me know about that furniture delivery today. Who the hell does he think he's playing with? Black bastard's probably got his ugly-ass face stuffed up in some stanky whore's pussy. Damn, I should've known better than to trust a bastard like him," he mouthed angrily as he snatched open the door.

As he was pulling out of his parking space, he spotted that bitch Lt. Woo walking toward her small compact car with her head bent down as she dug into an oversized purse. He smiled at himself as he felt a sudden impulse urging him to drive right over her publicity-seeking ass. Instead, he honked his horn and waved at her. At least he got to enjoy the look of shock on her face from being caught in his high-beam headlights. He veered around her and out of the garage, pleased with himself for letting that little bitch know that she was vulnerable.

Lt. Woo squinted at his departing car, wondering what she'd done to him to encourage him to try to scare her like that. The little smirk he had on his face as he drove by certainly gave her that impression. Little did he know that she wasn't the least bit scared of his antics. After all, she was extremely confident in her ability to avoid danger. Little did he realize that he had really piqued her curiosity, which was really dangerous on his part. Now she had to investigate his ass as a promising enemy. It'd only prove to sharpen her wits when it came to dealing with him from now on. She smiled as she settled behind the steering wheel, knowing that she always came out on top of all of her enemies.

CHAPTER TWELVE
The Boosting Queen Gets Her Man

Sparkle had little time to admire the lavish surroundings of Al's game room when Debra led him to where the poker games were really getting it on. The aroma of the combination of cocaine and reefer assaulted his nostrils immediately as they entered the room; bringing back memories of the other night when he had banged Al's head real decent. The three poker tables were full of players chunking money and talking shit.

In the center of the room, sitting up tall in his bamboo chair shaped like a throne, was Big Al in a black fedora munching on a big cigar jutting out of the side of his mouth. Percy and one of the twins, along with three other people, were bunched around the table concentrating on the cards they had been dealt. It was evident who was doing all the winning because of his cheerful attitude, much different from the last time that Sparkle was over there kicking his ass.

An over-smiling Al greeted them with a cheesy grin. "Well, how ya'll doing? About time ya'll jive asses got back. My man, Sparkle, let's see how your luck runs tonight. I'm on a real roll here. As you can tell by the look on some of these folks' faces, they're probably wishing they asses had chosen something else to do instead of fucking with Poker King Al," he finished in a husky Barry White tone.

JJ saluted him. "Do your thing, big man; do your thang. I'll be there in a few to rattle your money chain; believe that there."

"Yeah right, like you hope to do every time you enter my lair," he groveled like Vincent Price in one of those old monster movies before his attention was drawn back to the action at the table.

"Godayum, a nigga's luck be running like donkey shit around this here bitch." The familiar voice of his nephew, Stacy, drew Sparkle's attention to the far end of the room, as he slammed his cards on the table.

Sparkle shook his head. *Damn, this boy ain't learned a thing I've taught him.*

Then he looked around the table and spotted his boy "B," which got him to thinking about Violet. He smiled as he watched him pick up the deck and start to shuffle the cards, talking plenty of trash. Moans and groans erupted around the table as one of the two girls at the table snatched up the deck from him and started reshuffling them.

Sparkle walked up to stand behind Johnny B. "Yo, black, I don't appreciate folk taking advantage of my nephew again."

"Who da fuck," he said before he looked over his shoulder and recognized his boy. He put on one of his most brilliant smiles. "Nigga, I was wondering when your ass was going to get back around here. Fuck this game; we need to talk."

"B" got up from the table, grabbed his shoulders, then held him at arm's length. "Man, why you didn't let me know that you was coming over this way?"

Sparkle hunched his shoulders. "Shit, dog, I didn't really know myself until Sis there caught me getting off the bus on Candler Road. So what's up?"

The commotion drew the attention of the people at the high stakes table. "Come on, JJ, Debra and you, too," Al said. "'B,' I see you raking coins over there. Your black ass is welcome over here, too."

"I'm on my way now, big timer!" Debra shouted as she reached over Sparkle's shoulder with her palms up, wiggling her fingers.

Sparkle looked down at her hand. "What…what's that for?" He arched his brows with curiosity.

Debra spun around. "Damn, Bro, you hit up really good over here the other day. Give a bitch a few coins to chunk at these greedy muthafuckas."

Sparkle's eyebrows shot up in mock surprise as he smiled down at her. His thoughts immediately shot back to the days when he had first revealed to Debra the art of cheating. Ain't no way her ass was still in training and thinking that he'd go for that okey-doke move. He knew that she had bank in her purse. Otherwise, she wouldn't have been so anxious to get over here in the first place. But she was Baby Sis, so he gave in, reached into his pocket and eased a couple of hundred into her palm.

There were things he wanted to kick around with Johnny B anyhow. She batted her eyes and gave him a smirk of a smile and turned to the table. "Hold up there, playa. Can a bitch get a cut of them cards there? I ain't like a ho; trust any of ya'll dogs, know what I'm saying."

"Girl, your ass need to be paying attention instead of running your mouth at folk who ain't even tossing bills in that bitch!" somebody shouted. She ignored whomever it was and picked the deck up to reshuffle herself.

Al removed the thick cigar out of his mouth and mumbled, "Nigga, you know damn well that you need to let folk cut the deck whenever they want to. Uh-huh, yo dirty ass probably trying to sneak one of your deals in, but that ain't about to happen. Is it, girls?" His tone was gentle but persuasive.

A chorus of "fuck you" erupted around the table. Sparkle smiled at the banter and began studying the players to see whatever cheat tactics they were using. However, he would never reveal anything if he saw one of them doing something. That was straight-up taboo as far as he was concerned. Besides, it would only wire them up that he had those abilities, too.

Shortly afterward, he felt "B"'s gnarled hand grasp his shoulder as he whispered in his ear, "Yo, partner, we got a lot of updating to do, so whatcha say we go get a couple of foosball games in. Shit, this game is nearly done anyways."

Sparkle told him that he wanted to get in only a few hands just for show, which he acknowledged with respect. After getting off a few rounds, in which he won three hands without having to use any of his cheat tactics, he pushed away from the table and joined his boy at the mini fridge in the corner where they got a few cans of Olde English before they headed to the game room.

"Well, what have you settled into, partner, and have you caught up with Rainbow yet?"

Sparkle shook his head. "No, I haven't had the chance to see him yet." He put the beer down on the coffee table, belched and added, "I'm aight as far as aight goes. What I do need though is the rundown on a bitch I met."

"B" rubbed the stubble on his chin with the back of his hand. "That's all. Shit, depends on what ho you talking about. Let's see, I've already told you about that bitch Dee."

Sparkle took a long swig of the beer, picked up the remote off the arm of the chair and flicked until he settled for a video on BET. "Yeah, you have and…"

"B" interrupted him as he leaned back, laughing. "Yep, man, I remember her little ass from back in the day when we was trapping and robbing in Buttermilk

Bottom. I know you can recall back when she used to try to get us to buy reefer and those bootleg tapes at the poolroom beside the 617 Club."

Sparkle joined in the laughter and leaned forward on his knees. "Uh-huh, her little tomboy-ass bitch thought cowgirl boots were the only way to go."

"Yep, but hell, that girl ain't nowhere near little no more. Mmmhh, whew, that thang done grew into a brick house from the old school." "B" smiled, visualizing that fat ass of hers.

"Oh hell yeah, she definitely ain't," Sparkle joked before he got serious. "Anyways, I done gave her some shit to work with for me."

"B" cocked his head to the side and started rubbing his neck. "All I can say about that one there, partner, is that as long as the folk are flowing through her crib, your shit will be alright but—"

Sparkle cut him off, "But don't give her no fresh package after two on Saturday night, especially early Sunday morning because most folk be spent out by then and only looking for a nigga to do them a favor. And her ass is gonna keep getting high as long as there is some dope around."

"B" laughed at that one. "Well, at least she done wired you up on that, so she trying to play straight with you. Can't ask for much more than that there, dog. On those times there, just deal with her on a money-now basis. She'll understand, even though she'll definitely try you; that's for sho."

Sparkle sat back up straight. "Let me get this straight; you mean to tell me that there ain't no money to make except for on Thursday, Friday and Saturday."

"B" scooped up the beer Sparkle had been drinking and finished it off. "No, dog, there is plenty of money to make on what I call the cell phone route. And it's a twenty-four-seven job because folks out there in the suburbs, the ones with the real money, will be calling you at all times of the week. So what I'm really saying is for you to handle your dealers with a long one because when the traffic stops in the inner city that don't mean that they stop getting high. And most of them ain't got that long green like those white folk in the burbs, that's what I'm saying."

Sparkle nodded in understanding. "Okay, dog, I get whatcha saying. Thanks, partner."

"B" turned his mouth down like he was in some kind of junkie nod, with his eyelashes lowered as he scanned the room. Satisfied that no one was paying them any attention, he reached inside his jacket pocket and removed a cherry blend cigar. He thumped it on the back of his fist a couple times before he put it to blaze. After a few hard jaw-sinking pulls, he handed it to Sparkle. "Yo dog, hit this bitch here. It's reefer laced with boy and girl—the way we used to do back in the day."

Sparkle took the same room scan and then got his head blitzed right along with him. *Ah man, it sure do feel good being back around my real folk again*, he thought as the euphoria of the three-way hit massaged his senses.

He smiled at "B" in a dream-like daze from the rush. "B"'s words were coming out in a low buzz and his movement was in slow motion.

"B" smiled at him. "Now that we feeling kinda good, are you planning on doing any of your old hustles, because I still got the check machine we took out of that drugstore all those years ago—that is if you want to hang some paper."

Sparkle forced his eyes open, shook off the nod that was trying to take over. "For real, dude?"

"B" leaned back cheesing. "Hell yeah, and I can let you work some of my girls on the creep and snatch. Shit, ain't no way any of these shops at all the malls around here can be hip to your face. Hell, and besides, I need to have them lazy-ass whores get off their asses and do something other than laying around waiting for a geeker to come around to score; know what I'm saying?"

Same old "B" gorilla clocking muthafucking dollars, Sparkle thought. "All that'll work in time, my nigga. Just let me get my feet wet for a while first. Then it's on, for sho." He pinched his nose and started massaging the side of his face with his fingertips. "But check this here out. Whatcha know about this old lady that I met over Dee's the other night named Violet? She sure do seem to be a real sharp babe; know what I'm saying?"

"B" stared at him for a few seconds and then shook his head. *Shit, partner here is about to snatch up a real hood star. Sure do hope that he's still got his game together though because old "V" is definitely one of a kind and a handful for any nigga.* "Man, you got to be talking about old queen thief lady Violet, who be dressing all fly and shit; hair cut like Halle Berry; looks like a black Chinese."

Sparkle's face broke out in a wide smile. *Damn, he hit her right on the head with that one there.* "Yeah, that'll be about how I'd describe her fly ass." He started squirming in his seat, anticipating the reaction.

"My nigga, you ain't gonna believe this but that's Yolanda's aunt," "B" said matter-of-factly.

"On the real, man?" Sparkle replied with a frown.

"Yeah, man, on the real. And peep this here: She's the hottie that turned Yolanda and a lot of other whores to the boosting game. Shit, on the up and up, that old playette done turned out a lot of the best boosters in Atlanta, including all those bitches that Rainbow and a lot of other pimps be getting paid from."

"Damn, she like that, dog?" Sparkle inquired with sparks flying from his eyes.

"Hell yeah, and this one here is really gonna hit ya good. Mama's old man was big Joe Hankerson, uh-huh, and he used to march right along with Martin Luther King, Jr.—hell, like one step behind Jesse Jackson, Andrew and Ralph."

Now that had Sparkle thinking that his boy was tripping for real as he said shockingly, "What the fuck that's got to do with anything?"

"B" shook his head like he couldn't believe that he

wasn't getting the message. "Man, beside from stealing her ass off, she gets something like forty-five hundred dollars every fucking month for her and her son, JoJo, from social security. Shit, Big Joe was in the money, player. The biggest problem is that she always fucks up her digits buying dimes until all that shit is gone. Hell, all she needs is a real player nigga like you to manage her finances. You feel me?"

Still not quite believing his good fortune, Sparkle felt compelled to throw out one more tester to be sure. "Hold up there, partner. Are you really telling me that this is the Queen 'V' that all the old-head pimps used to hire to school their hoes to the boost?"

"One and the same playa." "B" smiled slyly.

Sparkle leaned back in the seat, cheeks glowing brightly as his thoughts shot back to the little time he and old gal had spent together. It was a click there, for real. He nodded his head in appreciation of the news he had just heard. "Shit, dog, Mama gave me all kinda come-get-it-nigga signs. Hell, dog, I got to hurry up and lock old girl up because a nigga could use getting all shined up and shit with some fly gear. Oh hell yeah."

"B" folded his arms, seriously contemplating, before he crossed his legs. "Check this, homes. I'll give you a couple of days to handle whatcha got to handle. In the meantime I'll get Yolanda to set up a run with Violet to get your wardrobe flashy like you like it."

Sparkle's cheeks rose that much higher. "Oh yeah, I sho nuff needs some rags, for sho."

"Damn, before it slips my mind, I'm gonna get the girls to go groom up some shops so ya'll can pull some checkbooks. That is by the time you get back with me in a couple of days." "B" plucked himself upside the head before he added in a more serious tone, "Mmmh, must be getting old, dog. I've even got a honey who can get a signature check on just about anybody who runs a business in DeKalb, Fulton and even Henry County."

Sparkle's eyes gleamed as he shifted slightly in the seat to face him. "When you wanna get down on this?"

"B" wiped a hand across his mouth and chin. "Shit, right after Lady 'V' gets you all dressed up. Give me a call when you ready to roll like that."

"That's a sho nuff, partner. You know I'll let you know."

"B" jammed an elbow into his ribs. "Just make sure that you look out for my bunnies. That's all I ask."

The words had barely escaped his lips when Stacy stuck his head in the room and hollered, "Yo, Unc, Debra wants to tell you something."

Sparkle leaned forward rubbing his knees and looked at "B." "Yo, man, we gonna do that. Give me that cell number."

"B" stood up, snatched a pen and pad off the end table, scribbled the number down and handed it to him. "Here you go, dog. Check this. I'm about to roll; got things to do myself. Just hit me when you ready," He strolled out the door.

"That's a bet," Sparkle said to his departing backside and followed Stacy back into the gambling room. They could hear the verbal battles at full blast as soon as they opened the door. Debra's voice shot up another octave when she noticed them while she was shuffling the cards. That let Sparkle know that she was putting a mickey in the deck. So like a proud teacher watching a prize student, he stood behind her to watch her put in work. At the same time he was also checking out the other players around the table to see if they were on point with what she was doing. None of them was up on her moves, which was all good.

He stood there like a ghost concentrating on their giveaway reactions, like facial expressions, lip twitches, eyebrow raises, and hand and posture movements— any telltale signs that most players didn't even pay attention to.

He was standing there for about a half-hour when he felt JJ nudging him in the knee. He looked down to see him nodding toward Stacy lying back on one of the bean chairs around the room.

Sparkle eyed his downcast young nephew for a moment before he eased over to plop down beside him. "Looks like those lessons I gave you didn't do you too much good from the way your mouth is all twisted up. Another bad night, huh?"

Stacy sneered before he looked over to see who was invading his solitary. "Hey, Unc, shit be rough right in now. That's for sure." He smiled for a brief moment before his face turned back into a disappointed sneer.

Sparkle patted him on the knee. "Oh, yeah, it gets like that sometimes—even when you are putting your thang down."

All Stacy could do was shake his head. "Man, it seem like that shit ain't working for me. I've still been losing like a bitch."

"That's okay."

Stacy sat up straight. "How in the hell is that okay, man?"

"Man, you can just chill with the 'tude, son." He waited for him to sit back before adding, "Good, now, how you been doing? Heard you been making babies by the car-load."

That got a quick smile out of him as his eyes lit up. "Shiiiit, Unc, honeys be blowing up on a nigga before I even get the dick in the pussy."

Sparkle laughed. "Nigga, you still wild as hell, just like your pops. What's up with old-ass Sam, anyway?"

"Hell, every time I go to the News, he and that bitch Rheta; they be nodding, man," he said full of sadness. "I sure do wish that he'd quit doing that shit, man."

Sparkle decided that it was best to change the subject back to happier tones. "How many babies you said you had, nigga?"

His face brightened as he smiled. "Hell, I don't know. Let me see—about three of them crumb snatchers that I know about for sure. A couple of claimers that bitches be trying to throw in a nigga's mack. I know it had to be Kym or Krys who had to bring that shit up."

Sparkle smiled with a nod. "Krys."

"Figures, Unc, those two be staying in my shit twenty-four-seven; talking that crazy shit about getting married and shit."

"I know you don't be paying them no attention with that there."

"You know that's right. They can talk all the shit they want to, but a player ain't about to be tying no knot with none of these crazy-ass whores. Oh, hell naw."

"You know how them girls be thinking, partner."

"Yeah, you right. They something else." His eyes suddenly started twitching. "Damn, Unc, is it just me, but I could swear we already had this conversation."

"Man, you know what? I was feeling that same déjà vu my damn self." He shook his head and pinched his nose as he took on a more serious tone. "Yo, man, you lose a lot?"

Stacy's face immediately balled up in frustration. "About thirty-five hundred or so. Shit, I lost count when that shit started getting stupid."

"Come on, man. It's time to give you a re-up on this gambling thing." He nodded toward the door; it was time to roll. A half-hour or so later they were leaving a hotel room with Stacy's refresher course, from false shuffles and deck switching to practicing in the mirror until he couldn't even see what he was doing.

Stacy, who had been sitting on the bed stunned as he watched Sparkle work his magic, finally spoke as they were heading down the balcony. "Yeah, I'll get it. How long you been knowing all this stuff?" The astonished look on his face was almost comical.

Sparkle snorted a short laugh and rolled his eyes. "Man, how you think your aunt and your grandmother been beating niggas for all these years?"

Stacy's shoulders shot up like they were shot out of cannon. He spun around with his fist pressed against his mouth as he said wide-eyed, "Naw, man, naw, you mean to tell me that Grandma be cheating, too?"

Sparkle gave him the "duh" look. "Shit, dude, she's the one that showed me how to run up the deck, false cut and steal cards way back when I was in elementary school. And then this nigga named Googie polished me up when I was in the joint."

Stacy placed his hand over his face and sighed heavily. "Well, I'll be damned."

A couple of hours and several grands' worth of winnings later, they were heading to Debra's car. "Damn, Unc, you really worked them in there," Stacy said. "I knew what you was doing and I still didn't see what you did. I have the worst luck in the world whenever I come over here fucking with that fat-ass Al."

Sparkle ran a hand over his head. "Nephew, that's the same way it'll be for you if you get serious about mastering the things I taught you. It gets real easy once you get those things down pat. I bet you didn't even notice that redbone in the blue dress. She was palming cards all night long."

Stacy frowned. "What the hell? I'm gonna kick that

bitch's ass for cheating on me." He started back toward the house before Sparkle stopped him with a very serious tone. "No, no, no, baby boy, lesson number two." He extended his finger to poke him the chest to drive in the point. "Never ever—and I do mean never ever—expose a cheat."

Stacy's frown remained, for he was definitely mystified now. "What the fuck you mean, man? I been playing fair with these bastards the whole time. To hell with that, player. I've lost big bucks fucking with these dogs."

Sparkle gripped his shoulder and said in a soothing tone, "Baby boy, baby boy, whew, slow down, man. Don't be sweating that chump change."

Stacy reared back. "Chump change, chump change," he interrupted.

"Chump change," Sparkle also interrupted. "By the time you get all this stuff down, as well as the mannerisms that go with them, they'll be the frustrated ones. I guarantee it. Just trust your old unc on this one here. You saw how fucked up Al got. I bet you ain't never seen your auntie or grandma get mad the few times you've seen them lose."

Stacy put his hand over his mouth and mumbled, "Come to think of it, I sho ain't."

"You ever thought about why they be so cool regardless?"

Stacy stared at the ground before answering, "No, no, I haven't. It be so rare. Nope, I sho haven't," as he concentrated on the last statement.

"That's because they win eighty percent of the time; the other twenty percent, it just be one of those bad nights. We all have them but the point is that you never reveal a cheater 'cause that lets other players realize that you recognize the cheat. That ain't good 'cause if you can recognize the cheat, it's possible that you can be cheating, too."

He quickly nodded in agreement. "Oh, yeah, that makes sense."

Sparkle reassured him. "Hey, nephew JJ don't even know that Debra be cheating, man. Hell, he don't even know that I do, too, and he was my gambling partner in the joint. That's how secretive you got to be with this shit 'cause a nigga or a bitch will let that knowledge slip out without even realizing they've done so. Trust me on that one there, too. I've seen it happen too much to other niggas who trusted their folk."

Sparkle pinched his nose, examining Stacy's reaction to make sure he'd caught on. When he nodded to show that he had he continued. "Man, I saw Al do a few things during the game. All I did was fold, that is unless I lucked up and had a hand that I could battle him with. That shit happens; catch a nigga short sometimes, too—part of the game. What I'm saying, little soldier, is to let folk get away with their thing and they be thinking that you ain't hip. And then they don't even consider you be doing your thang on their asses. Why? Because they be concentrating on doing their thing and just chalk you up to being lucky, which is what you want them to be thinking anyway."

"Okay, ya'll two, enough of that yap-yap shit! I got to get home for those horrible brats of mine, because Ebony will have Mike burning up bologna and shit with her fast ass!" Debra shouted as she fished in her pocketbook for her car keys.

Stacy headed for his Caddy and sped off ahead of Debra, who immediately flooded Sparkle's ear with this and that about what he should and shouldn't be doing. Whew.

✠ ✠ ✠

It was around noon the next day when Sparkle was stirred awake again by good smells coming out of the kitchen. This time he was lying on the couch instead of in one of the kids' beds. He opened his eyes and saw JJ doing his thang again at the stove. He lifted his head and immediately felt cramps crinkling along his neck from lying on the arm of the chair all night. The aroma of fish sticks, French fries and buttered biscuits helped to ease some of the discomfort, as he sat up and rubbed the crust out of his eyes and stretched.

JJ looked back at him and smiled. "I thought the smell would get yo ass a-stirring. Go ahead, wash up your mug and shit, this stuff will be ready in a minute."

A couple of minutes later, when Sparkle sat down at the table, JJ said, "Now don't be expecting this here that often, dude. I'm only doing it because you'll be getting used to these bricks again."

Sparkle nodded with a quick smile. "Thanks, bro, you know that I really appreciate it."

JJ waited until they were nearly finished eating to say, "By the way, your boy, Duke, and Johnny Dobbs called while you was over there snoring. Said to get you to call them when you got yourself straight."

Sparkle grimaced slightly before he nodded. "You get their phone numbers?"

"I left a note on the coffee table."

Sparkle eyed the table and gave him a quick nod. "Thanks again, dude. I'll holler at them niggas sometime today. They ain't going nowhere. Shit, I've got to go buy myself some clothes; can't keep wearing your stuff."

"Yea, especially since yo ass done hit up twice over here," he said with a good-natured smirk. "Oh, yeah, before I forget, Johnny said something about he had a thang set up for the rack-em thang ya'll used to work."

Sparkle snorted. "Rack-em thang, huh?"

"Yeah, the rack-em thang," JJ repeated.

Sparkle nodded with a smile. "That's my boy, aight, figuring that I want to get into stuff right off the bat. If he call back while I'm gone, tell him I said that we can do whatever; just like old times after I get myself straight."

He finished his meal and went into the bathroom to get himself ready to leave.

✠ ✠ ✠

A couple of hours later he was sitting on the bench in Five Points waiting for the train. He had spent an hour or so buying enough gear to last at least a week. He was rifling through the bags admiring his purchase when he heard Violet's presence. He looked up from the bags into her smiling face. She had on the same boosting gear from the other day. "Damn, shawtie, you stay on the grind, don'tcha?"

Her eyes lit up as she looked down at the bags between his legs. He could almost feel the warmth glowing from hers as she looked back up at him and said, "Mmm, looks like you've got the same taste I figured you for."

He rested his elbow on his thigh before he leaned back to look her up and down. As if she was reading his mind, she raised her head to check out the surroundings before she pulled one of the pleats in the dress back to show him a cluster of fine clothes packed the same way they were the other day. To his surprise most of the stuff was of the same brand and type that he had just bought. His mind immediately shot back to the talk that he'd had with "B."

She batted her eyes and gave him the kind of smile that women gave dudes they were really into—at least that's what he took it for. Then she said seriously, "Now tell me that you got some of that good shit on you. I'm sure there's some things in this stuff that'll hit you just like you like it."

He swiped the back of his hand across his mouth and

took a deep breath as he tried to stare her down. *Was she trying to throw him a curve here or what?*

She spread her arms. "What's up, playa? Cat's got your tongue or something?"

"Or something," he mumbled.

She leaned toward him, undaunted by his stare. "What's up, man? Do my breath stink or something?" She aahed on her hand and sniffed. "You smell some stale pussy, ass...I mean what the fuck, man." She reached between her legs and sniffed at her fingers.

He cocked his head to the side studying her for a few seconds before he shook it. "Girl, you crazy; you know that?"

"Well, that's sho good to know," she spat and sat back on the bench with her arms folded over her fake belly. She tried but she couldn't hide the smile creeping to the edge of her mouth.

He shook his head again. "Naw, shawtie, it ain't even like that, but have you noticed all the people down here?" He stretched his neck around her to emphasize his point.

She put her hands on her hips and pretended to struggle to her feet. "Shit, man, that's all that's putting the bug on you. Come on. Go with me?"

He even surprised himself when he followed her. After a few steps, he started having second thoughts and stopped. "Where we going, girl?"

"We going up top to catch the El to my car," she said over her shoulder as she waddled in front of him.

"Damn, step it up then 'cause there goes the train now."
She looked back. "Oh sure is, ain't it?"

She took a few steps and stopped, which caused him to bump into her ass. She turned her mouth down and smiled before she stepped to the side with a look of joy and surprise. "Mmh," she gasped as she felt his hand clasp hers as the train came to a halt.

They got off at the first stop, the East Lake station, where she retrieved her car. He noticed right away that they were proceeding on Memorial Drive. "So where we headed, if you don't mind my asking?"

She didn't answer and pointed to the glove compartment. When he didn't respond immediately, she reached over and started tapping on it with her designer nails.

Once he opened it, he didn't have to ask her what she wanted when he saw the glass-smoking bowl with the letter "V" engraved on it. He reached into his jacket pocket and pulled out a baggie full of rocks. He filled the bowl and ran his lighter up and down the stem before he passed it to her.

After blazing herself to Scottieville, she passed the bowl to him. "Playa, I can feel you digging me and I already know that I'm digging you, so I might as well show you where your fine ass is gonna be housing it, huh? Any objections?"

He was in the middle of getting blitzed himself so all he did was smile. After the rush, Sparkle lay back on the headrest and started checking out the scenery. Before he realized it, they pulled into a row of townhouses on Memorial Drive. Once they entered the apartment, she disappeared into one of the back rooms, only to reappear a few moments later with an armload of clothes. She dumped them on a red leather couch.

Sparkle, who had taken a seat at the glass dining room table, sat there in semi-shock as he watched her grab the hem of the maternity dress and pull it all the way over her head. Strapped to her body was a harness-like contraption with a huge plastic bubble with large holes on each side.

Violet's eyes glowed as she pulled clothes out of the bubble and added them to the pile. She waggled her fingers for him to check out everything she had unloaded. Then she licked her lips seductively. "I do believe that most of these will fit you."

She picked up a couple of outfits and held them up to his body and nodded. Satisfied about the sizing, she threw them down, picked up another couple of outfits and went to his back. Rising up on her toes, she pressed them and herself against him and whispered in his ear in a husky voice, "Nigga, ain't no need to try to front or try to fight it: Yo ass belongs to me." She cupped his ass cheeks in both hands, giving them a nice tight squeeze.

She gasped in pure shock when he suddenly spun around and grabbed her arms, pinned them to her sides, lowered his head to her neck and bit her. She aahed and melted up against him. Suddenly, he released her and turned back to the clothes on the couch. He picked up a gold silk pants set and held it against his chest, laid it back down and picked up several more pieces and did the same. It didn't take long for him to realize that almost everything fit him. Then he realized that he was looking at the same stuff that he had seen the other day at the Decatur station.

He felt her ease back slightly and breathe into his ear, "I told ya the other day that I had picked up some stuff for a new addition to my life. Didn't I?"

Of course he remembered and smiled down at her and to himself. "Damn, girl, you done put claims on a nigga already, ain'tcha?"

She wrapped her arms around his waist. "What a bitch gotta do? Get on her knees and offer your ass a ring or something? I feel you, motherfucker; it's as simple as that."

He continued smiling. "As simple as that, huh?"

She pursed her lips and smacked a kiss at him. "Yep, as simple as that."

His eyes were glittering when he said, "Okay, fly-ass mama, it's on then."

She reared her head back. "Okayeee, as simple as that, huh?"

"Yeah, sweetie, as simple as that."

His cell phone started ringing on his hip. He frowned and pulled up the hem of his shirt to peer down at the flashing number. A look of puzzlement crossed his face. "Damn, who the fuck number is that? Hold on a sec, shortie. Let me check this out."

Violet was disappointed. Her body hadn't been heated up like that in a long, long time—much too long. But she nodded and backed off of him.

He punched the return call button. His boy, Rainbow, picked up on the second ring. *Helluva timing, damn.* He listened for a few and then replied, "Damn, homie, it sho do feel good to finally hear that squeaky ass voice of yours again. When? Damn, I don't know. Wait a minute." He looked over at Violet, who had sat on the couch; frustration written all over her face. "Girl, how far are we from the DeKalb Mall?" With her lips turned down, she told him and he went back to his call. "About twenty minutes, playa. Sure I could meet you there, the Dairy Queen, right? Okay, I'll see you there in a few then."

He could tell that she was disappointed and was ready to get her fuck on, but he couldn't let his boy down. Hell, she'd be aight. He hung up, licked his lips and turned to face her. He didn't bother smiling for it was player rule time. "Damn, baby, I hate for shit to be snapped like this but I got to go see my boy. We go way back to the kindergarten days and I've like been waiting for him to contact me ever since I got up." She didn't show any expression but it was evident that she was pissed. *Oh well, playa to playette, she knows how it goes.* He reached down to pick up his bags and headed for the door.

She beat him to it and pressed her back to the door. "You ain't got to take all those bags with you. Why don't you slide into one of those outfits before you go see ya manz. Shiiit, I got them all for you anyway."

He looked her up and down and licked his lips. "You sho sure of yourself, ain'tcha?"

She lowered her shoulders, resigning respectfully to the game, then took a deep breath. "Hell yeah. I'm sure of myself; ain't you? Hey, it's been a long time since I've had the chance to feel this way about a nigga. You got that look, muthafucka, and I want to be the one you be looking at. I guess you can say that I know what I want, and I want you."

He stared into her eyes and felt hers dig deep into his soul. This was it and he knew it. Still he was on a cop-and-lock mission and had to stay with the script—no matter how hard his heart was thumping. He stared at her for several more seconds and turned toward the couch. He asked over his shoulders. "Okay, sweetheart, which one you want to see me in?"

Her face lit up like a candle as she rushed to the bedroom and quickly returned with some tan Timberland boots as she waved her hand at the bundle of clothes in grandeur. "Get fly, my prince, get fly."

He chose a dark brown silk outfit and held it up against his body for her inspection. She had settled at the dining room table and crossed her legs. Wiggling her fingers in excitement, she said, "Let me watch you put it on."

He laughed and did as she'd asked. Violet oohed and aahed. He walked over to the full-length mirror mounted to the outside of the hall closet. He quickly nodded his okay to the fit and the image before he headed for the door. He opened it to leave, leaned back in and flicked her a bag with four fifty blocks of rocks in it. "Okay, star, we gonna see where this here goes and takes us."

She put the bag inside of her bra, got up and walked past him. "You don't really think that I'm going to let my prince ride no damn bus, do you?"

He let out a short snort and smiled as he admired the way she swayed her sexy-old ass out the door. *Shiiiiit, nigga, you done caught yourself a muthafuckin' legend ho.*

CHAPTER THIRTEEN

The Boss Team Gets Reunited

Violet let him out at the BP station on the other side of I-20. He wanted to grab a pack of Kools and a sixteen-ounce bottle of Olde E. Sparkle also wanted to walk the remainder of the distance so he could clear his mind and calm his ego from the amazingly easy way that he had copped a hood star. He also thought he'd be a little cautious because of the drug bust he had witnessed the other night. He didn't particularly care for some leftover cops to see him getting out of Violet's luxury ride. Police still had the tendency to pay extra attention to black folk rolling on fine wheels.

He spotted his boy as soon as he trotted across the highway. Rainbow was stepping out of a dark green Cadillac in the parking lot of the Dairy Queen beside the Citgo service station. There were three snazzily dressed sex bombs following him when he looked up to see Sparkle approaching. Rainbow's Max Julien smile lit up like a ray of sunshine as he spread his arms out in welcome. "Sparkle, Sparkle, Sparkle, is that you, my nigga? Aaah fuck, I thought you had given up on your peeps there, dog. Come here. Let me squeeze the life out of your skinny ass." His smile was so genuine that Sparkle felt his heart flip with warmth as Rainbow leaned back against his shiny ride.

As he approached he raised his neck and started massaging his chin as he inspected the luscious bodies of the honeys. "You know how it is, partner. I got caught up in this and dat."

Rainbow started laughing loudly at the direction of his gaze. "Still sweating my bitches, I see." He waved his open palm with a pimp flair at the girls, letting him know that they were all up for his pleasure; like always with any bitch he had in his stable.

Sparkle pinched his nose and nodded sharply. "Good enough to sweat, dog."

Rainbow saw the way his hoes were watching his boy and went straight into his macking mode. "Bitches, how many times I got to tell ya'll to get out of range when I'm talking to a nigga? Get the hell on up to the room. Princess, you've got the key, so get!" he screamed at the one that Sparkle had seen earlier. It was at one of the hotels he'd first hit with the dope JJ had given him. She was the sexiest of the three.

All of them were dressed in some come-get-the-pussy gear. Sparkle felt like a piece of prime meat as they went straight into their ho struts and eyed him up and down seductively as they headed toward the Red Roof Inn.

Sparkle shook his head as he recalled Princess's jazzy-talking ass that night at the Motel 6. Under Rainbow's iron hand of discipline, her ass was like a lamb; the complete opposite of the bitch he'd dealt with earlier. *Man, I should have known that JJ and that nigga Percy couldn't handle a fine bitch like that. And that my nigga wouldn't let a ho of her caliber survive these streets without his guidance and instruction. She's a whole different bitch now. My nigga's got her ass in his mortal lock.*

His trance was broken when Rainbow grabbed him in a bear hug. "Damn, I miss your skinny ass, muthafucka. Boy, it's good that you finally made it back to these bricks, playa, for real yo." He leaned back and grasped his shoulders in a firm grip. "Man, I had us a lick jam up. Why didn't you holla at me when I hit that nigga JJ on the phone?"

Sparkle pinched his nose and smiled. "Joh…oops, I mean Lah… oh damn, it's Rainbow now. Man, who the fuck you going to be next week?"

Rainbow gave him a fake frown. "Whoever the fuck I want to be." He laughed and lunged toward Sparkle, putting him into a headlock up against the car. They wrestled around for a while until Sparkle grabbed his forearm and twisted it up until he screamed out loud in pain.

As soon as Sparkle had done it, he immediately thought, *Aw man, I forgot all about how his collarbone be popping out of its socket so easy.* Both of them slid down the side of the car and plopped loudly on the pavement.

Before he could go to bitching, Sparkle grabbed his arm and pulled. Rainbow grimaced in agony and squirmed around for several seconds until Sparkle finally heard the shoulder pop back into place. After the shocking pain subsided, Rainbow started laughing despite the tears that were running down his cheeks.

Sparkle couldn't hold back the laughter as he stood up and reached down to carefully help him up. "Ah man, I forgot all about that fucked-up arm of yours."

Rainbow grunted, straightened out his clothes and pushed him upside the head. Then he lifted his head to look around. "My man, my man, whew, I'm just glad that one of them wild-ass bitches didn't see that. One of them crazy muthafuckas might try that shit and I'd have to kill their stanky ass."

After frowning about that dreaded possibility, he stared at Sparkle for about thirty seconds, shook his head and draped his arm around his shoulder. "Damn, I miss you, nigga. Damn, those years was a long motherfucking time, dog." He ruffled the curls on the top of Sparkle's head. "Come on, let's grab one of them Waffle House specials."

They gathered themselves and sprinted across the street to get their grub on. Rainbow waited until they had feasted halfway through some pancakes and cheesy eggs before he finally spoke. "Yo, partner, I figured that you had gotten a little busy getting your groove back. But damn, you sure waited long enough before you hollered at me. Damn."

Sparkle nodded between bites of cheesy egg as he waited for him to continue.

"Taint no biggie, though. You still want to get down? I got a couple of construction workers lined up for a prime spiel. It's a pretty good lick too, partner."

Sparkle stabbed into one of the strawberry pancakes. "Man, why you keep doing that sting there, dog. I know you got money's mammy."

Rainbow's eyes started to glitter as he smiled across the table at him. "My nig, you of all people know that it's all about the sport of it, man—simply the thrill of the game, man."

Sparkle continued to play in his food as he shook his head. "You crazy, you know that, don'tcha? Just don't get enough excitement out of handling those hoes, huh?"

Rainbow arched his head in a circle as he sat back in the chair and rubbed his neck. "Man, I've been bored with this pimping thing for nearly a decade," he responded blankly; at a loss for words.

Sparkle leaned forward to place his elbows on the table. "Why the fuck you keep doing it then? You don't need the money; that's a fact. Hell, I've even heard about your buying up some slum apartment buildings and shit. Man, your ends are longer than a rainbow."

Rainbow blew his nose into a napkin and sucked on his teeth while staring at him.

Sparkle cocked his head to the side and started laughing. "Man, you know that you look just like that nigga Max Julien in *The Mack* when you do that?"

"Oh yeah." He smiled and sniffled.

"Damn, that sinus still be fucking with you, huh?"

Rainbow frowned. "Hell yeah, ever since you gave me this shit that day in the sand pit."

"What!" Sparkle retorted astonished.

"You heard me, nigga," Rainbow repeated.

"Shiiiieeet, you the one that gave me that shit."

Rainbow harrumphed and sniffled again. "Uh-huh, man, this shit been fucking with us like forever, ain't it?"

Sparkle squeezed his eyes shut and pinched the bridge of his nose. "Yep, and snorting that white mack don't be helping none, either."

Rainbow hunched his shoulders and stared around the restaurant before he sniffled. "Speaking of…let's hit the bathroom for a taste. Shit be the bomb, too, dog." When he got up, his black silk shirt spread open and revealed a gold digger's spade glittering on his herring-bone necklace. "Come on, let's do this." He got up and led the way away from the booth.

When they got into the bathroom, Rainbow took out a gold cigarette case. As soon as he opened it, the strong odor of the coke exploded into the air. It was some of that pinkish gold-flaked stuff Sparkle had seen that first night he had gotten out with JJ. Rainbow took two tokes and closed his eyes as the rush blazed through his brain and caused his forehead to bleed beads of sweat. He blinked several times and shook his head. "Oooh wee, whew! Man, this is the best stuff that I've ever had, dog." He yanked the necklace over his head and passed it and the case to Sparkle.

Sparkle took a quick one on one and frowned because that shit bombed on him the same way. He closed his eyes and shook his head. "Oh shit, man, what the fuck... where the fuck?" He sniffled and rubbed his nose. "Man, where ya'll niggas getting this stuff from? I ain't never seen no pink blow before." He started wiping the sweat off his forehead.

Rainbow grabbed a paper towel and started wiping the sweat off his head too. "Damn, that shit good. You about ready to go bang these hoes up?"

Sparkle scooped another hit to his nose. "Trying to keep me with ya 'til the sting, huh?" He took one more scoop and passed the case back.

Rainbow smiled. "That's right. Think ya'll know a nigga, don'tcha?"

Sparkle took the towel out of his hand and started brushing the excess powder off his nose. "How in the hell I can't know you, man. Come on, I want to try some of that black one anyway."

"Shiiiieeet cool, knock the bitch's back out. Let's roll."

As he followed him out the door, Sparkle placed his arm across his shoulder. "Man, I thought that ho was working for that nigga Percy and JJ."

Rainbow squinted his face up and flipped his shades off his eyes and perched them on his forehead. "Percy and JJ, nigga, please. Man, hell naw, them niggas be working for... Hold up, wait a minute. Now that nigga Percy be doing thangs for me, but who the fuck is this nigga JJ anyways?" He grunted and began rubbing his earlobe—something he always did when he was puzzled about something.

A hard frown creased Sparkle's forehead for a second or two before he answered, "That's the nigga you talked to the other day when you called Debra's crib. But fuck that, soldier; them two niggas gave me the impression that we all were going to be like triplets in this drug thang." He hunched his shoulders, wanting to know the real deal. He hated being lied to for the hell of it.

Rainbow smiled. "Naw, my nigga, I beep the twins with code to hit Princess whenever I want them to take her something. I had no idea that you was with them hoes. Hell, dog, I would've hollered at you then if I had known that."

Sparkle exhaled and lowered his shoulder. "Well, I'll be damned, and you know the twins, too?"

"My nigga, I've had them sneaky bitches for nearly three years now. Other than Lady, those two have been with me the longest." Rainbow smiled, exuding the same confidence he'd always shown.

At the sound of one of his favorite females, Sparkle's smile widened. "Lady…man, how my baby doing?"

Rainbow laughed out loud. "Following orders as usual."

"Following orders; nigga, you a mess." He smiled as he leaned away and punched him in the shoulder. It was good to know that his main man hadn't changed a bit.

"As always, and from now on, I might add." He laughed a little harder, so proud to be a hood legend.

They continued to kick it as they headed across the Kroger parking lot toward the hotel. Suddenly they heard screaming tires coming in their direction. They jumped out of shock and looked behind them to see a big sedan streaking directly at them. Instinctively they leapt out of its path onto the grassy area in the same direction to get out of the speeding car's path. They drew their guns as they spun in a roll. They were about to open fire at whatever fool who had come at them like that, when they heard a big Santa Claus-like laugh bellowing from the driver's window.

"What the fuck ya'll scary-ass old-timers doing out this way this time of night?" the husky voice of their ole doping partner, Duke, rang in the night air. He stuck his big face out of the window, cheesing hard for a mug.

"You big, crazy, fat muthafucka, you done lost your mind or what?" Sparkle screamed at the top of his lungs. Inside he was feeling good about seeing another of his boys.

Rainbow picked himself up off the ground and added, "Blind ass bastard, give me your insurance card. I'm going to sue your big ass for vehicular harassment."

Duke stepped out of the car jiggling with laughter, looking like a fat penguin in a full tux with tails and all. They embraced and started shooting each other body punches. Looking beyond Duke's massive shoulders, Rainbow saw his car rolling down the sloped pavement toward the wall and yelled, "Oh shit, big dude, you may need to get out your insurance card, for real, dog!"

Sparkle and Rainbow burst out laughing as big boy screamed like a banshee and bounced his big ass after the car. By the time he was able to lean into the car's window and jerk it into park it was only a few feet from the wall. With the sudden stop, his big ass bounced off the fender, slammed into the wall, slid down it and plopped loudly on the pavement huffing and puffing big time.

His buddies were laughing so hard that their sides started to ache. Rainbow looked over at Sparkle, who was down on his knees gasping for breath. He was laughing so hard that his eyes had started to water.

There was a real stupid look on Duke's face as he sat there spread-eagle against the wall like a battered penguin. He let out a heavy sigh as he stared at the pair for a few seconds before he burst out laughing himself, his big belly shaking like a gigantic bowl of Jell-O. After awhile he wheezed. "Man, I should've ran over the both of ya'll dirty asses."

The two of them grasped their sides and crawled over to the wall to sit on either side of him. The trio looked back and forth between each other and burst out laughing all over again.

Duke started hiccupping but still managed to repeat himself, "Man, what ya'll niggas doing out this way?"

Rainbow wiped the laugh tears from his eyes and cheeks. "We was headed to the hotel to enjoy some phat-ass hoes. You wanna come with us because there's three of them."

Duke wrinkled his nose. "Not if ya'll got some stanky-looking bitches with funky pussy up there."

Rainbow sniffled. "Oh hell naw, big fellow, I got black queen Princess, Sidney and a fresh new honey I just copped named Candy."

That surely got him excited as he sprang to his feet like a jackrabbit. Cheesing from ear to ear, he bent down and reached out with both hands to help them to their feet effortlessly. Bucking his chest out, he started shaking his waistband. "Candy, huh, is she good enough to eat for a sweet?" His eyes were bucked wide with anticipation.

Rainbow brushed himself down and proudly. "Yep, that's her name, aight, Candy. I bet your fat ass a grand that she can get that little dick of yours to spit in sixty seconds flat. Then again, nigga, what the hell you doing out this way in the penguin suit looking like a fucking pallbearer?"

Duke ran his big hands down his chest like he was ironing out the fabric and spread his arms out wide. "Man, that girl Cynt had me up at some banquet for one of her co-workers, some kind of black-tie affair...it was alright." He rotated his shoulders and pinched his nose as he narrowed his eyes at Rainbow. "Sixty seconds, huh; nigga, please."

Rainbow thumbed his nose and retorted, "What part you didn't understand, the six or the 'o'? Hell yeah, sixty seconds—that's what I said, ain't it? Guaranteed, straight up, playa." His poker face was set in stone.

Duke covered his mouth with his fist and stared at him for a while. "Naw, that's aight, no bet. Your ass is too damn tight to put up even a fucking penny that quick unless you had locks. Besides, why betcha when I'm about to taste the bitch's game for free? Hell, I'll dub my hat off to you if the bitch can perform that miracle."

Overly sure of himself, Rainbow smiled, flexed his shoulders and nodded. "I'm definitely sure, dog. The bitch is like that, man. Hmm-mmh, why you think I let her ride with Princess? She bad, playa. Oh hell yeah, she the real deal, dog, for sho."

Duke ran his eyes up and down Rainbow's body. "Damn, bro, why you so big on that black-ass ho Princess?"

Rainbow licked his lips, wiggled his nose and cocked his head to the side before he spat, "Because playa playa, she done pulled off some drastic shit for me that any ho wouldn't. Believe me, dog, she's definitely earned her stripes; especially coming from me. And even before you open your big mouth, you don't need to know what, know what I'm saying?" he finished with macking flair.

Duke gave him a curt nod. "Uh-huh, okay, I feel ya; sorta like me and that dirty bitch of mine, Cynt."

Sparkle interjected, "Damn, she like that? Hell, I thought my girl Lady was your one and only, dog," and playfully shoved his shoulder in disbelief.

Rainbow twisted his mouth down. "Man, Lady will always be my number one, just like 'B' and Yolanda, just like you and you know who. Who, by the way, came out on Auburn Avenue the other day and inquired about yours truly." His eyes bucked wide open as if to say, *Whatcha gotta say about that there, soldier?*

Duke smiled and punched Sparkle on the shoulder. "He must be talking about Lady Bev, huh?"

Sparkle grimaced. "Hey, fuck you, fuck both of ya'll. Come on, let's go tap some of that fine ass up there in the room waiting for a nigga to soak his dick in some stanky juicy juicy." He didn't want to discuss Beverly *period*—at least not with these two fools.

✠ ✠ ✠

After a full night of three-way swap-a-ho, coking, oiling both boy and girl, and smoking reefer-laced blunts, Sparkle stirred awake at the smell of a Waffle House breakfast box being waved under his nose.

The first thing that registered on his hazy mind was the three sex kittens prancing around in bras and thongs, sharing a shooter full of coke. He fought off a yawn, then wiped the crust out of his eyes. "Where my dogs at, ya'll?"

Princess sashayed her black sexy ass right up to him, the aroma of all-night fucking and sucking permeating the air around her. It intoxicated his senses because that shit was really good and stood between his legs. Her crotch was so close that he could feel the heat emanating from it. His dick started to rise as he thought of how she was riding him in reverse cowgirl style. That pretty shiny black ass spread wide across his thighs a few hours ago. He stirred uncomfortably on the bed with sexual tension.

She placed her hands on her hips, smiling seductively as she hunched her fragrant pelvis forward. "Baby, those boys been gone. Rainbow told me to get you up in time to get to Five Points before twelve."

He looked into her conniving eyes with the feeling that she was disrespecting his dog with the way she was acting out of his presence. He definitely didn't have time for that bull, so he grabbed her Lady Omega-laced wrist and twisted it around to face him. To his surprise it red 11 a.m., so he pushed her away and jetted for the bathroom to freshen up. He hollered over his shoulder as he opened the door. "Yo girl, ya'll got any mouth-wash or—" He nearly bowled right over Candy when he turned around for an answer. She ooohed when she pressed up against his semi-erect morning hardness.

With a sweet smile on her face, she cooed, "Here you go, baby; figured you'd want this." She handed him a small bottle of Scope from a pair of dainty little hands that were fashioned with designer nails and several gold and platinum rings.

Her feminine aroma was just as intoxicating as Princess's. He stepped back smiling at her glittering eyes. "Thank you, sweetheart. You're a real doll."

She batted those big brown puppy dogs at him, spun

around like a perky pixie and poked her round little donkey butt out as she sashayed away with a sweet smile dimpling her rosy cheeks.

He shook off the sexually induced trance the girls had caused and closed the door. After taking care of his hygiene, he bid them adieu. He considered calling Rainbow but decided to go to Debra's to check in first. His intuition told him that besides doing that scam, there was no telling what would come next. Rainbow was as wild as ever. As he crossed over I-20, he looked up at the gathering clouds and wondered if it was an omen of whether anything would go wrong.

CHAPTER FOURTEEN
A Gathering of Foes and Friends

The unexpected rain caught Black Don totally by surprise as he parked his dark blue Lexus. He took a quick peek into the mirror to check out the chinstrap he'd gotten the barber to trim up. Damn, he did favor that nigga 50 Cent when he angled his face a certain way. Maybe them bitches weren't bullshitting him when they teased him about the resemblance. Hell, both of them were top players so it was all good.

A pair of headlights flashing from the other side of the hotel snapped him out of his short reverie. The distorted vision caused by the rain and accompanying mist had him contemplating venturing across the hotel's parking lot to the hoes' room. The jittery feeling he was experiencing had him wondering if he was tripping off the heavily laced blunt he had sucked up earlier. This was just before he had gotten the call from Big Bertha about the attempted robbery.

As the rain started to bang harder on the windshield, he wondered why his little crew of niggas hadn't answered his calls. Now that really had him pissed. He was used to them being at his beck and call whenever he wanted them to be.

Fucking younguns. Damn, you can't rely on their unstable asses for nothing when you sho nuff need 'em. He kicked the door open. He pulled the hood of his leather jacket over his head and stepped into the downpour. In a crouch, he jogged across the lot. He hated coming to these haunts, especially this one with this mini-jungle surrounding the back and sides of the hotel. It really gave him the creeps. By the time he reached the walkway, he didn't know whether he was shivering because of the freezing rain or the paranoia effect of the blunt.

He rapped on the door and froze when a chilling sound made him shake from head to toe. He was leery but turned around curious with fear. He went into a defensive crouch when he thought he saw something move in the mini-jungle along the embankment sloping from the interstate. Was one of his enemies lurking in the bushes? Was this whole robbery bit a setup to catch him in a fucked-up situation? The goose bumps along his arms were no joke.

He jumped again when he heard the nerve-wrecking sound again. He squinted at what appeared to be movement for several seconds before he realized that it was only the wind.

"Damn, I've got to stop fucking with this coke so damn much. Shit's got me shaking like a leaf. Aw man, what the fuck was that?" he muttered before he realized it was his car keys dangling in his pocket. Heaving a sigh of relief, he wiped his face and blew into his fist to calm himself down. Shaking away the jitters, he cranked his neck in a couple of circles, turned to finally knock on the door and nearly jumped out of his skin when it was snatched open.

"I thought I heard—" she started to say when her breath caught at the sight of the gun aimed in her face. She flinched from the wild look in his eyes and stepped to the side.

"Girl, don't be scaring me like that. You can get yourself blown away with that shit," he spat angrily as he replaced the nine-milli Glock back under his armpit.

Frowning, she spat back, "Man, what's wrong with you? All I did was open the door because I heard something out here."

Ignoring her angry stare, he barged into the room. She backed up to the bed and sat down, in no mood for a nonsense confrontation.

Feeling the need to maintain his gangster image, he eyed Mercedes, one of the dancers who worked at the strip club he partly owned on the east side of town on Lee Street. In the short time she'd been dancing at the club, he'd really taken a liking to the little Vietnamese honey, but in an effort of hard playerhood, he refused to show her any weakness. He turned to his usual gorilla control and growled, "Why ya'll bitches wait this long before ya'll told me about this shit?"

Bertha, the big-boned honey, recognized the coke glaze in his eyes and mustered the energy to deal with the situation. There was no telling how they might react to any kind of defensiveness. She swallowed and started fidgeting with her white gold heirloom necklace as she muttered in a low voice, "We didn't really want to bother you, baby, because the niggas ain't get away with but three or four dimes. Shit, it was more like a snatch robbery but I figured you'd want to know about it anyhow." She batted her long eyelashes innocently.

He'd barely heard her, as thoughts of little Mercedes lapping between Bertha's big red thighs caused his dick to stir. And since he didn't want them to see his shit rising in his pants, he started pacing back and forth between them.

After a few anxious moments, he finally regained control of his dick and went to lean against the dresser under the television. He took a deep breath, bowed his head and started rubbing the stubble on his chin. "For one, I want to know if you've seen them niggas around anywhere; and two, why in the hell you ain't at work? Especially you, Bertha, because you know damn well that I don't trust those other bitches to be trying to run thangs. And three, you could've told me this weak-ass shit whenever I saw you again at the club."

He eyed the both of them very suspiciously for a few seconds before he started twisting his neck in short circles, enjoying the crackling sensation of the tension release. He straightened up and went to sit beside Mercedes. *Damn, this little thang reminds me of a delicate*

China doll. He placed his arm around her shoulder. He blinked several times, fighting off the hypnotic effect of her dark almond-shaped eyes as she looked dreamily into his. "You comfortable with your routine, cutie pie?"

She hunched her little shoulders, smiled demurely and said, "Uh-huh, but I wish I was getting more tips from the guys, though."

Her sweet voice sent shivers down his spine. He quickly smiled back at her. "You do, do you?" *Boy, I sure wouldn't mind sliding up in her little fine ass right now.*

Mercedes started fidgeting slightly because of the wicked glitter in his eyes and smiled innocently into his face.

He reached into his coat pocket to get a slim cherry blend cigar, took his time lighting it and blew some halos. Crossing and then uncrossing his legs, he leaned forward to rest his elbows on his knees. "Tell you what, little princess; I want you to start working on the pole... I mean *really* work the pole, like you fucking it." His eyes twinkled into an empty stare as he added, "Oh yeah, baby." He started nodding his head as his lips turned down like he was on a heroin high. "Oh yeah, fuck that pole like you riding the best dick in the world. I betcha them sex-deprived muthafuckas will make it rain green up in that bitch if they see that there." He was secretly wishing that he could be that pole.

She squinted at the wall for several seconds before she angled her head sideways with an ever-widening smile.

She began waggling her legs as she nodded, then mumbled, "I think I can do that."

"You think you can?" He frowned at her.

She opened her mouth into a sexy "O" and licked her pouty lips before she batted her lashes. "Yeah, I can do that, uh-huh, I'm gonna do that." She squirmed around on the bed and started bouncing up and down.

He smiled and used his elbows to prop himself up. "That's my girl." He stood over her thinking all kinds of freaky thoughts and gently squeezed her chin. Then he looked over to Bertha. "Damn, redbone, you really geeking, ain'tcha?"

Bertha was peeking through the curtains with a stern look. "Hell naw, man. I ain't geeking, like yo ass. I'm just making sure that everything's clear out there. Hell, them niggas didn't roll up on you; they rolled up on me and shortie girl there."

"So whatcha trying to say?" Black Don growled as he walked toward her.

She wasn't daunted at all now by his menacing stare and walked around him, mumbling.

He got pissed, feeling like she was straight up disrespecting him, especially in front of this little honey he was trying to impress with his gorilla. He growled angrily as he followed her sassy strutting ass. "What the fuck you say, bitch?" She continued on to the back of the room and started brushing her hair in the mirror.

He mumbled under his breath, "This big bitch ain't

fronting on me for the sake of this little ho, I know." He hissed between clenched teeth as he started toward her with his fists balled up at his sides. His paranoid anger got the best of him and he raised his hand to give her a hard backhand slap.

He froze in midswing as his eyes registered on the gleaming switchblade that had magically appeared in her hand. Her hissing lips were just as menacing as she growled, "Nigga, your ass must think that I'm one of them scary-ass bitches that be bowing down to your ass."

As he stood there shocked, she flipped the blade from one hand to the other like a real pro and sneered, "Go ahead, muthafucka, which side of your black ugly-ass face do you want me to start on? Don't make me a bit of difference, yo."

With her having the ups, he knew that it was best to chill, for the moment anyway. So he threw his hands up and backed away to give her some space. Still he had to save at least a little face and played it cool by pinching his nose. "Okay, redbone, I'll give you this one, but don't be making no habit of drawing no weapon on me."

She was psyched for battle if that was the way he wanted to carry it. She had enough of that bullying shit from her days of whoring for Rainbow; she wasn't about to bow down for him. "Yeah, what- ever, nigga. All I wanted to do was let you know that these niggas around this bitch was starting to disrespect your turf, so your ass needs to tighten up your game around here."

Realizing that she indeed had a point, he started massaging his brow and sat down on the bed. He leaned against the headboard to regain his composure before he sat up straight. "I thought you said that you didn't know the niggas that jacked you."

She squinted at him, trying to figure out how serious he was before responding, "I don't know who they were."

He tilted his head back and started at her for a moment. "So what in the fuck are you talking about then?"

She refused to turn away from his stare, knowing that is what he expected her to do. "I'm talking about other folk slanging out of this hotel. And I hate to say it but their stuff is better than the stuff you gave us, and the package is bigger, too."

That certainly got his attention as he stood back up. "Who? Where?"

She leaned her ample hips up against the wall and folded her arms. "Somebody is fronting some butch bitch and a black Amazon down there in the last room." She leaned forward and stared him directly in the eyes defiantly. "And that little butch bitch has the kind of look that'll make a nigga back the hell up if they ain't ready for some physical contact, if you know what I mean. In other words, the little bitch is ready to solve problems if they come up; you feeling me on this. That goes to show you that there's some serious competition going on around this joint. Whoever is backing these hoes, I think you need to hang around and check this shit out, man. That's all I'm saying."

He looked down at his watch before he set her with a cold icy stare. "Check this here out, redbone; you and shorty go on ahead to the club and I'll check on this little problem here." He turned away and walked out of the room.

He sat in the car, pondering what to do, until he saw Bertha and Mercedes leave the room a few minutes afterward, get into Bertha's red Mustang and split the scene.

His first thought was to follow them and see how that big bitch acted when he got the ups of her, but he quickly changed his mind. Checking out the competition was much more important. So he sat and watched the comings and goings of the traffic in the room they'd told him about. After it stopped raining, he didn't want to be sitting in the car looking all conspicuous, so he eased out of the car to go check out the competition.

✠ ✠ ✠

The noon-day traffic on I-20 was bumper to bumper as Beverly contemplated getting off at the East Lake exit even though she preferred not driving through her old neighborhood. While she maneuvered through the cars munching on a Wendy's egg and sausage biscuit and sipping gingerly on her steaming hot cup of cappuccino, a bolt of nostalgia hit her. She pulled over to the emergency median and sped to the exit ramp.

She was soon caught up reliving memories as she cruised past some of her old stomping grounds. The corner store where she used to lean against the old red oil pump with her sidekick Yolanda watching the old heads of the neighborhood schooling young lookers on and trash-talking to her three amigos in the fine art of playing checkers. Now it was a rundown, rusty, old building run by a Vietnamese family. She found herself wondering about the former owner, sweet old Mr. Mack.

She cruised by the old huckleberry tree when it dawned on her that her old kindergarten used to be there. Now it was an empty lot. Oh, how the times had changed. She found herself really longing for those days.

The nostalgia gave her the impulse to go by Mrs. Dobbs' house, Johnny's mother. He was the oldest of the three. Once she stepped on the porch of the old yellow house, she started getting warm thoughts of all the evenings she'd spent after school swinging on the porch, waiting for Mrs. Dobbs, her favorite baby sitter, to come home. She loved the hours they had spent sweet-talking all the potted plants hanging on ropes from the roof. They'd even sing to them to help make them grow and stay beautiful.

The door was suddenly snatched open by Johnny aka Rainbow. He had always been the instigator and pretty boy of the crew. Even though she had recently seen him, she was still somewhat taken aback since she hadn't expected to be there.

Clearing her throat, she blinked several times before she was able to gather herself to speak. "Hello there,

Johnny. I really didn't expect to see you here. Is your mother here?"

It took him a moment or two to get over the initial shock of seeing the chief of police at his mother's door. Naturally his first thoughts were those of suspicion, followed by tension; especially since he had talked to her the other day. He stood at the door silently, wondering what she wanted.

He finally spoke up, "How ya doing, Bevy? The last person I expected was you so soon," addressing her with the pet name they had given her years ago.

She scrunched up her face and blinked several times. "Trying to look out for our lovely city."

He returned the scrunch and blink as he responded in a low voice, "Well, I guess that takes up a lot or most of your time, huh?"

He glanced over her shoulder to see if anyone was within earshot. Massaging the week-old stubble on his chin, he said, "Why is it that you haven't been to see my moms in almost two years? You too ashamed to be seen in your old neighborhood since you done become the top cop?"

She despised his attitude and responded in kind, "Nigga, please, I stop by here to see Mama Dobbs at least once or twice a month. We just don't report it to your ass." She placed a hand on her hip wondering what suddenly had brought about this snappy attitude of his. She stared at him with an impish grin and was a little bit surprised that she was blushing. He always did have that effect on her. She was stuck between wanting to smack him upside the head with whatever she could get her hands on and hugging him.

She certainly didn't have to remind him that they were on the opposite sides of the law. She just couldn't hang around the hood like she used to.

The only way she could continually look out for them was to stay away; she could show her appreciation for all the years they'd looked out for her.

After airing out those thoughts, Beverly looked at him sweetly and asked, "Do I really have to stand in the door and wonder why you haven't invited me in? Or do I have to push your ass out of my way and holla at my mama?" She didn't even wait for a response and barged right past him.

Johnny cocked his head to the side, as he was forced to lean against the door to let her pass. Absorbing the impact of her sharp elbow, he rolled his eyes, smacked himself upside the head and growled at her departing figure, "Still a bully, huh, Miss Thang?"

She whirled around in the middle of the room and sat down sassily on the brown leather couch. All he could do was shake his head and smile as he closed the door and followed her to the couch. He sat down lazily beside her and propped his Gucci-clad feet on the coffee table adorned with delicate figurines.

Before he could even get off a satisfying aah, she reached

over and pushed his feet off of the table, catching him in the process of folding his hands behind his head. Caught completely by surprise, he sprang up awkwardly and gritted. "Girl, what the fu—?"

She didn't give him the chance to finish before she was frowning all up in his face, "Man, respect your mama's valuables, dang."

Raising his eyebrows menacingly, he jerked his head back and teased, "Dang." He whistled to stifle a laugh and repeated, "Dang," shaking his head.

"That's right, dang," she said and pushed his shoulder playfully. "Ugh, you make me so sick."

He straightened up and did a fake shiver. "Well, I'll be damned. The big tough cop's still got a little Bevy left in her after all."

"Aw, shut the hell up," she said as she leaned toward him and changed to a more serious tone. "I wasn't planning on seeing you here. I didn't even think about dropping by to see Mama until I got caught up in a traffic jam at the East Lake exit." She sat back and took a deep breath before she continued, "Baby boy, uh Rainbow, uh Lah, or whoever you are calling yourself these days, your business has found its way to my office which ain't good at all, player."

"What…" he started to say something but the look on her face stopped him. She knew him too well to even attempt to deny anything to her. She wouldn't turn on him unless her back was totally against the wall. Hell, he really doubted that she'd do it even then; they went too far back to even consider it. He leaned forward to place his hands on his knees and stared straight ahead. In his peripheral vision, he saw that she had begun to run her tongue across her lips. *Aw aw, that there was one of those looks she used to have when she was deciding whether to let him copy off of her test when they were in high school. The end result was that he'd usually have to do her a lot of favors in return.*

She noticed that look about him as the very same thought ran through her mind. Knowing him so well, she smiled shyly and took a deep breath. "Now you know that I'd do just about anything I could to keep your ass out of jail—hell, to keep all of ya'll out of jail."

He put a hand on her knee and started to speak before she put her hand on top of his and added, "Hold on, wait a minute. Let me finish. But ain't much I could even do if some of Atlanta's or Decatur's finest jam ya'll on something first."

The sincerity in her eyes had him feeling bad about what he and Sparkle were about to do. With his mind suddenly turned to Sparkle, he looked down at his watch wondering why his boy hadn't called him yet. He knew them bitches wouldn't dare disrespect that he'd told them to wake him in time to meet him downtown.

On second thought, he silently prayed that he wouldn't pick now to contact him, not with Beverly breathing fire down his neck. Damn, as if he had felt it coming, his cell started ringing on the coffee table. He cocked a wary eye in her direction only to see that her eyes were arched at him as well. Nonchalantly, he reached over to pick it up to check the number. And as he dreaded, it was Debra's number; Sparkle was checking up on his whereabouts. He immediately thought, *Damn, this nigga's got some bad timing,* and stood up.

"Excuse me for a second, Bevy. I've got to make this here return call and I'm not quite sure you'd appreciate my talking business right in your face. You feel me?" His face was wrapped in a phony smile as he headed for the kitchen. Boy, was he ever grateful that she had enough respect for him that she didn't say anything.

Johnny waited until he crossed the sill to the kitchen before he spoke into the phone, "Yeah, my nigga, you ready? Good, good, good. Hey, do you have a dark blue suit jacket? Well, see if you can get one from that nigga and then meet me at the entrance to Underground at quarter to twelve. You with that?" He held the phone pressed to his thigh and looked around the corner to see what she was doing. She was busy pushing stuff around in her purse.

He shook his head and mouthed lightly, "Women," and put the phone back up to his mouth and said, "Ya feeling them damn butterflies, ain'tcha? Hell, me too. Shit, it's been a minute since we've had the chance to do this together and, shit, I'm hoping that you still got it, dog... Okayeeee, you right. I wouldn't even be doing this if I didn't really think you still had it, so there, feel better, damn…. Man, big boy and me split up at the Wendy's around eight o'clock. Yeah, the one on East Lake. Why you ask? Yeah, okay anyway, he said something about going to pick up a package down there in Florida. Uh-huh, I gave him both of our cell numbers; said he'd holla when he hit land again. Come on, man, of course I got his, too. You'll get it when we hook up. Bet, in a few then…Hey and cherish the butterflies. Right, I'm out."

When he came back out of the kitchen, she was patting the sofa next to her. He glanced at the old grandfather clock on the far wall beside the television and prayed that she would leave soon.

Beverly sighed deeply and with the same sincere look that she had earlier before they were interrupted by the phone call, she said, "Johnny, my army of soldiers have no idea that I love you like a brother—hell, more than a brother—but baby, the best that I can do is to let ya'll know when ya'll activities are getting some serious airtime. So please be careful and check and then recheck yourself."

Man, how can I get rid of her without that super cop mind of hers going haywire, he thought.

"Well, it's evident that your mama ain't home yet or we'd have heard her by now."

He smiled gratefully when she got up and patted him on the shoulder. He immediately rose to his feet and escorted her to the door, kissing her lightly on the cheek as she departed.

He closed the door and slipped to the curtain to peek out of the crack as she pulled into the street and sped away. Once the car had disappeared around the corner several blocks away, he slipped out of the door and jogged across the street to his car and headed downtown. The butterflies had started.

CHAPTER FIFTEEN
Playas on the Scheme

Stacy felt like he had just conquered the world after finally getting to use the things his uncle had taught him correctly; especially after all those times he'd been cleaned out at Al's poker games.

While he was busy separating the fives, tens and twenties, one of Al's girls stuck her head in the door and said, "Hey, Stacy, your uncle's on the phone." She paused to run her tongue over her juicy red lips. "He says that he got to holla atcha like right now."

She held her head slightly down and forward with her hands on her hips as she waited for him to respond.

He acknowledged her with a nod, ran his eyes up and down her body, pausing at the puffy "V" between her flush thighs as his smile rose to reach his eyes. She shifted her weight to the other leg, being visibly moved by his intense stare. He made a mental note to get at her whenever the opportunity presented itself. Now wasn't the time, nor was this the place.

He pushed back from the table watching Al for a reaction. After all, he did have to respect the man's house. When a stone-faced Al nodded his consent, he slowly stood up and followed shortie out of the room. She led him into the living room, where he was directed to the phone laying on the sculpture of a naked black seductress. She excused herself and went to the bar and started mixing a drink.

He eyed the sway of her hips in some glittering crushed velvet red pants, knowing that she was putting a little more effort into it for his benefit. He quickly checked himself, lifted the phone to his ear and said, "Yeah, unc, what's up? Yeah, I'm doing pretty good. Just stuck their asses for the biggest pot of the night."

He sat down and crossed his legs as he eyed her while listening to Sparkle's reply. She narrowed her eyes and ran her tongue seductively around the rim of the glass. He squinted, wondering what her game was. Tearing his thoughts away from her, he listened intently to what Sparkle had to say and then replied casually, "Okay, I'll get out of here in a half hour or so… Okay, that'll work; I'll see you in a few then."

After hanging up, he headed back to the game, with the intent to play a few more hands before going on to Atlanta to meet his uncle. But honey had other plans. She waited until he got almost to the door before she hit a switch on the wall that caused the lights to start blinking rapidly. He froze, as he was about to turn the knob. Licking his lips, he slowly turned around to face her.

She was standing by the bar with two drinks in her hands motioning for him to join her. He stood at the door staring at her, waiting for her to make her move all the way. There was no way that he was going to play the aggressor in another man's house, especially when he didn't really know her full intentions. She seemed to be moving in slow motion as she swayed seductively across the floor.

Damn, those blinking lights be having a nigga wanting to bang honey girl like oowee, he thought just before it dawned on him that he didn't even know girlie's name.

She must have read his mind as she flicked her curly red-tinted bangs away from her pit black eyes with a dainty flip of her head. Her nose flared like a panther on the prowl. She licked her gorgeous lips and handed him one of the drinks. "Baby boy, my name is Mona."

When she didn't immediately follow up on her introduction, he smiled at her. "And?" He was really curious about her intentions for sure now.

"And I'd like to get to know you better," she responded while she sipped on her drink.

Stacy took a sip of his own drink and stared directly into her eyes. She batted her eyelashes a couple of times before she said, "Well."

He downed the rest of his drink in one big gulp, pinched his nose and started walking back to the middle of the room. She stood at the sculpture with one hand on her hip—looking like she could have been the model used to carve the goddess—and eyed him up and down. She silently wondered how he was able to resist her feminine charms because most niggas melted whenever she so much as smiled at them. She squinted her nose at his departing back, his hard-to-get act making her more determined to get her way with him.

Refusing to be brushed off so quickly, she started stepping after him. He suddenly spun around, making her freeze in mid-stride. With an intense stare directly in her face, he picked up another cell phone from off of a similar statuette and held it out to her. "Is this yours?"

She placed a foot on the carpeted step and nodded. Cocking his head slightly to the side, he nonchalantly punched some numbers and handed it to her. "When you get the chance and the desire, holla at a nigga." He didn't even wait for her reaction and walked out of the room.

Her eyes blinked rapidly at his departing figure until the door eased shut, and then she picked up the phone to check out the numbers he had punched. Smiling warmly to herself, she clicked the numbers to her save unit and started rubbing the phone against her cheek. She was definitely enjoying the chase already.

When Stacy stepped back into the room, he looked right into a harsh stare from Al. He didn't know exactly what to make of his reaction. He didn't think that he had been gone that long, so he decided to play it by ear.

Since Al had just cut the deck, his attention was drawn back to the game and chatter. He picked up his money and asked the dealer, "What's your game, CeeDee?"

CeeDee was one of his regular buyers, scoring at least a quarter of a kilo every three days or so, which was really good considering that he was dealing his package out there in one of the rural areas, Henry County—a real country hot spot about ten miles outside of DeKalb County. In his mid-thirties, the boy had locks on the cocaine trade on his turf; mostly farmland with widespread black folk projects and trailer parks dotted throughout the land. For a big country boy his pockets stayed fat with Al's product.

He was a big boy with a rounded face full of facial hair and thick cornrows gracing his fat head. He had a thing for plaid shirts that he kept buttoned all the way to the neck and matched the bandana he always had wrapped around his head. His real trademark though was a derby hat he liked to wear cocked acey-deucey. If you saw him, you saw the bandana and derby.

He peeked at Al over a pair of wire-framed sunshades. "Let's try some of that stuff you like, big man...some of that forty-four, ah low card in your hand is wild for a bitch," CeeDee said in his distinctive country boy drawl.

Stacy looked at his four cards and the four on the table. Right off the bat he knew that he would have a bad hand, so he folded and leaned back in the seat. After a couple of more hands, it was obvious to him that his luck had run out. Along with wanting to hook up with his uncle, he decided to call it a night.

Pushing away from the table, Stacy stood up. "Yo folks,

I'm going to catch ya'll another time. My moms wants me to do some thangs for her." He turned toward Brenda and smiled. "Hey, pretty lady, I'll catch you at the club later on tonight, aight?"

She stopped counting her money long enough to smile up at him. "Yeah, okay, baby boy, don't spend all the loot in one place. I'll see you there. Oh yeah, tell your auntie that I'll call her sometime today to make an appointment for my hair and nails."

Stacy nodded to the other players and walked out the room.

As he was backing out of the driveway, he noticed that Mona was watching him through a crack in the curtains. He smiled to himself but chose not to acknowledge her as he drove away. Besides, to his reasoning, anytime that a bitch would pull a stunt the way that she was, in a nigga's own house, how could he possibly trust her? Quickly recognizing the real for the real, he put his ego in check and decided to enjoy the chase.

✠ ✠ ✠

After all of the gamblers had departed, Al sent Mona to the Sonic convenience store down the street to get enough cases of brew to restock the refrigerator in the game room. He watched through the blinds while she backed out of the driveway and drove down the street before he went to the wall behind the jukebox. Lifting a secret panel to reveal an electronic keypad, he punched in his code numbers. There was a near silent whirling sound as the pool table started sliding along the floor, opening to a stairway that led to a sub-basement.

He had taken a couple of steps when a sudden ringing sound froze his leg in midair. *Stupid bitch done left her muthafucking key; that's what I get for fucking with a dilly ho* was the first thing to come to his mind as he spun around and rushed back to the top of the stairs. He fast-stepped back toward the panel hoping that he had enough time to close the secret stairway before she got back into the house. He didn't want anyone to know that the room even existed. By the time that he got to the juke-box, it dawned on him that the ringing sound was a different one from that of his doorbell. All he could do was stand shaking his head at his own stupidity when he saw the cell phone ringing on the pool table. *Damn, I must be slipping or something.* He couldn't remember putting it there.

With a huff of anguish, he stomped over to the table, snatched it up and saw Black Don's number blinking at him. Even though he needed to talk to him about some business, he clicked off and started back down the stairs. When his foot touched the bottom of the stairs, the pool table automatically slid back into place and the lights came on.

Feeling secure in his own little personal world, he sat down in front of a roll of monitors, pressed a series of buttons on the arm chair and sat back. He leaned back and massaged his mouth, chin and neck as he calmly viewed the screen for a couple of minutes. With nothing unusual happening during the poker session, he flipped over to the middle monitor. He touched another button that rewound it back to the time when Stacy had made his call. He listened to and watched the entire scene intently. Feeling good about his suspicions, he rewound several more times to cement the images in his mind, as he envisioned how he would repay the bitch for her dishonesty.

After satisfying his thirsty intuition, he called his boy Don. "What's up, partner? I heard that there was a little trouble out at one of your holes the other night."

Don, who had spent the previous night at the Omni Hotel with a couple of girls who had delivered him a shipment of cocaine from Miami, was just pulling into the BP service station on Candler Road. He had been on his way to see Al after his confrontation with Bertha. And finding out that the black Amazon and butch queen in the corner room were working for what he considered his main competition, hadn't left him in the best of moods. So when Al hadn't picked up the phone on his first call, he had turned around and was headed back to his crib in East Point.

I should make his ass wait the same way that he did me. Who in the hell do he thinks he's fucking with anyhow, like I'm one of his peons or something, he thought as he got out of the car and reached for the gas pump. By the time that the car was filled up, he figured that it would be best to go ahead and get their business out of the way. Before he pulled back out into the traffic, he went ahead and called him back. "Yeah, there was a little some-thing-something out that way but it wasn't no biggie. I handled it, no problem, but shit, how did you find out?"

Al held the phone away from his face frowning at his response but held back from a negative retort. "I've got my ways, but fuck dat. When you gonna bring me my half of that piece we ordered?"

Don stared at the phone for a second before he replied, "Man, since you didn't pick up earlier, I thought I'd drop some off at a couple spots until you called me back. Why? You in a hurry or something? You know the shit's good, dog."

"Naw, nigga, I ain't in no fucking hurry and I don't have to be, but my business is my business and I'd like to be able to handle my business when I need to, not when you choose to handle it for me. Just like you do!" he shouted into the receiver, showing his impatience.

"Okay, okay, you ain't got to blow a rod, damn."

"Man, just tell me when you gonna bring me my shit, simple plain."

"I just told ya, after I hit off a couple of my folks on my way over there."

"Aight, call me when you're really on your way then."

"Bet," Don said and hung up before he could say any-thing else.

After he heard the click, Al quickly dialed another number. "Hey, man, let me know when you want to meet on that thing." Since he was forced to use the voice mail, he hung up as soon as he'd left the message. "Damn, I hope this muthafucka ain't gonna play with a nigga, too," he muttered to himself and started back up the stairs. He decided to take a shower to freshen up for the freak show he had planned for Mona when she got back.

After clicking Al off, Don decided to call his aunt Rose to check in. He pushed in Little Wayne's latest CD and started bobbing his head to some lollypop music as his mind drifted to thoughts of his auntie. He was always in awe of the way she managed to hide her true self from the horde of niggas that occupied their world. Everybody thought that she was a goodie-two-shoe. Little did they know that his sweet-faced overseer was just the opposite, though looking at her one wouldn't think so. Beyond the grandmotherly exterior, there was a hard-core ex-street walker, who had turned him out to the hustling life. She had been raised herself under the strong hand of a veteran macking gangster in those mean streets in Miami. Those heavy-handed lessons had prepared her well for dealing with the thug life.

When he was brutally murdered some years ago by a rival pimp, she was forced to leave Miami, but not before she had made a major connection in the drug game. Some of those connections still wanted to get their hands on her good-playing ass for ripping them off. So it was up to him to maintain a bumper between them and her. He paid good money to keep them off her ass.

Still there were other dope connections, that couldn't care less what she had done to their rivals and had actually helped her to bring Don to Atlanta to expand their product—a new, more powerful kind of cocaine that got to be known as Peruvian golden flake. So named because of the pinkish hue and the way that it glittered with gold specks when it was tilted from side to side. No doubt, she was the real deal, brains and power behind Don gaining prominence in Atlanta's red light district.

Not long after his arrival he'd gone into partnership in the 617-skin house gambling establishment and the strip club. Through the years the club had become well known for its beautiful exotic dancers and as a hub for scoring cocaine in huge quantities. He'd always guessed, but could never really confirm, that Rose's Miami connects were the ones that had greased the skid for him to do all the things he had done. And truth be told, he didn't give a fuck how he got there; he was thankful that he was there.

To see her most people would never imagine her as being the vicious, conniving silent partner and tutor of one of the most dangerous players in the hood. Those that did know her only saw the owner of a neighborhood corner store. This was exactly what she was in College Park, as a cover to keep the police and hustling competitors at bay.

Even Al, his other secret partner in crime, had no inkling of her real status. And as far as Don was concerned, she would remain his ace in the hole. Besides, even with all the money, power and respect that he'd gained since his arrival in Atlanta, and despite his physical prowess and widespread guerilla tactics toward any opposition, he knew that deep in his heart that without her he was nothing.

Though he loved and respected her more than anybody else in the whole world, there was a special aura about her that could be described only as straight-up "fear factor" that he certainly couldn't ignore. He and he alone knew something that nobody in Atlanta even considered. That under the sweet old lady that masqueraded as the mild-mannered corner store owner, there was a scandalous, conniving, ruthless, cold-hearted, cold-blooded killer in disguise.

CHAPTER SIXTEEN
And The Game Goes On

Sparkle took a quick peek at the Omega watch he had just bought from a young hustler, who was hawking his wares at the entrance to Underground Atlanta for $100. It read 11:30, which meant that Rainbow was supposed to be there by now.

He took a another sip out of the strawberry milkshake he'd brought at the Hardees restaurant a couple of blocks down the street, before he looked up and down Peachtree Street wondering where his boy could be. He had just unfolded the newspaper under his arm when he heard Rainbow's familiar twang from behind him. "You can stop looking all around the place. No, no, no, don't turn around. I had to come and let you know that I've been warming the vics up for a meet at his worksite by the Peachtree Towers at twelve. You ready, nigga, 'cause it's about to be on?"

Sparkle frowned slightly. "I got this K-mart jacket on, don't I?" He wiped an anxious hand across his mouth to hide the smile that was edging up.

It must have been contagious because Rainbow faked a cough with his fist to stifle his own laugh. "Yeah, nigga, you K-mart, aight." Then he looked down at his feet and started scratching the back of his ear as he peered down the street. "Damn, you even got yourself some insurance man shoes on."

"Fuck you, man. I had to bow down and ask old man Lewie for these joints, man."

Rainbow arched his brow. "Damn, that old dude's still around. Shit, I thought ya'll two didn't get along."

"Uh-huh, the old grouch is still kicking. Shit, I told him I was going job hunting and wanted to look presentable, and this is what his old ass came up with." Sparkle said made a loud slurping sound through the straw.

"And he believed that shit there?"

He was tempted to turn to face him but caught himself. "Hey, fuck Lewie; let's get back on the sting. I'm a little pumped here, dog. We play it the same way as always from back in the day, right?"

"Oh yeah," Rainbow said as he handed him a Sears name tag over his shoulder.

Sparkle cuffed and frowned at the name on it. He couldn't even begin to pronounce it. He held the card away from his face. "Who the fuck...man, how you say this shit?"

Rainbow laughed again behind his fist. "U...ban... jig, just like it sounds, fool." He placed a hand on his shoulder and added, "That's right, homes, you are of African descent. Ancient history, my man."

Sparkle gritted at the hand pressing his shoulder. "Aw,

man, why didn't you tell me about this dumb-ass shit earlier?"

Rainbow snorted. "Shiiiit, what difference does it make who the fuck you is, dog? You still ready for the point, ain'tcha?"

Sparkle practiced a couple of lines in a foreign accent and rolled his neck. "Whatcha think?"

"I think that you still a pro, nigga." He looked down at his watch. "Got to go, hero, just browse around in the store until you see me with a couple of hillbillies. I'll be heading up Peachtree with a dude or dudes because you know that these crackers in these construction hats don't be trusting a nigga one on one."

Sparkle had heard enough. He was pumped and ready to get it going, so he cut him off, "I gotcha, I see you and the vics and shoot up to, uhhh damn, where do I go?"

Rainbow frowned and patted him on the shoulder again, then took a deep breath sighing. "He's buying DVD players and shit like that."

Sparkle squinted with understanding and started rubbing his thighs and knees, ready to roll. "Okay, gotcha, I'll be there. Let's do this."

Rainbow rolled his eyes to the sky, spun away and strolled down Peachtree.

Sparkle waited about five minutes after he had lost sight of his boy, before he started fidgeting and walking up and down Peachtree. After ten anxious minutes, he bought a *Sports Illustrated* and plopped back on the bench and started flipping pages. Five more minutes and his patience had worn paper thin as he began to wonder if Rainbow had called it off. Then he saw his boy bebopping down the street with two, yep, two white construction workers, who looked like they were straight off the farm. Talking about hillbillies, these dudes were exactly that.

He nonchalantly laid the mag on the bench and crossed the street, heading toward the Sears across the street from Five Points. He didn't waste any time browsing around as he went straight to the elevator, checked the directory and hopped on one of the three cars available to the sixth floor where the appliances were located. He quickly scanned the area with the radar of a veteran store thief on full alert for any store security, nosey salesman or anyone who may show him unwanted attention. He began to browse along the aisles as if he was interested in the products. At the same time, he locked the prices in his mind in case one of the vics needed to know.

He was about to make his third round when he saw the construction hats bopping up the escalator. The fluttering in his stomach took him by surprise for a moment, until he realized that they were the butterflies. *Ah, it is on for sho now*, he thought as he turned away and reached in his pants pocket to get the name tag and pinned it to his coat pocket.

He saw them coming his way out of his peripheral vision and walked over to stand close to an elderly couple looking at some televisions and pantomimed a conversation with them. When they got within earshot, he abruptly turned away, speaking in his best foreign accent "And-a dey will-a be on sale for only one-a more week, but just take-a your time. I could a really use da-a commission."

Rainbow was smiling as he walked up to him and leaned forward to squint at his name tag. "Hello there, my man, Mr. Uh, U. ban...aah whatever," he said with a wave of his hand and a wink at the vics. The hillbillies, straight out of Mayberry, acknowledged his wink with one of their own. Continuing with the smiley face, Rainbow said, "These fellas here wanna check out some of these DVD players, iPods and aaah." He looked toward the vics as if he was a little puzzled, then put the friendly smile back on. "I tell ya what, ya'll gentlemen go with my friend—damn, I can't never get his name right—he'll show you all the stuff I was telling you about." He paused to look around in a conspiratorial way before he leaned closer to them to whisper, "Just remember that everything you choose is like half price, so calculate this stuff like real fast. We can't be hanging around here all day, you know." He spoke with a smile and another wink that was returned by the vics in unison.

As Rainbow walked away, Sparkle cleared his throat to draw their attention so that he could duck behind one of the columns by the escalator. Once he had disappeared, Sparkle heard one of them whisper, "Gee, George, he's one of them there Africana dudes. You sho we can trust him?" That was Sparkle's cue to look around like he was kinda scared that one of his fellow employees might be paying them attention. He leaned over and touched the smaller of the two on the elbow and whispered, "Could ya'll please a keep a your tone down? I can't afford for to-a let nobody know what I'm-a doing-a here." He paused to look around some more to make certain no one was watching. "I've almost made enough money to-a get-a my little sister over here-a to-a this-a wonderful country of yours."

He still had it. He could tell the vics went for that shit hook, line and sinker by the way they started looking around themselves. Sparkle smiled to himself as he noticed the co-conspiratorial looks on their faces. It let him know that his boy had worked his magic on them and it also put him at ease to continue with his part of the scam, so he led them over to the DVD/VCRs. "Ya'll can check-a out-a these here. There's some iPods over in the other aisle if ya'll want to see some of them, too."

The bigger of the two, a redhead with lots of freckles across his nose, dressed in cement-stained khaki pants and a blue plaid shirt, pulled on his ear and said in a deep country drawl, "How much dose thangs gonna cost us, man?"

Sparkle blinked a few times. "Everythang you see can go for sixty percent of the price tag." No sooner had those words slipped out of his mouth, he knew he had made a booboo.

They looked at each other quizzically before Big Red said, "Your friend, Jimmy Ray, said we could get stuff for half price."

"Jim…" He caught himself right away. "Jimmy Ray said that, ooh well, I guess he really likes ya'll dudes if he willing to cut his part off that much then." The sudden look of shock on their faces let him know that he'd lost most of his accent. He was quick to regain himself though and added, "If-a Jimmy Ray says-a fifty percent, then fifty percent it is then."

Evidently Big Red's greed overrode his suspicions and he grumbled, "Okay then, how about letting us get about twenty of them DVD/VCRs, printers and cameras and—"

Sparkle cut through him, "Wait a minute dere. Ya'll sho do want-a lotta stuff. I hope ya'll got a van or something." He had a concerned look on his face, but what they didn't know was that he was setting up his escape.

They looked puzzled at each other before the little guy said, "You mean Jimmy Ray didn't tell you what kinda money we were spending?"

Sparkle did his best to hide the surprise on his face. He chanced a look over to Rainbow, who was sticking his head out beyond the column spying them.

He must have felt what was going on because he immediately held up two fingers, indicating how much they were supposed to be spending. Sparkle rubbed his finger under his nose and held up six fingers with his eyes bucked wide open. Rainbow mouthed "wow" and then ran his thumb under his neck to indicate bringing the sting to a close.

Sparkle saw the little guy getting ready to turn his head in that direction. He quickly cleared his throat, smiled at him and took out a pad from inside his coat and started jotting down the items they had chosen. After the quick calculation, he said, "Ya'll don't-a mind holding on for a moment do you? I'm gonna call Jimmy Ray-a so he can tell his cousin what to expect-a."

They both nodded their consent so he walked down the aisles and called his boy to let him know what was up. He whispered, "Partner, these boys got nearly six g's, dog." And then he said out loud for their benefit, "Okay, we'll see you in a few then."

Rainbow maintained his composed look. "Hmm, that's good, dog. They said that they had two g's but it looked about twice that much. But hell, that's even better. Gone back over there. Let's get this thang over with."

He walked up a few minutes later and pulled Sparkle to the side. "Oh yeah, check this out. They may try to split up and each of them try to roll with one of us. You got to pull both of them to you because I'll have the money mitted by then. You ready?"

"Shit, no problem, dog, no problem," he said full of confidence. He turned from him and walked straight up to the little blond guy, figuring him for the leader of the two since his khaki pants were starched, pressed and cement speckle free. He had a name "Greg" pinned to the pocket on his shirt. "Mista Greg, why don't you go handle your money biz with Jimmy Ray, while me and Big Red here-a recheck-a this list."

Greg patted Big Red on the shoulder and departed with a grunt.

While he checked the list with Big Red, he positioned himself where he could see Rainbow when he got his mitts on the loot. Didn't take his boy long at all and his eyes lit up when he saw Greg pass him a green money bag from under his shirt.

Rainbow arched his brows at him as he slid the bag into his coat. Sparkle hunched Big Red on the elbow. "Hey, I forgot to tell Greg something. Could you go get him for me?" It was time for the shake-off.

Big Red eyed him suspiciously for a second before setting upon the task. When they walked back together, Greg hit Sparkle with what he dreaded. "I'm gonna go with Jimmy Ray downstairs—"

Sparkle cut him off immediately with a sound of desperation in his voice. "No, no, no, his cousin won't make a deal with anybody but him. Come, we go to do the paperwork."

They looked at each other strangely; long enough for Sparkle to feel a little unease and doubt creep into their faces. He didn't give them a chance to concentrate too much. "Hey, if-a ya'll wanna call-a it off, it's cool." He looked around nervously like he was making sure that none of his co-workers were watching. "Aaah, man, a that's aight. I'll go get your money-a back. I can't do-a it like-a this because ya'll is a-making me a-nervous now. That's okay, that's okay, deal's off, deal's off." He started walking toward Rainbow who was about to step on the escalator.

Greg grabbed him by the elbow and said anxiously, "Okay, okay, we do it your way," as beads of sweat started to form on his upper lip.

'*W yeah, man, it's gravy now,* Sparkle thought as he nodded. "Okay, a-my a-way," he said, pointing his thumb to his chest. He gave a thumbs-up sign to Rainbow's departing head, as it disappeared down the escalator. Only he knew that he would wind back around to keep check on how things went until Sparkle made a successful shake-off; in case any trouble started.

He watched along with them as his head no longer showed and then nodded for the pair to follow him. When they got to the elevator, he stopped and bopped himself upside the head. "Goday-um I-a almost-a for-got. I still got to get the inventory forms to make this thing legit. I'll be right back-a in a second." He beamed a brilliant smile and started away until he felt Big Red walking with him and then put his hand on the door-knob to the business office. Sparkle quickly turned around with a frown on his face. "No, no, I can't-a take-a you-a in the office. Draw too much attention. I'll be right back out," he assured him with a manly pat on the shoulder.

Red looked back at Greg with a puzzled frown, but all

he got from Greg was a hunch of his shoulders and a what-else-can-we-do look. Sparkle nodded and entered the office feeling their eyes stabbing him in the back. As if it was an everyday affair, he walked up to the counter and asked the clerk for a credit application. Out of his peripheral vision, he noticed them staring at him. When the clerk bent below the counter to get the forms, he turned to them with an anxious look on his face and waved them away.

When they disappeared around the corner, Sparkle made his move and gently pushed the door open. On the balls of his feet he made a quick exit across the floor to the stairway. As he eased the door shut, he looked across the room to see Rainbow rushing down the aisles to the escalator. Closing the door he ran all the way down the stairs to the street level and cruised toward the exit. Just as he was about to step on the automatic door pad, he looked back to make sure that nobody was following him.

He saw several heads looking upward. A low murmur erupted as several shoppers turned toward the racket. He squinted his eyes, not wanting to believe what he was seeing and immediately bucked them wide open in astonishment when it registered on him that Rainbow was tumbling down the escalator. A moment of pure panic seized his chest before he was able to react, but he regained his composure fast and started toward the escalator to help his boy.

By the time that he had gotten halfway down the aisles,

he saw Rainbow roll out at the bottom. Even from that distance he could clearly hear the moan escaping his lips.

"Aw shit," Sparkle mumbled as he watched in anguish as he started to struggle to his feet as soon as he finished rolling. He continued to walk toward him when Rainbow looked up and spotted him coming. The look in his eyes stopped Sparkle in his tracks and he started having flashbacks to the days when they were young thieves stealing candy apples and other goodies out of the corner store in the old neighborhood. Even from his own mama's store. They had made a vow way back then—*Only one fall at a time*—and they all had stuck with it ever since.

After a momentary pause, he started scanning the surroundings for the vics and even worst, the store security guards. As he was radaring the scene, Rainbow waved him away, struggled to his feet and hobbled past him favoring his already bad left shoulder and leg. It seemed like everybody in the store had stopped to check out what was going on.

Sparkle waited until he got close to the door before he started to follow him. Unconsciously, he placed his hand on the .38 pistol inside his pocket, in case he had to ward off any interference if it occurred. He would protect his boy at all cost, regardless of that "one fall at a time" credo.

Before he stepped on the automatic door pad, Sparkle eyed Rainbow gently into the street and took one last look around. It seemed like there was a dozen pair of eyes watching him, but the vics weren't in sight. Nor was anyone in pursuit, so he walked out of the store and followed his still hobbling partner up the stairs to the MARTA trains.

Sparkle finally caught up with him when he was about to get on the down escalator to the subway. Since Rainbow was still walking gingerly, Sparkle lifted his arm and draped it over his shoulder.

"Ow, godayum, man, take your time, shiiiit, humph," Sparkle grunted, leaning against his own weight to try to balance himself before he looked down at his boy's grimacing face. "Damn, dog, you aight? That was a nasty fall you took back there."

Rainbow looked at him with the full intensity of the pain all over his face, pressed his lips together and growled, "Do I look like I'm aight? Damn, this shit hurts, dog."

Knowing now that they were out of any immediate danger, Sparkle sighed in relief and started snickering.

Rainbow glared at him. "Man, what in the hell do you find so muthafucking godayum funny?"

Sparkle halted their journey down the steps to grab his side, spitting all over himself laughing. "Dude, you should have seen the look on your face as your ass was tumbling. Damn, that shit was like three stories up— that's a long way, dog, a long-ass way. Whew! Man, I'll never figure out why you want to do this shit anymore. Your crazy ass got money's mamie. You just a wild muth-afucka; that's all I can say."

Rainbow leaned up against the moving railing and looked at him seriously for a couple of seconds before a small smile creased the corners of his mouth. He blinked a few times. "Yeah, I guess that shit was funny from where you was at. But dog, there wasn't a damn thang funny about it from my end."

Sparkle stared at him really hard trying to hold on to a serious face, but that wasn't about to work. He sprayed Rainbow's face with sprinkles as he burst out laughing again, even harder than before. "I betcha it wasn't, oooh shit. Hold on a minute, dog, damn." He leaned away and grabbed his side and the railing to keep both of them from falling.

They took a few more steps before Sparkle stopped again.

Rainbow grimaced. "What now, man?"

Sparkle cocked an eye at him, looked down the steps and then back at him. "This here ain't working, partner. Hold on for a second." Before he could respond, Sparkle grabbed him by the elbow and pushed up under his armpit with all his might.

The only thing that Rainbow could do was form his mouth into a silent scream until he heard his collarbone pop back into place.

With his mouth still wide open in shock, Rainbow leaned on Sparkle until the pain subsided. Finally, he took a couple of deep breaths and sighed. "Damn, thanks, dog. You sure remember this broken-down old body, don'tcha?"

Sparkle sat down on the moving steps. "How can I not? I've been popping that bitch back in place all my fucking life. But forget that, where we headed, man? We surely can't go get your car right now because those hillbillies have got to be roaming all up and down Peachtree hunting for us."

Rainbow rotated his shoulders around a few times, aahed and started rubbing his knee. He stepped up his pace heading down the moving steps alone. He got close to the bottom and said over his shoulder, "To the club at the West End stop."

Sparkle threw his hands up in the air. "Why am I not surprised to hear you say that? Junior and 'em still got that spot?" He reluctantly followed him.

Rainbow grunted his way down to the bottom, whewed and turned around to face him. "Oh yeah, those niggas still got paws in that joint, but they done really fixed it up from back when you was out. They got a funny-styled nigga down with them on it now, but shit still be popping on the regular."

"Yeah, I heard a little something about it, but words out that the showcase spot is Magic City. Now that spot there is hot for a mug, dog, even way down there in the penitentiary."

"For real, yo."

"Hell yeah, for real," Sparkle said.

Rainbow nodded his head in agreement. "That's the place nowadays, for real, but our boy's spot keeping paper rolling, too. Hell, they even had a couple of video shoots up in that bitch—Outkast, Usher and a couple of other hot groups. It be popping, yo, on the real."

"Well, speak no more. Let's roll up in there, my nigga," Sparkle muttered as the train was pulling up. Just before the doors closed, they heard some voices hollering at them and looked up to see the hillbillies running down the escalator. It looked like the big one started tumbling down as the train pulled out. Rainbow and Sparkle shot those muthas some birds as the train wheeled out of their sight. "Ain't that one lovely sight; serves the bastard right causing me all that their pain," Rainbow said as he elbowed Sparkle in the side.

CHAPTER SEVENTEEN

Browsing Enemy Turf

*L*ess than five minutes later, they were pulling into the West End station. Rainbow was still walking with a slight limp, so Sparkle slowly walked beside him in case he needed his help.

In the distance they could hear the rat-a-tat-tat of Morehouse's marching band throwing down on some funky cadences. They looked at each other and started bobbing their heads, marching to the beat. For a brief moment, Sparkle even thought of going to watch some of those young tenderoni majorettes and cheerleaders bumping and grinding the air to the jazzy rhythm, but let the urge slip away.

He noticed that the parking lot seemed to be a lot bigger than he remembered. Then it dawned on him that the bank was no longer there. *Damn, a lot of shit done changed in the years since I left,* he thought, admiring the assortment of luxury cars.

As they was about to cross the street, he felt Rainbow nudge his shoulder. "How about going over to the Krispy Kreme and hook us up with some of those chocolate and strawberry donuts and a couple of milk shakes? I'll be at the bar kicking it with Big Bertha."

Sparkle leaned away frowning with his mouth turned down and gritted. "Damn, she still here, man?"

Rainbow gave him the kinda look that said, *Damn, ya'll really don't be hearing about shit down in that joint, do you?* "Shiiit, man, Bertha's been the one running the joint ever since Junior and Mack got shot up right after you got busted. I can't believe you ain't heard about that there, man."

Sparkle stopped and gave him a puzzled look across his shoulder. "Man, I must have just been starting that bit, way up in Jackson somewhere not to hear about that there, dog. Why you just now hipping me to that? You know them my niggas, dog."

Rainbow hunched his shoulders and spread his arms apart before he covered his mouth. "Hell, man, Mack's been…hey, we can finish this when you get back with the donuts, nigga. Right in now all I can think about is getting off of this bum-ass leg, man," he moaned, limping his way across the street waving him on to get the treats.

"Aight bet, I'll see ya in a sec," Sparkle said over his shoulder as he headed for the doughnut place on the corner of Lee Street. After getting a dozen of each kind of doughnut, a chocolate and a strawberry milk shake, he headed back to the club. When he elbowed his way through the first set of doors, the first thing he saw was a "Girls admitted free on Thursdays" sign with silhouettes of exotic dancers in various poses plastered on the wall behind a podium. It was an exact replica of a drawing he had done for Junior, when he and Mack had first converted the cafeteria-gas station combo into one of the hottest strip joints in the ward.

It took his eyes a moment to adjust to the red, yellow and black blinking lights when he entered the main room. He heard Rainbow's voice over the din of loud music and crazed customers. Then he spotted him at the bar gulping out of a pitcher of Olde English.

He gave Bertha a warm smile as he placed the boxes on the bar and sat down beside Rainbow. She didn't even take the time to acknowledge his smile before she reached over and ripped open one of the boxes and crammed a donut between her ruby-red lips.

He leaned over the counter as the creamy filling started oozing out the side of those juicy lips. "Godayum, Big Red, can you imagine what that cream oozing around those red lips of yours makes a nigga think about, mmmmmmh." He arched his brow in mock excitement.

He flinched when she bucked her eyes wide open and slammed her big mitts on the counter. "Well, I'll be damned, my baby boy Sparkle, when did you get up, you muthafucka," she yelled in her squeaky little girl voice, sprinkling his face and shirt with particles of dough and cream. It was a voice that in no way fit her size and attitude.

Sparkle jerked his head back trying to avoid as much of the crumb avalanche as he could, brushing at his face and clothes. "Damn, girl, whatcha trying to do, give me a doughnut cream bath or something? I feel ya being happy to see a nigga. I'm just as happy to see your big ass but what the fuck!" he yelled as he reached over the bar and mushed her face playfully.

She snarled and snapped her teeth at his fingers. "Nigga, fuck dat, give me a hug with your little skinny ass." Her eyes glittered with joy.

He rose up off of the stool and spread his arms, only to find himself gasping for breath as she bear-hugged the air right out of his chest and devoured his face and neck with a series of sloppy kisses.

He was finally able to squirm his way out of her bear-like grasp and grabbed a napkin out of a dispenser on the bar to wipe the wetness off his face and ear. "Thanks, Red, I really needed that, damn."

Smiling warmly she reached out and mushed his face and whined, "Aw, bastard, you better cherish that sugar there. Ain't too many niggas are worth that." She lowered her face and started to pout.

Sparkle erased the frown off of his face and reached out to grab both sides of her face and gently kissed her on the mouth. "Don't look so glum, sweet stuff. You one of my favorite hoes."

Like a puff of magic her expression changed as she looked at him under eyed, batted her lashes and frowned, "Baby, I ain't been nobody's ho since I got from under this dirty-ass yellow nigga here." She nodded at Rainbow and rolled her eyes.

Rainbow cocked his head and brow like he couldn't believe what he'd just heard. "Aw, come on, baby, you know you'll always have my heart." He gave her his brightest smile and squeezed his heart to emphasize his point.

She wasn't going for it and rolled her eyes again and mumbled, "Uh-huh, fuck you, Lah. Oh damn, it's Rainbow now, ain't it? Man, you change your name more than Erica Kane changes husbands."

"That's right, and your big, fine ass better keep in mind that I'm that nigga that you're gonna always love." He paused to rub the side of her face gently before he continued, hypnotizing her with his penetrating stare. "And gonna always belong to me."

"Yes, daddy," she said demurely before she snapped her head back. "Nigga, you wish, those days been long gone." She finished with a snake roll of her head and three finger pops.

Sparkle and Rainbow looked at each other and said in unison, "Damn." All three of them burst out laughing hard as hell.

After the laughter subsided, Sparkle nudged Rainbow in the side. "Yo, partner, go ahead and finish up that shit you was telling me about Junior and Mack."

A reluctant Rainbow took a deep breath and rubbed his hand up and down his face, then twisted his mouth to the side. "My nigga Mack's been in a wheelchair ever since and Junior survived, but he's all fucked up in his left arm and leg."

Sparkle sat there staring off into space as a frown slowly crept to his brow. The pain in his eyes couldn't even be measured. Rainbow reached across his body and started waving his hand back and forth in front of his face until he blinked a couple of times. "Where the niggas that done that shit, dog?"

Rainbow sat back, pinched his nose. "Hell, man, you can see dem niggas every time you pass the King station."

That look in his eyes told Sparkle what he had already concluded, but he said it anyway. "Six feet deep, huh?"

"Oh yeah, me and Duke was in on that one, but that dirty-ass punk Wyatt Earp caught some fed time before we could catch up to his ass. Last I heard he was up there in Marion on super max."

Bertha, who had been silent up until then, placed a tray of glasses she had been shining up under the counter and got in a little growl of her own. "I never did trust that dirty-ass sissy no how; especially from the way that he did my baby sister. I kept telling that stupid-ass bitch that he was a punk but she wasn't' hearing me. That is until she caught all that fucked-up time dealing with his sorry ass."

Rainbow quickly added, "I don't blame you one bit, baby. That sorry muthafucka done put a whole dorm of good niggas and hoes in the joint with all that snake-ass snitching he be doing."

Sparkle added his two cents' worth. "Uh-huh, as much dope as that bastard used to oil up, I don't see how he got away with that shit he do and niggas let him live. Somebody should have given his bitch ass a battery shot years ago. But you know what, somebody had to be behind that there because that's all that nigga does is dirty stuff for other niggas."

Rainbow interrupted him with an angry cough. "That's exactly what I was thinking when that shit went down. And then right after that, this nigga named Black Don appears out of nowhere from Miami and provides enough coke that he ends up as Mack and Junior's co-owners." His words were laced with plenty of venom.

"And don't forget about him digging roots into the 617 and the Checker Club," Bertha added angrily.

Sparkle leaned back against the bar listening to them until his attention was drawn to a little oriental sexpot, who had just joined three other girls on the circular stage. He looked behind himself on both sides because shawtie's slanted cat eyes were staring right at him. When she was sure that she had his full attention, she started rotating her little golden-hued hips like she was easing onto a dickhead.

Her eyes were glued to his as she worked her way around the girls to the pole and pressed her cute little ass against it. She reached behind her to pull her cheeks apart and arched her back so that her pussy was sliding along the pole. She continued to eye him seductively like it was meant only for him. She reached up behind her to grasp the pole and rubbed it like she was urging someone to fuck her harder. With her other hand, she started massaging her small breasts.

As he sat there mesmerized, her eyes suddenly turned into mere slits as her mouth formed into an "O" of pure lust. Her gyrations against the pole got harder and faster and then she put one, two and then three fingers in her tiny mouth. She started sucking on them as if she was draining the last drops of cum out of a throbbing dick.

Sparkle's eyes were hypnotized to her movements and the lust she was urging his way. He hardly noticed when his hand eased to his crotch as he started rubbing his aching dick. When she realized what he was doing, she began fucking the pole to the rhythm of his stroking. They were so into each other, there was no doubt that they were making love at a distance.

Suddenly her whole body started shaking and she started rubbing her pussy, faster and faster, her eyes locked on him the whole time. To them no one else existed in the room. When it was obvious that she had started nutting, he exploded all down his pants leg. She honed in on his dick jerking through his pants knowing that he had cum right along with her. With her nostrils flared in lust, she gyrated to the edge of the stage. She squatted right in front of him and pulled the crotch of her thong aside, inserted two fingers in her pussy and showed him the pussy juice he had caused to flow.

"Damn, dude, you aight?" Rainbow said as he shook Sparkle's shoulder.

Sparkle flinched from the unexpected contact and shook his head out of the sexual trance shawtie had put him in. "Man, who the fuck is this hot little bitch?"

Bertha, who had been enjoying the show herself, leaned across the bar and whispered in his ear, "That's my little buddy, Mercedes. She's something, ain't she? And she's digging on you too, man. I ain't never seen that little bitch get off like that for nary a nigga, for real, yo."

Sparkle couldn't keep from smiling as he watched her sexy little ass twist that tight little booty off the stage. She twisted half around to watch him until she bent the corner toward the dressing room area.

Right after she disappeared, his attention was drawn to a figure hobbling with the aid of a black cane around the circular stage. His emotions were laced with both elation and sadness as he watched his old buddy, draped in a gold silk outfit, struggling with each step. Despite the obvious pain he was in, his face was lit up with a bright smile.

"I thought I heard some clucking hens out here that sounded familiar. What's up, Sparkle, my man? I heard you'd graced these old bricks again. What's up, Lah? Ah damn, I forgot yo crazy ass is Rainbow now." Old slick-ass Junior pinched his nose, coughed a few times, sniffled and started laughing as he continued in a gravelly voice, "Nigga, you change your name more than I change my CD player."

"That's the same thing I just told his ass," Bertha hissed.

Junior stopped in front of them cocked sideways leaning on the cane and beaming all thirty-two. "Man, I heard you had risen. Why didn't you let a nigga know you was out? We could've thrown down in this bitch."

Sparkle hunched his shoulders and replied, "Hey, bro, what can I say? I got caught up catching up. Hell, you know I was gonna get around this way sooner or later."

Junior rubbed the stubble on his chin nodding to Sparkle's reply and sat down at the nearest table. Laid his cane against it and crossed his legs O.G. style. Then he reached into his pocket and lit up a Black and Mild cigar. "Your boy Duke was just in here the other night."

Rainbow snapped to attention and started scratching his neck. "Oh yeah, what was up with that?"

Junior turned his mouth down and looked around the room before he answered, "Uh-huh and big bro left some good blow on the house, dog. Ya'll niggas wanna go do a few rounds, you know, to sorta celebrate my nigga here getting out of the stir?"

Rainbow cocked his brow and looked at Sparkle, who in turn cocked his brow at Junior. "Nigga, please, after a day like we done had, where it at?"

Junior sprung out of the chair and started hobbling to the back. When he got halfway around the stage, he noticed that they hadn't moved. He looked over his shoulder frowning. "Well, come on then, what the fuck ya'll waiting for?" He continued hobbling his way around the stage, greeting some of the regular customers along the way.

They followed him down the corridor through a door adorned with pictures of gorgeous girls dancing nude and semi-nude in various sexy outfits. They passed through another door into a room full of mirrors and dressing stalls. There were six girls in different stages of dressing and doing their make-up thang for their routines. Nearly all of them were clucking so it was like a pen of hens.

Instead of the conversations slowing down, they were greeted with a chorus of sexy hi's and hellos as they passed through, on their way to a door of frosted glass that prevented folk from seeing whatever was going on inside.

Sparkle spotted Mercedes in the last stall while she was changing into her street clothes. She winked and licked her lips seductively as she eyed him through the mirror. He made eye contact with her and mouthed silently, "I'm gonna get your little sexy ass, for sho," as he gave her a one hundred-watt smile.

She shifted her petite body on the stool, bit down on her bottom lip and mouthed back at him, "Come on, I'm waiting," and flared her nose like she could hardly wait.

Now wasn't the time, though, so he nodded and followed Rainbow and Junior inside the door.

The special décor in the room drew an immediate smile from Sparkle as he radared the area. The spacious office was laid out with a black cushioned circular sofa that nearly occupied the entire wall. The floor was made up of black marble tile with gold flakes that gave it a glittering effect. Behind a black ivory desk sat old man Mack sitting in a cushioned wheelchair chomping on a stinky cigar, blowing halos.

When they stepped in, he peeked up over the rim of a pair of oval red-tinted glasses and grimaced. "Well, I'll be damned if it ain't two of the muthafucking amigos. What's up, fellas?"

Rainbow smiled and responded quickly, "Just browsing the neighborhood scoping for some potential vics. Looks like we done ran into a pretty good pair with ya'll old fools."

"Yep, we heard that there was some good money snatching around these here hills, so are ya'll going to give it up nicely, or do we gotta go gangster up in this bitch?" Sparkle added his brand of humor with a brilliant smile.

Mack wheeled his way from behind the desk and spread his arms out wide. "My nigga, my nigga, feels good to see your narrow ass, boy. Godayum, you looking good, son. Whatcha doing, how ya doing?"

Sparkle responded quickly, "Just getting in where I can fit in."

Rainbow chimed in, "Hey, man, we been out there reliving old times downtown, know what I'm saying?"

Junior recognized that look on his boy's face and patted him on the back. "Mmmh, the way I taught ya, huh, baby boy?"

Rainbow caught his hand as it rose to his shoulder. "Hell, is there any other way? Of course, we did it like you taught, old man."

Mack started scratching the back of his ears. "I betcha

some foolish feeling somebody's out there mad as all holy hell looking for ya'll two snakes."

"Probably is, probably is, but we need to be hunting their asses because the bastards tried to play a playa. Sons of bitches had more than they said from the start. You reckon they didn't trust a nigga or something? Ain't that a bitch?"

They all looked at one another and burst out laughing.

After the laughter had petered down, Rainbow took a seat on the couch and pulled out the green money bag they had scooped off the vics and started leafing through the wads. He counted aloud until he got to three g's and handed it to Sparkle. Then he licked his finger and continued counting the rest. When he finished, his face balled up into a knot of anger and he recounted.

Afterward, he frowned in Sparkle's direction. "Aw, hell naw, Spark, we got to go back downtown and kick those muthafuckas' asses. The bastards done shorted us about twenty dollars."

A flustered Sparkle snatched out the wad he had folded in his pocket and recounted it. Feigning anger, he snarled, "That slick-ass country hick, he's got some nerve, my nigga. That was some Oscar winning Hollywood shit they paid for. You just don't get good acting like that every day."

Rainbow's nose flared as he agreed, "You damn right, partner; that was some fucked-up shit they tried to pull on a nigga who be out there giving it his best, know what I'm saying?"

They burst out laughing again. Junior joined them on the couch holding his side. Mack wiped the tears out of his eyes and placed a crystal ball on the desk top, unscrewed the top half off and took out what looked like at least two ounces of that pinkish blow. "Dudes, our boy Duke says that this be some new shit that he copped on his last trip down the way. They be calling this shit Peruvian golden flake. See how it glitters when you tilt it from side to side. The best shit I've ever had, straight up."

Sparkle got up and walked over to the desk and started to fondle the package. "It's that good, huh. Check this out, dog, makes you kind of wonder why he didn't say anything about it when he was with us last night," he said as he looked over at Rainbow.

"But he did say something about it. Yo ass was too busy getting triple teamed by the girls. Shit, you wouldn't have heard a bomb go off," Rainbow joked.

Junior started tapping his cane on the floor impatiently. Rainbow took the package out of Sparkle's hand, started fondling with it himself as he walked over and kicked his cane. He spat, "What, nigga, what?"

Junior slapped the cane against his ankle. "Man, what you babysitting that stuff for? Let's do this." He hobbled over to a picture of MLK and the Kennedy brothers on the wall, unhooked it off the wall and started working a combination on a circular wall safe. Then he reached inside and lifted out a brown leather shaving bag, hobbled back to the desk and placed the bag on it.

Mack unzipped it as Junior went to the bathroom to

get a glass of water. Then he pulled out a couple of test tubes and hypos soaking in a Ziploc bag full of alcohol, as well as a couple of hypos still in their wrappings. He placed the items on the desk. "Which way ya'll niggas wanna go? Help yourselves. I prefer oiling myself." He started scooping some of the powder into a big silver spoon.

Sparkle waited until Junior had registered a hit before he reached into the kit and took out one of the tubes and a baggie of baking soda. He scooped a healthy lump of the coke, along with some of the baking soda and water, into the tube. Then he shook it up hard and started to put a lighter to it. Junior tapped him on the elbow with the cane. "Yo, Sparkle baby, try this mixture here in it." He handed him a pill bottle full of liquid.

Sparkle eyeballed the bottle for a moment before he lowered the lighter, arched his eyebrows and asked, "What the hell is this, soldier?" as he rotated the bottle in his hand.

Junior retrieved the bottle and poured some of the liquid into the test tube. "It's Seagram's gin and lemon extract. Your boy Duke recommended that; it's supposed to remove all of the impurities out of the coke, increase the size and make it rock hard all at the same time."

Rainbow, who had been angling his head back and forth to get the best view of what they were doing, asked, "For real, yo?"

Junior eyed him for a second before he took the tube out of Sparkle's hand and put the lighter to it. "Uh-huh, shit works, too. Try it both ways and see for yourself."

Sparkle lifted the tube out of his hand and dumped a big rock out on the table. He then rocked up the same amount in the usual way with water and baking soda. After he was finished, he dumped the rock beside the other one for a comparison. After watching them nod in approval, he chipped off a small piece off of each rock and passed it to them.

They lit up one behind the other. After hitting the one with the so-called special mixture, Rainbow rushed straight to the bathroom and threw up. He came out a moment later wiping sweat off of his forehead. "Owee, whew, man, that stuff is the bomb, for real."

There was no way that Junior could let him off so lightly, so he spat jokingly, "Go ahead, try a bigger piece the next time. I love the way ya'll wannabe hard-ass niggas be stepping beyond what you can stand," just before he injected the plunger into his vein. He didn't even get the chance to jack the plunger twice before his eyes flew wide open. He jumped up, speed hobbling to the toilet, too, yanking the hypo out of his arm on the way.

Rainbow, Sparkle and Mack rolled with laughter as they listened to him gagging over and over again for what seemed like minutes. Soon he returned to the room drenched with sweat like he had just come out of the shower.

"You aight, dog? Looks like your old ass overdid it yourself." Sparkle said as Junior hobbled to the couch and flopped down with his legs spread far apart. After taking a few deep breaths, he started wiping the sweat off of his face. "Wooooo, weeeee, man, that's it right there; that's it, for sho. What was that you called this shit? Where in the hell did he hunt some shit down that potent? I thought I was going to die in this bitch for a second there," he wheezed between gasps of breath.

"You right, Sparkle; that nigga could've or should've let ya'll know what the deal was with this here. A nigga could die fucking with too much of this here. Mmmm-mmppphhh and ya'll was with his fat ass last night. Hell yeah, he should've let ya'll know about this here."

Mack took a small blast. "Man, he was on his way down there when he dropped by about a half-hour before ya'll showed up here."

Rainbow was finally able to straighten himself out enough to join in. "So that's what he was in so big a rush to get to." He paused to look at Sparkle, who arched his eyebrows in confusion as to why big boy hadn't come out on the real with them while they were together. "Dog, that's why I left the room earlier than I wanted to, because he wanted me to go over Cynt's house with him. But I knew that I couldn't do that, not with you waiting on me."

Sparkle took a blast with one of the glass shooters, then brushed a hand across his head. "Damn, I should've known it was something because you wouldn't have just left me like you did unless something was up." He didn't really want to feel that way about his boy but he had to wonder why Duke was acting all secretive.

CHAPTER EIGHTEEN

Violet and Mercedes: Wives-in-Law

As they were getting into their groove, there was a sharp rapping on the door, followed by the sound of a mumbling feminine voice. "Aight ya'll bastards, let a ho in this bitch." She began shaking the knob noisily when no one answered.

Junior, who was right in the middle of getting a third jack off the hypo, cocked his head to the door and growled, "Mack, let that old loud-ass bitch in, dog. Damn, she be fucking a nigga's high up with all that banging."

Mack, who was plucking his arm, trying to find a fresh vein to go in, looked at him over the rim of his glasses and said angrily, "Shit, I'm the one in the wheelchair. Get yo ass up and hobble over there and get it yourself, damn."

Junior snatched the hype out of his arm, frowned at his dog and started hobbling over to get the door. He looked back at them and then whispered through the crack in the door, "Damn, 'V,' can't you see that a nigga be busy up in here? Why you think we got the mutha-fucking door closed?"

She snapped on him immediately, "Why the fuck you

think I knocked on it for? I must have some business with your dirty ass, nigga." He only got the chance to crack it a nudge before she barged her way past him with a pair of large shopping bags tucked under each arm. Her hips swaying out of control, she sashayed over to the desk and dumped the contents out of one of the bags on top of it. "I know that ya'll cheap-ass bastards wanna see some of ya'll girls in some of this fly-ass shit here." Then she spun around like she was a grand dame at the ball and braced her ass and both hands on the desk.

It took her a few seconds before it dawned on her who all was sitting on the couch. When she did, she folded her arms across her chest and said directly to Sparkle, "Damn, player, seems like everywhere that I be you be; looks like we headed for a collision course."

"Looks that way, don't it," Sparkle replied, feeling like all eyes were on him. They were, with Rainbow being the main nosey body.

She batted her eyelashes at him daintily, smiled and then reverted her attention toward Mack as she started taking items out of the other bag, "Check out the tags, man. Ain't nothing there under three hundred dollars, high-quality stuff as usual."

Junior reached around her to pick up one the flimsy garments. "Yeah right, like we don't know that you keep boxes of these tags at your crib. Come on, 'V,' this be us, yo."

She snatched the garment out of his hand and pushed

the tag up to his eyes. "Well, check this stitching out, smart ass, Ain't nobody got no machine to baste tags in there like that 'cept the factory where they was made."

Mack continued to sift through several items as he arched one eyebrow at her. "Uh-huh, like your slick ass don't come up with new twists all the time with your good-playing ass."

She picked up one of the outfits and started fondling it as she leaned over the desk and gave him one of her warmest smiles. "Naw, dog, for real, man, you know how I keep it real with ya'll. Shit here be the real thang, right off the rack real. I just hit that real high-quality store next to the Peachtree Plaza, taint nothing but Victoria's Secret stuff up in there." She continued to spread the stuff across the desk. Finally she sat a hip on the edge of the desk and added, "Tell ya what, that there is ten outfits, guaranteed to have these freaky mutha-fuckas jacking on they shit while the girls flaunt the stage in all this hot-ass gear. Give me a c-note for each of them."

Mack leaned back in his chair and held his hands up in surrender. "Whoa, godayum 'V,' where you got the gun hidden because this has got to be the best robbery technique that a nigga done come through with in a century. I thought we were your friends, girl."

She certainly wasn't about to go for that lame-ass game there. So she brightened her smile another hundred degrees, circled the desk and put her arm across his shoulder. She pressed her cheek next to his and said sweetly, "Baby boo, don't be so hard on your peeps, playa. You know damn well she got to make some groceries."

"Uh-huh, yeah, and I guess it's mainly for that over-sized youngun of yours JoJo."

There it was, the opening she had been on alert for. "Aaaah, you do love your godchild, don'tcha?" she purred.

"Of course I love that big-headed boy, but look what that nigga T-boy did with that stuff you sent us that last time."

She leaned away from him and frowned. "Come on, Mack, you know that nigga switched that stuff on his own. I would never tell you some quality stuff is on the way and it not be what I say it is. That fool played both of us on that one there and you know it. And fuck that nigga T-boy from now on. His half-slick ass played me fucked up on some other stuff just the other day too. Come on, we both thought that fool was aight." She pouted and sat on the edge of the desk.

Junior started laughing from the couch. "Nigga, can't be that much of a chump if he played both of ya'll; especially you, the queen."

Violet tooted her nose up at his sarcasm. That Junior always found a way to pinch her last nerve.

Mack gave a short snort, pinched his nose and said, "Tell you what, V-girl."

She laid her head on her palm and whined, "Oh-oh, when this nigga hits me with the V-girl, you can bet some bullshit is about to follow. Go ahead, tell it."

Mack pyramided his arms on the desk, then rested his chin in the crock of his hands. "Naw, baby girl, this here is on the real. See that shit there on the table?"

She looked at the package on the coffee table, got up and walked over to get a closer look before she looked back at him over her shoulder. "Man, that look like some of that new shit floating around, so what's the deal, yo. I have never seen any pink stuff like that before."

Junior raised himself up on the cane and leaned on her shoulder. "That's because ain't none of it done really hit the ATL before now. Dat nigga Duke hit us off with that the other day, told us to spread the word around to our folks. But shit be so good we just been doing a little private hitting, didn't want that nigga Don asking us all kinds of stupid questions. You know how that youngun and his wild-ass crew can go on the silly for little or nothing sometimes, thinking he's the only one who is supposed to have the good shit and all. But fuck that, go ahead, girl; take yourself a good hit of that piece our boy Sparkle just cooked up."

She wasn't used to tight-ass nigga Junior offering a bitch anything but a hard time, so she was more than a little shocked when she realized that he was dead serious about her getting one. But fuck that, she sure didn't have to be told twice. So before he could change his mind, she reached into her bra and extracted a gold straight shooter, picked up what amounted to a good dime rock, hit it and just like the rest of them rushed to the bathroom hurling and gagging. And just like Rainbow she came out sweating raindrops, gasping, "Uh-huh, oh yeah, that be some real shit there, boy, for sho."

After she stammered back to the couch fanning her face, Mack wheeled himself over to face her. "Tell you what, fly gal, we'll put you a grand worth in hundred-dollar slabs in a Ziploc and take all of those cheap-ass outfits off your hands, since you went through so much trouble calling yourself looking out for us."

She squinted her face up and cocked her head to the side as if she was really contemplating the offer. Everybody in the room knew damn well that she was going to go for it.

One look at that glitter in her eyes and Mack was sure. He wheeled back over to the desk and picked up one of the skimpy outfits and displayed it for the fellas.

Hell, she knew she was going for it, but she took her time anyway. She purred in a doped-up hazy voice, "Sounds about right, but make sure that ho Pocahontas gets that red sequined one because I was thinking about her when I got it. Also because she made me promise to get her one."

Mack smiled as he picked up the outfit and started fingering it. "Oh yeah, I can see her bubble butt getting really funky in this one here. Whatcha think, boys?"

All three of them niggas hollered, "Hell yeah," before it even got out of his mouth good.

Junior hobbled over to pick up a couple of them. "Uh-huh, them horny-ass girls be causing a lot of nut busting with these thangs here." He looked over at Violet conspicuously, "You sho your slick ass ain't hooked these things from one of these other shake-a-booty clubs around here. We don't want no other bitches trying to stir up no bullshit around here, know what I'm saying?"

"Fuck you, Junior," she said before mumbling, "That's why yo short ass crippled up now, always throwing shit around."

He whirled on her growling, "Whadda fuck you say, ho?"

She blinked innocently. "Taint said a thang, dog, ain't said a thang."

"I thought so, bitch."

"I got yo bitch leaning on that there cane, bastard."

"What?"

"Nothing, man, nothing. Go ahead, handle your biz, dude."

"Mmmphh, I thought so," he said before he walked back over to the coffee table, snatched the dope up and went to the desk to start scooping some of the coke onto a digital scale. Mack replaced the outfits in the bags and wheeled over to a closet that was not even noticeable if one wasn't actually looking for it.

When she got the bag of dope from Junior, she rolled her eyes at him and sat beside Sparkle on the couch. She purred, "How about rocking us up a good chunk of this, baby," as she wiggled her hips up against him.

He smiled and said coolly, "Taint got a problem with

that there, sweetie, no problem at all." He walked over to the desk and picked up the bottle of special mixture and shook it at her. "This here's some special liquid some of my dogs claimed that they hipped me to. I came up with it but you know how some niggas are, want to be on top of everything." He looked around the room smiling as he started putting it altogether.

She leaned forward on the couch. "What is it?" as she reached for the bottle.

He arched his brow and waggled his finger as he sat back down beside her. Then he winked at the guys. "Can't give away all my secrets, sweetie, but it's guaranteed to swell yo shit up bigger and harder too. Just take your nigga's word for it, okay."

She sat back on the couch feigning dejection, folded her arms and snorted. "Go ahead and do your thang, playa."

He nodded to her show of respect and proceeded to rock up several twenty pieces, broke off a nice chunk and put fire to it to get it started before he passed it to her to finish up. Then he leaned back and said, "Girl, if you gonna be hanging out with me, you got to drain the stem. With me it's a straight trip to Scotticville."

When she hesitated, he sat up and reached for the shooter, which she handed to him right away. *Good girl, she's showing that I'm the man in front of these niggas; I like that,* Sparkle thought while he put fire to the shooter and sucked until there was no smoke filtering through the tube. Then he hung his head on the back of the couch and slowly exhaled the smoke in wispy halos.

Violet waited until he was totally relaxed before she said, "Damn, baby boy, I ain't used to killing it all on one draw."

He sat up, put his hand over his mouth and fought off the urge to hurl before he gave her a stern look. "Well, get used to it, sweetheart, because I'm a go-for-broke type of guy and my honey has got to be the same way, you feel me?" He wiped the sweat off his forehead.

"Okay, I'll try it your way, If I go out make sure my boy JoJo kisses my coffin," she said shyly and waited for him to fix her up another hit.

"That's my girl." He smiled and started fixing her one.

She lit it up, eyeing him the whole time as she sucked up the whole hit. The smoke was starting to thin out when she pulled off and grabbed her heart. While she was exhaling, he dove straight on her mouth and slid his tongue deep into her throat. He reached down to grasp her by the hips to pull her closer to him. She willingly melted right into him. When he finally pulled back, she was sweating and gasping for air. Her chest was still heaving as she wheezed, "Owee nigga, whatcha trying to do to this old lady? Godayum." Her eyes were filled with lust.

He got all up in her face, so close that their noses were pressed together. "Trying to pin down a star bitch; you got a problem with dat?" Then he grabbed her by both arms, leaned arm's length back and added, "You got enough left in you, old gal, to go on a joy ride with a wild nigga?" He looked straight through her eyes into her soul.

She could only sit there, mouth agape, staring at him all gooey-eyed for nearly thirty odd seconds before she lowered her gaze. "You sure you want an old bucking mule like me. Because I can be a handful."

He pinned her with a squinted gaze. "I'm so sure that I can see the future." He licked his lips. "Girl, you gonna be mine for life."

"For life," she mumbled as her eyes misted over like girls do when they're in the presence of their man.

"For life, baby, for muthafucking life," he repeated as he kissed her lightly on her eyelids.

She smiled sweetly. "Hmmph, I think I'd like that."

"You will, baby, you can bet your sweet ass you will…"

Rainbow mushed him upside the head and spat, "Damn, ain't this a bitch. Aight, mack daddy, put a lid on that shit."

Junior joined in, "Yeah, cut out all that mushy shit."

Mack added, "Ya'll horny muthafuckas need to go get a damn room somewhere, whaddafuck."

Sparkle popped out of his mystifying gaze and got up off of the couch, watching her eyes as they followed the rise in his crotch. *Oh yeah, I got me a real stallion now. Let's do this, nigga, let's do this.* He reached down to help her up, as he looked at his boys and said, "Yo fellas, ya'll have got to excuse me." He paused to jack up his pants. "I got some ho banging to do. We out."

She stood up and leaned into him, fitting like a glove under his arm as she looked at them and smiled. "What can a bitch say; I'm caught, ya'll." Then she patted him on the ass. "Let's go, stud, yo ass got some serious digging to do, believe that. And I'm ready to catch all that shit." She shoved the bag of coke into his jacket pocket. She leaned away from him and added, "Damn, baby boy, you gonna do something about this K-mart gear, ain'tcha. Whew." She pulled on the jacket as they headed for the door.

Rainbow yelled after them as the door was closing, "Call me, nigga, uh and niggette, when ya'll come up for air."

Sparkle looked over Violet's head and winked at his boy. "Don't know for sho when that'll be, dog."

Rainbow waved him off as Junior hollered, "Whenever, whatever, man!"

Mack got his jab in as well. "Yeah right, nigga like ya'll two old-ass dogs got a lot of fuck game left in those worn-down-ass bodies. Anyways, holla atcha, dog and uh, doggette."

While he was closing the door he overheard Junior whisper, "Man, ain't that a bitch. I've been trying to hook that super-boosting ass bitch for two, three decades and this nigga pulls her ass with the blink of a muthafucking eye, damn."

"Aw, stop playa hating, nigga," one of the others teased.

"I was just saying, damn."

He closed the door on the remainder of the conversation and looked down at Violet. With his arm draped over her shoulder, he smiled. "Should've tried a little harder, huh, baby?"

She reached across her body to clasp his fingers and smiled too. "Sure should've, then again he never would have made it here, not enough player juice for me."

"Daaammmnnn, and he thinks he's the player of the year type of nigga, I guess not. But fuck that; he too late now for sure because the love of your lifetime has got you now."

She looked up at him with glittering eyes. "Lifetime?"

He kissed her on the forehead. "Yep, 'cause you gonna love me harder than you've ever loved a nigga before."

She batted her long lashes at him teasingly. "You sure about that; I've had some helluva playas in my day, fool."

He pressed her tighter to him. "None like me, sweetie, none like me."

She reached up to mush his nose. "Whatever you say, stud." She smiled before they damn near walked over Mercedes. They both staggered back slightly to look down at the miniature vixen. Yep even Violet, all five-feet-three of her stood high over the little Asian doll, who barely touched the five-foot mark, if that.

Like a little puppet doll on a string she pushed her little hips out to bump each of them in turn before she stood back on her legs with her hands on her hips. She smiled up at them innocently. "Can I go, too?" she said in a little girl's voice with broken English.

The idea of ménage à trois certainly caught Sparkle's interest right off the bat and he didn't hesitate to show it as he smiled back and forth between them.

Even though Violet was a little surprised by the situation, she gathered herself rather quickly, leaned away slightly, eyed the little vixen under eyed and licked her lips in anticipation. There was something exciting about the little bitch's boldness. She admired that but she still wasn't about to share her first experience with Sparkle with any woman.

Out of her peripheral vision, she saw and then felt the excitement stirring up in Sparkle as well. She couldn't really blame him; what man could resist getting his freak on with two women? So she contemplated briefly on whether to play the selfish bitch or be the playette she knew she was. From years of experience dealing with street niggas, she knew it would be better to be the playette. What other choice did she really have? Dude would expect her to play the game and that was what she would do.

There was a bright side to the situation as well. It had been a while since she'd had a protégé to whom she could teach her boosting and other skills of the game. Smiling inwardly, she stood in front of Sparkle to show the little thing that she was the boss bitch and smiled demurely at her as the playette in her took over. She arched one eyebrow. "Sweetie, as bad as I want to grab your little ass and bite you on the neck, suck all the blood out of your ass and shit"—she paused to fake a growl before she licked her lips and winked—"and other things, we, me and him, have got something that we need to take care of right now."

Sparkle took over from there as her reached out to lift her chin up. "Baby doll, I know that you feel me like I feel you but mama here is sorta like a shot caller when it comes to our little family, so, wait right here for a second."

He unloosed his arm from around Violet's shoulder and went back into the office. He walked straight up to Rainbow and said, "Mack daddy, I got a little problem out here and I need your help on how to deal with it."

Rainbow got off one more jack of the hypo stuck in his arm, exhaled deeply, then wiped the sweat that started to pour down his face. "What's up, dog? Spill that shit."

Sparkle rotated his shoulders before he looked away and sighed heavily, "My nigga, that littler hot honey who just fucked me on the pole, she uh…"

Rainbow shifted in his seat and wiped his hand over his mouth. "Yeah, what about her?"

Sparkle licked his lips, stared at Mack and Junior and then turned his attention back to Rainbow. "Dog, little honey done just chose me, right outside the door, right in front of Violet."

Rainbow pinched his nose and rubbed his chin. "The little oriental doll?"

Sparkle nodded. "Yep."

Before Rainbow could answer Junior stood up. "You talking about little Mercedes in the pink cowgirl outfit?"

Mack looked up from registering a hit on his forearm. "What?" He shook his head and added, "Man, you asking for trouble with that one there."

Rainbow's head snapped around like that bitch Linda Blair in *The Exorcist* and eyed both of them, then blinked several times. "Why, ya'll niggas got a problem with my boy pulling that bitch or something?"

Junior started massaging his neck and spat, "Naw nigga, ya'll play that shit the way you want to, I'm just saying that little package has got Black Don's nose like wide muthafucking open. You can drive two, three tractor-trailers up that bitch when it come to that little ho."

Rainbow sprung from the seat like a jack-in-the-box, jacked his pants up and spat, "What the fuck that got to do with my nigga here? Shit, when a ho chooses a nigga, the loser nigga can't do a damn thing but give up respect for that."

Mack unwrapped the rubber tie from around his arm and picked up a bucket that was beside the desk and hurled into it. Then he took a rag out of his drawer to wipe his mouth. "True that, soldier, but that silly nigga ain't about honoring no rules, dog. All I'm saying is that I don't really think that little bitch is worth the shit you got to go through dealing with that clown."

Junior pulled off the shooter to throw his two cents'

worth in. "Hell, stud, that little ho just learned how to work the pole. She ain't all that if you ask me."

Sparkle frowned at him. "Come on, man, you got to be bull-shitting me on that one, the way she put it down on me out there."

Mack, who couldn't believe these niggas were tripping on that little bitch, jumped in. "Say what, my nigga, that was probably her second time doing that shit on it and that's for real, yo."

Rainbow snatched the shooter out of Junior's hand and started stuffing it with coke before scratching the back of his ear and sniffled. "Shit, ya'll, what that there tells me is that baby girl is really into my boy here. Yep, that's what it's telling me." He smiled an evil smile and lit up the rock. He really hated when so-called players hated on other players when they had pulled off stunts they weren't capable or willing to do themselves.

Sparkle ignored that bullshit they were saying and turned his full attention to Rainbow. "Yeah dog, I feel that shit too, but the problem is that I just pulled the Queen Bee. Shit, I ain't even tapped that ass there yet." He sat down on the couch and leaned back for a second before he continued, "Okay, feel me on this, Bow, I'm going to… Fuck it, I'll be right back." He spun away from them and left the office. It was time to face the girls.

Not wasting any time he pulled Mercedes up against him. "Check this out, little mama, you mine now. Fuck that nigga Don. You done chose me; that's that as far as

I'm concerned." He waited for her to nod yes and added, "But right now I've got to take care of some business with Mrs. V here, who's, by the way, gonna be your mama from here on out."

The girls looked at each other, surprised at what Sparkle had just said, but neither showed any sign of objection. They seemed quite cool with it. Picking up on their vibes like a real pro, he quickly added, "So, little angel, you gonna go with my buddy Rainbow until me and Violet—aaah, your mama—handle this thing we was about to do." He reached down and held her little face in his palms. "You with me on this, baby doll?"

A wave of sadness washed over her face as she mumbled, "But I want to go with ya'll. I wanna be with you," she said in her broken English twang.

"And you will, sweetie," Violet intervened as she pulled her to her side. "Don't worry about a thing. We gonna take good care of you, baby, okay?" she added in a motherly voice, then gave her a hug.

All Sparkle could do was smile as he saluted the player in Violet, then he put his arm around Mercedes' shoulder and walked her back to the office. He walked her straight up to Rainbow, who was looking back and forth between Junior and Mack. "Sweetie, this here is my main man Rainbow, I want you to hang with him until me and Violet come and get you, okay?"

She looked up at Rainbow shyly and then at Mack and Junior. "Ya'll not mad at me, are you?"

Mack looked at Junior, who had his eyes shut trying to figure out how he was going to explain this shit to that crazy-ass nigga Don. Mack finally said, "Baby girl, you know who you want to be with. Hell, all I can say is that you have to be you, so that's what you do; be yourself and yourself wants to be with my man Sparkle here. Don't even worry about that nigga Don. His ass will get over it. Fuck him."

Rainbow stood up bravely and pulled her to the side. "Fuck that nigga. Ya'll can tell him that I got her. His ass knows better than to approach me with that bullshit."

Sparkle patted his boy on the shoulder and pined, "Shiiit, that's that then, I'll catch ya'll boys later. I'm out of here." Then he leaned over and kissed Mercedes lightly on the forehead. "I'll see you in a short, okay, sweetie?"

She nodded sweetly and he split to rejoin Violet in the hallway. She was all smiles and melted right into his side like she belonged there all the time.

CHAPTER NINETEEN
The Action Heats Up

Beverly was at odds with herself with what to do about that nigga Sparkle. She knew that deep down she couldn't keep evading the inevitable. The same way that she had found a way to get with Rainbow, she could have just as easily gotten with him. But something was holding her back. Was she afraid that she was still madly in love with him? Hell, who was she trying to fool? Of course she was, had always been and probably always would be. So what was she so afraid of? It wasn't like he didn't know it. So why was he ducking her as well? She was sort of lost in those thoughts when the counter girl interrupted her reverie, "Will there be anything else I can get for you, Miss?" she chimed as she finished ringing up her purchases.

"Huh?" Beverly blinked a few times to bring herself back to the present and said with a bright smile, "Oh, excuse me, my mind was way out yonder, but no, that'll be all but could you please wrap a couple of them croissants in a napkin for me." *Oh my God, where is my mind;, what's wrong with me*? "Could you put one of them on a paper plate for me? I think I'll just eat one here right quick."

Smiling gracefully, she picked up the plate and ordered a small cup of cappuccino and took a seat in the rear of the Krispy Kreme. She was about to bite into her croissant when she noticed a familiar car pull into the fenced-in parking lot of the MARTA station across the street.

She recognized the driver immediately as Lt. Woo. But what really drew her attention was how animated she was in the conversation she was having with her passenger. It was someone that she wasn't familiar with but that didn't really matter. Beverly could tell that Woo was upset. And the passenger was obviously scared. Her police instincts automatically wondered why. Then again it may have been one of her snitches; every police officer had their lot of them. Yeah, that's probably what it was and she was using scare tactics to gather some information. But for some reason it didn't seem right. There was something odd that she couldn't put her finger on.

On the other hand what was she doing parked near the club where her three amigos frequented? Why was she putting them in the same thought with what she was watching? Was it her intuition telling her to check things out further? Those thoughts and others crossed her mind as she sipped on her cappuccino and settled back to observe.

Unbeknownst to Beverly, there was someone watching her watching Lt. Woo. The occupant in the dark blue sedan in the parking lot of the West End mall placed his cigarette in the ashtray and adjusted his binoculars to study her more closely.

It wasn't that RJ had been trailing her; he happened to see her entering the Krispy Kreme as he was departing the Pep Boys after buying some auto supplies. He couldn't really explain why he had chosen to spy on the chief at that moment. And when he noticed that her attention was directed at a red Mustang in the MARTA parking lot, he got that much more inquisitive and turned the binoculars that way as well.

Seeing Woo preoccupied in what seemed like a heated conversation, obviously with one of her informants, didn't surprise him at all. Where she was doing it did, though. It was just too close to the club to be a coincidence as far as he was concerned. He had invested too much into their secretive drug enterprise at the club to have that little bitch nosing around. He smiled evilly as his attention flipped back and forth between the lot and the donut shop, fully curious why two extremely ambitious police officers were in the area. As he watched them with ever-rising concern, he punched a set of numbers on the cell phone. When an unfamiliar female voice answered, his first instinct was to hang up. He was too anxious to find out what the holdup was with the furniture he needed to furnish the condos that had recently been built. Arrangements had already been made to get rid of the hijacked furniture rig. And paying the driver extra for having to wait was out of the question.

The timetable was getting too close for comfort, so throwing caution to the wind he said, "Could I please talk to Al? Well, do you know when he will be available? No, I don't want to talk to anyone else, just tell him to get in touch with Mr. Tombs as soon as possible. Oh yeah and make sure that you tell him that it's quite urgent that he do so. Thank you." Hanging up without waiting for a reply, he clicked off the scrambler. Always being cautious was his number one motto.

Lighting up a cigarette he noticed that the occupant in the car with Woo had gotten out. Moments later she was sprinting across the street to the club. The look on the girl's face really piqued his curiosity.

Once the girl disappeared into the club, his attention reverted back to the chief, who was still calmly observing the scene as well. He wondered if she was as curious as he was why Woo didn't pull away after the girl had left. Was her reason for being there other than regular police business? Or could it be that the little bitch was in some kind of an affair? Especially since he had never seen her in any kind of a relationship with a man, there was certainly the possibility that she was into women. He wished that he had noticed her earlier; maybe there was some freaky stuff that could have been observed. That would surely be some ammunition to be used against her in the future, if it became necessary. One never knew when or how they could use a go-getter like her. And a go-getter she surely was. That, he had no doubt about at all.

Maybe, just maybe he had better keep a closer eye on the chief as well. Being near the top of the list to replace her in case anything went awry was something to consider. There was enough at stake to think about all the possibilities and he would gladly step on whoever got in his way to the next step up the ladder.

He continued to watch anxiously as the chief got out of her seat when Woo pulled out of the parking lot. He wondered briefly if he should follow her following Woo. But she veered in the opposite direction down Lee Street. Something in the back of his mind told him to follow one of them. His dilemma was which one.

✠ ✠ ✠

Even though she didn't see any immediate danger, she felt it. She'd always relied on her razor-sharp instincts to survive in the harsh world of law enforcement. As she passed the East Point city limit sign, her thoughts drifted back to the events that had occurred.

Lt. Woo had parked under the MARTA rail line on Lee Street across the street from the club and lowered the visor to take a pack of Newport cigarettes from under a rubber band. As she pushed in the car's lighter, she smiled across the seat at Crystal, a jet-black version of Beyoncé. She reached into the pack and removed a perfectly rolled blunt of reefer and cocaine and lit it up. *I wonder what the high and mighty Chief Johnson would say if she knew about this. Fuck it, a bitch has got to have some kind of secret pleasure.* After sucking up a long drag, she passed the blunt to Crystal and said, "Whooosh, whoosh, hmm, dat-a be some good-a shit there-a, home girl."

Crystal harrumphed her way through a couple of long tokes and passed the joint back to the little Vietnamese, who waved it away and said, "Naw-a, baby girl, enjoy-a yourself. You can-a duck that joint there, do that shit-a later on."

Not quite knowing how to react to her sudden generosity, Crystal pinched her nose between fingers that were glittering with recently done designer nails, sucked up some more of the smoke and purred in a squeaky voice, "Taint no problem with that, home girl, no problem at all."

Woo narrowed her eyes as she laid her head on the steering wheel, licked her lips before she smiled at her and said, "Hmmm, I can-a still taste-a your musky-a pussy, aaaah." She took her head off the steering wheel and reached across the seat to pick up Crystal's left hand between both of hers and placed them in her lap on the top of her pussy mound. Crystal felt an immediate tingle run up her arm as the heat radiated from Woo's lap. She shivered when Woo leaned across the seat and said, "You-a know dat-a you are-a special to-a me, don'tcha?"

"Of course I do, sweetie," Crystal murmured as she gently removed her hand from Woo's grasp and pouted her lips. She ducked the blunt, wrapped it in some tissue and deposited it in the bra of the costume concealed under her leather jacket and repeated, "Of course I do."

Without any warning, Woo's face suddenly hardened as she said sternly, "That's a good-a, that's a good, that's why I need-a you to prove-a that I am special to-a you too." She retrieved her hand and placed it back in her lap. "You-a understand me?"

Crystal answered with a shy nod.

Woo continued, "You-a stay-a real wid-a me and I-a stay-a real wid you," as she put the hand to her mouth and gently kissed it.

Crystal was confused with another sudden change of her attitude and nodded again, mumbling, "No doubt, no doubt."

Eyeing her intensely, Woo licked between her fingers and scraped her teeth along her knuckles. Her tone got harsher. "Then you-a shouldn't-a have a problem finding out-a what I-a asked you-a to then?"

Crystal felt a terrifying chill tickle the nape of her neck when she made eye contact. The fire shooting out of those eyes seemed to burn right to the fear factor in her brain. She blinked once and then again as her mind registered the psychotic image of how crazy this bitch actually was. She rubbed her kneecap nervously anticipating what could be coming next.

Before she could even comprehend what was happening, Woo's arm shot out like a striking cobra and gripped her neck with nails that felt like steel talons. The intense pain cut her breath off, causing her to gag as tears stung down her cheeks.

Her eyes bucked wide with fear and she instinctively reached for her throat. She felt the heated spittle from Woo's snarling mouth hissing in her ear, "Then slut-ass bitch, don't be playing no fucking games with me and get that information I told you to." All of her broken English was gone now.

Crystal had never been so scared in her life as she felt the sticky warmth of her own blood oozing from the iron claws that were choking her. The darkness of unconsciousness was a welcoming relief from the overwhelming pain when the death grip finally eased.

Stars circled dizzily as her body convulsed and jerked forward as her head rammed into the dashboard. She bent forward grasping her burning neck with both of her hands and blinked back to awareness. She sighed heavily at the spark of relief.

And then she felt Woo's hot slippery tongue slide in and around her ear. In a lustful reflex she aahed and arched her back when she felt those same deadly claws ease down to her lace panties to cup her hairy mound and snake into her damp pussy lips. The realization that she was sloppy wet caused her to gush cum all over the slender fingers that started plunging rapidly in and out of her now humping pussy.

The combination of fear, pain and ecstasy, along with the thought that it was another woman, nearly caused

Crystal to faint with pleasure. She had never had a nut so intense in her whole life.

As the tingling subsided she heard Woo say in a soft whisper, "You-a my baby-a right-a, sugar?" The sultry accent had suddenly returned, soothing her as the uncontrollable trembling ran its course. After several moments she was finally able to find enough of herself to nod.

"Okay-a then, go do whatcha-a supposed to," Woo cooed and reached across her to open the door.

Crystal, still visibly shaken, eased one leg out of the car and turned to Woo with dreamy eyes and purred, "I'll get that the first chance that I can."

"Yeah you-a do-a that, sweetie. I'll-a holla atcha." Woo smiled, closed the door and backed onto Lee Street and sped away waving. She didn't realize she'd pulled straight out into oncoming traffic until she heard several horns honking in protest. She threw a bird over her shoulder and kept pushing her souped-up Mustang until she pulled into a Hardee's restaurant in East Point. For the entire ride she couldn't shake the feeling that she was being watched. "Fuck it," she mumbled as she stepped out of the car and reached for her cell to gather her troops. As she headed for the restaurant, she smiled to herself as she thought about the rendezvous she would soon be having with an old friend.

✠ ✠ ✠

As she watched Woo's car disappear around the bend, Crystal raised her head to the sky and thanked God for allowing her to escape from that crazy bitch. Her shoulders slumped and she pressed her hand to her chest wheezing with relief. She walked to the club massaging her neck and dreading what else the evil little woman could, or worse, would do if she didn't do what she wanted.

She put Woo's threats to the side and thought about that ho Carol, who had disappeared suddenly after she'd heard Don tongue-lashing her about his package being short or something or other. There were rumors flying that Carol's head was in Henry County and other body parts in College Park and Marietta. What really shook her nerves was that it took days for those parts to be put in those places. She gave an involuntary shiver at the thought of having to go through days of torture like that.

But those were rumors; however horrible they sounded, they were still rumors. What she had just experienced with Woo was real, as real as real could get. The tingling ache and drying blood on her neck attested to that. *Damn if she did and damn if she didn't*, she cursed her predicament as she passed through the doors into the blaring blinking lights and booming sound of T.I. and Young Jeezy rocking the air waves.

Her thoughts brightened when she saw her running partner Gina gyrating on the stage. She was off into that other world that strip dancing provided, smiling seductively at the hands stuffing dollars in the garter belt of her Egyptian girl outfit. Her petite, well-shaped body and almond-shaped brown eyes reminded her of a slightly larger Mercedes.

Crystal paused in the din of lustful men to light a Virginia Slim cigarette wondering what Mercedes was doing at that very moment. The rumor had her slipping away with that fly-ass nigga Rainbow. Whether that was true or not, she really didn't know. Then again it was none of her business what a bitch did or who she done it with. *Hell, she's probably somewhere getting blitzed with that fine-ass nigga they called Sparkle that came back on the scene a couple of months ago. Boy, was Don gonna be pissed when he found out that little ho done split wid another nigga. That is if he hadn't already gotten word of it. Shit, I might have to be dealing with that attitude too. That bitch Woo don't know what her ass done got my ass involved in. Hell, she probably don't give a fuck what I got to go through to get what she want,* she thought as she continued to watch her girl doing her thing.

The intoxicating effect of the atmosphere was mellowing and starting to calm her nerves when she accidentally bumped into one of the girls playing waitress. Like all of the girls who had to take their turn browsing amongst the horny customers, the girl wasn't the least bit enthusiastic about toting a tray of drinks among the yelling, smelly throng of mostly male customers. Unfortunately one of the glasses tilted over and dowsed Crystal's cigarette and breasts.

Crystal's face tightened when she looked down at the

damage the drink had caused to her outfit. Her mouth formed to match the curse words erupting from the other girl before she noticed Big Bertha waving and hollering at her from the bar. Her frown overmatched the importance of dealing with the girl, so she brushed by the screaming bitch who continued to yak bullshit at her departing back.

Before she could get comfortable on the stool, Bertha gave her a reluctant smile and threw her palm toward one of the customers yelling an order. "Girl, you barely got five minutes before you gotta be on the stage! You best to shake a leg."

She pursed her lips to the side and leaned around Bertha's wide girth to take a look at the clock on the wall and sighed. "Whew, damn, I didn't know that it was that late." She leaned further over the bar to give Bertha a noisy air kiss and added, "Thanks, hon, luv ya, gotta go, gotta go."

She turned away and stepped quickly around the crowd of groping, horny men crowding the stage and headed for the dressing room. Just before she stepped around the corner she took one last look at her girl Gina. Only, she didn't look like Gina anymore. She shivered at the image of Woo instead. *Aw fuck, what am I gonna do*, she thought, wiping the muggy sweat off of her brow. She shook her head to try to clear her mind and continued on to the back ignoring all the lusty overtones behind her.

She grimaced, fanning at the acrid fumes of musty balls,

piss and cum pouring out of the door left open to the men's restroom swinging back and forth. She was suddenly nauseated by the combination of the stench, the paranoia effect of the come-down from the coked-up blunt and the fear of disappointing Woo, mixed with the dreaded task of crossing Don. She pinched the bridge of her nose and leaned against the door of the dressing room. Sighing heavily she pushed her way through thinking horrible thoughts. *What am I gonna do? Oh, my God, what am I gonna do?*

CHAPTER TWENTY

What's Love Gotta Do With It?

Violet was all smiles when she hooked her arm under Sparkle's and led him to her Thunderbird parked in front of Hechts in the West End Mall. She clicked the button to unlock the car and tossed him the keys before she went to the passenger side.

He deftly snatched them out of the air with his eyes glued to the swell of her hips in her cowgirl dress. He smiled and shook his head. *Oh yeah, mama's sho feeling good about hooking a nigga. Hell, I'm feeling just as good hooking her boosting legend ass,* he thought as he pulled out. "Where to, boss lady?"

She wiggled in the seat, stretched her neck, looked around the parking lot and said, "Since you couldn't find your way back to my crib earlier, do you know where the Holiday Inn is at on Wesley Chapel? I've got a friend there that keeps me a room ready at all times."

He nodded and steered into the traffic on Lee Street. Nearly thirty minutes later, they were entering a room on the second floor overlooking I-20.

"Go ahead and fix us up a good brick. I'm going to wash some of this grime off of my ass," she said, tossed her jacket on the bed and went into the bathroom. A few seconds later she marched back out and stood over him with her hands on her hips. She stared at him like she had some kind attitude for a moment, squinted and returned to the bathroom when he didn't respond.

He sat there considering how crazy her move was but when she didn't return, he shook his head and started on the coke. By the time she came out some fifteen minutes later, he'd cooked up four slabs and was blasting away. Afterward, he lay back chilling against the headboard.

She strolled back in the room with *rip-the-runway* flair, acting as sassy as you please with a shopping bag swinging under her arm. Smiling, she posed in front of him, rolled her eyes before she flipped her head back and went back to the bathroom rifling through the bag. He was more than a little curious but since it was obviously her show, he relaxed to enjoy the evening as it unfolded.

Seeing that glitter in her eyes, he started cutting the slabs into smaller pieces and put them in the ashtray beside the lamp. He picked up the remote and flicked channels until he found an episode of one of his favorite shows, *CSI: Miami*. He folded his hands behind his head and lay back to enjoy the show.

Fifteen minutes later, she came out strutting, smelling like a freshly picked rose, in a baby blue man's silk shirt that went past her knees. Half the way to him she popped her fingers and went back into the bathroom to get the bag. Smiling brightly, she began taking the folded clothes out of the bag and placed them on the vanity.

She sat down beside him. His attention was immediately drawn to the shirt sliding along her butter pecan-colored thighs. The thought of her being naked under the shirt made his dick jump. Her eyes lit up when she noticed the rise in his pants. She smiled sneakily and folded her legs under herself like an Indian. Then she reached across him to get the shooter and the ashtray full of rocks off of the dresser. Intentionally rolling her breasts against his chest, she felt a tingling along her arms when he sucked in his breath from the contact. His eyes narrowed when he felt her nipples harden as she rolled back and forth on his skin.

Dirty teasing-ass bitch, he thought when she sat back and lit up the shooter. After exhaling the intoxicating smoke, she started to eye him dreamily. Sharing three hits together in silence, he finally got up and sat on the other bed facing her.

He sat back, folded his arms across his chest, crossed his legs and slowly started gazing up and down her body, smiling. Squinting lustfully, he gently grasped her hands in his, uncrossed his legs and started kissing her fingers. He alternated kissing along one arm and then the other, working his way up to her neck.

With his dick throbbing, he sat beside her and started licking around her ear. Encouraged by the low moan that escaped her parted lips, he started caressing her breasts.

His warm touch brought an even louder, more intense moan. She leaned away and shifted her legs from under her, revealing her hairy pussy. The sight of her nappy-nappy and slight feminine aroma caused his dick to drool.

He gently laid her on the bed and started slowly sucking her breasts through the silk shirt. She wrapped her hands around him and started rubbing the back of his head as their breathing got heavier. He kissed and licked her trembling flesh down to each button of the shirt, opening each one deliberately slowly, one by one. He intentionally left the last one closed and started on her navel with her stomach flexing with each circular motion of his tongue.

He worked his way down, blowing warm feathery air along her inner thigh until her trembling increased. He then started back up to her neck before going back down until he got to her hairy, musky pussy mound. He started blowing hot, and then cold, air in her hairs. She responded by grinding her hips to meet his tantalizing tongue.

He got a whiff of her strawberry douche when he opened her glistening pussy lips. He blew lightly into her hole, followed by light feathery licks all around her mushy lips.

Then he worked his way back up her body, pressing his now constantly drooling dick against her hot, smooth skin. He tongue massaged one nipple and rubbed his throbbing dick at the edge of her pussy. He luxuriated in her womanly scent as she began to grind her wet pussy lips along his length. She gasped with pleasure and grabbed his ass cheeks with both hands and started grinding harder and harder, faster and faster, moaning louder and louder. His mind swirled enjoying the feel of her pussy muscles gobbling at his dick as she let out an even louder moan, dug her fingers deeper into his ass and leaned her head back as she nutted. *My God, this old lady is hotter than a firecracker, whew*, he thought as he slid his entire length along her pussy lips until he felt her juices soaking his hairs. She gasped with pleasure and grabbed him by the neck. She stuck her tongue deep into his mouth moaning loudly without shame as a second wave of nut erupted in her, drenching his balls and the bed.

As the feeling eased off, she moaned, "Damn, your dick feels good sliding along me like…" Her breath was taken away when he jammed himself all the way into her in one hard thrust. Her mouth flew wide open and her legs began to tremble when he lifted her thighs and placed them on his shoulders as he began to ride her clit. She started cumming all over again as he thrust high and hard, pulling his dick out to the edge of her gaping pussy and slamming it back into her squishy hole. He pounded that pussy mercilessly for about five minutes, lowered her legs and started hammerjacking it from the side.

After a couple of minutes, she clamped his dick and thigh between hers and started fucking his dick as if it was the last one she would ever have, pressing her clit hard against his pelvis. "Aaaaaah, uggggghhh, oh baby aaaaaaah, oh my God, oh my God, so good, so good, so gooooood, oooooh, ooooooh," she moaned wildly as she rode the feeling to the very end and flopped back on the pillow. Her passion urged him on as he grabbed her creamy soft thighs, raised them up and started thrusting anew into her now sore and aching hole. The popping, squishing sound of her sloppy wet pussy, as he pushed in and out, scorched his brain as her gripping pussy lips pushed him closer to the edge of exploding.

The pleasure in his balls got so intense that he hooked his arm around and cupped her breast with one hand, and with the other he raised her thigh until he was able to get a death grip on her waist and went berserk with pleasure. "Oh shit, oh shit, goddamnit, girl, ugh ugh ugh…here it comes, baby, here comes that juice all up in your pussy. Squeeze it, baby, squeeze that dick, baby. Yeah, like that, just like that. Oh hell yeah, oh hell yeah, oh aaaaaah ooo whew!!" He collapsed holding her in that position, rubbing and massaging her sweaty body. He left his softening dick pressed deep into her and started kissing the sweat from her neck and face.

After lying still for a couple of minutes, enjoying the aftershock, holding and caressing each other, Violet maneuvered her body to face him. With half-closed eyes she smiled the smile of a well-fucked woman and said, "My God, man, where you learn to put it on a bitch like that? Shit, I ain't got that many nuts since I was a young bitch getting my first taste of dicks."

Getting cooed like that rubbed his maleness to its highest point as he continued caressing her, saying a bunch of nothing as he looked up at the ceiling, letting the warm wave subside.

Sighing huskily, she pressed her head under his chin and purred, "I sure do hope that you are going to be doing that there for awhile, hustler; that there was the bomb dick I've been looking for like forever."

He stared at the ceiling for a few more minutes before kissing the top of her head. "Girl, let me tell you something"—he paused to take a deep breath—"You have been blessed with what us dudes call the super pussy."

He untwined his body from around hers and went to the basin, knowing she was sweating his nakedness as he checked himself out in the mirror. He turned into the bathroom smiling to himself, knowing that he had dug up in that pussy the way a bitch wanted a nigga to do. *Ain't a damn thang easy about locking a star bitch, but somebody has got to do it, might as well be little old me.* He splashed some cold water on his face, took a rag and wiped their mixed juices off of his body.

Afterwards he walked over to the bed, put his silk drawers back on, sat on the bed facing her and started fixing up their shooters. He passed her one of them and patted her on the thigh, "Come on, shawtie, I've got to go check on some of those spots to collect my money and re-up those bitches."

She frowned slightly because she wanted to fuck some

more, but she understood how it went, so she got up and went to cleanse herself as well. Smiling brightly she took the clothes off of the shelf and tossed them on the bed beside him. "Put on the one that you like the best."

He leaned back and squeezed the weariness out of his eyes before he took a deep breath and picked up the baby blue silk pants that obviously went with the shirt she had had on and tossed it on top of the shirt that was on the other bed. Then he lifted up a gold shirt and pants and nodded. While he was getting into the outfit, she tossed him a bottle of cologne. "See if you like the smell of that there; I think it's sexy as hell."

After getting dressed, he sat in the chair beside the dresser and started rubbing the material, then smiled at her. "Feels good, smells good…I guess you done hooked yourself a nigga now, huh?"

She gave him a cute little curtsy and smiled. "Oh yeah, and it's been a helluva long time in coming too." She began folding the rest of the clothes and put them back in the bag.

"Huh," he said, leaned back and crossed his legs.

She put her hands on her hips standing on the back of her legs, fluttered her long lashes and glaring at him under eyed. "Whatcha looking all surprised for?"

He pinched his nose. "Because of what you just said." He picked up the pack of Kool cigarettes she'd laid on the dresser.

She picked up the lighter and flicked him a light. "Baby

boy, I done had some booty calls every now and then, but I ain't had a man I could feel in years. There, you satisfied?"

He blew a few halos of smoke into the air. "So how you know I ain't just a booty call?" There was an impish smile on his face.

She tooted her nose at him. "Call it woman's intuition; hell, call it whatever the hell you want to, I just know it that's all."

He stood up, smiling, and planted a kiss on her forehead. "Yeah, old lady, I'm satisfied and you do know. Come on, you ready to ride?"

She didn't bother answering and scooped up the bag and followed him out the door yakking, "Yeah, let's go and keep this in your mind, I got your back." She stopped suddenly, wiped her hands across her face and said through her fingers, "Aw, damn, I forgot your mutha-fucking shoes."

"My shoes, what you talking about, woman?" he said over his shoulder, puzzled.

She pushed through the door mumbling, "Nigga, I was so godayum anxious to get me some of that dick that I forgot to get you some shoes to go with these clothes." She quickly added a smile, grabbed his ass and gave it nice little squeeze as she passed him at the door. "Don't worry about it, though. I already got you several pairs at the house, which you would have known if your ass had come back."

He shook his head smiling as he eyed the new bounce to her step as she headed for the car. "You were just real sure of yourself, weren't you, girl?"

She looked over her shoulder, squinted her nose, stuck her tongue out and said real sassy-like, "Yep."

✠ ✠ ✠

Mona heard a muffled whirling sound coming from Al's game room while she was placing the cases of beer on the kitchen table. She thought the garage door was malfunctioning, but it was to close that. With piqued curiosity, she fast stepped to the game room.

She eased the door open and jerked back when she saw the pool table sliding along the floor, followed by the sound of footsteps coming from under the floor. A sneaky girl by nature, she closed the door to a crack and watched wide-eyed as Al's head appeared coming up some stairs. Her hand instinctively flew to her mouth as she silently backed away anxiously wondering what she should do. She definitely couldn't let him know she was there or what she had seen.

She retraced her steps back to the kitchen, her instincts telling her to get the hell out of there. Her head swirled around anxiously before she headed for the door, but no sooner had she touched the knob, she thought about the beer. "Damn," she mouthed to herself and ran back to the table and picked up the cases. She had made two steps toward the door before she realized that she couldn't open it with her hands full.

She huffed, spun around and laid the cases on the floor. Fighting desperately to control her shaking hands, she managed to get the door open. Wide-eyed with nervousness, she scooped up the cases and broke into a silent sprint for the car. Tossing the cases into the back-seat, she quickly started the car up and backed out of the driveway and drove back in the direction from where she had come. The adrenaline rush she was experiencing kept her from seeing Al's face watching her through the garage door's curtains.

Look at that silly-ass ho. She forgot to close the damn door. Al smiled as he wondered what kind of game she'd bring back with her. "Bitches," he mouthed as he headed for the kitchen, but changed his mind. He wanted to see her expression when she tried to figure out whether she had left it open or not. Already trusting only himself, he decided to act dumb to see how long she would go or if she would reveal what she had seen. He had been dealing with lying, conniving bitches all his street life. So the length of time it took for her to reveal it would go a long way into determining how far and how much he would let her into his game or kill her ass.

There was one major strike against her; it was what he'd witnessed on the video. The only time that a bitch leaned at a nigga the way she had leaned at Stacy was when she really wanted to lean all the way into him. There was no telling what a ho would tell a nigga that she went in the deep for. A few more strikes and he'd have to get rid of her the only way he knew how to get rid of a pest.

He shook his head and muttered, "Damn," cursing himself for the wicked thoughts he was having. Was he becoming some kind of a psychopath or what? Was he actually beginning to enjoy getting rid of people, or problems? Hell, people, problems; they were quickly becoming one in the same to him. Or was it a way of him securing his survival in this human jungle of money first and foremost? Or was the spilling of other people's blood over the years finally getting to be an ambition for him? He smiled insanely as he saw Mona pulling back up into the driveway. *Let the games begin*, he thought as the telephone started to ring.

It was one of his business associates who was wondering whether he was gonna keep his end of their bargain. He assured him that everything was falling into place. After hanging up he placed a call to Henry County. The response he got caused him to rush to his room to get some money out of his wall safe behind a picture of Hank Aaron hitting homer number 754. Then he headed to the closet to get his coat and Glock pistol. On his way out the door he brushed by Mona. She opened her mouth to speak only to have him put up one finger to indicate that he'd catch her in a few as he dashed to his car and drove away. He'd decided to let her stir in her thoughts for a while longer. Besides, he didn't feel like she was going anywhere. So he'd deal with her after he took care of his business.

✠ ✠ ✠

As Don turned from the counter after paying for his Big Mac and fries, his attention was drawn to a burgundy Mercedes at the red light. He stretched his neck to get a better view of the driver but was unable to tell who it was. The light turned green as he exited the fast-food restaurant and started walking in that direction as the car pulled off. He hunched his shoulders and headed for his own ride. As he pulled into the street, his first thoughts were to follow the car but then he said under his breath, "Naw, that couldn't have been Al because he was too anxious to get his share of the dope to leave his house." He turned down the street in the direction of his crib.

As he pulled into the driveway several minutes later, he couldn't help admiring the layout of his boy's spot. *Partner really has his shit together*, he thought as he pulled up behind a brown Mercedes in the driveway. *Damn, bro sho do have a thing for the Benz.* He got out of his candy apple-red Thunderbird.

As he walked to the front door, he could've sworn that he saw a shadow move across one of the windows in the garage. Maybe it was his imagination. *Oh well, what the fuck does it really matter?* he thought as he rubbed his stubble waiting for someone to open the door.

After knocking three times, he got impatient and walked around peering in the windows. He stopped when he got to the corner of the garage, figuring that he was pushing it with the coke under his passenger seat. There was no telling what some nosey neighbor, who might be peeking out of their curtains at that very moment, might be thinking. Or do for that matter. He'd give the doorbell one more try and then head on back to the club and let Al catch up with him later on.

As he started for his car he was sure he'd seen a movement at the curtains in one of the windows. When he took a step back to get a better look, he heard, or rather he felt, the door crack open. His eyes immediately reverted back to the door, which was ajar just enough for him to see an eye and the tip of a feminine nose peeking out.

He saw Mona's beautiful face, her still damp hair plastered to the side of her face. She gave him a weak smile and motioned for him to come on in. His naturally suspicious nature had him cutting his eyes to each side and behind before he advanced to the door.

She had a towel wrapped into a turban around most of her hair as she used her hip to push the door open barely enough for him to squeeze through. He stepped over the doorsill and took one last look behind him and closed the door. When he turned toward the room, the sight of Mona's voluptuous body made him arch back admiring the seductive sway of her hips as she walked ahead of him, tightening the sash of her red silk kimono robe. She was still damp with the way the material was clinging to every curve as she headed toward the bar. Several drops of water slid down her coffee cream-colored calves.

The thought of her curvaceous nakedness under the robe made him take a deep breath as he tried to control the sudden ache in his groin. That didn't do much good, especially when he saw the smile on her face when she turned and lowered her jet-black eyes to the swelling bulge in his pants.

She let out a short snort and asked, "What's up, Mr. Black Don? Beyond the obvious," in a husky voice that sent shivers down his spine.

He braced his shoulders and arched a brow. "You must have left those angel wings upstairs on your way down here, angel." He paused to wipe a hand down his face before adding, "Naw, naw, on the real, sweetie, where's Al? He was supposed to be here waiting for me."

She smiled demurely, appreciating the comment and batted her long lashes to show she had. She started feeling the power of her feminine glow over him and figured that she could possibly persuade him to reveal some of the answers to the questions that were running through her mind. She mixed them both a large glass of crème de cacao and Bacardi rum. Then she sashayed to the couch and slowly crossed her legs, briefly exposing part of her soft, slightly muscular thighs.

Daintily she handed him one of the glasses and purred,

"He was pulling out as I drove up. He did seem to be in quite a hurry, at least that's what it looked like to me."

"In a hurry, where to?" he asked as he sat down in the love seat directly in front of her, took a sip of the drink she had made and placed the glass on the coffee table.

She arched her brow, thinking, *What the fuck, did he not hear me or what?* She turned her mouth down before she answered, "Well, he did indicate that he'd be back shortly, but no, I don't know where he went." She paused and turned her head sideways to look at the miniature grandfather clock over the fireplace. "Which was about a half hour ago."

Staring down into the drink, Don was wondering why he hadn't called to let him know that he had taken off so suddenly, especially since he was rushing him to get over there. Then he reasoned that he'd probably be back in a little while. In the meantime what was he to do about this fine-ass woman sitting in front of him that obviously didn't have any inhibitions about displaying her feminine attributes.

Mona watched him over the rim of her glass for several minutes knowing that he was trying to figure out how to deal with the sexual vibes she was shooting at him. She licked her lips and said, "Is there something in particular you want me to tell him when he gets back?" She crossed and then immediately recrossed her lovely legs.

He started contemplating if he had enough time to make a play on her. He reasoned that she was all but asking him to get up between those creamy thighs of hers.

"Do you have something you wanted to give him? You could leave it with me if you in a hurry, you know," she said and smiled sheepishly.

Having never dealt with her before he was really skeptical if he should. Or if Al even had her in his business like that. On the other hand, it could be the key to getting under that silk robe to those soft-ass thighs and all that was in between.

She knitted her brow and asked, "Are you aight?"

"Huh," he responded with his eyes glued to her thighs.

"Whoa there, man, I've asked you several questions," she purred as she uncrossed her legs and leaned forward, spreading her legs even further apart, enough so he could almost see her hairy vee between them. The widening of his eyes let her know that she had caused the desired effect. "And you haven't answered either one of them yet." She inched a little closer to the edge of the couch. "So what's wrong?"

He cursed to himself, *Bitch, you know damn well what's wrong. What the fuck am I supposed to be, a fucking android or something.* He was mesmerized with the possibilities.

She cleared her throat, and when he didn't respond, she cleared it again and purred, "Well?"

He didn't divert his gaze one iota as he answered in a static voice, "Uh, uh. Ain't nothing wrong."

She sat back and opened her legs just a little bit more and pouted. "If ain't nothing wrong, then why haven't you answered me then?"

He stared at her thighs for a few moments more and

then braced his hands on his knees. He pushed himself up to a standing position right in front of her. His swollen manhood was directly in her face, throbbing through his pants.

She recoiled slightly and gasped in surprise—a reaction that he automatically took as her getting excited by the mammoth size of his dick. Most women were stunned when they saw that he was hung like a horse. And she was no different as her nose flared and she became glued to his crotch. She tilted her head to the side and squinted her eyes, not believing that anyone could really be that big. With her mouth gaped wide open, she looked up at him and the animalistic gaze in his eyes both scared and excited the hell out of her as she felt her pussy juices dampening her panties.

He smiled down at her knowing that she was in shock. "Well, whatcha gonna do, leave the python in its cage? Go ahead, touch it, it's real."

Swallowing, she raised her hand to rub it through his pants and shivered when it throbbed to her touch.

"Go ahead, take it out," he commanded with his voice coarse with excitement.

She looked from his crotch to his face, too stunned to say a word.

He hunched his hips forward. "Go ahead, free it, before I cum in my pants."

She took a deep breath, slowly unzipped him and reached inside and tried to wrap her small hand around it, her body tingling all over when she realized that she couldn't.

The warm trembling feel of her touch almost made him cum right then and there, but he held on and stepped back a fraction and pulled it out himself. He enjoyed the look on her face as her eyes widened, full of lust.

She gasped, "Oh my God," while her mind was saying, *How in da fuck? Man, that damn thang can't fit in me; it's got to be at least…*

"Thirteen inches," he said proudly.

She frowned as she tried from different angles to get her hand around it. It was thicker than her arm; how could he ever think she could take something like that.

To answer what he knew was on her mind, he inched forward and pressed the monster head to her lips. She responded by gently lapping her tongue around the enormous tip. When he started rotating it in her mouth, she moaned and began waggling her legs. He slowly started to hunch it into her mouth: first, the gigantic head, that stretched her mouth as wide as it could go; then an inch, then another, then another until she stopped his forward motion with her other hand and started bobbing her head, swirling her tongue. Her mouth was being stretched wider than it had ever been and caused her pussy to start gushing foam at the lips.

She had bobbed on it four or five times when she heard him grunt and felt him swell up even bigger in her mouth, which she thought had to be impossible. He started spurting huge gobs of cum down her throat, so suddenly that it made her gag and choke. But she didn't pull back; instead she started sucking him even harder and faster. Through his slanted eyes of pleasure he saw her hand pistoning rapidly under her robe. As he felt the last drops being pulled out of his dick, her thighs started to shake. Her hand gripped his dick even harder and the edges of her robe fell to the side. He gave up a real gorilla grunt as he saw her fingers getting wetter and wetter with each plunge of her glistening digits.

His dick started throbbing anew as she began moaning louder and louder as she inserted a couple of more fingers to join the other one and started fucking them passionately. He saw tears running down her cheeks when she started cumming and cumming as she stuffed more and more of his giant dick down her throat.

Just the sight and thought of her cumming that hard with his dick throbbing in her mouth caused his knees to buckle. She actually had to brace her hands against his stomach to keep him from falling on her.

After hosing her throat with nut, he moaned, "Whew, godayum, girl, you something else," and wheezed as he tried to catch his breath.

"Naw, you the one that's something else." She breathed huskily, as he straightened up and started to push his semi-hard dick into his pants.

"Whatcha think you doing?" She pushed his hand away and started stroking him. "Hmmm, shit, nigga, momma needs this muthafucka in her hot pussy now." She moaned huskily and got on her knees on the couch and hiked her fantastic ass in the air. She didn't even wait for him to say anything as she grabbed his dick to guide it into her dripping pussy. When the aroma of her female musk assaulted his nose, he blinked with passion and started slowly circling his dick in. She grabbed one of the pillows off of the couch and bit down on it as her pussy started to get stretched beyond her endurance. He took his time, just feeding her a little at a time until he felt her pussy getting wetter and wetter, taking in more and more. Inch by agonizing inch he slowly pushed up in her until all thirteen inches of his massive dick was slowly plunging into her spasming pussy. She began wagging her head from side to side in blissful agony and pleasure.

His pleasure was taken to another level when she began rotating her jelly ass back at him in rhythm with his stroke. He gripped her by the hips and started stroking faster. It took only a few of his faster strokes before he was massaging her g-spot, which caused her to moan louder and louder. Soon she was trembling in climax and arched her back with her mouth opened wide in a silent scream.

He started trembling himself when he looked down and saw her grinding back on his dick for all that she was worth. His nose flared in passion as he watched his gigantic dick getting coated with more and more woman nut. Wanting her to receive the maximum dicking, he slowly started pulling back to the rim of her pussy before slowly plunging all the way back in.

She began swaying her head back and forth, out of control as she screamed in the ecstasy of cumming yet again, "Oh my God, fuck me, man…Push all that big-ass muthafucking dick in my hot-ass pussy. Oooh goda-yum, I'm cum, mmmmm, innnng again, daddy. Oh God, oooooooooooh, your dick is just too goddamn big, nigga, Give me all of it, fuck me, fuck meeeeee."

He couldn't hold back any longer as he saw more and more of her juices coating his dick with every plunge. He pushed in for all he was worth one more powerful time, holding all of his pulsating, sperm-spewing dick as far up in her as it would go as he came and came, spurting glob after glob of hot cum until he fell over across her wide ass. Then he gathered enough strength to pull out to finish nutting along the crack of her ass. For a brief moment he thought that he was going to faint when she reached behind her and started milking the very last drops out as she continued to grind her fat, milky ass up against him.

Finally he collapsed on top of her and rode her soft body down onto the couch. She was still grinding back slowly when the telephone started to buzz. It was hooked onto his belt with his pants bunched around his ankles. At first he started to let it ring until he heard her wheeze from under him. "That might just be that nigga right there." She breathed in gasps as she tried to wiggle from under his pressing weight.

Feeling her discomfort he rolled off of her to the floor

and took in several heavy breaths to regain his composure before her reached down to pull the phone from off of his belt. He immediately frowned at the face and breathed, "Damn, it's his ass, for real." He placed the phone at his ear as she scrambled off the couch and sprinted up the stairs. He took one more deep breath, shaking his head as he admired the way her fat ass was jiggling and bouncing with each step.

"Yeah, what's up, dog? Where the fuck you at? I zoomed by your spot about three minutes ago; nobody answered. What the fuck is up, dude? You acted like you was in such a muthafucking hurry. Damn, playa, you could've at least hit a nigga that you was on the move. That's fucked up, yo."

He nodded a couple of times to whatever Al was saying before he replied, "Yeah, man, I can go back, but I'm gonna grab me something to eat first, fried chicken. Hell yeah, but when she gonna be there. ...She's there now. Why she didn't answer the fucking door then? Okay, dude, I'll be there in a few. Hey, man, don't have me waiting over there too long. I got stuff I need to handle just like you do, okay, later, bet."

He clicked off as Mona was coming back to the top of the stairs, with her head leaning toward the telephone in her hand. Her robe was opened as she wiped her voluptuous body down with a pink flowery towel.

She clicked off the phone and walked down the stairs at him with a seductive smile on her shiny beautiful face.

She pressed her body to his and started rubbing his monster through his pants and said in a husky voice, "You know you got to keep giving mama a lot of this big muthafucka now, don'tcha?" Then she ran her tongue up his neck, arched her back and pulled the robe away to show the full roundness of her hips and ass. She turned around and started jiggling that entire ass as she sashayed to the kitchen. She purred over her shoulder, "Got to fry my man up some finger-licking-good chicken." She licked her fingers as she disappeared around the corner.

"I know that fine-ass, good-pussy bitch is going to be the death of me," he moaned as he walked to the bathroom to wash the pussy scent off. He came back out a few minutes later and picked up the remote to click on the big-screen television. He lit up a blunt to try to masquerade the scent of fucking in the air and flicked the remote until he got to ESPN.

He sniffed the air until he was satisfied and then sat in the love seat to wait for Al. He noticed that she had changed into a pink jogging outfit and had an apron tied around her waist as she went about her business of cooking them up some hot chicken to chow down on.

He lay back enjoying the basketball highlights while his mind concentrated on how he could steal that fine piece of woman away from Al. After a short time, he started smiling to himself as a plan started formulating in his mind, just as he heard a car crunching the gravel on the driveway.

✠ ✠ ✠

Beverly felt compelled to know what Lt. Woo was doing. Rumors of her guerilla warfare tactics were well known around the station. Okay, she was definitely making a huge dent in the drugs flowing on I-20. And her means and ways were suspect, but having spent many years dealing with the street vermin herself earlier in her career, she was well aware of the stresses and demands of the job.

'Wah,wah,wah…' the jarring sound of a police siren tingled along her neck and jotted her out of her mini revelry. She jerked her attention back to the wildly erratic drivers in time to keep her from ramming into the rear end of a black Escalade.

Her hand instinctively flinched toward her own siren button, but she wasn't really in the mood to be harassing folk so she maneuvered around dude. Shortly she was exiting down the East Lake ramp.

With all the stress she'd been through lately, it felt good to get away from police activities for a while.

She decided to drop by Mother Dobbs' house to get herself an energy boost from the lovely older woman. Her thoughts turned to the possibility of running into her son Johnny, or was it Rainbow. *Damn, he has more names than an orphanage.*

She was several blocks from her destination when she saw a group of young hoodlums giving a pair of guys a vicious beat down at the entrance to an alley next to a Laundromat. Her hand eased to her service revolver as she slowed down and put the car in reverse.

Five sets of angry eyes blazed at her when she came to a halt and kneed the door open. Those eyes turned into shock when they saw the big gun whipping up from her side and the glittering badge attached to her belt when her jacket flew open. Shock quickly turned to fear as several froze in mid stomp and the angry mob sprinted down the alley. One of the boys looked vaguely familiar to her but in the heat of the moment she couldn't place him.

In hot pursuit she leaped over the two balled-up youths on the ground and gave chase to the fleeing boys. "Halt, freeze, stop, police," she shouted to no avail as the boys widened the distance, turning over huge garbage cans into her path. The years of sitting behind desks started to quickly take its toll and she realized that a snowball had a better chance in hell than she had of catching them. Once they hit the end of the alley, the mob split in each direction.

Beverly felt her ankle twist awkwardly when she hurdled over some cans and landed on a huge rock. Her head flung backward with her arms waving wildly as she slowed to a halt and bent over to rest her elbows across her knees, sighing in disappointment. Squeezing her eyes tight, she took several deep breaths before finally raising her head and blinked them open. She squinted at a figure in a car across the street whose head was swerving back and forth at the fast-moving youth. She knuckled the corners of her eyes, snorted and stretched her neck toward the car. If only it hadn't been the beginning of dusk, she could've been more certain of whom she thought she was seeing.

She strained stiffly to her feet and started toward the car. As if they had recognized her for the first time, the driver shot the car into reverse and squealed tires to the end of the street, straightened out and screamed away.

I know damn well that wasn't...Naw, it couldn't have been. No way, she thought as she hobbled to the middle of the street. She looked in the other direction in time to see three of the boys disappear around the corner. For some reason she couldn't shake the icky feeling that whoever was in the car was connected to the beat-down crew.

She pinched the back of her neck, twisted it from side to side to relieve the tension, and then headed back down the alley. *What the fuck?* she thought when she noticed the boys who had gotten the beat down were gone. As she neared the spot of attack, her attention was drawn to a object leaning against the wall of the Laundromat. Her brows were wrinkled in concentration as she walked to the end of the alley and looked in both directions for the fallen youth. They were nowhere to be seen. Full of caution and concern she turned around and walked over to get the object that turned out to be a plastic bag full of what she suspected was cocaine and an envelope. She opened it and saw a stack of money and a note that was written in some kind of code. Placing it inside her jacket she walked back to her car and drove around the block several times in search for any sign of the youths. Her police mind was running wild now with all kinds of suspicion. Did this have anything to do with her boys? Why was that the first thing that came to her mind? Was she playing the overprotective mother hen when it came to those fools again? If her impulses were on point, as they usually were, what connection was there to those that raced into the night when she spotted them? She decided to put her car search to an end and headed for Mother Dobbs' house. Her mind was working overtime with whos, whats and whys. As she pulled up to the house of many adolescent memories, she saw Mother Dobbs swinging back and forth on the porch swing where she'd learn how to be a woman.

It had been quite a while since Beverly had felt such warmth. Seeing the sweet, gentle older woman's glittering eyes and smile made her sigh with joy. As she shifted the car into park, her attention was drawn to Rainbow's shiny red pimp-mobile down the street at old man OJ's corner store.

Gray-bearded Mr. OJ, the neighborhood's ultimate gossip, had his cream-colored Stetson cocked acey-deucy over his outdated Jheri Curl was plopping on his red suspenders and laying a checkers whipping on some young hoodlum draped in dark blue Rocawear gear. Beverly had an immediate flashback when she saw his profile but dismissed it because she couldn't put her finger on where it could have been. She could tell the old pro was getting the better of the youngun when he started flashing both fists full of money around like he owned the hood. The trash talking was very loud and brash to the point where she could make out nearly every word.

Even without seeing him, the sight of Rainbow's car made her naturally suspicious. *Why hadn't he just walked to the store from his mother's house?* It didn't make too much sense to her unless he was up to no good, which was usually the case.

"Hey there, Bevy sweetie, how ya doing? What brings ya around these parts? Mmph, don't get to see ya that much since you turned *'Wonder Woman'* for the whole city." Mama Dobbs' chirpy voice broke through her concentration down the street. Beverly's cheeks glowed as she turned toward the still gorgeous and loving woman.

Mama Dobbs sat there smiling as pretty as an early ray of morning sunrise. A granny version of Alicia Keys twinkled before Beverly's eyes. She was knitting a colorful woolen sweater as she rocked back and forth to whatever beautiful music was flowing through her head. Beverly instantly recalled the days when they'd sit in that same swing for countless hours after she'd come home from school while waiting for her nana to come home. Mama Dobbs hummed to the Temptations or the Supremes and she bobbed her head to some LL Cool J, Run-DMC, Prince or Michael Jackson.

Beverly scooped up a blue, roughly scarred plastic pitcher off the edge of the stoop. She began prancing up and down the porch watering Mama Dobbs' array of beautiful flowers suspended from different colored ropes from the roof.

Beverly luxuriated at the mixture of wonderful scents caressing her nostrils before she sat beside her favorite teacher. "You mean to tell me that hard-headed son of yours didn't let you know that I'd stopped a little while back?"

Mama Dobbs pursed her lips and sucked on her teeth. "Girl please, you know that boy don't nevah tell me nuthin'."

Beverly shook her head and sighed. "Yeah, I guess you right..." She froze in mid-sentence when Mama Dobbs continued to talk right through whatever she was saying. All she could do was smile. Suddenly her attention was drawn to the sound of Rainbow's familiar voice as he stepped out of the store and blended right in the mix of the old man and youngsters' banter.

✠ ✠ ✠

Sparkle's eyes gleamed with pleasurable pride as he watched his two women in the rearview mirror. His veteran street queen Violet was giving his new honey

Mercedes some more 4-1-1 on the boosting game. He was smiling because he knew that the old lady was a genius in her field and Mercedes was like a sponge absorbing every drop.

Yep, Boo done really got into her mother hen role with little shawtie, for sho. "Whaddafuck dat ho doing around her?" he muttered when he spotted Lt. Woo's Catwoman-mobile and her two cop henchmen parked across the street from his planned rendezvous spot with Rainbow. Sparkle knew Woo hadn't spotted him yet. His intuition told him to slow down and observe.

Rainbow's loud boisterous voice diverted his attention away from Woo just in time for him to see his boy coming out of the store. He started cursing under his breath. "He know damn well he was supposed to wait 'til I got in the store. Shit." The girls arched their brows at each other and grimaced at his sudden change of attitude. He wondered if Rainbow had spotted Woo and her crew. Or did he come out as a warning for him to keep away? Or was it something else?

He frowned. "Oh shit; what the hell." Somebody's car tires were smoking as it screeched past them.

✠ ✠ ✠

Beverly saw and heard the car's tires screeching as it veered around the slow-moving traffic and sped down the street. There was something familiar about the silhouette of the man in the driver's seat of the one it had passed. She was straining to see who it was before her instincts were drawn to the windows of the speeding car. As the windows started lowering she saw all the passengers' heads turn in the direction of the store. *Were those guns they were pointing out of the window?* She sprung from her seat as adrenaline rushed to her head. She barely heard Mama Dobbs' next few words.

Beverly knew Mama Dobbs was stunned by her sudden reaction. From the expression on her face it was evident that she wasn't aware of the danger nor that Rainbow was possibly in the line of fire. She'd do whatever it took to keep her from seeing her son get hurt.

When Mama Dobbs' head started turn toward the commotion, Beverly reached down and grabbed her wrist. "Come on, Mama; I sure could use some of that special lemon juice stuff you be hooking up."

"What, girl? You mean to tell me that you came all the way over here for some of the dangnamit juice? Honey please, just tell me that the moon's out for the day and the sun's gonna be here tonight."

Beverly's smile brightened as she helped her up and led her into the house. It disappeared immediately as Mama Dobbs headed for the kitchen. She had to get her to safety and then spring out the door without her becoming too suspicious. "Hmm, go ahead and hook that up. I got to get something out of my car right quick."

"Huh?" Mama Dobbs turned around but Beverly was

already about to go out the door. She pressed her gun to her thigh and peeked out the screen door. She still couldn't see clear enough into the other car but she could definitely feel the vibes. *Was it that nigga? And if it was who were the others with him?* Was that a tinge of jealousy running down her spine? *Boom, boom, booooom.* She sprung out of the door with her pistol raised high with both hands.

✠ ✠ ✠

Sparkle looked beyond the speeding car for a brief second toward Rainbow's mother's house. He squinted at the familiar figure leading Mama Dobbs into the house. *Was it? Could it be? Oh no, it damn sho is. Man, I ain't ready to see this woman.* Why was that? And what was he afraid of?

He checked the mirror again just in time to see the girls' expressions change from wide-eyed exuberance to shocked concern. He spun around frowning. "What's wrong with ya'll.....?"

He paused when their mouths shot open and their arms pointed down the street at the same time they heard the *pop, pop, pop* of gunfire. He spun back around in time to see Rainbow diving for cover beside his car.

Automatically he reached under the seat to get his piece. The girls screamed. He kicked the door open and rolled out of the car into a crouch. But before he could let the lead fly, the speeding car made it around the corner with several arms sticking out of the window with their guns blazing.

He sprinted for Rainbow's car. His boy was pressed to the side of the vehicle. The shock on his face told it all before it turned into a gasping smile when he saw who it was.

Sparkle looked toward the store. The old man was leaning back in his chair with blood spewing from a red blotch on his chest. Rainbow sat up and followed his partner's gaze. His mouth suddenly formed into a big "O" before he blinked several times and croaked, "Man, where the hell that nigga go?"

Sparkle leaned down and grasped his elbow to help him get up. "What nigga, dog...?" He froze when he spotted Beverly sprinting across the street with her gun held high. He wasn't ready for this and let his boy's elbow go, ignoring his waving arms as he plopped back into the car and ran for his car.

"Man, what the fuck!" Rainbow screamed as his head and back banged against the car. He raised his head to look over his shoulder through the window to see what had frightened Sparkle so much. "Oh shit." It was all he could mutter as he ran his hand down his face, sighed heavily and plopped his head back against the door.

✠ ✠ ✠

Beverly shivered when she heard the glass splatter off the floor. Through the screen door she could see the frightened look of shock on Mama Dobbs' face. She motioned for her to remain in place, not really knowing whether the sight of her gun or the loud report of the other ones, had scared her so. She cocked her gun to make sure a round was ready to fire and rushed toward the car speeding down the street. She immediately saw that it was no use as it swerved around the corner several blocks away. Her attention swayed to Old Man OJ slumped in his chair.

She scanned the entire area for any more gunmen. She saw someone running away from Rainbow's car. *Yep, it was that nigga, aight. Sparkle. Why in the hell is he running?* She growled at his departing back, "Halt, muthafucka." She shouted in despair as he jumped in the car with what she could now see were two females. He sped backward down the street until he had enough room to make a wildly spinning U-turn and jetted out of sight. Before he could do so Beverly grimaced at the two women with him. They stared back at her until their heads were jerked every which way when he maneuvered the car out of sight.

She had immediately recognized one of the women as Violet, her best childhood buddy Yolanda's aunt, but she couldn't place the other face. Dejected and disgusted she ran over to where Rainbow was groaning against his ride. "Why'd that fool run away like that? And who were those niggas that tried to do yo ass?"

Rainbow spread his arms far apart frowning. "Girl, how in the hell am I suppose to know that?"

"Know what? Who those niggas were or why he got the hell out of here like that...?" She froze when she noticed him trying to look around her. She turned around, sighed and rushed over to Old Man OJ. It was too late. She checked his pulse; Pops was a goner. She started shouting over her shoulder as she headed for her car to send for an ambulance and backup. "You tell that muthafucka there ain't no need to be running from me..." She was halfway across the street when she heard his tires screaming in front of the store. She stopped and looked around. He was waving at her as he bent the corner with a mask of death creasing his features.

Oh, here we go again, damn. She turned back toward her ride. Before she could make another step, she heard another car rev up and spin tires after Rainbow from the adjacent street corner. She strained her eyes at its occupants. It was Lt. Woo and a couple of her henchmen. *Now what in the hell is she doing around here? Had Sparkle or Rainbow spotted her? Was she the reason they had jetted out so abruptly?*

"Oh shit," she muttered and covered the mike. *That youngun flashing the green was with those niggas down the street giving those other boys the whipping.* She fingered the drugs in her pocket as she pondered the connection. *Old Man OJ is shot up, the youngun disappears. Woo, Sparkle and Rainbow are all mixed up in this shit together.* No doubt she had her work cut out for her. Whatever was going on she had to get to the bottom of it before her beloved city was turned into a bloodbath. And because her boys were in-volved, it would definitely have to be a solo mission; for their safety as well as her own. She sighed and took a deep breath. "Oh well, Miss Police-woman Chief, get on your muthafucking job," she mumbled just before the static from the police band hit her.

As she was about to start shouting orders, she suddenly felt strange and icky. She stared past the mike down to her crotch. It was glistening with her juices even through her pants. She shivered, more than a little embarrassed, because she knew why she had gotten so excited. She'd seen her man again—Sparkle. Whether he was with another bitch or two or three, he was still her man and she was going to get him. *Hell, and he knows it, too, the sonofabitch. That's why he was running from me, or was it? Whichever way this is going I've got to have him. I've waited all these years and I ain't about to let no other bitch have him—period.*

About the Author

L.E. Newell was born in Atlanta, Georgia. He is the author of *Durty South Grind* and *The Grind Don't Stop*. Visit him on Facebook.

IF YOU ENJOYED "DURTY SOUTH GRIND,"
BE SURE TO CHECK OUT

The Grind Don't Stop
The Continuing Saga of Durty South Grind

AVAILABLE FROM STREBOR BOOKS

CHAPTER ONE
As The Hood Turns

The persistent static racket on the police band was really starting to get on Beverly's last nerves as she spun around the corner in pursuit.

In pursuit of what? Who? Her thoughts were twisted in a whirlwind of scenarios. *Am I following Lt. Woo because she and her squad of police hoodlums were trying to bust one of my boys? Or am I chasing Rainbow to see if he'll lead me to that bastard Sparkle? Or does he know or have a hint of who took out Old Man OJ? Or was the hit actually meant for him?*

✠ ✠ ✠

It was a hit that Rainbow felt; naw, a hit he *knew* was meant for him. What other reason would that nigga Joker be sneaking gritty sneers at him while he was shooting the breeze at the store counter with Junior's brother "Big Guy," the longtime co-owner of the store with OJ?

Add that grit with watching Joker's reaction and facial expressions as he dashed from his and OJ's checker game right before the shooting had started. The circumstances and consequences added up to a hit; no matter how you wanted to see it.

Rainbow's thoughts were in straight-up killer mode of revenge as he jumped into his Caddie and jetted in hot pursuit of those niggas. He hadn't paid the least bit of attention to Lt. Woo and her hoodlums parked near the end of the block as his tires screamed around the corner. He was only concerned with finding out where those niggas were headed. As he pressed on the gas pedal to possibly overtake them, he chanced a look into his rearview mirror and spotted that worrisome little bitch and her henchmen. *Oh shit, I got to shake this little bitch first. Because when I catch these little muthafuckas, dey asses have got to go meet their maker. Dey ass got to die, leave this earth. Try to take me out like that…and kill one of my childhood idols. Oh hell yeah, ya'll niggas got to die, for sho.* Rainbow was way beyond shook up. He had to get rid of the bitch *and* her hoodlums; no doubt about it. He surely couldn't take the chance of them witnessing him blasting on those fools. He shot down the next intersection and sped up, hoping to lose them.

✠ ✠

Regardless of how things had gone so far, Beverly knew she had to get to the bottom of it; and without Woo or anyone knowing. Talking about skeletons in her closet, this mess was really getting out of hand. She realized she had to make sure that Woo didn't see her. But how was she going to do that and keep up with Rainbow? She was following Woo chasing Rainbow while he was following the niggas who'd thrown down on the drive-by.

Oh shit, has that bitch spotted me? Beverly thought as she narrowed her eyes when Woo's silhouette angled upward toward the rear-view mirror. Had the little bitch slowed down to get a better look at who was following her?

Beverly knew that she could no longer take the chance that she'd been spotted. She made a quick left at the next intersection knowing that she was giving Woo the worst possible angle to recognize her. As she was making the turn, she saw that the car involved in the drive-by was making a right some three or four blocks ahead. She pulled to the curb, jumped out of the car and sprinted to the corner. She pressed her back to the brick wall of the paint store and did a quick peek. She ducked back around the edge of the building in time to see Rainbow make a right turn a couple of blocks away. Beverly presumed that he was either trying to cut them off, or that he had spotted Woo chasing him and was trying to put a move on her. Either way he pressed the pedal to the floorboard, speeding down the street at double the limit. She could hear the rubber screaming and see the smoke spiraling in the air from his tires as he jetted away.

It shocked Beverly when Woo didn't follow him but zoomed down the street the shooters had traveled. Even though she was puzzled why Woo had responded this way, Beverly had seen enough and rushed back to her car.

From the sounds of the radio, some of her troops had already arrived at the scene of the shooting. What should she do now? Go back to the scene? Follow Rainbow to keep his crazy ass from getting into any more trouble? Follow Woo to find out what the little bitch was really up to? Or put some more troopers on their trails?

While she was contemplating her next move, another familiar vehicle jetted past her and turned left speeding down the street. She shot her car into gear and pulled up to the corner in time to see the car following the path of Woo and the shooters.

She blinked several times at the antennae sticking out of the trunk, knowing that it was a cop's car. She zoomed in on the license plate and the silhouette of the driver. It hit her like a ton of bricks. *That bastard.* She grimaced as it dawned on her that it was JR, the deputy chief. "What in the hell is he doing here? What's his connection with all of this?" she mumbled to herself.

The light was red. Normally she'd flip on the siren and speed by all traffic signs. But her intuition kept those responses at bay because she knew that she couldn't draw any attention to herself. So what should she do now? There were definitely too many things happening to handle all of them.

She took a deep breath and started across the intersection. For some reason her eyes shot to the rearview mirror. "Now ain't that a bitch." She cursed at the image of Sparkle in the car trailing hers. Why had the fool jetted away from her in the first place? From what she could tell, he hadn't recognized her. So what now? Should she keep going to see what would happen?

She maintained her concentration on his face for several blocks before she decided to circle the entire block to get behind him. She saw that Violet and the other girl were both still in the car. For a brief second, she considered pulling them over just to fuck with them and display her power; to let them bitches know that she wasn't anything to play with. She also thought about how the girls would react. If they got loud, it would certainly defeat her purpose of secrecy. Besides, she didn't really trust how her jealousy would make her act.

After all, she was not only hiding from the authorities but from the street gossip as well; especially knowing how cops always maintained their own personal crew of snitches. She had an army of them herself.

She followed Sparkle and the girls to the house by Turner Field and settled in the parking lot. She pulled out her mini binoculars to check out the activities of the house.

A huge lump roughed its way down her throat as she watched Sparkle pull up to the curb in front of the house. He leaned forward in the driver's seat to let the other woman out. From where she was sitting it seemed like the girl pushed the seat forward with a little attitude. Violet jumped out of the other side and eased into the front seat with a smirk on her face. One that said, *Aw, little bitch, handle it.*

It only meant one thing to Beverly: both of these girls had to be Sparkle's woman. She shivered with jealousy as the car sped down the street. She followed them to a small set of apartments on Memorial Drive. She knew she couldn't park there so she drove across the street and stopped in the supermarket parking lot facing the apartments.

No matter how long it would take, Beverly was going to find out what the hell Sparkle was up to. Her heart pounded with grief and anger as she settled into the seat and pressed the binoculars to her eyes. *It might just be a long night.*